John Watson was born and brought up in London and began his working life as a messenger boy in an advertising agency. He progressed slowly up the ladder as a copywriter for direct response advertising. He founded his first company in 1978 at the age of twenty-nine and his second three years later, which he recently sold with a turnover of £100 million.

He lives in Sussex with his wife and two childen, and is working on his second novel.

THE IRON MAN

John Watson

WARNER BOOKS

A *Warner* Book

First published in Great Britain in 1998 by Warner Books
Reprinted 1998

A CIP catalogue record for this book is available from the
British Library.

ISBN 0 7515 2147 7

Typeset by Solidus (Bristol) Limited
Printed and bound in Great Britain by Clays Ltd, St Ives plc

Warner Books
A Division of
Little, Brown and Company (UK)
Brettenham House
Lancaster Place
London WC2E 7EN

For Karen, Robert and Emily

All but one of the battleships in this novel are real. *Yamoto*, the biggest battleship ever built, lies, now a war grave, in deep water several hundred miles south west of Japan. *Iowa* and *Missouri*, together with their sister ship *New Jersey*, were until recently kept in commission and repeatedly modernised. *Iowa* saw action in the Gulf War. The *Stalin* is fiction, of course, but it is based on the specifications of *Yamoto*, and then 'stretched'. Given the Russian fondness for the gargantuan, and given the extraordinary achievements of the Soviet Union in the war years, there is no technical reason why the *Stalin* could not have existed, just as described here.

I am grateful to many people who have had a hand in bringing *The Iron Man* to the slipway: Mike Owsley, and Carey Schofield's *Inside the Soviet Army* for military help; Tony Sanford, and Carolyn Griffiths and Charles Swan of the Simkins Partnership for legal help; Jeanine Berigliano for sorting out the typescripts; and Christopher Little and Hilary Hale for making the whole thing possible.

J.W.

PROLOGUE

Yakov Zof was staring at the TV with disbelief. They were tearing down the Wall.

Kids with filthy jeans and long hair, boys and girls – though it was difficult to tell the difference, thought Zof – were balanced on top of the uneven breeze-blocks, long ago splashed with fading graffiti. Some of the youths had pickaxes and were swinging at the topmost level of breeze-block. Dusty gobs of rubble trickled downwards. In the background, emerging into the stark light of the TV cameras, they had found a wrecking crane. A great cheer went up as the machine unsteadily positioned itself.

There was a close-up of a group of Vopos, now in plain clothes but obviously security police all the same. They watched the crowd helplessly as it swirled around them. Bloody Germans. Zof wanted to yell, 'For Christ's sake do something,' but he kept quiet. There were five others in the mess, all Navy men, watching the scene on the snowy black and white set they had clubbed together to buy. Their world was falling with each lump of rubble wrenched from a wall on the other side of the world, and they were powerless to stop it.

Then they heard it, rolling in from across the vast parade ground: the distant sound of singing and cheering. The nearby barracks had come alive with the voices of hundreds of conscripted ratings from the far corners of the Union, who were watching the same pictures on TV. But unlike Zof and his fellow-officers, every one of them was delirious with joy, helped by plenty of cheap Navy vodka. The singing grew louder: a crowd was heading for the mess. Zof stayed sitting, watching the TV, a smoking cigarette in his nicotine-stained fingers. The others became nervous and jumped up. The crowd was now outside the door.

There was a crash and a metal crate flew through the window, which exploded into daggers of glass that cascaded through the air and scattered spinning to the ground. Still Zof remained sitting. There was a heavy beating at the door; it flew open, and a handful of young, half-drunk sailors pushed into the room, less confident now as they entered the mess, the forbidden ground where none of them had ever before been allowed to enter.

Zof calmly got up from his chair, ground out his cigarette under his foot and walked straight up to the youngster who was first through the door. The kid froze. Zof was a big man, whose black Captain's uniform and scrub of crew-cut hair made him look even more forbidding. He stopped a foot in front of the young sailor, casually rested his hand on the black leather holster of his service automatic and stared into the kid's now frightened eyes. Their faces were no more than six inches apart. Zof didn't blink once.

There was an angry silence. The other sailors stared at Zof. The officers stared at the ratings. Zof wasn't a man you treated like this; they all knew that. What would he do? Behind them, on the screen, the Berlin

Wall continued to crumble. The sailor looked at Zof, fearfully at first, and then it dawned on him. Zof and his officers were now the past. Their world was ending. There was no point. Why waste the effort? The youngster smiled, shrugged and turned round, leading his comrades back out into the warm Pacific night.

Zof was left standing there. The world he had been born into nearly fifty years ago was breathing its last. This was the final humiliation: ignored by a snotty-nosed kid who six months ago would have been proud to serve under him. He buttoned up his jacket and smoothed his cap neatly on to his crew-cut head. Captain First Rank Yakov Zof lit another cigarette and walked out into the night. His small group of officers, every one of whom would have followed him to the ends of the oceans, were left behind, nervous and confused. No one had ever ignored Zof before. It was just not possible ... not with someone like Zof.

Along the winding quays, the vast Red Banner Pacific Fleet was already tied up and silent. Famous ships lay tired and forgotten. The colossal *Kiev*. The huge *Admiral Gorshkov*. The great *Stalin*, still towering above them all even from this distance. No ship had moved for a month. Probably they would never move again. It seemed a lifetime ago that the port was a mass of ships and of people and of noise, and the sweet smell of fuel oil hung in the polluted air, and nobody cared; the rambling naval port was one of the biggest in the Soviet Union, and for all the years since the revolution and for many years before had been Great Russia's maritime fortress against the threats from the Pacific – first the Japanese, and lately the Americans. It was a whole life here, remembered Zof bitterly. He was born here. He did much of his training here. He married here. And now his life was collapsing in the same place.

In the distance, young sailors were still singing. Zof had struggled all his life in this place now haunted by the ghosts of his past. The years of training, the years of working under officers he hated, the long months spent at sea that had cost him – so recently it still hurt – his marriage and his child, then that final glorious moment a month ago when his commission came through and he finally made the rank of Captain. Now, no crew, no fleet, no Navy, no family. They hadn't even found him a ship.

Mother Russia had taken everything he had to give, and now the bitch had turned round and spat in his face. But what really burned deep in Zof's darkened soul was the foolishness of the fact that, bitch or not, Mother Russia still mattered. Crazy, he thought. Crazy. What was she going to ask from him next? He flicked the crumpled stub of his cigarette into the dark, still water of the dock. He wasn't sure that Mother Russia could speak any more. He wasn't sure he even wanted to listen.

1

MOSCOW, 4th DECEMBER 1938

The tension in the glittering hall was making most of them sweat, even though the temperature was barely above freezing and their breaths hung in the air in damp, slowly-drifting veils. The walls glimmered with shining mosaics: the Granovitaya Chamber of the Kremlin, where for centuries the civilised world's ambassadors had gathered nervously to present lavish gifts to the latest Tsar, had become since the Revolution nothing but a vast, echoing waiting room.

Of the party of seven, only Maslov was looking relaxed. A stocky, grim-faced man with an awesome reputation as an Admiral who wouldn't give an inch to anyone, he was hunched in an almost soundless conversation with Badaev, Chief of Procurement of the Soviet Navy – both men keeping their voices low in a habit as old as the Kremlin itself. This was a country where you knew for certain that, behind the wall or the pillar, there really was someone straining to catch your thoughts. Maslov's easiness was far from shared by the only member of the group in ill-fitting civilian clothes: the slight, bespectacled, nervous figure of Mikhail Kishkov, accepted even by Maslov as the most talented warship designer in the country as well as a complete pain in the backside and a spoiled brat whose temper and eccentricities had to be tolerated.

Kishkov remained stiff and silent, his stomach churning with nerves; he jumped when a sullen Mongolian suddenly appeared and then silently ushered the party through a set of massive oak doors into a smaller, plainer room, dominated by a huge table and surrounded by heavy chairs each one of which still displayed the Romanov double-headed eagle carved into the black oak. The doors closed silently behind them. The time had come.

Even Maslov was quiet now. He stood with arms folded, and closed his eyes as if in some ritual meditation. The rest of the party remained standing and nervously produced files from their briefcases which they each started to arrange neatly on the table in front of their chairs.

Maslov had taken up position behind the chair in the middle of one long side of the table. On his left stood Badaev; next to him was Kishkov, Chief Designer of the Bureau of Naval Construction. Then came Belov, Deputy Chief of Procurement and an accountant by training.

On Maslov's right was Vorov, head of Naval Intelligence, accompanied by his deputy Rodin. Then there was the Political Commissar for the Naval General Staff, fat Vlasik, who wore a uniform, although he was not entitled to one, because he thought it made him look better.

At the end of the room opposite the doors through which they had just come was a smaller door of the same black oak, polished to a deep gleam, with shining brass handles. Several minutes passed, then there was the sound of several sets of footsteps approaching the other side of the door. The footsteps went silent, one by one. Kishkov started to feel physically sick. The door opened softly. Through it came three men with an air of relaxed importance, two in unusually well-cut dark civilian suits, double-breasted and neat.

Kishkov recognised one of the men immediately. Short, balding Lavrenti Beria, his eyes almost invisible behind thick wire pince-nez: the head of the KGB, the most frightening man in the Soviet Union. Behind him walked Poskrebyshev, a lumbering, time-serving bureaucrat who had risen through the Party ranks to become a member of the Central Committee.

The last of the three through the door, shorter than the other two and walking slowly with a relaxed air, was dressed in the felt boots and loose tunic of the kulak, the Russian peasant. But the boots were made of an unusually fine felt and the tunic was clean, expertly tailored and appeared to be made of silk instead of the usual rough wool. The two civilians quietly moved to each side of the peasant, leaving him to take the central chair, the one with a higher back than the others and a carved double-headed eagle that was richly gilded. As Beria and Poskrebyshev waited respectfully for the short man to sit down, there was a steady, complete silence in the room.

Kishkov was rooted to the spot as he watched the figure approach. The heavy eyes, the thick-set face, the drooping, luxuriant black moustache so thick it virtually covered his mouth. It was a face that had stared at him from almost every street corner in Moscow. As Kishkov watched, the man pulled out the chair and sat down, waited for a moment, looked around him, then motioned that the others might sit too.

'Good morning, Comrade Admiral,' said Josef Vissarionovitch Dzhugashvili, known since his early days as a communist revolutionary in Georgia as the Steel Man, Stalin in Russian. The dictator had started the meeting.

*

Kishkov watched Stalin with fascination. He had never been this near the father of the nation, and he was surprised that the General Secretary wasn't at least six feet tall and as handsome as the posters showed him. His hair was not the rich black that the pictures portrayed but grey, and thinning on top, and his face had a tired pallor. He was fatter than his pictures, too.

Maslov started to introduce his group one by one, each giving a little bow as their names were mentioned. Stalin nodded silently back, looking at each man under the heavily-lidded eyes. When it came to Kishkov's turn his neck muscles froze and instead of bowing all he could do was hunch his shoulders like a cripple. But Stalin didn't seem to notice.

Maslov thanked Comrade Beria and Comrade General Secretary Stalin for their time; appreciating how busy they were with great matters of state, nevertheless this was something he was sure they would want to know about. Beria and Stalin watched Maslov silently, without acknowledging his flattery, and the Admiral then briskly started his presentation. The third man – Poskrebyshev, Stalin's faithful assistant – was hunched over his notebook and scribbled down every word that Maslov spoke without once looking up at anyone.

'The General Secretary will hardly need me to remind him of the policy laid down by the seventeenth plenary session of the Communist Party two years ago where the secret protocol regarding naval superiority was agreed. As I recall, the Comrade General Secretary was instrumental in ensuring that the Navy was granted the mandate to start its new building programme,' continued Maslov, and Stalin acknowledged the compliment with a lazy move of his hand like a monarch idly waving to the crowds.

'Gaining and then maintaining naval superiority in all four fleet theatres was insisted upon to protect the motherland from the aggressors of the capitalist countries. The General Secretary is of course aware of the plans of our enemies to build bigger and bigger ships. Up until now we have matched our efforts against those of the British, the Americans and the Germans. The threat in the east was not seen as so immediate, but nevertheless was carefully watched by my staff, and today I have news which I think you will find as disturbing as I do.'

Beria's eyes narrowed behind the thick lenses. Intelligence was his domain, and he would violently defend any encroachments on his territory. He should have known about this. The head of his eastern section would find himself inside the Lubianka prison by nightfall if what he was about to hear was really new.

Maslov saw the look in Beria's eyes with some amusement. The battle between the KGB and the military intelligence organisations had been going on for years. Victories for the military side were rare, and all the more pleasurable for being so. 'Comrade Vorov will explain,' continued Maslov, and sat down, leaving the floor to his respected head of Intelligence.

Vorov was a classic Navy man, tall, square-jawed, dedicated and absolutely ruthless. Beria had been watching him for over a year now and had carefully compiled a detailed dossier on his dalliances with at least two other officers' wives. He would soon arrest the husband of one of the wives for spying for the Germans, which would leave Vorov in the spotlight. Not long now, my naval friend, not long now. Beria removed his pince-nez glasses and started to polish them with a clean white handkerchief as Vorov stood up and opened a folder, reading from it like a hymn-book.

'Last March,' Vorov began, 'we had reports from reliable sources that the Japanese were planning a new class of battleship which was to be something altogether more ominous than simply an upgrading of existing ideas. Our reports suggested a battleship of 70,000 tons, a speed of over thirty knots, massive armour-plating rendering it virtually indestructible, and nine eighteen-inch guns on three massive armoured turrets. Our own naval experts were clear that a ship like this would be bigger, faster and more powerful than any vessel afloat or planned to be afloat, by us, the Germans, the British or even the Americans.'

Vorov looked up at Stalin. 'Clearly, any nation with a ship such as this would pose a massive threat to our security. And, indeed, anyone else's. However, our intelligence services were convinced that although plans existed, there was little evidence that building such a ship had commenced, or was even likely given the costs and technical difficulties involved. Indeed, the latest eastern intelligence digest – issued last week, I believe,' and he held up the thick document with the KGB initials prominent on the front cover, 'specifically states that construction was nowhere near ready to commence and, even if it did, it would be at least six or seven years before the ship was complete.'

He placed the intelligence report carefully on the table in front of him. Beria continued staring coldly at him, the thick lenses making his eyes bigger. Stalin folded his hands together and looked slightly amused. He enjoyed seeing little scraps like this; it left him feeling secure.

But Beria was less relaxed. 'Comrade Vorov, I do hope you haven't dragged us into a meeting to play a fantasy game over this fairy tale. The Navy's been peddling the super-ship story for years now. You realise it's just a plant, don't you? The Americans have tried to scare us with that one since I don't know when. Don't tell me you've gone and fallen for it?'

'I appreciate Comrade Beria's concern. However, we can now update the situation with some solid evidence. The situation is worse than we had been led to believe,' replied Vorov, returning Beria's smug look with a cold and contemptuous stare. 'Our latest intelligence tells us that Doctor Hiraga of the Imperial Japanese Navy drew up the final detailed plans for this super-ship just about the same time as we received the original reports. We have now had confirmation that the plans are, as we speak, being put into effect, and work on this monstrous new ship has now started at Kure naval yard. We were alerted to this by the deepening of the dry dock by over a metre and the erection of a special roof to screen the work from view. We understand that three other vessels of a similar class are being started shortly. We believe construction will take about four years, which would mean the first vessel being in active service towards the end of 1942.'

There was a pause. This was a lot sooner than anyone had thought possible.

'So the Japanese are building a big battleship. Surely we have many ships in our fleet that could dispose of such a vessel?' said Stalin, looking slyly at Beria as he spoke.

Maslov took up the comment, looking directly at Stalin. 'Comrade General Secretary, this is perhaps the biggest threat to our naval power this century. Consider these drawings.' He handed across sketches of the Japanese battleship. 'It will have a top speed of thirty-one knots. It can outrun any ship we have. Our fastest vessels will reach only twenty-eight knots. And even if we did catch it, we could do nothing, even with our biggest guns. The ship is an armour-plated box.

The sides of Vickers hardened armour plate are over eighteen inches thick. Our biggest sixteen-inch shells would bounce off it like rubber balls. And then, if it chose to shoot back, its eighteen-inch projectiles would rip apart any vessel in its way. It would have the run of the world's oceans. It is not a thought that I, as Commander of the Pacific Fleet, care for one little bit, Comrade General Secretary.'

Stalin thought for a moment and then shrugged. 'I presume you're telling me this so that you can present your solution, Comrade Admiral?'

Maslov smiled. 'The Comrade General Secretary understands the naval mind. We can counter this threat, but we need your authority to get the project going any further. Since we heard of these developments, we have had our esteemed Chief of Naval Design, Comrade Kishkov here, develop a set of plans of our own. A great deal of work has been done already, Comrade General Secretary, and fortunately we are able to make some very positive recom-mendations.'

Maslov was promptly handed a sheaf of papers by Badaev; he in turn handed a set to Stalin, to Beria, and then left the others on the table, pointedly ignoring the still-scribbling Poskrebyshev who carried on with his careful note-taking.

'If the Comrade General Secretary would be so kind as to inspect these drawings and papers, we have prepared a list of the attributes of the Japanese ship on the left-hand side of the paper, and a list of the attributes of the Soviet ship we plan to build on the right-hand side. You will see that the Japanese vessel, designated A-140, will have a displacement of 69,500 tons. We propose a vessel with a displacement of 75,000 tons. The so-called A-140 has a top speed of 31 knots. We propose a top speed of 35 knots, using steam turbines producing 250,000 horsepower. The A-140 has 22,000 tons of armour. We propose 34,000 tons, up to two feet thick in places, capable of dealing with eighteen-inch shells. The Japanese ship is to have an armoured double bottom against torpedoes. We propose a triple bottom, with thicker armour and a honeycomb watertight structure that will withstand any torpedo attack,' continued Maslov. 'And to prevent the ship being disabled by having its rudders or propellers blown off by a lucky torpedo strike, we propose a unique arrangement of armoured cages as well as hiding the propellers in armoured tunnels under the hull.'

The Admiral paused for a moment to let the pile of facts sink in. He looked up at Stalin, who remained silent and impassive, and then carried on. 'Lastly, Comrade General Secretary, we propose to counter the A-140's nine eighteen-inch guns with nine twenty-two-inch guns, the biggest ever made. They will be able to hurl a four-ton shell over thirty miles. No ship could withstand such a force. With this vessel, we will be able to dominate the oceans. It will become the undisputed master of the seas.'

Maslov left the final words hanging in the air, looked at Stalin and Beria, and then sat down.

There was a silence while everyone waited to see if Stalin would speak, but he remained silent, looking carefully at the list, right-hand, left-hand, weighing up the threat and the counter-threat laid out on the single sheet of paper.

Beria broke the silence with a snort. 'The Comrade Admiral is noted for his optimism. What makes him think the Japanese really are going ahead on this project? It's far too big and far too costly. Why does he think a bunch of orientals can build such a monster? I understand that Comrade Vorov's resources in Japan are somewhat thin. Of course, I would be happy to help out. We in the KGB have a number of excellent agents in the Kure area. Perhaps, you'd like me to give them a call?'

Vorov smiled. 'Comrade Beria is most generous. However, we are fortunate in having a very highly placed source in the Kure shipyard itself. Naval Intelligence has been working with him for some years. Naturally we asked for substantial proof, otherwise we would not be wasting the Comrade General Secretary's time. Perhaps these photographs would help?' Vorov's trump card, or cards, were inside the enormous envelope. As Beria balefully watched, he opened the envelope with a hint of ceremony and produced four very large black and white photographs, which he turned round and laid out carefully on the table in front of Stalin. Stalin looked through heavily-lidded eyes at each photograph, carefully inspecting one, then another.

'The first photograph was taken some months ago and shows the main keel being laid. You can see the size of the ship from the smallness of the Japanese workers in the picture. You can also see the start of the armour-plating on the bottom. The next three pictures were taken a few days ago. You can see the surprising degree of progress made, with the hull plating already more or less complete. We have analysed the pictures with our engineers and they confirm the dimensions we have already heard about. Given the progress shown in these photographs, we have no doubt that this ship will be on the high seas by 1941 or 1942 at the latest.'

Stalin slowly put down the pictures. Beria refused even to look, but stared across the table at Vorov with undisguised venom. Less than a year later, Vorov was arrested and charged with being a German spy, to which he confessed fully following a day of interrogation at the hands of one of Beria's more talented thugs. He was shot one warm, sunny July morning a few days later.

Stalin looked up at Maslov with half-closed eyes, but stayed quiet. Then he turned his gaze to Kishkov. Kishkov's heart suddenly jumped and immediately started pounding in his chest.

'So, comrade, you can take on this Japanese monster? I'm glad to hear that communist ship-building and engineering is up to the task. How's it to be done? Exactly?' he asked, leaning back in his chair, waiting for the most obviously nervous member of Maslov's team to mess things up.

But Kishkov suddenly felt more confident. Though he knew that building such a ship would be far from easy, he did at least know that it could be done. In detail – exactly. Well, almost. 'Comrade General Secretary, we certainly have the ability to build this vessel. We have been working on designs for some time, and have most of the detail sorted out. I have built scale models and tested them in tanks. I see no major problems. We know more or less exactly how to build such a ship.'

Badaev looked skyward at Kishkov's last statement and waited for the inevitable.

Stalin jumped in with surprising speed for someone who gave the appearance of being half-asleep most of the time. 'More or less, Comrade Chief Designer? More or less? Perhaps you could indicate those parts of this ship you know more about building and those parts you know less about?'

Beria's look of contempt suddenly brightened, but Maslov quickly rescued Kishkov with an airy wave of the hand. 'A figure of speech, Comrade General Secretary. Chief Designer Kishkov is a modest man. His plans are worked out to the last detail. If the Comrade General Secretary would care to inspect them, I can have the drawings sent over within the hour.'

Kishkov nearly died. No such drawings yet existed. Early drafts, scribbled on with his crude demands to re-draw this or that, were all that he had. And it would take him a lot longer than an hour even to find them.

Stalin went silent, and looked carefully through the list that Maslov had handed over. A full minute passed. 'It looks expensive,' he said finally. 'We have many demands on our slim resources, Comrade Admiral. Many of them are more pressing than joining in an arms race with the rest of the world.'

Maslov spoke softly. 'Of course, it is finally a political decision. However, we have costed the project carefully, Comrade General Secretary. My staff and I believe so strongly in this project that we would be happy to delay the building of the two heavy cruisers that we were due to start next year. This will save around one hundred and fifty million roubles. We will, however, need an additional budget of some fifty million roubles. I appreciate that this alone is a substantial sum, Comrade General Secretary.'

Kishkov was astonished again. This was nothing like the estimates he had gone over with Maslov just two days earlier. The Admiral had cut a full half from the price.

Stalin grunted with what must have been a laugh. 'Well, well, Maslov. I've never seen a Navy man give up two new ships so easily before. This must be important. Bring some tea,' he ordered and Poskrebyshev, without pausing or even looking up from his notes, immediately pressed a bell-push on the table near his hand. Two servants must have been waiting outside; within seconds they entered the room with glasses of tea. There was a stiff silence as the two

Asians, both improbably tall and heavily built and obviously Beria's KGB thugs, quickly distributed the glasses and then silently left the room, closing the big oak door behind them with a clumsy thud. Stalin slowly sipped his tea. It looked to Kishkov as though he was filtering it through his big moustache.

'Well, comrades. Thank you for your efforts today,' said Stalin eventually, putting down his tea. 'I will put your plan to the Central Committee and see what they have to say. And I would like Comrade Beria here to go over your intelligence, Comrade Vorov. You will make your information freely available to officers of the KGB.' Vorov glared at Beria. 'I also want a few things understood.' Stalin turned to face Kishkov. 'I want none of your cost overruns on this if the Central Committee agrees with me and we go ahead. I'll hold you personally responsible, Comrade Chief Designer, for every rouble you spend over your budget. I'll ship the entire team to Siberia if you ask for so much as an extra kopeck. I'm fed up with seeing these projects get out of hand. Do you understand?'

Kishkov was barely able to speak. He nodded, his heart pounding.

'Also,' continued Stalin, 'I don't want this ship built at Odessa or at Archangel. I know they're the only two yards capable of handling such a project at the moment. If we go ahead, I want the ship secure from the enemy. Those yards are just too near the Germans. Find somewhere on the Asian coast.'

Stalin was as good as conceding that the expected Imperialist War would get as far as the two major seaports of Continental Russia. Maslov, and indeed the rest of the military, knew that if the Germans attacked at the moment it would be a rout; this was the only time he heard Stalin admit as much.

'Find somewhere secret and out of the way,' Stalin

continued, then smiled darkly at Kishkov. 'Of course, Comrade Chief Designer, your team will be be going there too. Make the arrangements. And remember what I said about costs.'

As Stalin stood up, the rest of the meeting almost jumped to their feet. He turned and walked towards the door without murmuring a word. Poskrebyshev hastily closed his notebook and got up, gathering the papers and the photographs, and walked quickly towards the door, following Stalin and Beria. The big door flew open yards before the dictator reached it, but suddenly Stalin stopped and faced Maslov again.

'By the way, Comrade Admiral, what is this Japanese ship to be called?'

Maslov paused. 'I believe it is to be called *Yamoto*, Comrade General Secretary. I am told it is a poetic Japanese name for the land on which the first seeds of empire were sown. It is a name revered by the Japanese people.'

Stalin nodded wisely. 'And tell me, Comrade Admiral, do you have as good a name for our new ship?'

'Indeed, Comrade General Secretary. What else could we call it but *Stalin*?' replied Maslov, smiling.

Stalin grinned hugely, and even Poskrebyshev looked up at Maslov with a smile. 'Well done, Comrade Admiral, I knew your talent for flattery would not desert you. But I accept the honour graciously. Let's hope the Central Committee will share your enthusiasm for the ship. And of course the name.' He hurried briskly from the room with a sly smile across his face, the slight figure of Beria hurrying along beside him. As the big door closed there was a sudden release of tension like a tightened rope being suddenly severed, and Maslov began to put away his papers. 'Thank you, comrades. I think that went rather well. I cannot imagine that the Central Committee will disagree with our analysis. What do you think, Vlasik?' he asked the fat Naval Political Commissar, who disliked Maslov as much as Maslov disliked him.

'Our leader cares only for the safety of the motherland, Comrade Admiral. If the Comrade General Secretary recommends it, then I am sure the Central Committee will want to support him.'

Maslov snorted contemptuously. 'The same old bullshit, Vlasik. You should do something useful and lean on a few of your friends in the Party to make sure they agree.' Vlasik shrugged and ignored the comment. His time would come.

They were led out of the room by the two Asian thugs who had brought in the tea, and were deposited back in the Granovitaya Chamber, amongst the glimmering mosaics and the curious stares of other groups of military men waiting for their turn. The two Asians vanished.

Kishkov was agitated. As Maslov was pushing his arms into his tailored greatcoat, so long that it brushed the floor, he confronted the Admiral. 'Comrade Admiral, forgive me, but this is simply impossible, quite impossible. You cut the budget by millions of roubles. I cannot build the ship for that kind of money. He'll kill me if I overrun,' hissed Kishkov, keeping his voice down in case Beria's men were behind a convenient pillar.

Maslov glared at Kishkov. 'Listen, Comrade Chief Designer,' he growled in a threatening whisper, 'let me tell you one fact of life. If Comrade Stalin wants it done that way, that's exactly the way it gets done. If he wants it for ten roubles, that's what we give him. Our accountants are just as clever as our engineers, and far more creative. Now shut up and leave it to me.' Maslov winked and walked off, leaving only Badaev behind.

They walked from the great hall out into the freezing Moscow morning. The dirty snow lay deep, piled up against the ancient walls of the Kremlin fortress, covering the domes of St Basil across Red Square with a greyish white. Only the granite mausoleum of Lenin, swept every day, remained clear of the grubby snow, stained with the smoke of a million stoves and chimneys that struggled to keep the inhabitants of Moscow warm. They watched as Maslov and his party climbed into the black limousines flying the Red Banner, the naval ensign of a yellow star surrounding a small hammer and sickle on a blood-red background. Badaev bade farewell to Kishkov before getting into the last car of the small convoy. 'Cheer up Mikhail Mikhailovitch. Think about Vladivostok. I hear it can be quite pleasant in the summer.'

'If I live that long,' replied Kishkov, using an old Moscow saying that was the standard reply to any promise of anything remotely pleasant made in the depths of the interminable Russian winter.

'Trust Maslov, Mikhail Mikhailovitch. He wants this ship. Leave the politics to him and you won't go far wrong.' The fat black limousines pulled away from the Kremlin, rattled over the cobbles and drove at speed out of the gate, to go the short distance down the road towards the big building between Ulitsa Frunze and Kalinin Prospekt known as House Number One, the Ministry of Defence main building.

Kishkov turned towards the Moskva River, still and white, frozen to a depth of two feet, and walked quickly to the newly completed Metro. He would remember Badaev's last words, but it would be for a lot longer than he could have guessed.

2

VLADIVOSTOK, 10th JUNE 1997

Feliks Zof was as different from his stiff Navy brother, Yakov, as it was possible to be. He was a short, sweaty, unshaven man who tried to look like one of the boys, except that he still had plenty of cash for vodka. In an attempt to defeat middle age, he wore faded Levis and a T-shirt that bore, dubiously, the name Armani. Now on his fifth drink, he would peel thousand-rouble notes from a wad as thick as a paperback book whenever the waitress brought another glass. He had dollars, of course, but why waste them if they took roubles?

It was still only two in the afternoon. He'd woken up feeling dreadful and got himself down to the bar as quickly as he could to get a few vodkas inside him. The churning in his stomach was only now starting to subside. As he drained the chipped glass, the sullen waitress replaced it with his sixth, swapping the glass for more of the creased notes. It was almost a challenge: bet you can't make it seven. But he would.

Feliks began to feel more cheerful and ignored the waitress. The sun glimmered off the oily, debris-littered sea in the harbour. The sky was a hazy blue and the smell of sulphur from the nearby steel-works scented the lazy breeze with its familiar flavour. His head had stopped feeling as though it had become detached from his body overnight. A distinct improvement, he said to himself, and lifted the next vodka to his unshaved mouth. He was so improved, in fact, that he began to take some notice of his surroundings, and in particular of the three strangers who kept glancing in his direction.

To Feliks Zof, strangers were people to be treated with great caution. The men sat at the other end of the grubby terrace. The only other people in the bar were hidden inside the gloomy interior; a bunch of old men, reading a single newspaper divided up into sections amongst themselves so that everyone got a bit to read. The three strangers were separated from Zof by the distance of half-a-dozen grubby white plastic tables. Two were neatly dressed and intense-looking. The other one was surprisingly fat, wore shorts and shirt and, oddly in this weather, a white scarf around his fat neck that completely covered it, and he was smiling broadly in Zof's direction. They had to be tourists: a novel sight on the streets of Vladivostok. The numbers were small and most of them were Japanese or even American, and so were stuffed with yen and dollars; either currency was worth more than gold as far as Zof and the gangs that ran Vladivostok were concerned, and thus were fair game for any plan that could be hatched to relieve them of some of it.

But these looked different from the usual tourists who wandered by mistake into the bar and then quickly finished their drinks and got out again as fast as they could. The usual kind were dressed in ridiculous shorts and loud shirts and hung cameras from their necks. But two of the men seated opposite Zof wore pressed slacks and respectable shirts, and there wasn't a camera in sight. With their careful haircuts and expensive shoes, they were definitely not ordinary Russians. And the KGB couldn't afford to have people sitting around in bars; not these days.

Zof wondered uneasily what they were doing and then, with a sudden flush of adrenalin, it dawned on him that they were looking very directly at him with a worrying level of interest. As he stared back at them, they made no attempt to avert their eyes. He glanced quickly away and started to panic. The effects of the vodka rapidly vanished.

He told himself to calm down. They were only tourists, after all. But no tourist he'd ever seen was dressed like that. He glanced up quickly and felt his face flush as he met their gaze for a brief moment before looking away again. Jesus Christ, they were still staring at him! His mind filled quickly with all sorts of terrors. Did he owe them money? He couldn't remember. He'd ignore them for a few minutes and then, if they were still staring at him, he'd go over and sort them out. He settled back into his chair and took another generous swig at his vodka glass, trying to look unconcerned. Maybe they just wanted girls or drugs and were too shy to ask. Maybe he should offer to help? If they were still looking at him ... which, of course, they were, the moment he looked up at them again; the fat one continued to beam happily directly at him.

Zof finished glass number six and stood up. What the hell, he thought. Maybe they need a good kicking. Feeling brave, he sauntered across to their table, pulled up a chair and sat down confidently. He beckoned to the sullen waitress.

In his bad but recognisable English, of which he was extremely proud – learned from his brief time at Navy school before he got thrown out, the influence of his respected older brother Yakov notwithstanding – he asked, 'Drinks with me, yes?' He hoped his English would impress them.

The three tourists looked at each other. One was tall, you could tell, even though he was sitting down, and thin and bony. He had long elegant fingers and a generous mop of dark hair. Close up, Zof noticed he was not quite so neat as he appeared from a distance, and for some reason this made him feel friendly towards the man. He wore crumpled white slacks, but they still managed to look expensive.

The second was shorter and older, with a rough weather-beaten face and thinning curly hair; he was wearing a Ralph Lauren Polo shirt that Zof would happily have mugged him for, showing thick, hairy forearms that although devoid of a tattoo reminded him of Popeye. The very fat man with the scarf was still smiling at Zof, but there was something sinister about him and Zof quickly decided he didn't like the look of him.

The shorter, older man replied in a broad New York accent, which Zof didn't recognize. 'Sure, we'd love a drink with you.'

Zof was hugely pleased with himself that he had spoken in English. He felt he had made a good impression; this was important.

Zof ordered drinks, in Russian, from the hovering waitress. As she walked off into the dark interior, he relaxed and introduced himself, now settling into the part of the friendly host, though the inane smile from the fat one made him feel nervous. 'Welcome to Vladivostok. You Americans? Call me Zof. Where you come in America?'

It was the shorter, older one who spoke again. He seemed to be the leader. 'Nice to meet you, Mr Zof. We come from all over. My friend here comes from England. I come from New York. You heard of New York?' he asked, smiling at Zof, but the smile was cold and deliberate.

'Sure I heard New York. No problem. Washington, Chicago, Miami, Mexico, all that kind of place. So what you do here, huh? Why you look so long at Zof in the corner, for instance?'

There was a pause. 'Mr Zof, I'm glad you asked that question. You see, me and my friends were looking for someone to help us out with a business proposition. We heard that Feliks Zof was the man to see. Now I wonder if we're right or wrong in that information?'

Zof went silent. They had come here to find him; this was bad. 'Sure. This all depends. You're buying what, exactly? Maybe you should buy Zof to start with, Zof knows everyone,' he laughed, but he wasn't joking. 'Zof gets you good deal, no crap. Everyone else fuck you. Anything you want, Zof will get. Within some reason you understand. Atom bombs not possible. Maybe next year,' he chortled. Two of the men enjoyed the joke hugely and raised their glasses to Zof's humour. The fat one remained silently smiling.

'Well, Mr Zof, I guess you could say that we're kind of interested in all sorts of things. We had heard from some of our friends that Feliks Zof was well known hereabouts for being able to fix things up. In fact, we had hoped to meet you here. We were told you could be found in this bar. Now isn't it just great that we found you?' The American's face hardened and changed quickly from being that of an innocent tourist to something that Zof felt a lot less comfortable with.

'So you found Zof. Lucky boys. Who tell you this?'

'Mr Zof, there's no need to worry. Me and my associates here are looking to do some good business with people we can trust. We'd like to discuss our proposition with you at your convenience. If that's OK with you.'

'Business is what Zof does. What business though? Only certain business that Zof can do. You need certain things in Vladivostok, maybe Zof can help. Certain other things, not so good. Other people's business, understand?'

'We perfectly well appreciate your situation,' replied the tall Englishman. Vladivostok was divided up amongst the gangs who each had their own areas of business. Zof had to be careful not to tread on other people's toes.

Zof shrugged. 'OK. You talk. Maybe Zof can help.'

'We'd greatly prefer it if we could discuss our business matters somewhere a little more discreet. Perhaps you'd like to meet at our hotel? We're staying at the Imperial. Join us for dinner perhaps?'

Zof didn't like the idea of meeting three strangers on his own, but dinner at the Imperial was a very status thing to do. And whatever dangers lurked around the street corners of Vladivostok, he had not yet heard of anyone being machine-gunned in the Imperial. The Japanese gang bosses would never stand for it.

'OK. Zof will meet you at Imperial for dinner. Eight. No trouble. We talk good business. Perhaps you give Zof some idea of business now?'

The stocky American ignored his question. 'That's excellent, Zof. We'll very much look forward to meeting you tonight. Very much indeed. I'm sure you'll find it most interesting. Now, if you'll excuse me, me and my good friends here must make our way back. A great pleasure to meet you, a very great pleasure indeed.'

The strangers stood up before Zof could reply, and one after the other they left the bar as he stayed sitting carefully watching their departure. The fat one looked back over his shoulder as they disappeared around the corner towards the seafront; his face was hidden in shadow from the bright sun behind him and Zof couldn't make out his expression, but he still felt the strange smile from the dark figure as he followed the other two around the corner, leaving only his slowly receding shadow pulling along the ground until it too vanished.

*

The Imperial was an impressive pile of stone and glass put up at the end of the last century by a Scottish architect and a Russian hotelier. It was a Victorian vision of a baronial mansion transplanted to the East, where the Scottish turrets had got tangled up with Chinese dragons and ended up looking like a film set. Most of the buildings in Vladivostok had a similar flamboyance. It was a city where cultures clashed, and it couldn't make up its mind if it was East or West; it looked remarkably similar to San Francisco, even down to the trams struggling up and down the hilly streets overlooking the sea.

Since the Revolution the Imperial had slipped slowly into decay like the fading member of an exiled aristocracy, poorer and poorer as each year went past. It had reached rock-bottom by the time Gorbachev assumed power and had lain derelict until Japanese property developers, seeing which way the wind was blowing, bought it for next to nothing and rebuilt it as one of the grandest hotels in the East.

Feliks Zof had ironed a shirt for the occasion, though he couldn't manage to find a tie. He took the trouble to shave for the second time that week and, stopping briefly to admire himself in a mirror, then drove erratically back to town, with the music from the 8-track tape-deck beating through the open windows. He parked the dented BMW 630 Csi outside the grand front entrance the way they did in the movies, to the obvious disgust of the Korean doorman, and walked into the lobby. He was the only Russian in the building.

The entrance hallway was vast as a palace, and small groups of Americans, Japanese, Chinese and Japanese stood around: tourists or businessmen anxious to lay their hands on the decaying corpse of the Soviet Union; long-lost relatives gathering around the bedside of a dying millionaire.

The older American was leaning against the reception desk, arms folded, as Zof walked in through the doors into the cool, air-conditioned foyer. He made no sign of recognition but looked steadily at Zof, and carried on leaning against the dark walnut veneer desk, making the Russian walk the full distance of the hall to meet him.

Only when Zof was within a couple of yards of the man did he stir himself, although he kept his eyes on him all the way. Suddenly the American pushed himself away from the desk to stand upright, smiled but only with his mouth, and swung out a hand towards Zof's. 'Mr Zof, it's good of you to come. A pleasure to see you again. My colleagues are waiting in the restaurant. I guess we should go straight through,' he said loudly and enthusiastically, making sure that anyone who wondered what this scruffy Russian was doing in this hotel understood that above-board, perfectly legal business was about to be done.

Zof took the American's outstretched hand and let himself be led towards the restaurant down a long, thickly carpeted corridor. The American was talking in a loud voice as they went about how much he was enjoying his stay in Vladivostok and what a wonderful city it was, though Zof found it difficult to keep up with his chatter. He was talking fast, even for an American.

As they drew level with a door signposted to the toilets in English and Japanese, but not Russian, someone was coming out; it was the fat one Zof had seen with the others in the bar and he was smiling broadly, straight at Zof. He was dressed more formally this time but his suit didn't fit well, and he still wore the white scarf. Then it all happened too quickly for Zof to react. With a powerful push Zof's escort, still chattering, shoved him bodily into the alcove that partly concealed the door to the toilets. The fat one, ready and waiting, grabbed Zof by both arms and the Russian, still stumbling from the first push, was then jolted upright as his arms were held in a surprisingly powerful grip. He was almost lifted off his feet as he was turned round and pushed towards the door which the fat man shoved open with a fast but soft kick. As the door bounced away, Zof was pushed through and into the silent, deserted marble-lined toilets. His escort quickly pushed the door shut behind them, and the American leaned against the dark wooden door to prevent anyone else from coming in.

The snatch was over within seconds. Zof was only now beginning to react. The fat one, a smile still fixed on his face, stood calmly away before Zof could grab him, but the American had already produced a small automatic gun which he was holding with both hands, arms outstretched, a foot from Zof's face. Just as Zof was thinking of aiming a kick at any one of them, he looked at the gun and stopped dead in a semi-crouch, his eyes wide and his hands clenched together in small, angry fists.

'So unpleasant, I'm afraid, Mr Zof, but I'm sure as you'll appreciate you can't be too careful these days. Such a sad reflection on the times. Now, Mr Charlie, how do we find our good Russian friend here?' The American spoke with a smile but held the gun steadily a foot from Zof's eyes, and Zof slowly straightened up. As he did so, the American followed him upwards with the gun.

The fat one, Charlie, now warily approached the Russian. He laid his hands on his shoulders and then quickly body-searched him, running his hands down his back, round the waistband of his trousers, round his groin and finally around the tops of his feet. For a man of his size he was surprisingly light with his touch. Zof stood stock-still while the search was taking place. The fat man stopped as he felt around the top of Zof's right sock; he carefully lifted the bottom of Zof's trouser-leg and removed a five-inch knife that Zof took with him on all occasions as a matter of habit. His smile broadened and he shook his head at Zof.

'That's all, Mr Able,' said the fat one, in a hoarse, gravelly whisper that owed nothing to a need to be quiet. He handed the knife over to the American, who lowered the gun. It was the moment Zof had been waiting for. He ducked down and swung a fist at the fat man, who leaned coolly back while the fist flailed harmlessly past him. Zof froze again, wondering if he should swing again or make a run. While he was thinking about it, the fat man moved back towards him with a speed and precision that took him by surprise, and soundlessly rammed his outstretched hand into the bottom of Zof's ribcage, pushing inwards and upwards, a smile creasing his plump, shiny face. Zof's knees gave way instantly like a cow being slaughtered, and he flopped to the ground in a tangle of collapsing limbs.

They both stood over him while Zof wheezed and coughed, trying desperately to catch some breath. His throat made a soft screeching sound as he fought to draw some air into his chest. Finally he managed to breathe deeply for a few moments and then, as Able and Charlie stood away from him, he pushed himself slowly to a kneeling position. He waited for another blow but when his attackers made no move, he painfully got to his feet. Zof had been in gang scraps before but had never experienced a blow quite like that. The pain was absolute and overwhelming. He thought at first he had been stabbed with a long knife, but he saw no blood and when he carefully touched the spot he felt no wetness.

Mr Charlie put a hand under one arm to help him up, the look on his face one of smiling concern. Zof pushed it away with a threatening stare and the older man, Mr Able, raised a hand to ward Charlie off. Zof turned round and propped himself up against a marble-effect wash basin. He was still trying to catch his breath and he made a croaking noise as he pulled air into his lungs. The two men hung back from him, watching carefully, keeping their distance.

Zof's breath was becoming easier. His face, which had gone the colour of plaster after the blow, now gradually warmed up to its previous patchy redness, and shortly he pulled himself up and took a final deep breath.

'Some fucking welcome, you guys,' he said slowly, nodding his head with each word to emphasise his disgust.

The man called Able replied. 'OK, Zof, you're still alive. Mr Charlie here was being a pussycat with you today, isn't that right?'

Charlie just smiled, and Zof wasn't at all sure if he was agreeing or not.

'What the hell, Zof. Kiss and make up, huh? You OK?' asked Able.

'Sure. OK. Great,' Zof replied.

Able motioned the fat man to check outside the toilet; he pushed open the door, and looked out into the deserted corridor, and turned round to nod at Able who ushered Zof out into the hushed passage. With Able on one side and Charlie on the other, they walked Zof carefully down the corridor towards the polished brass doors to the restaurant; the Japanese owner had decided to call it The Romanov, and had the place done out with four-foot-high plastic double-headed eagles and photographs of the last Tsar's family decorating the walls. The tourists looking at the happy family pictures had no idea that the family lay dead in a bloodstained cellar just a few weeks after the photographs were taken. The irony was not intentional, of course.

With broad smiles they guided Zof past the Korean head waiter, who ignored them all, and steered him to a far corner of the dimly lit restaurant to a secluded table where they sat him down. The tall, thin Englishman was waiting for them, nervously, Zof thought. Zof was still breathing carefully, but more colour had returned to his face and he felt almost normal.

'Zof, I'm sorry about Mr Charlie,' said Able, leaning across the table towards Zof. 'He shouldn't have done it so hard, maybe. We got to be careful, though. You know what I mean, Zof? You look as though you could use a drink.' He beckoned over an attentive waiter and ordered vodka for all of them, and then the food: steaks all round. They could have been anywhere. The waiter scribbled the order and disappeared.

'Now, while we're waiting, maybe I should introduce my associates here. Mr Charlie you've already met. He really shouldn't have hit you like that, but never mind. This is Mr Baker,' he said, indicating the thin Englishman with his mop of hair. 'And, of course, my name's Able,' he smiled. None of them offered a hand to Zof.

'Sure. Able, Baker, Charlie. My name's Lenin. Whatever.'

'Hey, Zof, pretty good. You're feeling better already. You'll feel like a new man after a few drinks,' said the

American who called himself Able. The waiter arrived with five vodkas in fancy glasses with a neatly made twist of lime floating in the top. Zof looked at his glass, then fished out the lime with a nicotine-stained finger and drained the vodka in one long pull. The others didn't touch their drinks, and watched Zof silently.

'Perhaps another. Just to help the blood get flowing.' Able pushed the second glass towards Zof, who repeated the process. 'Now maybe you're feeling a little better?'

'OK. Great. It's wonderful. Like you said. Now maybe you talk business or maybe Zof gets fed up and fucks off. You not so friendly, you know? Maybe Zof takes a dislike to you guys already. No offence.'

The American looked at the thin one, then back at Zof. He leaned forward in his chair and dropped his voice.

'Listen, Zof. We have to be very, very careful. I'm sure you'll understand. We're talking about business that's worth maybe several hundred thousand dollars. Maybe more. In hard cash. Used hundred-dollar bills, the old ones, just like we hear you Russians are so fond of. Me and my friends are talking about a great deal of money, Zof. Now, I'm sure you'll understand the need for our most regrettable precautions just now. Perhaps you'd like to think about it? I mean, maybe it could be too big for you?'

Zof sat silently and thought about several hundred thousand dollars, maybe more, in hard cash, in old-issue hundred-dollar bills that were better currency than gold, and half a second later decided that, what the hell, these guys were right to be careful.

'Sure. No problem. Look, hey, for hundred-dollar bills, Zof can do almost anything. What you interested in? Guns? You want guns, I think. Plenty of guns in Russia now. Zof knows people. Maybe you want girls? No problem.'

The food arrived; it was so quick it must have been microwaved. Zof didn't want it now, but the American launched into it greedily. 'Zof, we're most impressed by your helpfulness,' mumbled Able through a full mouth of steak which he was cramming in as he spoke. 'My associate, Mr Baker here, would like to make you a proposition. Go ahead, Mr Baker. Our good friend here must be eager to hear about our idea. How you feeling now, Zof – OK, huh?'

Zof nodded. The vodkas had repaired much of Charlie's damage, though the pain under his ribcage made it difficult to breathe at all deeply. He started on the third vodka that Baker had politely pushed in his direction.

The mop-haired Englishman called Baker was eating elegantly, carefully cutting up his food into small morsels and putting them discreetly into his mouth. He glanced up at Zof, put down his fork and wiped his mouth delicately with a white napkin. Then he looked at Zof with clear blue eyes, and spoke for the first time.

'Hello, Zof. Look, what I'm about to say is deadly secret. We really don't want anyone to know about this. I mean, not anybody. I do hope you understand. Our friend here,' he nodded to the fat one, 'would be very, very upset if we found out that anyone else had got to know. I am making myself clear?'

'Hey, what do I know? Trust Zof, OK? I don't talk to no one. No problem.'

The Englishman nodded his head. 'That's excellent, Zof, excellent. I'm sure we can trust you. Anyway, I hear you know people in the Navy here. We're told you have some good contacts. In fact, we hear you have a brother … what's his name – Yakov? … who we understand is pretty much respected as a Captain. Are we right?' The Englishman had frankly no idea if he was right or not;

the American had told him it was so earlier that evening. He had seemed very certain, though God knows where he had his information from.

Feliks Zof looked pained. So Yakov had come back to haunt him even here. His older brother had pulled himself up by his bootstraps to escape the back-streets of Vladivostok, had shone at Navy school and had gone on to become a Captain, no less. Yakov had always outshone Feliks. Even at home when they were small, their drunken father would tell Feliks to be more like Yakov. Yakov this, Yakov that. The trouble was that Yakov, his great and very respectable brother, was sitting alone in the Navy yard without a kopeck to his name and Feliks – the family failure, drinker and not-very-successful crook – was sitting here with these guys talking big, big deals. And still his brother dominated the whole conversation. Even here.

'Sure,' said Zof, annoyed. 'My brother Yakov is big deal in the Navy. But no one pay any more. My brother is fucking Captain and not paid for two years. No fucking ship either. Some shit. What you want Navy people for anyway? Navy people got nothing.'

'Oh, they've got a few things, Zof. Plenty of weapons. Plenty of ammunition. Quite a few ships as well, so I hear.'

Zof grinned. 'You want some ship? Jesus, mister, you take what you want. Hey, listen, they even pay you for taking the crap away, for chrissake. Which ship you want? I bring you any ship you like!' he laughed, and all of them laughed with him politely.

'Well, it wasn't just any ship we were after, Mr Zof,' continued the Englishman after a polite pause. 'We were after a rather special ship. And someone to take command. And a crew. Ready to go, as it were.'

'No problem. Any ship you like. Tell Zof, ship ready next day.'

'You can arrange any ship at all?'

'Sure. Any ship. I keep saying. Any one,' said Feliks, holding both hands upwards in a mock gesture of exasperation, but he was careful to keep his eyes on the fat one who stayed smiling throughout.

'How about the *Stalin*? How about if that was the ship we wanted?'

Zof looked carefully at the Englishman. He had to be joking. But he didn't look as though he was joking. He *wasn't* joking.

'Oh, Christ,' groaned Feliks Zof.

*

'You said any ship, Zof. It's the *Stalin* we want. Is that a problem for you? If it is, say so and we'll talk to other people,' said the Englishman, resuming his eating and looking unconcerned.

'Christ, you guys. The *Stalin* is one fucking big ship, you know?'

'Well, now, that's exactly why we want it,' said the American with an edge in his voice.

'It's the biggest thing in the yard, you know this? For instance, *Stalin* disappears one morning, all sorts of shit flying around. It's like some kind of museum thing, you know?'

'So you can't get it? No problem,' said the Englishman.

'Hey, that's not what I'm saying. Jesus, why you want ship like that for chrissake anyway?'

'Do you need to know?'

'Oh no. I wander in, see my brother, drive ship out, no questions asked, crew and all. Forgive me. No offence. For smart guy you got some stupid questions.'

Now the Englishman laughed. 'Fair point, Zof. OK, we'll tell you why later. First, we want you to agree the deal. Listen carefully. We want the ship, we want your brother to captain it, and we want a crew. We want to sail away in *Stalin* in two months' time. You organise that, there's a hundred thousand dollars in cash ready for you now, hundred-dollar bills, and another hundred thousand when we get the ship. If you need more cash to keep people quiet, let us know. No problem. We expect you'll take a good slice of anything that's needed, of course. In other words, if we get our ship ready to go, you make two or three hundred thousand dollars, cash. Good clean currency. How's that sound?'

It sounded too good to be true. It was more money than Zof had ever even thought of in his life. He could retire a wealthy man; he could buy his heart's desire, which at that particular time happened to be a Ferrari F40 in bright red. Now he knew this had to be some kind of a joke. But they looked serious. Very serious.

Zof stared quietly at the Englishman, who had picked up his fork again and was toying with the food. He looked at the others, who looked back at him, the American with an expectant expression on his face and the fat one called Charlie with his broad, vacant smile.

'You joke? You really want *Stalin*? It's a pile of junk, you know this?'

'We're very keen. Very keen indeed,' replied Baker, looking absolutely serious.

'So what the fuck for?' asked Zof finally, looking equally serious. 'Exactly what kind of deal do we have here?'

'Let's just say we have some interesting uses for such a ship. You'll appreciate just how sensitive this is, I'm certain,' the Englishman replied.

Zof thought for a moment. 'Hey, you know, even for that kind of cash, Zof not so sure can be done. You go off in ship like that, someone in Moscow chase after pretty quick. Big risk. Maybe not possible. Maybe too crazy even for Zof.'

'Not something you'll really worry about, though, is it?' replied Baker. 'The way we see it, we get your people in the Navy yard to get the ship ready for sea. We understand it's been kept in good condition. No one should know it's not under direct orders from Moscow. We gather there's been very little communication since Yeltsin anyway. Your brother can make it happen. He can arrange the crew, as well. We hear he's pretty popular with the officers. There will be good money all round. The sailors can think it's perfectly legitimate. Moscow wants to get *Stalin* running again. Then we sail off. No one sees us again. You're several hundred thousand dollars richer. So what's the problem?'

Zof thought carefully. The plan still sounded crazy, but he had to take them seriously. 'My brother is problem. He's not like me. Not businessman. Very military. Polished shoes. Wears uniform every day. Still not paid, but carries on anyway. Think Lenin shit-hot guy. How I get him to do this crazy plan?'

'Maybe give him money?' suggested Able, ironically.

Feliks laughed. 'Money? Hey, you guys never met my brother. Yakov and money are not friends, you understand. He don't give a shit. Only one thing get my brother going, that's ships and Navy stuff. He's crazy. He sits there all day staring at fucking ships while the world pass him by. Not money. Not a chance.'

'So, Feliks, tell us about your brother. What would persuade him?' asked the American, looking hard at Zof, who didn't like this one bit. He didn't like his brother, but for Christ's sake he wasn't going to put him in the firing line with people like this. Somebody had to look after the poor bastard. Not that Yakov would see it that way.

'Find out, you so clever,' said Feliks sullenly.

The fat man called Mr Charlie slid along his seat to

move nearer. Feliks' belly still throbbed. He put his hands up in front of him. 'You keep him away, OK?' he demanded.

'About your brother?' asked the American again, insistently.

'Sure, no problem. Listen, Yakov got some kind of fixation. Ever since he was a kid he had ideas about ships, getting someplace, getting out of this fucking dump. He quits school at sixteen and joins Navy. This was when Russian Navy was some pretty big deal. Then spends next couple of years pestering everyone for place at officer school. Imagine a kid like Yakov an officer? Some joke. So he spends all night reading books, doing all kinds of strange shit. This is not to my mind normal. Rest of the guys think he's crazy but like him anyway. Big guy. Good at football. Good at fucking everything.'

'So he made it?'

'Sure he made it. Gets himself in Nakhimov Naval School in St Petersburg, where they train the officers. Nice place. Big old palace on the river. Yakov only dock-worker's kid in the school. Rest all officers' kids.'

'How did he do that?'

'Yakov don't give up, you know? Wrote letters, saw people. Kept getting turned down. Then one day disappears, gets on plane to Leningrad, finds old Admiral or whoever runs the school. I mean, finds his house, would you believe? Old guy gets back three in morning, finds Yakov waiting in uniform. Won't leave until he gets place at school. See what I mean? Yakov gets away with it. Story gets round, Yakov some kind of big hero, best guy in the world, everyone loves Yakov Zof.'

'Then?'

'He gets himself through the place, top marks, star student, all that. Then he manages to get me in, after speaking in very positive way to man who runs place,' said Feliks, now looking almost proud of the brother he hated so much.

The American arched his eyebrows.

'So it didn't go so well,' confessed Feliks. 'Maybe I'm not the kind of guy who's made for Navy shit. They told me one day I should fuck off. Learned English, though, pretty good,' he said. It was an embarrassing time in both their lives. Out of a sense of duty Yakov had virtually forced the school to take him on, to get his brother out of the slums. But Feliks hated every minute of it and quickly started dealing drugs. Even Yakov couldn't protect him; it got to the point where he didn't even want to.

'Sounds like a bit of a bastard,' said the Englishman.

Feliks shook his head. 'Listen, Yakov got some trick. His guys love him. Go anywhere. Do anything. He just got to stand someplace and next thing, he got people round him.'

'He could get a crew together for the ship, then?'

'Yakov yell, they come running.'

'I thought they'd all gone?'

'Hey, where to? Load of Navy guys still around. Most of them working the markets, doing deals. Christ, you got loads of the guys still living on the ships, illegal. Yakov can sure put crew back together, but even Yakov got to pay them. First thing Yakov wants to know: how I gonna feed the men? Some of these guys living off nettles, you know? Yakov gets some good food together, you got line of guys already.'

'So will he do it?'

Feliks looked at them. He knew his brother well. 'If you make some kind of deal that's not just money, yeah, sure, I guess Yakov might listen. Maybe, maybe not go for it. Who can tell? Yakov wants to get Navy back again. Yakov wants his crew back. Yakov wants a fucking ship. You know he got made Captain and they never got him a ship before the whole thing breaks up? Some bastards, huh? You offer Zof a chance to bring Navy back, maybe you got a chance. Maybe not.'

'Maybe we just take his wife and daughter and threaten to shoot them unless he agrees?' said Able quietly and reasonably, as though it was the sort of thing you'd do every day without thinking twice.

'We could do that,' whispered Charlie, almost enthusiastically.

Feliks Zof laughed. 'Hey, you gotta find them first. She quit a few years back. Too much time at sea. Not enough with the family. So she said. Yakov comes back from some long trip or other, takes big presents home like always, opens door, no wife, no kid, but fucking letter. I hear she's somewhere in Moscow.'

'No girlfriend?'

'Yakov? Don't kid me. The girls try, you know? What the fuck they see in him I don't figure, but they fall over themselves. Yakov takes no notice. He still loves his wife and girl, for chrissake. See what I mean? He's crazy.'

'Maybe we should just go and talk to him?'

'Hey, leave that to me, OK? I'll go talk to my crazy brother, see what he says. Who can tell, you know? I'll talk to him. But listen, how do I know you guys are serious? You could be full of shit, no offence.'

'We understand, Zof. Mr Baker, perhaps you'd like to give Mr Zof here a small sign of our intentions?'

The Englishman took a narrow white envelope out of an inside pocket and handed it to Feliks, careful to keep it at table height. 'Listen, Zof,' continued the American as Zof looked into the envelope from under the cover of the table, 'there's twenty thousand bucks in nice old hundred-dollar bills. Come back, you get piles more. Don't come back, we know addresses of all sorts of people round here. We have other friends. You got until this time tomorrow. Back here, in the hotel. OK?' The American looked serious, and the fat, smiling one was staring not at Zof's face but at his throat.

Zof hid the envelope on his lap and quickly looked inside it. As promised, there was a thick wad of green $100 bills, clean and crisp, wedged inside. He had never seen $20,000 in bills before, and it didn't look that much. But he thought he'd be pushing his luck by asking to count it. The best thing now, he thought, was to be very, very nice to these very mad people and get out of the restaurant and away from the foreigners. The place felt as though it was closing in on him, and even several large vodkas had failed to calm his taut nerves. And his stomach was hurting like hell.

Zof closed up the envelope, looked around him and stuffed it quickly into his inside pocket. 'OK, it's fine. It's good. I see you tomorrow, no problem.' He got up and thought about shaking their hands but, looking at their faces, decided against it. He looked nervous and gave a small wave of his hand. 'Tomorrow,' he repeated, 'no problem,' and backed away before turning and getting quickly out of the door past the glare of the head waiter. He could feel the fat man's smile still grinding into his back as he walked away.

Once he got outside the hotel the heat of the evening hit him, but at least he felt he could breathe again. Where was his car? Someone had moved it. After a brief row with the surly Korean doorman who pointed round the back of the hotel, he found it down the end of an alley that held the reeking dustbins, and drove away trying to make the tyres screech in anger; but the car's clutch was shot and all that happened was that a cloud of pungent blue smoke poured from the exhaust and drifted slowly down to the waterfront on the still night air.

The three men watched Zof's panic-filled departure

with some amusement and then resumed their meal, the fat man eating with noisy relish. 'So, Kelley,' asked the Englishman, looking at the American, 'what do you think? Is our boy on or off, or does he just run to the police?'

The American looked relaxed. 'Don't worry. Harvey. He's not going anywhere near the police, not with his record. I hear he's wanted for half the petty crime in Vladivostok. In any event, in this city you only go to the police when you've got a business proposition and plenty of cash behind it. No, he's OK. He can't resist the cash. Anyway, it's not him we should worry about now. It's the rest of them. The brother and the other guy I told you about. They're not all like Mr Zof. Not so easy to buy.'

'How on earth did you find out about him anyway?' asked Harvey. The American carried on eating and just shrugged his shoulders.

They finished their meal without talking any more, both men carefully thinking through the options. Would Zof just disappear with the cash? Would his greed bring him back? Could they get him to persuade his brother anyway? At times like this, the whole idea seemed completely crazy. But then, so was the money they were due to make. The vision was one of staggering wealth, enough to make all three of them amongst the richest men in the world. And now, the first move having been made, the vision was slowly but inexorably turning into reality. This might, thought Harvey to himself, this might just work.

Pine, the fat one, remained in his corner with a gentle smile on his face like a contented Santa Claus in plain clothes. It was hard to tell what he was thinking. Harvey sometimes wondered if he thought at all.

3

The next morning Feliks Zof found his brother in his small office in the naval yard. There was no security on the gate, and there were no uniforms anywhere in sight. The place was all but empty; a few groups of skinny kids were playing football in distant corners, and a couple of old flatbed trucks were struggling under loads of what looked like beets down an access road. The smell of boiled cabbage in the air mingled with the sulphur from the nearby steel mill.

He parked the BMW in the middle of the deserted parade ground where just five years before the ranks of sailors had been ruler-straight, massed fifty deep, saluting the ministers and admirals with the spotless ships posing behind them. Now the ground was specked with small piles of debris: lengths of red plastic rope, fragments of smashed wooden crates, and brave weeds that had forced their way through the splitting asphalt, starting the slow process of turning the site back into Pacific scrubland. He didn't bother locking the car.

Since the break-up of the old Soviet Union, the military had suffered not just a breakdown in discipline but a financial breakdown too. No money came through from Moscow to pay wages. No money came through to pay anything. There was a story that a general was forced to take a detachment of troops to occupy his local power station because they threatened to cut off his base's electricity supply as the bill had not been paid. No matter how many calls to Moscow were made, the excuses were always the same. Lately, they didn't even bother to answer the phone. Some wag said the Ministry of Defence had had its phones cut off, too.

The mighty Red Banner Pacific Fleet, head-quartered in Vladivostok since the days of the Tsars, suffered along with the rest. Having the fleet had turned a primitive fishing village into the major eastern city of the Russian empire. But once Moscow ceased to have any interest in the place, the fleet and everything to do with it simply drifted quietly away as though a tide had turned. Shortly after the Berlin Wall came down, Moscow had quietly removed most of the nuclear warheads from the arsenal there: Vladivostok was just too far away from Moscow, they said, as they moved them to Archangel where they could keep an eye on them. One by one the sailors went off and got other jobs, such as there were. Most slipped into petty crime and joined the gangs that controlled Vladivostok, like so many other Russian cities. The ships themselves, from the greatest warship to whole fleets of submarines, were simply tied up, rafted against each other, packed into the oily water like fat steel sardines.

Some sailors, those with families, had taken up residence in a few of the ships. Drifts of smoke rose lazily into the air from the stoves they lit on deck. Washing hung from lines strung across the decks, looking from a distance as though the ships were dressed overall for a state visit. Kids played football on the quays and the big decks of the aircraft carriers had been turned into pitches; the only hazard was that the footballs kept disappearing overboard. It was a mystery how the squatter families survived. Sometimes they collected nettles to make soup; often the men would make up raiding parties, but instead of fighting naval actions the battleground was a local farm where the ground was stripped of anything eatable which was taken back in triumph.

The ships had long ago been looted of anything movable, mainly small-arms and ammunition, and anything electronic: those arms which weren't sold quickly to the highest bidder, no questions asked, were kept to become the gangs' impressive arsenals. Some of the gangs had sufficient armament for a small army.

What remained was left to rot. Engines were left exposed to the salt water. The few electronics that were left were ruined by the ravages of the salt air. The summers in Vladivostok were blistering affairs when the temperature would hit 90 degrees for months; the autumns were drenching downpours of warm rain; the winters were long and bitterly cold and ice would hang from the masts of the ships in stalactites.

Few vessels would last long in such conditions without proper maintenance, and anyone who even knew how to look after the ships had long since wandered off.

But the great *Stalin* survived.

Throughout the war the Soviet Union poured resources into building the massive ship, almost at the expense of every other project. Even with the Germans at the gates of Moscow, the ship led a charmed life when it came to getting the latest equipment and the latest armaments. Clearly, Stalin himself wished the ship to be finished.

During 1944 and early 1945, Marshal Zhukov's Red Army began to clear the Germans from the soil of

Mother Russia. Like avenging angels, they slaughtered their way across Poland towards Berlin. The great ship continued building. The Kremlin saw the *Stalin* as an answer to the growing power of the Americans after the War, and was keen to have the ship finished by the time peace was declared.

But on 7th April 1945, the first reason for the *Stalin's* existence was abruptly cancelled out. American aircraft attacked the *Yamoto* in the Bungo Strait for two hours, during which time she was hit by bombs and at least seven torpedoes. With Rear-Admiral Kosaku Ariga aboard, she withstood attack after attack, her thick armour absorbing most of the blows. But eventually, damage was done. A fire started which began to spread. With torpedo after torpedo ripping holes in the hull, she began to develop a severe list, though she still had her main engine functioning, albeit providing just 10 knots. Ariga ordered 'Abandon Ship'. The list increased to 90 degrees; the great ship lay helpless on its side. Finally, the stern ammunition magazines exploded with such force that the blast was seen by sentries on Kagoshimne, over 100 miles away. The *Yamoto* broke up and sank in 350 metres of water, taking with her 2,498 officers and men. Just 280 were saved. The blast was so huge it brought down several American planes engaged in the attack.

And then, just four months later, on a sunny morning on the 20th August, a B-57 called 'Enola Gay' dropped an atomic bomb over Hiroshima. It took a few weeks to realise it, but the battleship was now as obsolete as the bow and arrow. Desperate to build his own bomb, Stalin diverted every available resource to the task. The ship was put on hold. But by this time, it was virtually finished. It had already been out on sea trials, and achieved the breathtaking speed of 35.3 knots, but that didn't make any difference. The *Stalin* was towed to a quiet corner of the Vladivostok yard.

But the world's biggest, fastest, most powerfully protected and most powerfully armed warship was too big and too powerful to be ignored for long. If for no other reason, the fact that the ship carried Stalin's name meant it had to be kept up to a standard that would not disgrace the Father of the Nation, even if it never went to sea again. In any event, somebody in the defence ministry in Moscow suggested that it might be useful to hang on to it. Look at the Americans hanging on to the big *Iowa*-class battleships, they said – Second World War ships they should have scrapped but didn't, carefully laid up just in case. You don't see the Americans throwing these things out. Why should we?

And so the *Stalin* started a new career as a static training vessel. Every navy has a passion for training its sailors in the most old-fashioned way it can. Even though they will never sail on one, ratings are still forced up the rigging of four-masted schooners in an effort, presumably, to inject some kind of camaraderie. To the Russian naval mind of the time, therefore, the appeal of an old-fashioned battleship was impossible to resist. Thus the great battleship was neatly moored, its machinery and equipment carefully preserved. Year after year, raw conscripts were dumped on the teak decks, shouted at for an hour, and then hustled into their bunk areas to begin six months of intensive, mind-numbing training. Every part of the great ship had its trainees; from the very bowels of the ship in the dark bilges where the water and the oil slopped to the tops of the masts sprouting ageing aerials, the young sailors were bullied and pushed.

So it was that although the *Stalin* never again went to sea, she was kept cleaner, more polished, better maintained and altogether more shipshape than many another vessel in the Pacific Fleet. It didn't matter that the navigation equipment was becoming antique and that the electronics were non-existent; everything was tended and polished by generations of homesick seventeen-year-olds who simply followed their orders to the letter. Day in, day out, they had followed a carefully prescribed routine of oiling, cleaning, emptying, tightening, replacing and polishing. Nothing was changed: the ship had to be kept exactly as it was the day it was launched.

And then, the collapse. One morning the conscripts failed to arrive. The officers in charge, one by one, packed their bags and left. The full-time maintenance crews who were kept on to do the jobs that couldn't be trusted to the recruits were last to leave. The gleaming brass and glinting steel began to discolour and tarnish. The name 'Stalin', welded in steel letters to the stern, had been painted over when the dictator was finally disgraced. But today, the paint has started to peel off, and the old name is becoming visible once more. She is listing almost unnoticeably to one side; the hull is slowly starting to take in water – not from any leak, the hull being too well built, but from the rain starting to seep in through portholes and doors that were left open.

She is moored with huge chains in one of the remotest corners of the naval dockyard, on a big rusty mooring buoy well away from the quayside. Nearby, obscuring the view of the *Stalin* from the more public areas of the harbour, lies the aircraft carrier *Kiev*, aircraftless, left where she was the day the patience of the crew finally snapped and they departed to try to make some sort of living. But the prow and the stern of the *Stalin* show clearly behind either end of the carrier. And the single grey funnel, like an enormous round tower, and the equally huge superstructure, rear high above the

Kiev's vast deck, dwarfing the ship that was itself the biggest aircraft carrier the Russians had ever built.

Overlooking her, sitting day after day in a ramshackle office that no one now ever visits, and watching a phone that never rings, Captain First Rank Yakov Zof busies himself with paperwork that simply sits in the files. He spends as much time as he can there; it makes him feel as though he is still part of the Navy, though the bastards never pay him. The rest of his men have gone. One by one they had nervously shuffled up to him to explain that they didn't want to go and that they would have followed him to the end and that they loved the Navy but, well, you see, the wife was nagging and the kids were hungry and ... he had nodded his head sadly and let them disappear.

Zof alone had stuck it out as the mightiest Navy in the world crumbled before his eyes. He had to: he had no choice. Not now. Zof had fought his way up through the ranks with a determination that astonished the people around him. He had lived for nothing else. It gave him promotion against the odds, but it slowly destroyed his life: as the Berlin Wall was tumbling, so was Zof's family. He had returned from four months at sea – a duty he had volunteered for, much against his wife's wishes – to find a letter from Polina, his wife. She had finally given up on him, taking Yekaterina, their daughter, with her. Now, if he left the yard like most of the others, then he was nothing. He might just as well stay in his small, untidy office.

Sometimes the massive shape of the great ship, visible in the distance from his window, dominating the harbour, pushes itself into his view. Yakov Zof and the great ship saw the world change together; Yakov had been born in the same year that the *Stalin* was taken out of active service. His father Nikolai had spent twenty-four hours drinking to celebrate his son's birth and then had staggered back to his dreary docker's apartment in the back streets past the silent ship being carefully moored in position – not that he had noticed a great deal.

And so both Yakov and the ship together saw Josef Stalin die and be reviled by Krushchev. They watched Krushchev replaced by Brezhnev, who governed the Soviet Union with absolute power though he was barely able to walk or string more than two words together, and had to be fed by nurses. They saw the KGB reach the heights of power when Andropov became General Secretary, and then watched the attempts of Gorbachev to take the Soviet Union into the twentieth century. And then they saw the greatest military power in the world slowly collapse upon itself, the only empire in history to commit suicide.

It's a magnificent ship, he muses to himself when he's in the mood to indulge his fantasies. What on earth must it have been like to command a ship like that?

In the hot summer of 1997, though he has no inkling of it, Yakov Zof is about to find out.

*

'Feliks? What the hell do you want?' demanded Yakov, stubbing out a cigarette and looking up from his desk as his brother Feliks pushed through the office door without knocking.

Yakov Zof was a big, powerfully built man, quite unlike his short brother. He had dark hair that still covered his head, and had he not kept it in a crew-cut it would have made him look years younger. He had a square, weather-beaten face and piercing dark eyes, and women found him almost irresistible although few had ever managed to break through his cold reserve. They thought he was arrogant; in fact, he was nervous with women though no one in the world would have believed it. He had fallen in love with a beautiful school girl, Polina, from Moscow; they married early, had a daughter and then Yakov virtually disappeared to sea.

Which was why Polina had left him. Once the daughter had almost grown up, she decided enough was enough and took off back to Moscow, still a good-looking woman. Yakov was too proud, and too hurt, to go looking for them. His world had just about ended. And then everything else collapsed, more or less within weeks. Zof was not the sort of man to be bitter; but he wanted his revenge. Quietly and calmly he waited, hoping without any real foundation for his hope that one day his time would come.

He smoked almost constantly – his fingers were stained yellow – but he had no other vices. He hated vodka and would only drink the stuff to be polite; he remembered too well his drunken father, who had come home one night and beaten their mother to within an inch of her life before slumping, drunk, into his bed. Yakov was just fourteen, but was big already. The next night, he waited up until his father staggered back from the bar and met him on the steps of the block of flats where they lived. His father was too drunk to see him.

Yakov took advantage of the darkness. 'Your wife. Don't touch her again. This is for last night,' and he coldly pounded his fist into the man's face, three times. He could feel the bone cracking under the last blow. His father collapsed senselessly to his knees. The next evening, he stayed in, his face a black mess. He looked strangely at Yakov and didn't say a word, but he never touched his wife again.

And now here was his brother, standing before him

like a fool. Yakov was not pleased to see him. They were used to keeping their distance, mainly because Yakov thought that Feliks was a total crook who only came to see him when he wanted something – which was invariably true – and Feliks thought that Yakov was a stuck-up idiot who would rather strut around in a uniform than get on with the serious business of earning a living, which wasn't true: Yakov called it a sense of duty.

The truth was, duty and patriotism, and even a total loyalty to communism, were what gave Yakov Zof a reason for living. Having spent his life escaping the slums of Vladivostok, he had a lot to be grateful to the old system for. He had fought his way into the Nakhimov Naval School for officers at Leningrad, in spite of his background. He had pushed himself to the top, graduating just third in his year. He had volunteered for the postings no one else wanted: the Arctic, where he did four years on the icebreakers; Mozambique, in the 1960s and 1970s, where he survived the sullen local despots and the overpowering heat; even a spell on submarines, lying submerged for a month at a time off the coast of California. Slowly but steadily, it took Yakov Zof very near to the top.

It didn't take him long to realise that an allegiance to communism would be useful in the process. Stalin and the rest of them, truth to tell, left him cold. But it would help his career, and so he became an enthusiastic Party member. And Yakov Zof also realised early on that without a dogma, Russia was nothing. It was the glue that held the nationalities together. If it gave, then the might of the Soviet Union would be destroyed. The empire would collapse into dozens of warring states and the greatest Navy that the world had seen would vanish like smoke in the wind, and with it would go everything that Zof had fought for over the years.

Year after year, his rank had slowly improved. He did his last six years as a Captain Second Rank under an ogre named Zheltov who bullied his crew. It didn't take long for Zof to persuade the man to be a great deal more considerate. One evening in the mess, Zheltov began to scream abuse at a new young engineering *bay-chay** commander, Zhadanov. The rest of the bay-chay commanders stayed quiet. Zof let the old man rant on for a minute or two and then suddenly stood up; he towered over the Captain. Zheltov looked up at him, paused, then started to scream at Zof too. Zof motioned to the others to leave the room and they quickly left, young Zhadanov last of all, closing the door behind them. They couldn't hear a thing – the door was insulated.

Five minutes passed, then suddenly Zof opened the door and beckoned them back in. Zheltov was sitting silently at the head of the table. They shuffled back into the room and resumed their seats while the stewards carried on serving dinner. Zof just continued eating. Zheltov toyed with his food: he was pale as a ghost and his hands shook, and Zhadanov noticed with some amusement that one of the gilt buttons at the top of his tunic was undone. Christ knows what Zof had done to the man, but he remained more or less in his cabin for the rest of the voyage, leaving Zof to run the ship. Rumours spread like wildfire and Zof became something of a hero, not just on the ship but throughout the rest of the Fleet.

His commission to Captain First Rank finally came through as he returned to Vladivostok. He remembered the day well. The letter confirming his

---

*bay-chay: familiar expression for a *boeviye chasti* or combat department appointment was the second letter that he had read that day; the first was the terse farewell from Polina. It took him several days to order his thoughts sufficiently to go back to the base. He had brought back a stereo for his daughter and several Rolling Stones tapes – of which he thoroughly disapproved but knew that she would love; and for Polina, still the most beautiful woman he had ever known, he had saved months of pay to buy a small but exquisite emerald ring from a jeweller he found in Cape Town.

He had sat with her letter until it got dark, hardly moving. Then he stood up and walked from the flat for the last time, down to the harbour, where he flung the stereo and the tapes and finally the ring into the dark sea, and went back to the dockyard.

But there was no ship for him. He waited for weeks. Then they pulled down the Berlin Wall, and his world started to fold in upon itself. Just as he knew it would, once the binding of communism became unravelled, the individual states and even the smaller nationalities within those states started to split. Lenin had been right – the real enemy was not the capitalist outside the borders, but the nationalist within.

And now the years of service, the sacrifices, the prestige – all thrown away. The lunatics were running the madhouse. He hung on, going into his office every day, because an insistent voice in his head kept telling him it couldn't last. At some point the whole thing would start to collapse. Then people like Yakov Zof would be needed once again.

Feliks, on the other hand, thought capitalism and the free market economy was the best thing ever to happen to Russia. He had made full use of it, so far. The fact that he espoused the freedom so enthusiastically, and appeared to be making a little bit of money – he drove around in a BMW for Christ's sake – irritated Yakov no end. His brother was a lazy bastard, and now even he seemed to have the upper hand.

'A fine greeting for your loving brother, I must say,' Feliks replied. 'I thought I'd just come along and see how you were getting in your splendid office. How's the glorious Russian Navy these days?'

'This is just a social call, Feliks? I would have thought you had better things to do. I certainly have.'

'Like what, Yakov?' laughed Feliks, winding up his brother as much as he dared. 'You know something? You're crazy sitting around here all day. Moscow has forgotten all about your precious Navy, everyone knows that. I hear they're trying to sell it to the Americans. Why don't you just lock the door, chuck away the key and come and have a drink? You're the only one left here, you know that?'

'Thanks, Feliks. At least I have a job to do. So what's the problem? Who's chasing you for money? Or have the police finally caught up with my little brother? If you want somewhere to hide, tough,' said Yakov. Feliks always wanted something.

Feliks laughed again, but it was a nervous laugh and the smile was shallow. Abruptly he turned round so that he didn't have to look directly at Yakov and stood with his back to his brother, looking out of the cracked window, a shadow now to his brother's eyes against the glaring yellow light. Behind him, in the distance, the towering superstructure of the *Stalin* was visible above the cranes and gantries.

'Listen, Yakov, I do need something,' started Feliks. 'I have a little proposition. Please listen very carefully and think about it. I'm your brother and I know we've had our differences, but with this I need your help. I'm in real shit this time. Don't say a word. Just listen. OK?'

Yakov shrugged his shoulders and lit another cigarette. His brother always tried to pitch him some mad, illegal scheme when he visited, but usually he didn't sound quite so serious. This time Feliks seemed shaken and genuinely worried. He hadn't seen his brother lose his blustering confidence like this since he was small boy. Their father had caught Feliks stealing from the shops and beaten him until he was almost senseless. That had shut him up for almost a week.

Feliks started relating, detail by detail, the story of his dinner with the strangers the previous night. How they struck him as very powerful people. How absurd the names were, as if they clearly wanted him to know that they didn't really care about hiding behind false identities. How threatening they were. How they'd punched him in the toilet, which Yakov thought very funny but decided it was better to keep a straight face. How much money they were offering. How ridiculous the idea was. How crazy the whole thing seemed. How they threatened to shoot him and probably Yakov too, though to spare his brother's feelings he left out the bit about his wife and daughter. And exactly how shit-scared Feliks actually was, right now. The only detail Feliks omitted was the twenty thousand dollars, which was already safely hidden behind a brick at the back of the kitchen in his shabby apartment.

Yakov listened carefully. When his brother had finished, he just sat there and nodded to himself, blowing plumes of bitter cigarette smoke into the air.

'So, what the hell do I do now?' Feliks asked finally, expecting to get a mouthful of abuse from his brother regarding his unreliability, his weakness, his stupidity for even listening to these crazy people, his complete lack of patriotism, and several other faults besides.

He was not at all prepared for Yakov's reply. 'What do they actually want it for?' asked Yakov at length.

'What do they want it for? They didn't say, for Christ's sake.'

'No indication? No guesses?'

'Jesus, Yakov, a bunch of crazy foreigners say they want the *Stalin* and slap me around into the bargain. I didn't get their full life histories, know what I mean? What the hell do I know about why they want it? They want it, that's all I know.'

'OK, so let's find out why they want it. I'll come with you tonight when you see them and we'll ask.'

Feliks could barely believe his ears. 'Are you crazy, Yakov? You don't want to get mixed up in this shit. Get away from here. I can let you have some money. Maybe a few thousand dollars if you need it. Take it and clear off. I'll deal with these crazies. I'm used to this sort of thing, you're not.'

'Come off it, Feliks. You're useless as a crook. You never were any good. These people will roll all over you. You and I will go and see them and find out what's really going on. Just as a matter of interest, how much are they willing to pay?'

Feliks turned round from staring out of the window, eased himself down into the chair opposite Yakov's bent metal desk and leaned his elbows on it, staring his brother full in the face.

'Don't tell me you'll actually do it? You, the big patriotic Captain who never bent a rule in his life? Why, brother Yakov, I do believe you're actually beginning to see some sense at long last.'

Now it was Yakov's turn to stare out of the window at the almost hidden *Stalin*. The biggest, fastest, most powerful ship when it was first launched. And, astonishingly, still bigger than any warship afloat today, still faster than any other big ship around, easily the most heavily armed and the most heavily armoured. *Stalin* was bigger than anything Yakov had ever dreamed of commanding. It had been the pride of the Soviet Fleet in the days when the world feared the motherland and Russians didn't take any bullshit from nationalist hooligans and European fascists. Yakov could almost see the great ship as it sliced its way through the oceans. The idea that he would be in command was a difficult one to resist, however crazy it sounded. He had sat for too long, brooding, in this rundown office. No one was going to come and get him. The fools in the Kremlin had been bought by the Americans and their demise had been postponed. It was time to do something. What these people who had put the wind up his brother wanted was anybody's guess. But it was worth finding out.

Why the *Stalin*? Why so much money? Why a full crew? To Yakov Zof, it was of course irresistible. The *Stalin* would sail again, with Yakov Zof taking command of the ship he never had – a ship that no other Captain in the Soviet Navy had ever laid their hands on. Feliks could keep the money. All Yakov wanted was that ship – and a chance to show the world that the might of Mother Russia was far from spent.

He took a deep breath and turned back to face his brother. 'You know, Feliks, for once in your life I think you've got it right. Tonight at eight? I'll be there.'

4

They met in the Imperial, in one of the comfortless bars furnished with square black leather sofas where you get a small dish of stale nuts each time you order an overpriced drink. The three foreigners were huddled around a corner table, talking to each other in low voices until they saw the two Russians approach. They stopped talking immediately.

Feliks walked nervously up to them, leaving Yakov waiting.

'My brother, Yakov, the Captain. He wanted to come. He wanted to know more about your deal. This is OK, I hope, with you people?'

Kelley was surprised and then delighted. 'Sure, Zof, that's fine. Introduce us. We'll be delighted to meet him, won't we?' Harvey nodded. They stood up and smiled widely, shaking Yakov's hand, one after the other, with all the friendliness in the world, as Feliks introduced them as Mr Able, Mr Baker and Mr Charlie. Without asking either of them if they wanted a drink, which Feliks badly did, they then hurried them straight through the wide lobby into the almost empty restaurant and seated the two brothers at the same secluded table as on the previous evening.

Feliks was uncomfortable. The place was oppressive. Strangely – to Feliks at any rate – Yakov seemed quite calm, relaxed even. In fact, he gave every appearance of looking forward to the evening and had dressed in his one good civilian suit; he had even thought of going in his black Captain's uniform, but it would have been too conspicuous.

'Well, Mr Zof, here you are back again with your eminent brother. Welcome to our little gathering, Captain. We're delighted to see you,' started Kelley, looking at Yakov Zof carefully. He was wearing a pungent Russian aftershave, which Kelley fleetingly imagined to be called something heroic and Soviet.

Yakov shook the American's hand gravely. Even in his civilian suit, he was a dominating, forceful character. Kelley was impressed. He stood a good six inches bigger than Kelley, and when he spoke it was in the cultivated, American-accented English that senior naval officers had to learn to get their commission. Somebody thought they would need it one day.

Yakov Zof didn't waste any time. He was not here for small talk. He lit a cigarette. 'My brother here tells me that you have an interesting proposition to make. I'm keen to hear about it, Mr … er …' he halted, forcing Kelley to identify himself.

'Able. This one is Able, Yakov,' hissed Feliks. He was trying to remain in charge of the conversation but it was slipping quickly away from him.

Kelley looked at Feliks with some irritation. The little man was getting in the way. 'Sure, that's right. For now, call me Able,' he said. He could see Yakov Zof's sceptical look. 'I mean, once we know you a little better we can use our real names. But for now it's Able. We have to be careful. You understand?'

'I understand,' replied Yakov. 'But whoever you are, my brother here has told me all about your scheme. Frankly I am intrigued. What on earth do you want with the *Stalin*? It's a museum piece. You realise it has not been to sea for nearly fifty years?'

'Is it important what we want it for, Captain? We're offering a great deal of money, after all. Where I come from, that sort of cash normally entitles you to some privacy for your plans.'

Yakov Zof snorted loudly. 'This is not America, Able. I know that many of my countrymen have become very materialistic these days. But that does not mean all of us have. I don't give a damn about your money, though I imagine that whatever crew I can get together will be interested. I want to know what you need *Stalin* for. I want to know what the job involves, particularly if you ask me to command the ship. That's my condition, my friend. Take it or leave it,' said Yakov.

Able raised his eyebrows and looked inquiringly at the one called Baker. This man ain't kidding, said his expression. Baker shrugged his shoulders and nodded, looking carefully at Yakov Zof. Charlie, the fat one, shifted in his seat and began to slowly crush a white linen napkin absently-mindedly. His smile was not so broad as it had been with Feliks.

'Fine, Captain, fine,' Able continued. 'I just thought we'd get around to the details a little later. There's no harm in you knowing now, I suppose. You see, we represent a consortium of film producers from Hollywood. They're thinking of making a big film about the war. Sea battles, that sort of thing. The director has insisted that we get hold of a real battleship; he wants the realism. *Stalin* seems to us to be perfect. And quite probably for sale, or so we were led to believe.'

'I see. You want *Stalin* for a big movie. What happens to the ship?'

'Oh, you know, some shooting, some big bangs, that sort of thing. At the end it gets sunk, blown up, goes to the bottom with all hands. That's why we're willing to pay so much. It would cost a fortune to film it otherwise.'

Zof paused and nodded, and appeared to be thinking it over. 'Able, your idea is pure horseshit. Three strange men with ridiculous names turn up, offer vast sums of hard cash, threaten me and my family and want everything done in complete secrecy. My brother may look stupid, but do I? You want *Stalin* for a movie, why don't you contact the Navy in Moscow? They'd sell it to you for a lot less than my brother tells me you're offering. They'd be so delighted just to get rid of it, they'd probably give it to you. My friend, please don't waste my time.' He jabbed out his cigarette on a plate and immediately lit another one.

Feliks could feel hundreds of thousands of dollars slipping quickly through his fingers. He prayed his stiff-necked brother would shut up. Why oh why did he always have to have his own way?

'Sorry, Captain,' replied Able. 'Not much of a story, I guess, but we have to be careful, you understand? But let me just repeat what we said to your brother yesterday. If you're not in, keep quiet and no harm will come to you. Or to your brother here. Talk to anyone, Captain Zof, anyone at all, and I assure you that you will have a very big problem. Do you understand?'

Zof's face changed almost instantly. Feliks knew it was the wrong thing to say to his brother; he should have warned them. Yakov leaned forward and stared hard at Able. 'Don't threaten me, Able. I want to know what the deal is first. Then I'll think about it. Then I'll let you know what I think. And if I don't like it, you can fuck off, as I think you say in America. Now, do you tell me or do I just walk out of here?' Zof leaned back in his chair and blew a plume of smoke, clearly not even slightly worried by Kelley's threat. And he simply ignored the fat man who was smiling intently at him. Kelley's secret weapon was having no effect.

Feliks wanted to vanish quietly into a hole in the ground. His crazy brother was getting into an argument with these very dangerous and unpleasant men, for God's sake. Surely the fat one was about to lean over and snap Yakov's neck for him, if he wasn't very careful, though right now it didn't look as if Yakov was in any mood to worry about it. This arrogance and confidence ... it was something else that annoyed him about his brother. Feliks thought of himself as the fighter when they were kids, but in truth it was always Yakov who came to rescue him. None of the other kids would fight Yakov; they didn't like the look of him.

Able shrugged. There seemed no point in arguing with the man. 'If that's how you want it, Zof. My promise, not a threat as you suggest, holds good whether you want to hear it or not. But here's the deal. I need you to take command of *Stalin*, and I need you to get her ready and with a crew big enough to run the ship and its systems. One-way trip only. For that we pay plenty of dollars to you, to the crew, and leave you enough cash to square things with the authorities here if you need it. We want the ship ready to sail away in about two months' time. Can it be done?'

Zof looked at Able with some astonishment. He was almost laughing. 'You do not expect very much, my friend,' he said.

'Can it be done or not?' demanded Kelley. Time to get this proud Russian down to business. If he's so goddamn clever, let him sort this little challenge out.

Zof's face grew serious again. 'Maybe I can get the crew. I don't know if I can get the ship ready in time or even at all. I've been over it a few times, but it's been sitting there for fifty years. I cannot think that it will run without a lot of work.'

'Our information is that the *Stalin* has been kept in very good order.'

'In that case you have no problem. I have no idea if that is true or not. I will need to go over the ship with an engineer to tell if what you say is possible. Even if it was, I still have no idea what you want this ship for.'

'We can arrange an engineer tomorrow. As for what we want the ship for, here's the idea. It used to be called "privateering", so my friend from England here tells me. I guess it's really called piracy. Quite simply, Captain, we intend to use *Stalin* as a pirate ship to make ourselves, you, and whatever crew you can get together, as goddamn rich as we can and then disappear.'

'Piracy? And what, my friend, is worth becoming a pirate for these days? Japanese videos? Oil?'

'Better than that, Zof. Out there, right now, are hundreds of ships sailing the Pacific. Most of them carry shit like you say, not worth bothering with. But I happen to know that quite a few of them carry objects a great deal more valuable. What if I told you that most international gold transfers are made by ship? The guys in London that insure this stuff insist on it. They seem to think that if a plane goes down, there goes the gold, melted into the goddamn soil or something. A ship goes down, it's easier to find and they stand a chance of salvaging the stuff. See what I mean? The same applies to diamonds, Captain. De Beers insist that diamonds are carried in small parcels on merchant-men steaming around the world, but particularly from South Africa up towards India and Japan. We estimate that at any one time, at least one billion dollars of gold and jewellery are out there on the high seas in unarmed, anonymous little ships, just waiting to be got at. One billion dollars, Zof. Think about it.'

'And how do you propose to find these valuable little chickens with their golden eggs?'

'Simple, Zof. We have a friend in London at Lloyd's.

They carry the insurance for these shipments, so they need to know which ships are carrying what cargo and exactly where they are, all the goddamn time. Our friend works for a major syndicate in Lloyd's that handles a lot of these special cargoes. The vessels are required to report their positions back to Lloyd's every day. Most of the ships with these cargoes are just ordinary ships carrying ordinary loads, so they're not exactly well protected, arms wise. They like them to be ordinary ships, Zof. They think they're less conspicuous. Our friend in London simply lets us have the sailing plans of the next big shipments, keeps us up to date on progress, and we then turn up in some lonely little spot and relieve them of it. What could be easier?'

'If it's that easy, why a ship like *Stalin*? Why not something more modern?,' asked the Captain. '*Stalin* is very old, not to say very conspicuous.'

'Because it's fast, it's powerful, it's well armoured and, above all, exactly because it is conspicuous. It's going to frighten the life out of anyone who sees it. We don't want any trouble, no heroics, no brave fools looking for a fight, Captain. Not if we can avoid it. My colleagues and I have some experience in these matters. You need to wave a very big, very frightening stick to avoid trouble. Gets them shit-scared, you see. Stops them playing at heroes. Safer all round.'

'And exactly how do we get away with our earnings from this interesting little enterprise?'

'Easy. When we've got enough to satisfy everyone, we run for a small group of islands off the Australian coast called the Monte Bello Islands. It's where the British tested their atom bombs, so the place is deserted and surrounded by keep-out signs, but they haven't been radioactive for years. We run the ship aground, and we'll have transport to get us out. We can arrange passports for those who need them.'

'I see. And who exactly are you? Now you can give me your real names, I think.'

'My name is Kelley. Mr Baker here is actually called Harvey. And Mr Charlie here is what you might call our muscle. He's called Pine; he's an old friend of mine.'

The brief introductions didn't do justice to the three men. It was not a sense of modesty on Kelley's part, rather a well-developed sense of security. He saw no point in giving too much away. He'd already given the main story to this stiff Russian, and he didn't even know if the guy was in the deal or not.

James Kelley, called Jimmy when he was younger but now simply known as Kelley, was born in the Bronx and had become a policeman in the New York Police Department. He had displayed a fine sense of controlled violence and restrained corruption that had given him a good living and brought him regular promotions. When Kelley set out to solve a crime, he usually did so because he had arranged it with the local hoods. He would bring a fugitive to justice as a service not just to the law-abiding citizens of New York, but also as a service to whichever of the gangs wanted that particular individual taken out of circulation.

Then, for reasons Kelley could never understand, the NYPD decided it had to clear up the worst of the corruption. He had little choice but to get out before he faced the new breed of college graduates who thought you fought crime with degrees. He had then gone out on his own. For a few years his awesome reputation for violence helped him overcome most difficulties, and his old friends at the local precinct helped him when they could, which wasn't very often. The whole thing came to end when Kelley, drunk, had overstepped the mark and badly beaten some little snot during an argument in a bar. The kid was too well connected.

After the beating that Kelley in turn received, it was decided to give him a little holiday, and he spent several unpleasant years inside a tough prison where his previous career had made him few friends and lots of enemies. He came out a harder man. Quietly, and maintaining the lowest possible profile, he turned away from petty crime and began planning bigger and bigger armed hold-ups, at which he became spectacularly successful, and where the rewards began to match the risks he ended up having to take. He had, as he would tell you after several whiskies, finally turned professional.

Jeremy Harvey was a very different character. From a middle-class family in Hampshire, one of the more pleasant counties of southern England, he had gone to a bad but nevertheless expensive public school where he didn't distinguish himself greatly, mainly because he was too uninterested. But in his last year, he suddenly found his real calling was for drug-dealing, and it wasn't too long before he was thrown out.

The school was persuaded to keep it quiet to avoid a damaging scandal, which – desperate for wealthy parents and their offspring – it was only too keen to do. Harvey managed to join the Navy and attended the Dartmouth Royal Naval College, where he started to do reasonably well: he quite liked the sea, he had to confess, and he progressed, becoming third in command of a small frigate until a dispute with another officer one night, over that officer's wife, led to his being thrown in jail by the Provost, only to be released on the strict understanding that if he quit the service quietly all would be forgotten.

With the lazy elegance and the accent that only English public schools can teach, he didn't find it difficult to get a job in the City, where he began to develop a taste for earning money. He was, as his contemporaries would admit, bloody good at his job though with a reputation for being a clever bastard. But the great financial bubble burst in the late eighties and Harvey's debts, run up in the good times, meant that once again he needed to depart in some haste. He ended up in the South of France, just outside St Tropez, where his obvious English charm and his seagoing experience persuaded a small yacht-charter agency to employ him.

One sunny morning, Harvey looked up from reading a yachting magazine to see Kelley, who'd walked in wanting to charter a fast motor-yacht. Harvey offered him a selection. Not fast enough, said Kelley. Harvey dug out out a huge 80-foot Magnum that could do 60 knots. Perfect, said Kelley. And how many weeks would he like to charter it for, asked Harvey, to which question Kelley looked surprised, opened a case containing more francs than Harvey had ever seen, and said just for the night.

Kelley needed crew for the smuggling run, and it didn't take Harvey long to prove his worth. After a few months and a few runs, Harvey realised he had found a very pleasant way to make a very good living.

Pine, the fat man the others called Charlie, had been with Kelley even in those days. Kelley had found him hanging around the wrestling scene on the lower West Side, looking for bouts that could be easily fixed. He had almost lost his voice in one bout when his opponent stamped on his throat, which had left him with a permanent whisper and his opponent with a widow. The damage done needed several operations to repair and his neck was a mess, which is why he wore the scarf. He had to keep taking cortisone to help with the problem, but it had made his bulky frame balloon up to over 250 lb. He had a truly awesome sense of violence, coldly savage, capable of destroying another human being in the bloodiest way imaginable without the slightest fear; but until he decided he needed to use it he remained placid and silent, grinning at everybody, and when something struck him as funny he would giggle, but in the high-pitched way that was even more alarming.

Pine and Harvey never really got on with each other. Harvey thought Pine was just too creepy and too violent. He'd seen some of his sickening handiwork at close quarters. But you couldn't separate Kelley and Pine, and he had to put up with the 'dreadful pig', as he called him, even to Pine's face. It never seemed to both him, he just carried on smiling. It was as though Harvey didn't exist; just Kelley.

It was Harvey who had introduced Stanley Price, their contact at Lloyd's of London, into the plan. Price was another public school dropout who had wormed his way into the City, where he met Harvey. Like Harvey, he had been fired following the market collapse on Black Monday; but he lacked Harvey's entrepreneurial instincts, and ended up with a dull but well-paid job in the shipping movements departments of Lloyd's, though they had stayed in touch.

It was one night in a small café in St Tropez that Harvey told Kelley about Price in passing. Kelley, who normally found the Englishman's company boring after an hour, suddenly became very interested. Which department? Who was he? Was he, as Kelley politely put it, 'buyable'?

Harvey didn't know. What was the great interest, anyway? Kelley then outlined his piracy plan. He needed to know where the ships carrying the gold were located. Could Price help? A month later, Harvey had taken a short lunch and one bottle of cheap

Chablis to establish that Price was not simply buyable but running a January sale. Kelley was duly impressed and the scheme, which sounded like sheer madness to Harvey, began quickly to take shape.

Somehow, Kelley had found out about the *Stalin*, and even about Zof and his disaffection. Quite how he knew about these things, Harvey didn't know and didn't presume to ask. But a week ago they arrived in Vladivostok via Tokyo and the plan started to gather pace.

Now they were sitting opposite the Captain, waiting for him to make his decision. Both Kelley and Harvey knew that Zof was critical to the deal. No one else, according to Kelley, could put the crew together. Zof's hard, angular face had an angry expression; but he always looked like that. After fifty years of fighting his way up from the slums to the top of his profession, and then being dumped in the yard, Zof had plenty to look angry about.

'So, Captain. That's our plan. You in or out? Or do we ask someone else to do it?' asked Kelley. It was the crunch question. Both Kelley and Harvey knew that Zof would find it impossible to resist.

Yakov sat back in his chair and put his fingers together. He was thinking hard as he looked back over his career. How he had watched, powerless and horrified, as concession after concession was made in the name of *perestroika* and the fleet was reduced and reduced again. How the drunk Yeltsin simply sold out to the West. All his life he had given his loyalty to the motherland, and now the motherland left him sitting in a stinking hut, surrounded by rusting ships that didn't work, forgotten and ignored. His last request for payment hadn't even been answered. And now, here were these crazy people who wanted to make him into a pirate. In truth, the money didn't concern him. What was now running through Zof's mind was the prospect of getting a crew together and commanding the mighty *Stalin* at sea. It was the ultimate command. If these madmen wanted to loot Western gold ships, fine by him. They were bound to be insured anyway.

He knew he could do it. He knew he could sail the ship, knew he could get a crew together; most of his bay-chay, or divisional, commanders were still around the port, moonlighting, driving taxis, some even squatting on the ships in the dockyard. It was, it seemed to him, a fine irony. From not being paid for months, he could turn most of his crew into wealthy men – at least by Russian standards – overnight. More than that; he could cruise the mighty *Stalin* through the high seas and nobody would be able to stop him. He thought carefully about that last point, suddenly realising that the modern weapons and electronics of the new ships would be useless against that pile of armoured steel; it was built to take 18 inch shells in its stride, and a modern missile would probably just bounce off the thing. God almighty, he thought; turn one of the massive guns on anybody and you'd blow them out of the water. All the electronics in the world couldn't stop those shells flying through the air. It was a good thought; the mighty *Stalin*, pride of the great Soviet Navy, running rings around the panicking Westerners.

And what could keep him now? There was nothing left here. He knew he could never find Polina, was not even sure he wanted to any more. Maybe, with the money, he could find Yekaterina. Help her through university; get her out of Russia to somewhere better where they still had real values. He looked at Harvey, who seemed easy enough to control. Kelley was just a stupid American who didn't worry Zof too much; at least he seemed to know what he was doing.

He remembered walking down the lonely quays on the night the Wall came down, the distant singing of the drunken sailors, the gentle creak of the ships as they pulled slowly against their mooring lines. What in the name of Mother Russia am I supposed to do now? he had thought. Now at last, six years later, six years of waiting and watching the slow collapse, six years of seeing his life disintegrate ... now, at last, he had his answer.

Yakov Zof looked Kelley straight in the eye, then Harvey. 'OK,' he said simply.

'OK? Is that it? Think about what you're doing, Yakov,' said Feliks in Russian, now worried. He was alarmed how easy it was for his so-straitlaced brother to turn suddenly into a criminal. 'You don't know where this could end up. I mean, it's dangerous. You're not into this sort of thing. Come away and talk to me for a few days. Cool off. You really don't want to do this.'

'I have thought about it, Feliks. I'll do what they ask. It's not for the money; I don't give a damn for the money. It's something you could never understand.'

'What the hell's it for, then?' asked Feliks, getting angry because he'd already guessed the answer.

'Feliks, you idiot, do you really think I'm going to sit around waiting for these Kremlin bastards to decide what to do with me? You've been on at me for months to get off my arse and do something. Well, this is something I really want to do. Take the old ship out, get her up to scratch, and show the world what the Soviet Navy can do when it wants to. Even if we happen to be pirates. Shit, little brother, I hear even the famous Sir Francis Drake was not above a little bit of piracy in his day. I'm doing it. Not for them. Not for the money. For me. Maybe even for Russia ... and don't you dare say a word, Feliks, or I'll cripple you!'

Feliks knew his brother well enough not to take him on in this mood. Maybe he'd see sense later. He shrugged and turned away.

Yakov turned to Kelley. 'When do we start? I need to get an engineer's report on the ship, and the engines in particular. It's going to take some time to find a good man, particularly someone who knows about these old turbine systems. Then I need somebody to go through the armaments systems; they haven't worked in years. There's a lot to do, Mr Able or Kelley or whatever it is, if you want this thing running in two months.'

'Captain Zof, we're delighted, truly delighted,' said Harvey.

'You'll be a famous man, Zof. And you'll be richer than you can believe,' Kelley told him.

The fat man smiled, but it wasn't his usual wide grin, and he fingered the top of the white scarf wound around his throat.

'I don't give a damn. All I want is that ship. And an engineer. I'll ask around first thing in the morning,' said Zof.

'There's no need, Captain. We already have someone in mind,' Kelley said.

'Who is this? It's got to be someone I can trust.'

'Oh, I don't think you need have any worries on that score, Zof. Have you heard of Mikhail Kishkov, by any chance?'

'Kishkov? Never heard of him,' Zof replied.

'You never heard of the Kishkov who virtually rebuilt the Russian Fleet before the War? He built the *Stalin*, of course. He was still a young man then. A bit of a whizz-kid, they call them in America,' said Harvey.

'*That* Kishkov? Stalin had him shot just after the ship was launched,' said Zof, mystified.

'Stalin didn't shoot Kishkov. He had him locked him

up in a labour camp in some god-forsaken hole in the middle of Siberia until 1959 when he was released. He's still alive. He's crazy as a mad horse, but he's definitely alive and he lives here, in Vladivostok. We're meeting him tomorrow to see if we can get him to help with our project. Come with us.'

'My God!' said Yakov, with a broad grin across his face for the first time in months.

*

Pine had already retired for the night; he never stayed up late. Harvey and Kelley sat alone in the bar, toasting their success. The show, as Kelley put it, was now on the road. The biggest theft in history would soon take place, and both of them would be wealthy beyond their dreams. Delighted and a little bit drunk, Harvey clapped Kelley on the back, telling him how fortunate it was that they had met. Kelley nodded happily. Harvey clapped him on the back again. Kelley nodded again. Harvey beamed unsteadily at the American and finally decided that he'd had enough to drink. He bid Kelley a warm good-night and weaved towards the lifts and to his bed. Kelley stood up and stretched. Time for some air. He wandered out of the air-conditioned lobby into the warm Pacific night.

A gentle breeze was drifting in from the dark sea, bringing with it a clean scent that pushed away the sulphurous reek of the city. A few small lights glimmered far out on the invisible horizon, fishing-boats out looking for squid, tempting them on to their hooks by shining yellow gas-powered lanterns on the sea. The Imperial stood like a palace amongst the cracking façades of the other buildings around it. Hanks of wire hung from the fronts of buildings, looping around poles, carrying electricity and telephones. A few pink sodium street-lights flickered in the uneven current, spreading a hot but weak light across the dusty street. Kelley walked aimlessly across the big square in front of the hotel, savouring the gentle breeze. He turned to walk back again, but suddenly stopped and looked carefully at the hotel. Nobody was around. Even the doorman had retreated inside. There was no one to see him.

Kelley turned again, and now walked quickly away from the hotel. There was a wide pool of shadow beneath a failed street-lamp, and he vanished from sight into its gloom, then turned a corner. Walking fast now down a narrow deserted street, he reached another corner and turned into an alleyway, completely dark. The dim pink light was behind him as he walked into the blackness. At the end of the alley, two small white lights blinked on, like a big cat's eyes caught in headlamps, and then blinked off. Kelley hurried towards the lights.

When he reached the car at the end of the alleyway, the passenger door was pushed open and he got inside. 'You're late,' murmured a voice heavy with accent.

'The Englishman wanted to keep drinking. I couldn't get rid of him,' replied Kelley in the darkness. There was no reply. The man started the car and drove quickly out of the alleyway and down the street, away from the hotel. In just four minutes they left the street-lamps behind and were into the rural backwaters of the city. The car carried on for ten more minutes and then parked down a trackway that didn't, as far as Kelley could see, lead anywhere.

The driver switched off the engine, and a stifling silence surrounded them. They were too far from the sea now to get the benefit of the breeze.

'So,' asked the driver, 'what's the story, Kelley?'

'All's well. We made contact with the Captain and

he's gone for it. His brother is a lush, and I suggest you sort him out once we're gone. He's not to be trusted. We see the old engineer tomorrow, but the Captain seems to think he can get the ship going.'

'Careful with the man, Kelley. We have been watching him. Treat him well. He is a strong man. Strong mind.'

'I had noticed, Tariq. Don't worry. I can cope.'

'That's very good, Kelley. Our people will be very pleased. But you do not have long. We have heard about the ship we want,' said Tariq.

'Which is it? I need the details.'

'It's called *Jackson*. She is a new ship, just launched, and she's on a flag-waving cruise, I think the American Navy calls it, in the Pacific. According to our information she will be in the western Pacific in eleven weeks' time, heading for Hong Kong. The fourteenth, to be exact. It matches up with the cruise liner's schedule and the French ship. It's the perfect chance, Kelley, and our people want to make sure you don't miss it.'

'Jesus, Tariq, that gives me under three months to get the ship ready,' protested Kelley, turning to face the man.

'Less than that. We think you will need three weeks to get into position once you sail, taking things easy and so on. So you get two months to get the ship ready. It can be done. Our people have assured me that it can be done,' replied Tariq. He seemed confident enough.

'So what's the *Jackson*, exactly? What am I taking on?' asked Kelley, hardly more relaxed.

The man handed Kelley an envelope, which he ripped open. Inside was a set of colour photographs and a drawing. It showed a sleek, slim-hulled warship with a huge afterdeck, presumably to take a large helicopter.

'It's a new anti-submarine cruiser, Kelley. Lots of electronics. Should be no trouble for your ship. She carries a perfect cargo, about two dozen nuclear depth-charges. The warheads are kept separate from the depth-charge carriers, so you should find it easy to get them on board your ship.'

'I still don't know why you just don't do a deal with the crazies here. This dump must be awash with warheads, far less heavily guarded than the Americans' will be. Jesus, Tariq, for a couple of hundred dollars they'll even deliver the damn things,' said Kelley.

'Kelley, don't argue. You want the money, my people want these warheads. Nothing else will do. Just make sure you deliver on the day.' Tariq knew, but wasn't telling because it would drive the price up, just how important it was to get these particular warheads. Yes, he could have bought up dozens of Russian weapons: great, heavy, lumps that would wreck a city and were almost impossible to move, and which leaked radioactivity that any UN inspector with a Geiger-counter could detect from twenty miles away. The American weapons, RRS-Bs, were small, could be carried by a man, were leakproof, and would mount splendidly on top of a Scud missile, while the Russian equivalent would probably crush it. Best of all, with their small yields it was far more likely that the Americans would believe they would be used. No, my friend, thought Tariq – for what we want, it's vital to lay our hands on America's very finest.

Just as important was the fact that the US intelligence agencies were well aware that Tariq's masters were out shopping for nuclear weapons. But like Kelley, they too assumed that they'd be after the stockpiles scattered around various loosely guarded corners of the old Soviet Union; with no idea that they would go for the lighter, smaller American weapons, therefore their intelligence resources would be concentrated in all the wrong places. That made Vladivostok an attractive place, too: because it was so far away, two years ago the tottering Russian government had quietly transferred all of the modern nuclear weaponry back to Archangel, closer to home where it could be kept well out of the way of other interested parties. That explained Moscow's almost total lack of interest in the place any more – and it explained anyone else's lack of interest, too. Tariq explained none of this to Kelley; he surmised, rightly, that then Kelley would feel less pressure and the job would start going sloppy. He wanted the American to feel the heat.

Kelley was clearly feeling it now. 'Listen, tell them I can't guarantee anything. It all depends on getting the ship ready on time. We're busting some guts to get this done. I'll try, but no promises, OK? It's too early to be certain.'

'We don't want promises, Kelley. We just want those warheads. You've been paid well. Just don't fail. Understand?'

There was no point in arguing. As the man said, he'd been well paid. Over a million dollars, so far. And more to come.

'Sure, I understand. I'll manage it. What about the rendezvous?'

'Everything will be ready. We'll have a disguised ship standing off over the horizon ready to send in a squad of marines by helicopter as you're heading for the Monte Bellos. They'll secure the place ready for your arrival. Just turn up with the warheads, Kelley.'

'Your people had better be there, Tariq,' replied Kelley tersely. The man was irritating him.

'Don't worry, Kelley, don't worry. This is too

important for us.' The man Kelley called Tariq looked straight ahead out of the windscreen into the dark night. Kelley could just make out the gleam in his eyes. He took some comfort from the fact that it really was too important for them to screw up. So important that they'd spend almost any amount of money to make it go right.

'I need more cash, by the way. Same route as before.'

'How much?'

'Make it another half million. In the usual hundreds.'

'Sure, Kelley. No problem.'

Kelley wished he'd asked for ten.

'And the others, Kelley? How are the others?'

'Fine, Tariq. No trouble. Harvey still thinks it's a big fucking game, playing at pirates.'

'None of them know?'

'Christ, Tariq. What do you take me for?'

'Your friend Harvey worries us, Kelley. We don't know why you need him.'

'Listen, Tariq, I'm no seaman, OK? I wouldn't know one end of a fucking ship from the other. Harvey's my expert. And he speaks the language, for Christ's sake. Don't worry about Harvey. He's too thick to cause any trouble, he just wants the money,' growled Kelley. These people kept wanting to interfere. They should leave him alone to get on with it.

'And you think the *Jackson* will fall for the bait?'

'They have no option. It's part of their training, part of their code or whatever you call it. I checked all this out with Harvey. If they didn't respond to a distress call, then they'd be court-martialled.'

'And then shot?'

'No, Tariq, not shot. But locked up for a long time.'

'In my country we would shoot them. It keeps better discipline,' said Tariq. Kelley didn't get into the argument. In your country you'd shoot fucking everyone, he thought.

'Well, I guess we're different. Now get me out of here. It's giving me the creeps.'

Tariq started the car and bounced back down the track, turned round and headed off towards the pale glow of the street lights in the distance. He pulled up around the corner from the hotel, still in the dark so that Kelley's exit would be hidden. Kelley opened the door, and the driver leaned across and grabbed his arm.

'Kelley, don't fail. *Allah akbar* ... God is Great!' murmured the voice with a sudden, urgent passion.

Kelley pushed the man away. 'Yeah, sure. You'd better believe it. Just pray that ship keeps to its schedule. Now get out of here,' he said as he left the car. He could see the driver looking at him in the dim light, the thick black hair and the full, dark beard, and the gleaming eyes of a man who believed totally in his mission. The car accelerated quickly away, the tyres squealing in the silent night air.

'Crazy bastard,' murmured Kelley to himself as he headed back for the Imperial.

5

Mikhail Kishkov lived in a crumbling jerry-built apartment in an ageing block that should have fallen down years ago. He had been given the apartment rent-free by the Navy, who were also supposed to be responsible for his miserable pension since his release. It was intended to be some form of compensation. Inadequate as it was, it was all he had ever been offered.

In the baking summers the place stank, the water rarely ran, the electricity was intermittent and now, these days, he was plagued by kids on drugs hiding out on the balconies. In the long winter the raw Siberian wind pushed its way in through growing cracks in the prefabricated structure, and sometimes, when the wind was in the right direction, the snow would blow in as well. Last year, it even managed to form miniature drifts in his cramped kitchen. The heating, run from some hidden communal boiler that he could never find, was on for three hours a day at the most, and sometimes not at all when it was particularly cold. That was when the water also stopped working.

Over half a century ago – and just three weeks after his fateful meeting with Stalin himself – Kishkov had moved, together with his entire design team, to Trudovoye, a small town twelve miles north of

Vladivostok. Under Maslov's orders, the Navy had already started deepening and widening a huge dry dock in Vladivostok's vast naval yard. Just three months later, the first armoured keel plates were laid, screened from view by corrugated-steel walls and the watchful eye of a complete detachment of KGB Asian border guards, thoughtfully provided by Beria. Kishkov mercilessly drove his design team, and the workers in the yard, to finish *Stalin* by the required date.

In spite of his efforts, and although the project had almost absolute priority in getting scarce labour and materials, he couldn't avoid running some months late, mainly as a result of constant changes to the specification from the naval staff in Moscow. And as he knew he would be, he was massively over budget. Neither of these things would have mattered had Maslov still been around to protect him. But Maslov was gone, replaced by the commissar Vlasik. Badaev, one of the few people whom Kishkov regarded as a friend, had also disappeared, like Maslov, in one of the purges where Stalin had ripped the bloody heart out of his own military command structure. So when it came to it, it took very little to dislodge Kishkov. He had gained many more enemies than friends. He was young and callow, and to get things done would tread on anyone's feet. He was also brilliant, and made those who worked around him – particularly the older and more experienced engineers – look as dull and plodding as in truth they were. Somebody promoted so quickly, at such an early age, had not had the time in Communist Russia to build up his network of protective contacts. And Kishkov, still in his twenties, displayed an alarming political naïvety, even though he was such an enthusiastic supporter of the regime.

Just after the invasion by the Germans, the *Stalin's*

hull was ready for launch, now some three months behind schedule. Stalin himself was to launch the ship in great secrecy. The day before he was due to arrive, Kishkov received a telegram from Admiral Vlasik telling him that the cost of the over-runs and delays was his fault and that he was replaced with immediate effect. It was early July.

An hour after the telegram arrived, before Kishkov even had a chance to think about running, two sullen KGB officers walked into his office and in front of his entire staff took Kishkov away. He was left in a cell for five days without food. Then early one morning he was pushed on to a filthy military truck that bashed its way through the poor roads for three days to a labour camp in Shologontsy, a bleak township in the tundra of north-east Siberia, where his already angular frame was soon reduced to a skeleton by hard physical work and a diet that consisted of water and potato peelings. They called it soup.

His deputy, Vishkin, got his job; Vishkin had never liked Kishkov, and everyone in the yard knew that Vishkin had talked to Vlasik about Kishkov's constant complaints. Shologontsy, where Kishkov was eventually dumped, lies just below the Arctic Circle where in the brief summer the temperature rarely gets above fifty degrees and in winter the soil is frozen to a depth of twenty feet. For nearly twenty years Kishkov laboured in conditions that were, quite simply, meant to kill. Somehow he survived, and with the downfall of Stalin and the start of reform he was quietly released without a word one bitterly cold May morning, with a train ticket back to Vladivostok shoved into his hand.

And in between times the great *Stalin*, Kishkov's dream, the mightiest ship in the world, carried on being built. However incompetent Vishkin was, he had

Kishkov's detailed blueprints for the entire ship, and it was almost impossible for him to get it wrong. Thus the construction continued throughout the war; and at every moment Vishkin was there to take the glory. Once, a few years after his release, Kishkov happened upon a picture in an old magazine of the commissioning ceremony. There was Vishkin, decorated for his heroic efforts, telling the world how he had built the great ship, while Kishkov at that very moment had been scraping through a waste heap looking for potato peelings. The tears in his eyes as he looked at the picture were far from tears of sadness.

During his endless years in the tundra, Kishkov discovered a deep hatred of the world, found God, and went gently mad with the reassuring words of Badaev echoing like a distant bell in his ears. 'Trust Maslov,' said Badaev in the icy Moscow morning over fifty years ago. 'Trust Maslov. You won't go far wrong.'

He did not emerge from the camp as the same Kishkov who twenty years earlier had been carried off, shouting his innocence and weeping with frustration and bewilderment. He was now a deeply angry man, far from broken, and he had turned his anger to a fierce, revivalist religious belief that managed to blend a vengeful Russian Orthodox Christianity with a peculiar Russian nationalism that, had he been younger, would have had him hurling bombs in the cities. Like many Russians, he went to the extremes.

Every morning, the 82-year-old Kishkov would slowly take himself down the crooked steps of his apartment block to the nearby church of Saint Volodomyr and sit at the back, refusing the sacrament but watching the handful of old women who kept up the old traditions. The fat, bearded priest knew him and kept clear of him. The manic light in Kishkov's eyes frightened the priest, and he always felt nervous whenever the old man shuffled into the church.

This particular morning was no different. Kishkov had lurked at the back of the church for an hour until the service was over, then slowly lifted himself from the hard wooden bench and, leaning on his stick, hauled himself round towards the door. The interior of the small church was pitch black and the brilliant summer sun blazed through the small door, blinding him as he left the gloomy sanctuary.

As he came out he was dimly aware of the outline of four figures below him, waiting half-way up the old steps, their faces in deep shadow from the bright sun. He noticed that one of them was tall and thin, and another unusually fat. And one of them, who stood in the background, seemed to be wearing a uniform of some sort, though the light was too bright to be able to see what it was. He shuffled slowly down the steps and moved to pass them.

'Comrade Chief Designer Kishkov?' asked one of the figures, the tall one, in an educated, formal Russian accent that suggested an individual of some authority. Harvey had learned his Russian, in the same way that Zof had learned his English, as part of his naval training. It had been assumed by either side that one day, on the day of the final victory, they'd need to speak the other side's language. No one had made it clear whether they needed the language to negotiate in, or for command.

Harvey's question halted Kishkov, leaning on his stick. He had not been called Comrade Chief Designer since 1941, and it sent a cold shiver of fear through him. Who were these four people? Why had they spoken to him on the church steps? Why had they called him 'Comrade', now almost a term of insult?

'And who exactly are you, comrade?' replied

Kishkov, shading his eyes from the fierce sun and peering towards the face who had spoken, deep in shadow. He still couldn't see the man properly.

'We are friends of yours, Comrade Chief Designer. We have come with some good news. Can we speak with you for a while?'

Kishkov looked again at the men. His eyes were becoming accustomed to the bright light. Now he could see they were well-dressed, not normal kinds of people at all. The tall one who had spoken to him had a flop of hair across his thin, elegant face. Then there was a shorter, powerful-looking older man with short scrubby hair. Standing next to him was an extraordinarily fat man who seemed to be smiling at him. These three stood together on the steps. The fourth was tall too and stood behind the other three, and was wearing the black uniform and gold braid of a Naval Captain, First Rank. There was something about his bearing that seemed to make him seem more important than the others, though he remained silent.

'Good news, comrades? Perhaps you are from the pension office and you have come to pay me what you owe me? Good news indeed,' he grinned, a cynical look on his face. It would be a miracle if the Navy pension people even replied to his angry notes pushed through their door in the town, let alone send four people including a Navy Captain to talk to him about it.

'No, comrade, sadly we are not the pensions department. But we can do much better than that. Here, lean on my arm and we'll walk to that park. We can tell you our good news sitting in the sun. Come with us,' and Harvey offered his arm to the old man.

'Get away,' said Kishkov angrily. 'I don't need your arm. Twenty years in a Gulag and I can still walk, comrade, even if it is slowly. Walk alongside me and tell me what you want. If you've not come to pay me my money, what have you come for?' Like all old men, Kishkov's world had shrunk to the small problems that occupied most of his mind.

They all walked slowly across the street. A shady group of umbrella pines stood on a square of rough brown grass scattered with waste paper and small curls of dog-shit baked black and hard in the strong sun. There was an old bench under the pines with most of the slats of the back missing. They seated Kishkov in the middle of the bench, Harvey to one side, Kelley and fat Pine on the other. Zof stood behind them.

'So now will you tell me why you have come to annoy an old man?' demanded Kishkov, growing concerned. The pines shaded them not only from the sun but from the street as well.

Harvey had to get to the point before the old man shuffled off. Kelley had warned him that Kishkov was a temperamental, touchy character, though God knows how Kelley found out about these things.

'Comrade Chief Designer, it is an honour to meet you,' started Harvey in his most formal Russian. 'We have taken a lot of trouble to seek you out, comrade. You see, we need your help.'

'My help? What can an old man like me do for such good people as yourselves? It is I, comrade, who need the help.'

Zof had stayed in the background behind Harvey, and now he stepped forward to stand in front of the old man. He folded his arms and spoke as though he was addressing a meeting of his crew. In his black Captain's uniform he was a commanding sight which greatly impressed Kishkov – just as Kelley had said it would: he had insisted on Zof wearing it for the meeting.

'Comrade, we represent a group of people who, frankly, are sick and tired of what's going on in Russia these days. We are fed up with the way that the young people do not recognise the great sacrifices made by the older men who built this country into what it is today. We are greatly concerned with what is happening to this once great nation under those drunks at the Kremlin. What has happened to our great state, comrade? What has happened to us as a world power? What has happened to our armed forces? What, we want to know, has happened to the great Soviet Navy, once the most powerful in the world? Gone, comrade, all gone. Perhaps you agree, Comrade Chief Designer?' asked Zof, trying out the pitch he had agreed with Kelley and Harvey earlier. It was easy for Zof, thought Harvey. He actually appeared to believe this stuff.

The old man listened to Zof carefully. It looked to Kelley, who hadn't followed a word of what any of them were talking about, as if he was lapping it up. Kishkov looked up at Zof. 'What are you? Old communists? Listen, comrade, I did my time for Stalin. I met him once, in the Kremlin, with that bastard Beria. I hope their souls are rotting in hell.' Kishkov spat on the baked ground.

Kishkov would have strayed into the past given half a chance; his mind was filled with the glories of fifty years ago and he found the present uninteresting. But Zof wasn't going to indulge him. He leaned over him to keep up the pressure. 'Comrade, would you like our good news?' he asked sternly. Play the Captain, play the officer, said Kelley. It wasn't the kind of officer that Zof was, but he knew what Kelley meant and did his best to be the firm authoritarian that they assumed the old man would respect.

'Good news? Of course, Comrade Captain. If it's not

my pension, what is it? My apartment is very bad. The roof leaks. Have you come to fix it? Have you found me a new apartment, for instance?'

'No, comrade. Not your apartment. Not your pension. We'd like you to help us get *Stalin* going again. It's time to get that magnificent ship back on the seas. You remember *Stalin*? You built her. You designed her. *Stalin* is your ship. Your creation. Would you like to see her sail again in all her glory?' asked Zof, keeping his voice low.

Kishkov sat forward on the bench and leaned on his stick. This was too much, too much. He stared up at Zof. 'The *Stalin*? You want the *Stalin* to sail again? Pray that God does not strike you down for playing jokes on an old man like this,' he said angrily. But there was a gleam in his eye.

'No joke, comrade. We are very serious, and we need your help. We want you to become our Chief Engineer. There can be nobody better, after all. As for money, of course we can help you. We could make you a rich man, comrade, if you were interested. No more shabby apartments, not for the man who built the greatest battleship the world had ever seen,' said Harvey, taking over the pitch from Zof. The old man had turned to listen to Harvey, who was sitting next to him.

Kishkov nodded. It was still crazy: better humour these people. 'It sounds as though I have struck a great good fortune, comrade. But what, if you would be so kind as to tell me, is this all about? What exactly do you want from me? And who are you? You sound like Navy people but there are none left, so they tell me. All gone. Tell me a little more. I am trying to see the catch. There has to be one, comrade. There always is.'

'There is no catch, comrade. We are Navy, as you have guessed. But we are acting in an unofficial capacity. We have certain plans for the ship which must remain secret for a little longer. It is a very special project. What we need to know, Comrade Chief Designer, is if you want to help us. If not, we can look elsewhere. Our plans need advancing quickly. *Stalin* has not moved since 1945. She needs to be got back into commission. The new commander, Captain Zof here, wants you to look over the ship with him tomorrow to see what needs doing. Can you do that?' asked Harvey. He was enough of a salesman to know that you gave as little time for the decision as possible. Get action before they can change their minds.

'Can I do that? Comrade, let me tell you, I know that ship from stem to stern. Of course I can do that. I built her to last. Nobody ever built a ship as well as that, I daresay. She was the biggest battleship in the world, did you know that? I see her every day. From my apartment window I can see the funnel and the upperworks. She's starting to list. It's a disgrace to leave that ship rusting there. Tell me, what's she like inside? They would never let me through the gates, you see.'

'Oh, pretty good, we're told, comrade. You did an excellent job. The ship was well looked after, at least until recently.'

Kishkov was nodding again and Harvey thought he saw the old man's eyes moisten. Clearly, they were crazy. Or maybe they weren't. Kishkov looked at them again. The one in the uniform, he didn't seem crazy. Was it a trap? Were they KGB trying to imprison him again? Kishkov's suspicions were hardly settling. But he was surrounded by these people. And then, the *Stalin*! He never even saw the ship launched. That bastard Vishkin had stolen everything, even his final moment of glory. So, why not? Maybe they were crazy. Maybe they were KGB. Who cared any more? My life is nearly ended. Here is one last moment of glory; one last chance. 'Very well, comrade. I think I can help you.

I will look at the ship for you as you ask. Then you will tell me what this is all about, if you would be so kind?'

'Of course, comrade, of course.'

'You really mean to sail her again?'

'With your help, we will be on the high seas within a few weeks.'

Kishkov nodded again. 'And now, are you finished with me?'

'Thank you, comrade. You won't regret this. It will be a great achievement.'

Kishkov leaned forward on his stick and pushed himself upright from the grubby bench. 'When do we meet?' he asked.

'Tomorrow morning. The dock gates at eight,' said Zof.

'Not eight!' Kishkov suddenly stopped and faced Zof. 'At eight I will be at prayer. You should be too. I will meet you at ten. Then you will take me around my ship.'

'We will look forward to it, Comrade Chief Designer. Here's some money. Come by taxi – save your energy,' said Harvey.

'God will remember you, comrades, God will remember you,' said Kishkov. Without looking back at the four men, he walked slowly out of the park and across the dusty road towards his apartment, his head full of thoughts of the *Stalin* coming back to life.

*

At ten the next morning Kelley, Harvey, Pine and Yakov Zof were waiting anxiously at the dock gates. They had to wait for another half an hour until eventually Kishkov arrived in a battered Zil taxi dressed in a thick black suit he hadn't worn for twenty years or more. He struggled from the cab and proudly paid off the Asian driver, flourishing the wad of rouble notes that Harvey had handed to him the day before; they weren't worth more than a few dollars in total. Kishkov carefully buttoned his suit jacket and came slowly down towards the gates, where Zof saluted smartly and formally welcomed Chief Designer Kishkov to the yard.

The group walked slowly along the quay and managed – with some difficulty – to get Kishkov down a flight of stone steps to a stained inflatable with a Japanese outboard engine. With the weight of Pine, first aboard, it was already low in the water. The small boat rocked and tilted dangerously as Kishkov stepped on to it, nearly pitching him overboard. Zof pushed the old man down into a sitting position and the boat settled. He started the engine with an experienced pull and then expertly steered them across the oily stagnant water, passing groups of mooring buoys and taking them under the thick ropes and chains that connected the rafts of ships to each other, out towards *Stalin*, moored way out in the middle of the harbour.

The harbour and the quaysides were crowded with rust-streaked Russian warships, lying desolate and silent in the harsh, still sunshine. Moored bow-on to a quay were eight *Kilo*-class diesel-electric submarines, all identical other than the numbers on the fraying pennants, their doors and hatches half-open, lengths of cable and pipework snaking from various openings. Old wooden boxes and empty steel cans, too big for paint tins, were strewn around the decks, and scraps of rubbish floated in the water around them, clinging to the sloping hulls at the waterline as though some kind of magnetic attraction were at work.

One submarine had its stern almost under the water, so that its fat bow rose above the others like a displaced cigar. Another sat level but much lower in the water than the rest. They were all slowly sinking;

the crews had long since walked off in disgust. Next to the submarines was a group of missile frigates, square boxy ships with squat missile launchers on the big foredecks. The missiles themselves had long since gone, sold to the Bangladeshis on the black market. Like the submarines, the frigates were a mess. Anything removable had long since been unbolted or torn off for scrap or for souvenirs.

Some of the ships – the newer, more comfortable ones – had families of squatters living on board. The conditions were a great deal better than the run-down apartments that the Navy provided. All of the families were Navy people; senior officers had commandeered the best accommodation and ratings had been left with the ordinary crew quarters. The wives had lit fires for cooking on deck, and some of the men had rigged up generators to supply electric power. Zof knew many of them on the ships; he turned a blind eye and helped where he could, though he had little enough power left.

They puttered across the glimmering oil-slicked water, their wake disturbing shoals of tiny silver fish. The sweet, sickly smell of fuel oil drifted across them in waves as a light breeze disturbed the stagnant water of the harbour. *Stalin* came closer and began to loom menacingly above them.

She was a massive, ugly, grim-looking ship, the product of her times as much as her purpose. She lacked the graceful elegance of modern warships; instead, she was heavy and ponderous, and gave the impression of being just an enormous block of solid steel. She sat low and menacing in the water, her bows suddenly rising to a wave-crushing peak, angular gun barrels like fingers grasping outwards across the decks and a massive central citadel that rose, deck after deck, high into the clear morning air, black and shadowy, even though the sun shone brilliantly; she was tethered into place like a dangerous bull with massive chains that sank into the still water.

The ship had a huge length and beam, and also – especially seen from the small inflatable down on the surface of the water – an extraordinary height ... the single central citadel, prickling with anti-aircraft guns, rose some 170 feet into the air above the main deck. There were three bridges in the citadel. At the highest point, commanding a panoramic view of the ship, was the flag bridge reserved for the use of the embarked Admiral, *Stalin* having been built as a flagship. The height of the bridge was particularly useful for docking the big ship, so the pilot and the commander could see both ends of the huge vessel at once.

Several decks below the flag bridge lay the compass bridge, where the commander and officers would run the ship while under way. And below that, further down towards the deck and only just visible above the forward turrets, lay the battle bridge, surrounded by two feet of armour plate pierced by armoured periscopes and shuttered, slit windows, where the commander would retreat to in battle. Even a direct hit from an 18 inch shell was supposed to leave the occupants shocked but alive, and capable of keeping the ship fighting even if the rest of the vessel was just a pile of smoking wreckage.

At the very highest point of the central tower, two thirty-foot-long arms stretched out sideways, turning the top of the tower into a crucifix. Each arm had a small window set into the end. This was the optical rangefinder system for the main guns, invented long before radar gun control and, given the precision of the German optics acquired during the brief friendship treaty, it proved remarkably accurate for the huge 22-inch guns of the *Stalin*, capable of dropping one of its four-ton high-explosive shells within a hundred-yard circle at a range of thirty miles. On top of each arm sat a delicate spider's web of wires: the rusted remains of the radar antenna, installed just before the end of the War. The *Stalin* was equipped with one of the first sea-going operational radars used in the Soviet Union, but fifty years in the salt-laden air had long since eaten it away leaving just a ghostly web of wires.

Zof steered the tender at a sharp angle towards the steps – or ladder, as Zof insisted on calling them, though to Kelley's eye they didn't look anything like a ladder – that had been left suspended down the side of the ship by the departing maintenance crew. Within two feet of the bow ramming the lowest step, he smartly threw the outboard engine into reverse and pushed the steering arm hard over. The boat slowed, tucked its stern round, and came to a gentle rest neatly alongside.

Zof jumped off and secured the tender, then turned to help the others on to the ladder. Kishkov was last, and it needed Kelley and Pine to manhandle him off the boat. The flight of ladders facing them was forbidding; the deck was nearly forty feet above the level of the water, and both men had to help Kishkov slowly climb them, one each side of the old man supporting him by the elbows. Pine pushed a little too fast, so Kishkov was physically lifted up many of the steps.

He had not been so close to the *Stalin* since he last saw it in July 1941. For Kishkov, there were ghosts on the ship. He could see the men he had worked with, and he could see even more vividly the very few friends who had watched him being carried off by the KGB. Once he had walked this very deck and had been absolute master. Now he walked the same deck, slowly and stiffly, the teak beneath his feet bleached

after fifty Pacific summers. It was as though he had
aged those fifty years in a single step. He was silent,
and his eyes were watering.

The first place Zof and Kishkov wanted to see was
the engine room, deep down in the bottom of the ship.
How had the engines stood up to fifty years of
idleness? It was an echoing cavern, and steel ladders
and guard-rails twisted and turned in a maze, with
bundles of pipes and tubing like arteries and veins
running from deck to deckhead and hung in festoons
from the bulkheads. Zof had organised a couple of
men earlier that morning to run a generator barge
out to the ship, and hook up the power supply. The
generator thudded quietly away outside, and the old
wiring of the ship was just capable of dimly
illuminating the interior from twenty-watt bulbs
mounted on bulkheads in brass cages.

Dominating the huge engine room were eight
massive Parsons steam turbines imported from
Newcastle, painted green, and each one the size of a
house. The turbines drove the four shafts, each
turbine capable of delivering over 60,000 horsepower
to its shaft through a massive reduction gearbox; each
shaft needed two turbines, one for forward
propulsion, one for astern, interconnected through
the gearbox system. Feeding each turbine through
tubes the size of tunnels were four banks of boilers,
but these were contained in separate watertight
rooms forward of the turbine hall. They were fed in
turn by the thick, treacly oil that would be pumped up
from deep tanks that lined most of the bottom of the
ship. At full power, each bank of boilers would burn
over a ton of fuel a minute to superheat the water to
over 300 degrees centigrade of steam which was
blasted across the stainless-steel turbine blades at
massive pressure.

Besides the main machinery to propel the huge vessel, the turbine hall contained four further turbines, much smaller, each one driving a large generator. Without electricity *Stalin* was a dead ship; she could use as much as a small city, and just two of the generators could supply all her power, the other two acting as back-ups. Kishkov had carefully studied the sinking of every major battleship since Jutland, and he was amazed to see how many had become disabled through the lack of electrical power, leaving them at the mercy of their attackers. Beside redundant generating capacity he provided separate boilers away from the engine systems, and separately armoured too, to ensure that *Stalin* would remain powered even in the most extreme circumstances. Just for good measure he added two smaller generators, well away from the main machinery, that would provide just enough power to enable the ship to steer and to run the gun mechanisms, in case all the other generators went down.

They walked slowly around the vast cavern. The machinery was in good condition – though with its bulk, its huge fittings and its gleaming brass connections, it was all of a different generation. Everything was oversized. Even the bolts were big; huge pieces of carefully machined iron and steel that looked as though they would last for centuries. Over the years, generations of conscripts had been set to work cleaning and oiling every part; maintenance crews had dutifully checked every bolt and nut, and the insides of the ship were as well kept as the best museum exhibit. The neglect of the last two years was little more than dust and cobwebs; but whether the ancient machinery would actually work … Kishkov, looking at the product of his labours which he had never seen before, had no doubt that the whole thing would run like clockwork with a little effort.

Kishkov now seemed lighter on his feet the more he moved around the huge space. He scraped grease away with his hands as he examined the enormous turbines, the gearboxes and the generators, together with the spaghetti of piping and wiring that made the engine room look like the interior of a gigantic old radio set. He talked to himself as he moved around the machinery, reporting to himself what he saw and the condition of the equipment. As he poked and lifted and peered, he was oblivious to the rest of them.

From the engine room Kishkov stumped into the boiler rooms, the others trooping after him as though he were a tour guide. He stopped in front of one of the big boilers and tapped the front with his walking stick. 'You, I need to get inside here,' he said abruptly to Zof, who forced down a handle and opened the boiler inspection door. It didn't even creak. Kishkov peered inside at the condition of the tubing and withdrew again, still muttering; Zof couldn't tell if it was favourable or not.

After a couple more hours of peering and prodding, Kishkov demanded to be helped up to the main deck. Having struggled with the old man up several twisting, winding flights of ladders, they eventually emerged towards the stern of the ship near the after main turret. It was a relief to stand in the sunshine again after the oily, damp smell of the bowels of the ship.

'Well?' demanded Kelley once they were all out in the open, getting irritated with this old man's mumblings. 'Does the damn thing go or doesn't it?'

Kishkov looked at Harvey. 'I understand your friend's question from his tone. He's too impatient. But I have looked carefully and I think we can get my ship going again without much trouble. It looks as though whoever was left in charge of the ship did a good job.

Not perfect, but adequate. But we will still need to do work.'

'How much?' asked Harvey.

'Most of it is cleaning out the boilers with fresh water and cleaning out the turbines. I cannot yet guarantee the pressures.'

'Which means what?' asked Harvey again.

'It means that I think we can get power but I don't know how much. Perhaps some of the turbine blades are weak, perhaps some of the boiler tubes are corroded. We won't really know until we run them to full pressure. We are in God's hands. He will decide.'

Harvey decided against arguing the merits of God as an engineer. He translated for Kelley: 'He thinks it will work. He just doesn't know how fast yet, that's all.'

'Jesus, Harvey, I thought he designed the fucking thing. Is that the best we get? "I think it will work?"'

Harvey ignored Kelley and again followed Kishkov, who had set off once more down the deck towards the stern of the ship.

The after gun-turret was the old engineer's next call. The turret lay with its three enormous guns pointing slightly downwards to ease the strain on the mechanism. Kishkov told Zof to pull open the access door which had been left slightly ajar for ventilation. Like the engine room, all the machinery had been carefully looked after and polished over the years. Inside the turret, the cramped dimly lit space was densely packed with machinery and there was little room to move around. Dominating the interior, gleaming in the dull light, were the three vast breeches of the 22 inch guns, sealed by thick hardened steel doors with complex latching mechanisms to hold the doors in place when the huge gun was fired. Enormous hydraulic rams were connected to each gun to absorb the recoil; the rams filled the upper parts of the turret space and Kishkov and the rest of them had to duck beneath the gleaming steel and brass.

Behind each breech mechanism sat the shell cradles and rams that would push each four-ton shell, followed by its propellant in silk bags, into the gun. And behind the rams were the shell lifts that brought up the ammunition from the heavily protected magazines deep below, which had space to hold 300 shells and propellant bags.

This was one of the most powerfully armoured places in the ship. The turrets were surrounded by fifteen inches of armour plate, the magazines below were encased in two feet of it. Kishkov had calculated the impact from the biggest guns afloat at that time: the *Yamoto*, with its 18-inch guns, was the obvious threat, and he laid on enough armour plate to ensure that the turrets and magazines could withstand a direct hit by a shell from a gun the size of *Yamoto*'s.

While *Stalin* was being built, Kishkov constructed a full-scale replica of one of his turrets on a nearby army proving ground. He fired the biggest artillery shells he could lay his hands on – 16-inch-calibre monsters left over from the First World War – at the turret, and then dropped 1000 lb armour-piercing bombs on it from a mile up. The 16-inch shells tore splinters off the armour but did little else. The bombs gouged deep craters but left the turret unpierced. He calculated that three bombs would have to fall in exactly the same position before the armour was breached, which was unlikely even in the best conditions, let alone at sea. It was difficult enough to hit the replica turret on dry land from an aircraft; it took eight bombs before one connected for his test.

Kishkov tried one other test while he had the chance. Through the local KGB, he was provided with four political prisoners: they were scum, enemies of the state. He had them locked inside the turret and then blasted away at it with ordinary high-explosive shells, scoring eight direct hits. After twenty minutes they stopped shooting and unlocked the door. The four prisoners stumbled out, alive but with blood trickling from their ruptured ears, permanently deaf. Kishkov noted the results carefully, and then made sure that there was accommodation in the rest of the ship for at least four teams of trained gun-crews per turret.

Now Kishkov looked carefully at the machinery. He inspected the electric motors and the hydraulic pistons that would drive the turrets and elevate the guns. He blew insects from the eyepiece of the turret gun director that in an emergency allowed each turret to aim independently of the main director high on the superstructure. He poked at the wiring that ran around the turret interior. The ancient rubber insulation had started to perish in places, and the red copper underneath gleamed in the dim light.

When they emerged from the gloom of the turret, blinking in the strong Pacific sun, Kishkov looked pleased. 'The turrets are good. But I don't think the wiring has lasted very well.'

'But can it be fixed, comrade?' asked Zof, who so far had been impressed by how well preserved most of the ship appeared to be.

'Of course,' replied the old man sharply. 'I designed the wiring for multiple redundancy in case part of the circuits became damaged in action. It will be easy to re-route if we need to. We need a lot of good electricians and plenty of wire, that's all,' he went on, also pleased that his handiwork had so far stood the test of time so well.

As they walked forward towards the main

superstructure, Kishkov was becoming excited and was forgetting to lean on his stick. There was an ancient lift running the full height of the tower up to the flag bridge, but after two years of idleness no one wanted to try it. Struggling up the narrow stairway, they helped Kishkov to the lower combat bridge, but then his legs got the better of his enthusiasm. 'No further, if you please,' he gasped. 'Zof here can go and see what the rest is like. Leave me here to get my breath back.' They sat him down in the small armoured room, built like a bunker, and pushed the heavy steel door fully open to let a little light into the musty interior. Kishkov didn't seem to mind it.

'I'll go,' said Zof. He wasn't volunteering but ordering; he wanted to check out his new command for himself. Kelley and Harvey waited with Kishkov while Zof carried on up three flights of ladders to the second bridge, the compass bridge. It was a long, wide compartment, stretching a full forty or fifty feet. Doors at each end led to wing bridges that stretched out for a further ten feet, giving visibility of the sides and after part of the vessel. The bridge was rimed with dust, like a hoar frost. Insects scuttled around the floor as Zof pushed the wooden door open and walked in. The windows, angled forward to defeat reflections, were filthy and he rubbed a finger across them. In the centre lay the wheel and compass; the ship's telegraph and other instruments were planted around the wheel. They were all coated in grime and heavily tarnished but otherwise looked serviceable. Zof tried pushing the handle on the ancient telegraph to 'Full Ahead'; the bell rang clearly inside the brass column, but there was no answer from the engine room.

To the back of the bridge was the navigator's room and the radio room. He pushed open the radio-room door. It was packed with vintage radio equipment:

metal cases with ventilation grilles, big glass valves the size of church candles; dials three inches across made of white enamel with thick metal indicator needles, rheostat knobs like saucers of dull black bakelite, coils of wire covered in brown fabric insulation.

He was surprised the ship hadn't been stripped by souvenir hunters. Perhaps it would have been if left another year and more Japanese and Americans, for whom this stuff had a high antique value, had got a sniff of its existence. To the average Russian, it was still the kind of stuff he was throwing out to buy the latest Japanese equipment. The maintenance crews and the conscripts had looked after all of it lovingly. Nothing could be changed: those were the orders. Unwittingly they had preserved one of the finest collections of 1940s electrical gear in the world, except none of it worked any more: however well maintained and looked-after, most of the parts hadn't been made for decades, even in Russia's backward electrical factories.

Further up the central tower, up another three flights of ladders, was the flag bridge where Admiral Maslov would have had his command if the KGB hadn't got to him first. It had no instruments other than a big brass compass, and several telephone sets all made from bakelite, with thick twisted wire cords that looked as though they were insulated with a sticky black cloth. There was leather seating, but the leather was mouldy and had rotted away in patches. The bulkheads were lined in mahogany which had stood up well to the recent neglect, but the carpet across the steel deck was now just a spongy mass where damp had got at it, and it gave under the feet like turf. Zof wandered around, fascinated by the age of the place and how well most of it had survived. The place was a living museum, untouched by modern technology.

The view from the windows was breathtaking. He was almost at the highest point of the ship. Forward he could see the two massive turrets and then the long bulbous bow, festooned with chains and anchors all neatly stowed. The deck was made of teak that had bleached a brilliant white in the salt and sunshine. The windows ran all the way round the bridge, giving a panoramic view. Aft was the huge grey single funnel, with a gigantic star surrounding a hammer and sickle forged from steel and welded to each side. Behind that, half obscured by the small seaplane hangar, was the after turret with its three big guns.

Below the bridge at each side were the smaller turrets of the secondary armament and the anti-aircraft guns. Zof counted sixteen twin-barrelled anti-aircraft gun muzzles down one side alone, together with eight 6-inch secondary guns, and a further six larger guns. Each gun was housed in its own bulbous armoured turret; they ran down each side of the ship and clustered around the base of the central tower, a mass of grey steel blisters.

Zof stood silently for a moment, looking out across the wide decks of his new command. She had never sailed in anger, and had only ever joined the naval list as a training establishment. Now, after fifty years, she would move again; and Zof's final voyage would be his greatest. His couldn't help but grin as he clenched a fist and gave a silent salute, more to himself than to anyone. 'OK, Comrade Stalin,' he muttered. 'Time to show them what we can do.'

Slowly he made his way back down to the combat bridge where Kishkov and the others were waiting expectantly. Zof told them about the bridge systems. They were dirty, they were old, but they were all there and, apart from the ancient electrics, most of them looked as though they would work. The truth was, no one would know until they had the main generators running and the ship had full electrical power. Harvey, Zof and Kishkov started talking enthusiastically about getting the ship up and running, leaving Kelley – who understood little of the technicalities – and Pine – who gave the impression of being happily uninterested in the whole thing – standing outside looking out across the foredeck. After twenty minutes of sometimes heated discussion, Kishkov announced that he wanted to go back to shore.

They left the tower and walked across the bleached deck. After they had slowly helped Kishkov back down the ladder and got him comfortable in the tender, Zof motored them expertly away from the huge ship back towards the quay. Their tour around the *Stalin* had taken nearly four hours; the clear sun was now high in the sky and the temperature in the eighties. Zof landed them at the stone quay and they manhandled Kishkov up yet more steps. They finally reached Zof's ramshackle office and crammed inside, Pine shutting the door for security but ignoring the open windows that allowed a gentle though hot breeze to drift into the small room.

Kishkov had remained stubbornly silent throughout the trip back, and Zof knew that he was over-playing the whole scene, presumably to make him feel more important. He didn't like the small old man; he felt he was less than honest. Mind you, he thought, I'm standing here with a bunch of crooks in my office and I'm worried about honesty? He smiled inwardly; this was the biggest meeting he'd been at in two years, and here he was, a Captain First Rank of what was the mightiest Navy in the world, seriously considering stealing a fifty-year-old battleship. Oh well, thought Zof. Let's see what the bunch of lunatics make of the whole thing. He knew perfectly well the ship would sail; he could see for himself that most of it, though old, was pretty much in working order. Zof settled at his desk, arranged a sheaf of papers in front of him and waited for the rest of them to begin.

'So what's the verdict?' asked Kelley eventually, when it was clear that Zof wasn't going to lead the meeting. 'Do we have a ship or don't we? What does our friend here actually think?'

Kishkov looked at the others and then spoke; Harvey translated for Kelley as he did so. 'The Chief Engineer is very satisfied with his work. He is happy to see that everything has lasted so well, but naturally he expected it to do so. His standards of engineering were quite exceptional and he expects no problems. He is sure that everything will work but cannot be certain about actual performance until he gets a sea trial in the ship. It will, he says, need at least a week to get the muck out of the systems and the generators going. Given that they were in use until recently, he is happy they will perform. Once he has power back up, he can be more sure about the rest of the ship. Naturally, he says, he will need many good men, trained he must emphasise, and they will need to start quickly. Otherwise he sees no problem.'

'No problem? Where does the old fool expect to get trained mechanics in this dump, Harvey?' demanded Kelley, not impressed with what he had been hearing. 'What do you say, Zof?'

Zof shrugged his shoulders. 'I don't see why it can't be done. A lot of the old maintenance crew are still around the port somewhere. I am not very happy about the timings, however. I think I can get thirty or forty crew back by the end of the week, but it will take longer to get the others. Some weeks, perhaps longer. They will need to be well paid, of course. Cash. In hundred-dollar bills.'

'The timing, Zof, the timing is vital, for chrissake. We gotta get this ship ready no later than nine weeks from today,' said Kelley. Tariq had been more than clear on that particular point, he thought. The whole thing was a waste of time if they couldn't meet that date.

'Explain, please, the big rush? The ship will not run away, Kelley,' said Zof, annoyed at the American's pushiness. Kelley explained the importance of the timing, or at least as much of it as he wanted to reveal: Price, their contact at Lloyd's, had warned them of a big shipment of bullion coming through the South China Sea in exactly eleven weeks' time, on the fourteenth. That gave them just nine weeks to get the *Stalin* ready to sail, and then two more weeks to get into the right place. The ship must set sail within the deadline. Zof just shrugged his shoulders and repeated that he would try, and that he thought it would be fine, but these days, who knows? It was clear that he would work in his own time, not Kelley's.

Zof was more worried about what would happen when hundreds of sailors and workmen started on the ship. He was happy that the crew wouldn't talk because he'd make damn sure that they didn't, but he wasn't so sure about everyone else. Harvey came up with a cover story: put the word around that the ship had been sold to the Japanese as a tourist attraction, and was being got ready to sail; given the state of the Navy it was completely believable and, frankly, most people around the port were far too busy scraping a living to take much notice of even a vessel like *Stalin* getting under way. The story would be enough to keep them quiet.

As for the authorities, Zof didn't give them a second thought. Kelley was most worried about this: Zof found it difficult to explain to the American the scale

of the collapse. A few years ago, you couldn't spit in
Vladivostok without hitting naval top brass. But Zof
hadn't seen a senior officer in months: they had
simply disappeared. Moscow wouldn't know about the
Stalin getting ready, Zof was bitterly sure of that. Even
if they did find out, he doubted if anyone would care.
A museum piece like *Stalin*? No, said Zof, that really is
the least of your problems. But Kelley wouldn't give
up. What about American intelligence? What about
satellite spies? Zof snorted again. You think the
Americans are worried about this dump? There are
piles of nuclear missiles and rusting reactors
everywhere in the country to keep them busy; why
would the marvellous technology of the Americans be
wasted on this pile of old iron? Even Kelley had to
agree with Zof's logic; Tariq had insisted on exactly the
same points when Kelley had raised them at the start
of the enterprise. He doubted Tariq then, but was
greatly reassured by Zof's emphatic certainty that the
Stalin could probably sail out with the crew singing
the '*Internationale*' accompanied by massed Navy
bands and no one would take any notice.

As for the crew, Zof was looking forward to
bringing his men together again. He reckoned he
would need around 400 crew for the one-way trip.
There were plenty of experienced crewmen still
around, many of whom had worked on the *Stalin*
recently and knew the ship well. He was pretty sure
he could sell the idea to them. Men who were virtually
starving would do anything for food. Besides, Zof
knew a lot of them personally; they had sailed with
him before, and they treated him like a hero. But this
time, he could at least promise them something more
tangible than the glory of the motherland.

'And fuel? We'll need thousands of tons of heavy
fuel oil. Where do we get that?' asked Harvey.

Zof remained unperturbed. 'No problem, my friend. This yard has plenty of fuel oil sitting around. It's not been touched for months, remember? They kept a reserve supply for half the Pacific Fleet. All we have to do is load it. Won't take more than a day or two at the most.'

'Ammunition for the guns?' Again, Zof assured him that there were supplies within the dockyard. He'd found where they kept the 22-inch shells, lying forgotten in a distant corner of the arsenal. He wasn't sure about the explosives in them, but Second World War bombs were still exploding after having been buried for the best part of fifty years, and in any event, if Kelley was right, they'd never be used in anger. It was worth a chance. And there was plenty of cordite around the place, for propellant. Whole buildings were full of the stuff, just waiting to go off.

Zof was now sitting back at his desk with Harvey and Kelley facing him and Kishkov sitting quietly in a corner. Pine stood with his huge bulk against the door.

Harvey turned to Kishkov. 'Well, Comrade Chief Designer?'

'We are in God's hands. But if the Captain here can manage everything I will require, then I am content with the arrangements,' the old man replied slowly and carefully in the formal Russian he used for speaking to Harvey.

Harvey was about to shake his hand when Kishkov spoke again. 'But now, of course, you have to tell me exactly what it is you want with my ship? If you would be so kind?'

Oh shit, thought Harvey. He was about to embark on a long explanation of exactly what they wanted the *Stalin* for when Zof stood up.

'I think this matter concerns two Russians, my friend. Go for a walk and come back in fifteen minutes,' he said. Harvey was going to argue, but one look at Zof's face told him there was no point. He told Kelley that Zof wanted to talk to Kishkov on his own and they filed out, Pine following like a cheerful dog in their wake, and closed the door behind them.

'Jesus, Harvey, how the hell is our Captain going to sell the old man this idea?' asked Kelley. But he wasn't asking a question; by now, both of them were slightly in awe of Zof's power to get things done. His brother had been right – Yakov yelled and people came running. On Kelley's part, it was more a fascination with the man's methods. Truth to tell, he was beginning to admire the man. He seemed able to exercise power without violence, and this to Kelley was something quite new and extraordinary. He just wanted to know how it was done.

They wandered around the parade ground like naughty children cooling their heels. After ten minutes Kelley got bored. 'Fuck this. I'm going in,' he said, and headed back to the office. Either Zof had seen him or else he knew he'd be tempted to come back. The Russian was leaning with his back to the door, and all Kelley could see were broad shoulders and the fur of his crew-cut head. He wasn't going to try pushing the door open. They paced around for another five minutes, then the door was opened and Zof beckoned them back in.

'The Comrade Chief Designer is very flattered by your offer, my friend. He gratefully accepts and hopes our enterprise will go well.'

'What the hell did you say to him, Zof?' asked Kelley. The old man was sitting on the chair, smiling, and Harvey swore he could detect the dried streak of a tear down the wrinkled yellow parchment skin of his cheek.

'You wouldn't understand. It was about duty,

patriotism, the glory of Mother Russia and what things used to be like. Old-fashioned ideas like that.'

'Not money?'

Zof looked as though he would explode. 'Money? Yes, money too, Kelley. Very much money. Work out which one did the trick, eh? Now, here's your Captain, here's your Chief Engineer, and there's your ship. Satisfied?'

Kelley grinned. Pine smiled happily from the corner. 'Captain Zof, welcome back,' said Kelley. 'I think you got yourself your first command.'

And now it was Zof's turn to smile.

6

The *Stalin* came steadily to life. And as it did, Yakov Zof came to life too.

His first task was getting the crew together. He reckoned he would need at least four bay-chay, combat divisions – one, navigation; four, communications; two, artillery; and five, the all-important engineering bay-chay. That would mean around 400 men to run the ship; in full commission, the old battleship would have had a complement of all the bay-chay: nearly 2,000 officers and men. But, reasoned Zof, they were hardly going to battle, although he wanted a big enough bay-chay to run the guns if required; and it was a one-way trip in any event. The ship had to be sailable. He'd have to live without the thing being scrubbed and polished, and pointless cleaning, although a habit of the Navy, was not Zof's style; this was one of the things that endeared him to his crews.

He needed two things to start the ball rolling: Zhadanov, his old engineering bay-chay commander, to act as bait; then the best cook in the fleet, together with an ample supply of the best provisions he could find. He knew his men. Good food first, then the rest would follow. Most of them had not eaten a proper meal in months.

The cook was easy. He found Blokhin working in a tourist restaurant in the city centre.

'Pavel!' he grinned, as the rotund figure of Blokhin appeared from behind the beaded curtain that concealed the not very appetising kitchen. Blokhin looked worried and wiped his hands on a greasy once-white apron. He hadn't changed, thought Zof. The dirtiest cook in the Navy, as well as the best.

'Comrade Captain?' said Blokhin nervously. 'What brings you down here?'

'Pavel, I need a good cook. It's time to go to sea,' said Zof. Blokhin looked even more alarmed. He had never officially left the Navy, of course, and was technically – like the thousands of other sailors in Vladivostok – a deserter.

'Comrade Captain, of course, any time. I have not been paid, you see, so I simply took this job to fill in. Of course it is not a problem. But I must let . . .'

'Pavel, for heaven's sake stop panicking,' said Zof, interrupting the nervous cook. 'I need you as a cook, and I'll pay you well. Look, here's five hundred dollars to get you started. Meet me Wednesday night in the old mess at the yard. In the meantime, I need provisions for four hundred men for a few months. Can you get the best?'

'Comrade Captain! Four hundred men? It is not possible! Nobody supplies the Navy any more. They don't pay the bills.'

'Let's call it private enterprise, Pavel. I'll put up whatever money it takes. Dollars, mind you. Hard cash. But I want the best. And I want you to cook a meal for thirty in the mess on Wednesday night. I'm getting some of the lads together. Can you do it?'

Pavel Blokhin looked at the cash in his hand and then up at Zof. The Captain was not the sort of man to play jokes.

'It will be a pleasure, Comrade Captain,' he beamed, stripping off the filthy apron. One down.

Next on the list was Zhadanov. He was younger than

Zof and had worked with him for some years. He was a brilliant engineer, and Zof knew he needed someone he could rely on. Kishkov might know the ship inside out, but he was insufferable; there was no way he was going to let the old man try to run the engineering crew. That would have to be Zhadanov's job, whether Kishkov liked it or not.

He walked back to the yard and down to the quay. Zhadanov had a wife and three children, all boys, and he had moved them on to the *Vikin*, one of the newest missile cruisers in the Navy, where he had made himself and his family comfortable in the Captain's quarters. Zof strode up the gangplank, ignoring the stares of the small boys, and found the quarters; the door was open and Zhadanov was sitting with feet up, watching a colour TV he had somehow laid his hands on, a can of Chinese beer in hand. He was wearing old jeans and a T-shirt.

'Zhadanov!' yelled Zof at the top of his voice. His entry had been masked by the noise from the TV. Zhadanov spilt the beer down his front in panic, leapt to his feet, and the moment he saw the black uniform froze and wondered if he should stand to attention. Then he saw it was Zof.

'For fuck's sake, Yakov,' complained Zhadanov. When he wasn't on duty he never bothered with the formalities as far as Zof was concerned. It was one of the things that Yakov liked about him.

'Sorry, Yuri,' grinned Zof. 'You looked far too comfortable sitting there.'

'Want a beer? No? Silly question. Sit down. What's up?' asked Zhadanov, calming down.

'What are you doing Wednesday night?'

'Sitting here, watching the football. Stupid question, Yakov. There's not much else, is there?'

'Fancy a job?'

'What sort of job?'

'Getting the biggest battleship in the world out of mothballs, getting a crew of four hundred men together, stealing the ship, sailing it off, relieving the decadent Westerners of several million dollars' worth of gold and retiring wealthy men. That sort of job.'

'Fuck off, Yakov.'

'I'm serious.'

'Sure you are. Sure you don't want that drink?'

To keep Zhadanov happy, he accepted a freezing-cold tin of the beer. He turned off the TV and told the increasingly astonished engineer the whole story.

'You?' asked Zhadanov, eventually. 'You of all people would do this?'

'What else have I got left, Yuri? Polina's gone. The Kremlin's sold out to the Americans. Nothing's happening, Yuri. It's finished. The money isn't important. It's a chance to sail again, to show the world what you and I and the Russian Navy could have been. Take it, Yuri. You'll never get another chance. Nor will I.' Zof was more serious than Zhadanov had ever seen him before. Leaning forward in his chair, he'd even forgotten to light a cigarette in his enthusiasm. Yuri knew he had to go along with Yakov; when he was in this mood he was unstoppable.

'OK, Yakov. Sold. I'm in. You're crazy, but you always were. When do we start?'

'Wednesday night. Here's what I want you to do,' and Zof and Zhadanov started working through the details.

*

Zof and Zhadanov spent the next two days contacting around a dozen of their old officers, their previous bay-chay commanders and other specialists. The story was that there was to be a reunion dinner, one of Blokhin's finest, back at the mess. They would be able to discuss arrears of salary – Captain Zof had some good news for them: tell your friends. It was an irresistible promise. On Wednesday night, Blokhin excelled himself with the kind of meal that only tourists ate these days in Russia; he'd even managed to get several cases of Georgian wine, an unheard-of luxury.

Zof let them eat and drink until they had all reached that pleasant, relaxed state when they would buy almost anything. They were sitting at a massive oak dining table which seemed to have survived the looters, probably because it was too big to move. Zof sat at the head of the table, and Zhadanov at the foot. The remains of Blokhin's meal littered the dark wooden surface.

Zof suddenly stood and rapped a glass. 'Comrades, a toast, please. To Comrade Blokhin for one of the finest meals ever to grace the great Russian Navy!' and he lifted a glass of water while the others raucously raised glasses of vodka.

'And now, a moment of your time. I have a small proposition to put before you. But first of all, your arrears of salary ...' said Zof. He reached down under the table and produced a cardboard carton. 'Perhaps this will help?' And he started walking down one side of the table, behind the astonished officers, shaking the contents of the box down the middle. Bundles of crisp old-issue $100 bills, twenty to a bundle, cascaded down on to the plates and into the wine glasses, littering the table and the meal. No one had ever seen as much money in their lives.

The room went deadly quiet. Had their famous Captain finally cracked under the strain? Was he drunk? It was the most incredible thing any of them had ever seen him do, and Zof had done some extraordinary things in his time.

Zof returned to his seat, savouring the astonished

silence. 'Oh, it's real all right. Pick it up. It's all yours. And more. Much, much more. You deserve it. The way you have been treated has been disgraceful. There is not a man round this table who has not been insulted beyond endurance. Take the money. It is nothing compared with what you are owed. Listen, comrades, and listen carefully. I know the money is nothing to you. It is nothing to me. It is but confetti …' and to show his disdain he started ripping up some the bills in front of them. 'What is important? I'll tell you, comrades. What is important is Russia. Our great country, our great Navy too. All of you have trained for years. All of you have made sacrifices. Good god, men, who stood between the evil empire of the Americans and the motherland? You did, comrades. We were defeating them in every corner of the oceans. No one was mightier than we were. Then? Gone, comrades, all gone.'

Zof was enjoying himself. Don't overdo it for Christ's sake, Yakov, said Zhadanov to himself. But Zof knew his audience.

'Given away, comrades. Sold to the highest bidder. The drunks in the Kremlin have sold you out. Look at you! The pride of the Russian Navy, and you've just had the first decent meal you've eaten in months. Where are you living? On the hulks? In the slums? The men who stood up to the world have become beggars? Enough, comrades, enough,' and his voice fell to a low, pleading tone. 'Surely you've had enough? You, Morin? You, Alenski? Tell me?' he demanded.

Morin was Zof's old bay-chay two commander, missiles and artillery. Alenski had been in charge of bay-chay one, navigation. 'True, true, Comrade Captain. We're fucking beggars. It's true,' they replied mournfully.

Zof crashed his fist on the table; the plates jumped and the cutlery rattled. His audience's eyes widened.

'Well, I've had enough. That's it! Here's what I plan to do about it. Listen carefully, comrades. Every word I shall tell you is true.'

The audience sat spellbound as Zof carefully related the story of Kelley and Harvey and the ship. He told them, bluntly, what the *Stalin* was to be used for. He told them how he disapproved of the plan but was going to help, not for the money but because he wanted to show the world what the Red Banner Fleet was still capable of. He told them it was their last chance, and how he quite understood that their need for money was greater than his. He was doing it for Russia. For the Navy. For them. Forgive me, he asked them, for suggesting you turn into pirates. He was sad it had come to this. But as it had, let's show them what we can do.

He sat down abruptly. The officers were now even more astonished and no one knew what to say. Zof was the straightest of all of the officers they'd worked under. Unbendable, most would have said. And here was Zof, the great man himself, now suggesting piracy. He saw their faces ... and he also saw that each man had worked out his share of the millions of dollars' worth of gold that Kelley was promising. He waited quietly.

They looked uneasily at the dollar bills around the table. Nobody said a word. Suddenly, Yuri Zhadanov picked up a handful of the cash and held it in the air.

'I have bills to pay, Captain. My kids haven't had a decent winter coat for two years. I trained for seven years for the Navy, and now I have to sell cabbages in the market to make ends meet. I'll take the money, Captain, because I need it. But I'm still a Navy man. It's time to sort this out once and for all. I for one have had it up to here with this shit. Engineering Commander Zhadanov reporting for duty, sir!' And he snapped off an exaggerated salute. It broke the silence. Every man in the room was behind Zof, and they were also stuffing wads of notes into pockets and down their shirt-fronts. Zof shook many hands. He told them to report for duty first thing in the morning. Satisfied with at least the first phase of the operation, he walked smiling out of the room, Zhadanov with him. Once they were out of earshot of the others, Zof clapped him on the back.

'Well done, Yuri. You'd make a great actor,' Zof whispered quietly, smiling.

'No problem, Yakov. Glad I could help,' the officer replied.

The speech they had rehearsed just an hour before had done the trick. Zof had his officers.

Each of them went off into the night and started their own recruitment drives with Kelley handing over bundles of $100 bills almost on request. Within a week, more than 200 men had started working on the ship. Over half of them had been working as *Stalin*'s maintenance crew up until the collapse, and they knew every corner and every peculiarity of the great ship. More were joining them every day. The *Stalin* was coming steadily back to life.

*

First, they had to get the electrical power running. The generator tender provided enough dim light to work by, but the ship's main generating plant had to be functioning to provide the power for the rest of the systems, and it hadn't worked for nearly two years.

The main generator room had four massive diesel engines, each driving an alternator the size of a small truck. There were two standby generator systems as well, locked away in their own watertight compartments to provide enough back-up power to run critical systems if the main installation was knocked out in battle.

A small crew was set to work to pump diesel fuel into the generators' tanks from a supply barge, and another party was set to work to get the big diesels running again. As Kishkov had judged, they had been laid up well. Inhibiting oil had been poured into them, so the innards were clean and bright once the oil had been drained off. New engine oil was added, the injectors stripped down and cleaned, and the fuel pumps stripped into the bargain.

The enormous alternators driven by the diesels were also in good condition. The thick carbon brushes had to be replaced, and plenty of new grease packed into the bearings, but the only problem was the wiring. The central copper core was fine, but the rubber insulation had perished in many places. Kishkov insisted on a party going round the entire ship rewrapping the mains cabling with insulating material. He wasn't worried about anyone electrocuting themselves; he just didn't want a bare wire shorting itself against a bulkhead, which would throw out the main fuse system. It subsequently took a team of twenty men the best part of two months to complete the task, concentrating on the vital systems first.

Three days after starting, Kishkov was ready to fire up the first of the four diesels. The batteries had been replaced with new ones, but there was not enough power to charge them fully, so they had to start the engine by hand. They opened the compression levers and five of the strongest men that Zof could find started to turn the big handle to crank the engine. With the compression levers open, the load was reduced and the huge engine turned easily. They cranked faster and faster while another man, standing on a ladder, waited for Kishkov's instruction to close the compression lever on the first of the sixteen cylinders.

Kishkov gave the signal; the lever was closed. Now, instead of the cylinder pumping the fuel out through the open exhaust valve, the fuel was compressed to firing point and the cylinder coughed into life. It popped irregularly. The man on the ladder closed the other compression levers now, cylinder by cylinder, and each one sprang to life. Now the engine had gathered its own momentum and the five men stood back, sweating and breathing heavily.

Soon all sixteen cylinders were firing. The massive diesel had lumbered into life, and Kishkov eased open the throttle himself. Soon the engine was whining rather than stuttering, and the big alternator was spinning faster and faster.

Kishkov waited until the whole plant was running smoothly, and then closed the big mains switch. The dim, flickering light from the generator tender was suddenly overwhelmed by a brilliant white light that burst from the new bulbs in the generator space. A cheer went up. They had power. Now they could get to work.

*

Zhadanov had organised a long snake of piping from the main fuel dump out to the ship. Filled with diesel, the pipeline floated comfortably on the water, quivering as the electric pumps hauled the fuel nearly a quarter of a mile across the harbour. They would run for nearly two days until the tanks had as much fuel as Zof reckoned they would need for the one-way trip, plus a bit extra for safety.

In the vast engine room, Kishkov already had the main turbine covers off. Every blade was being examined carefully. One weak blade, snapping under the immense pressures inside the turbine assembly, would be enough to smash the whole thing apart. Kishkov didn't want to take the risk. All but a handful were pronounced fine, and he had found supplies of high-grade stainless steel which he transported to the ship's well-equipped machine shop where new ones were cut. He could remember the exact dimensions to the nearest thousandth of a millimetre, and he checked each one personally, rejecting nearly all of them the first time round as being out of tolerance.

The machinists, having spent hours on each blade, looked murderously at the old man; but they kept silent and remade them, and stood aside while he pounced on them every ten minutes with his old-fashioned micrometer, checking the tolerances time and time again. Eventually, even Kishkov was happy, and the turbines pronounced fit. The big covers were swung back into place, the bearings checked, the valves opened and closed to make sure they all worked.

Kishkov couldn't check the pipework for pressure until he could get some steam through them; his next task was to get the boilers working. Like the turbines he ordered every boiler stripped down as far as it could be done. He wanted to look at every copper tube in the boiler to ensure it could take the pressure expected of it.

Zof watched Kishkov with increasing irritation. Was the old man going too far? Although Kishkov had accepted Zof's orders that Zhadanov was in charge of the men, he ignored this in practice. Zof was called down to the boiler rooms one evening and found Kishkov screaming abuse at one of the mechanics, a lad of about twenty who was standing there in tears.

'You useless bastard,' screamed Kishkov. 'Never ever go near my boilers again. You're useless, useless! Get out of my sight.'

Zof walked up to Kishkov. 'What's the trouble, Comrade Chief Designer? I know this boy. He's a good worker.'

The mechanic looked gratefully at Zof. 'Sir, I just dropped a spanner, that's all. I've been working down here since six this morning. I was tired. Then this old idiot starts yelling and screaming at me. I've just about had enough of this. Tell him to stuff his fucking boiler.'

This was far from being the first time when Zof had needed to calm down an angry crewman. 'Off you go, son. Take a break. Come back the day after tomorrow.' The lad looked triumphantly at Kishkov and walked off.

Kishkov spat. 'Kids,' he said to no one in particular. 'Don't know one end of a hammer from the other. Not like my day, Comrade Captain.'

Zof put a big hand on Kishkov's shoulder. It wasn't exactly a friendly gesture. 'Comrade Chief Designer, listen for a moment, will you?'

Kishkov waited.

'The problem, Comrade Chief Designer, is that you are a cantankerous old bastard who is driving people harder than you need to. You carry on like this and every man on this ship will quit. I, for one, will not let that happen,' said Zof, matter-of-factly. 'In fact, Comrade Chief Designer, the next time I hear you shouting at a member of my crew, I think I'll come over and snap your little neck.'

Kishkov went silent. Zof towered over him and his grip on the old man's shoulder tightened.

'You may be brilliant but you're still a pain in the arse. Change the habits of a lifetime, comrade, you'll get things done even better. And next time you want to bawl out a member of the crew, you go through Zhadanov, understand?' Zof released his grip. Sometimes he felt sorry for Kishkov; he was awesomely clever, but he hadn't got the first idea of how to treat people. He loved cold machines better.

Kishkov scowled for a moment, then spoke. 'Comrade Captain, I'm sorry. The pressure is perhaps too much for us all. This is my ship, after all. She is a part of me. I find it difficult to see other people messing her around.'

'I understand, comrade. But soon the ship will be ready; then she is mine, not yours. Understand that, comrade, understand that very clearly.'

Kishkov sullenly nodded and Zof left him to it, turning and walking out of the boiler room. The old man watched him depart, and scowled again. Once he'd disappeared up the stairway and was safely out of sight, Kishkov spat again on the filthy metal floor. It's always my ship, Comrade Captain in your fine uniform, he said to himself. I didn't spend all those years in a labour camp to have it taken away again. My ship, Zof, never yours. He turned back to the vast boilers and carried on the task of inspecting and cleaning every inch of the miles of copper tubing that would turn raw water into superheated steam in the roaring furnaces of blazing oil.

*

It was like an animal coming to life, a dumb beast made of steel and rivets with intestines of piping and nerves of thick insulated cable. The damp steel bulkheads began to warm up like skin. Pipes that had lain empty and unconnected for years suddenly tautened as fluids started to course through them.

As the lights came on, the innards of the ship were dull at first, uninhabited, dusty and lifeless. But the grime was slowly cleared away, and once more Zof was astonished how well preserved everything was. Stainless steel was rarely used in the days when the *Stalin* was built: everything that needed to be corrosion-proof was made in yellow brass or grey gun-metal.

Now they gleamed and glimmered. Long passageways looked like vaults of gold as the bright brass and shining copper were revealed. It was no longer a museum piece.

The ship started to take on a human dimension. Zof had Blokhin's massive but ancient galley high on the list of the jobs to do. Within two days the place was spotless and the fires lit, and Blokhin had his teams of cooks working flat out to provide an endless stream of good food for anyone who wanted it. Zof inspected the galley and the mess every day; he kept the officers' mess closed and insisted on everyone eating in the big ratings' mess – even Kelley, who hated it.

The storerooms were filling, too. With Kelley's $100 bills, finding provisions was far from difficult. The head chef at the Imperial had been particularly helpful. In exchange for a thick envelope he had arranged for cases of Japanese tinned goods to make their way to the ship. There were things that most of Zof's men had never seen before; tinned fruit was particularly popular. Frozen meat was more of a problem; the *Stalin* had no freezer equipment that worked. But one of Blokhin's streetwise cooks solved the problem when a truck turned up one dark evening with twelve supermarket freezer cabinets that were quickly installed in one of the storerooms, and were speedily filled with meat of a quality that even Zof had never eaten before. Sacks of flour were loaded; but not the coarse stuff that most of them were used to. With the money available they could afford pure white refined flour; but no one liked the bread it made so Blokhin had to swap it for the more traditional stuff, to the bemusement of the Imperial's chef.

The sleeping accommodation was just as important. With 2,000 men on board, the ratings would have been confined to cramped living quarters where they had to sling hammocks every night; that was how it was when the *Stalin* was running as a training ship. It was desperately uncomfortable but was considered good for the soul. Zof would have none of· that. With just 400 men to accommodate he could do a lot better. There were 120 cabins of various sizes for various ranks of officers. Harvey, Kelley and Pine had already picked off the best and the biggest. Zof gave himself one of the smaller ones and made sure the most experienced men had the rest. He then turned over the officers' mess and various disused storerooms, and the old lecture theatre, to sleeping accommodation for the rest of the crew. He had them scrubbed spotless and then brought in several hundred iron bedsteads from the empty naval hospital. They might not have much privacy, said Zof, but at least they'd have decent beds to sleep in.

They'd even dug up a modern cinema projector and installed it in the now-empty crew quarters, together with a supply of films. By the time Zof had finished, he was determined to turn the *Stalin* into the kind of ship that would make its men proud to be on board.

Zof had brought it off brilliantly. His men had come running. Maybe it was the food; it was certainly the money. But everyone noticed the way the ship hummed with energy and life from the crew when Zof was around – which was most of the time, as the man seemed to be everywhere. From early morning until very late at night, Zof was watching, talking, encouraging and as often as not taking off his jacket and pitching in with various tasks. He started up a night shift and even showed up in the middle of that, although he'd been around all day as well. He had promised Kelley his ship would be ready. And even if he had to do it himself, it would be.

7

Within three weeks they not only had the electrical systems up and running, but now they were ready to raise steam as well. The main problem worrying Zof and Zhadanov was not if the boilers and turbines would work, but what onlookers would think when they saw smoke coming from the smoke-stack. They decided to run the test at night, when the dense, thick oily smoke would simply add yet another industrial stink to the port's usual collections of odours. The gloom of the overcast sky added to the sense of drama as Zof, Kelley, Harvey and Pine descended in a line from the upper deck down winding passageways into the bowls of the ship, and gathered in the engine room's control area. Kishkov was already there, excited and flushed like a small child on Christmas Day. Zhadanov sat quietly in the corner.

The control area was a mass of pipes, tubes, levers, valve wheels and immense brass dials. For each boiler, situated on the level below them, there was a pressure gauge, a temperature gauge and a water-level gauge. The three rows of dials covered a whole bulkhead; each dial was a foot across, and red pointers like weathervanes indicated the reading.

On an adjacent bulkhead were the turbine gauges, slighter smaller than the others, showing pressure, temperature, RPM and bearing temperature. And in between them all were dozens of other indicators showing the chief engineer the state of all the other systems that were vital to the ship. Most of the dials were direct – in other words, they were connected by tubing to read pressures and levels, rather than being connected by wires to sensors. The result was a spaghetti of brass and copper tubing snaking around the compartment with an awesome complexity. Harvey, brought up on modern ships, had never seen anything like it. It didn't look as though it could possibly work.

But it did.

Kishkov already had two boilers lit, enough to provide sufficient steam to test out the system. They'd been running for nearly six hours. The big dials showed the temperatures of the water and the pressure – already the temperature had reached 110 degrees Centigrade: the pressurised system meant that the steam could be superheated so that it was far above the ordinary temperature of boiling water, which gave it more power. At 160 degrees the steam would be hot enough, and the dial was slowly creeping upwards as tons of fuel oil blazed in the boiler.

The control room was eerily quiet. The steam had not yet been released to the turbines and the only sound was a distant rumble from the two working boilers.

'How's it looking?' asked Kelley when they reached the control area. Zof in turn asked Kishkov.

'Good, good, so far, Comrade Captain. The boilers lit well, the water pressure is fine and the steam pressure is coming up as specified. We'll only really know when we open the valves and run a turbine up. That's the real test, of course.'

Zof translated for Kelley.

'So when do we start the turbines?' demanded Kelley, who wanted to know if this monster would ever run.

Kishkov looked at the dials and did a quick calculation. He reckoned it would take another eight minutes before the temperature and pressure reached the right level. Then the test could commence.

As usual, Kishkov's calculation proved exact. Precisely eight minutes later, the dials had reached 160 degrees. Kishkov beamed, and ordered the valves slowly opened.

The superheated steam was led towards the turbine in stages. Four valves had to be opened, one after the other, to build up the pressure in the steam line between the boiler and the turbine. As each section of two-foot-diameter piping filled with the steam under a pressure of 3.2 bar, the pipework creaked and groaned under the stress. One weak point, one seam that had rusted through after fifty years of idleness in the sea air, and the whole line would explode violently under the pressure, spraying steam that was hot enough to kill and then cook anyone near it. Kishkov knew perfectly well what the danger was; but if he was worried, he was giving nothing away.

Three valves were open now, and the final valve was ready to release the scalding, pressurised steam into the last run of piping, the section that ran into the engine room itself where the turbines lay silent and still, waiting for the sudden blast of steam to start them spinning. Kishkov gave the order. A mechanic slowly opened the valve and the 40-foot length of pipework began to creak and grind, now just a few yards from the control area where Zof was smoking anxiously and the rest of the party waited and watched.

Then there was an ear-splitting shriek. It was

followed by the sound of metal plating ripping apart, like a sheet of thick metallic paper being slowly torn up.

'Close the valve,' yelled Kishkov, hobbling out of the control area. The others had instinctively ducked at the sound. The mechanic hastily screwed the valve down into its seat again. Kishkov was already peering along the length of the pipe. He stopped for a moment at one section and then yelled for the valve to be opened once more; then he returned to the control area.

'Don't worry,' he said, grinning at Kelley and Harvey who were still looking nervous. 'It was just a support bracket. The pipe expanded and tore an old bracket off the bulkhead. I'll have it patched up later. The pipe is fine,' and he carried on watching the steam pressure build. Kelley looked less than impressed.

Once the pressure had reached the right level at the turbine inlet valve, the time had come to see what the fifty-year-old turbines could stand. Kishkov had warned them about the noise, but when the inlet valve was opened the sound was like a whisper.

The released steam blasted against the steel blades of the turbine rotor. Although the whole rotor assembly weighed 12 tons, it was supported on precision bearings and would turn in a breath of wind. The giant rotor began to move, lazily at first, as the fierce steam squeezed between the tightly packed blades. The inlet valve was opened a little more; the pressure increased and the rotor began to spin, faster now, building up speed with every revolution. The inlet valve was opened further – now the huge blades were whipping round in the screaming torrent of steam. The noise in the control room began to make conversation more and more difficult. Kishkov watched the big RPM counter: he was aiming to get the 10,000 which was the maximum the big turbine had been designed for. He reasoned that if it could sustain the maximum pressures and speeds while idle, it could easily take the lower speeds demanded to actually drive the ship. The needle was nudging the big numeral '7' on the dial as he ordered more steam fed into the turbine.

The spinning rotor began to shriek. The outer tips of the blades were reaching the speed of sound, and each one was creating a miniature sonic boom which added together made up the characteristic shrieking whine of a big turbine being driven near the maximum. The rotor was connected, via a massive steel shaft, to the reduction gearbox that turned the high RPM into lower, usable revolutions to drive the propellers. The gearbox was permanently engaged to the shaft, so as to make the running of the huge system easier. It was normally impossible to run the turbine in 'neutral'. The astern turbine, next to the turbine that Kishkov was testing, was also engaged to the shaft: when one turbine was running, the other was forced to run too. Kishkov had to get the whole system unbolted to allow the test to take place. Even with the disconnected shaft idle, the gears inside were still turning, and the rumble of the gearbox added to the racket that was now shaking the whole area.

'The fucking thing's going to blow, for Christ's sake,' yelled Kelley almost directly into Harvey's ear to make himself heard. But Kishkov looked happy enough. The needle was now just touching '10' and the noise was stunning. But the turbines and pipework were all holding together. Nothing was leaking. Nothing was coming apart, other than two more supporting brackets, but the sound of their failure was drowned.

Kishkov let the turbine wail and scream for another two minutes before slowly reducing the pressure. Soon the noise began to drop back to a level that allowed them to talk.

'Well, Comrade Chief Designer?' asked Zof. He had to admit to himself that even though the old man was making a meal of it, the whole thing was impressive. He'd been in engine rooms before, of course, but they were clinical places. Modern diesels and gas turbine installations had little character; he'd served on a nuclear-powered ship for three months and the whole engine room ran with two people. This – this was very different. It seemed almost to have a soul. The machinery was a work of art; things moved, hissed, spun, shook and quivered, and you could almost watch it for the pure enjoyment of seeing machinery in action. In the old days, things were not hidden. The innards were exposed, almost as though the designer was proud of his creation. Frankly, thought Zof, the ship was less of a problem than this madman who was supposed to make it all work. Exactly how reliable was he? How could he cope with the curious voyage they were about to undertake? Zof looked at the hunched old man before him and asked the question again. 'Well?'

Kishkov looked up at Zof. He remembered the rebuke from the other night. 'My ship is fine, Comrade Captain. The boilers, the turbines, all are well. I'll check the others out later. Don't worry. My ship will perform to expectations.' He wiped his wrinkled hands on a rag, threw it casually over a thick pipe and walked slowly out of the control room to inspect the boilers, leaving the rest of them in the room.

The turbine had reduced to idle speed and the sound was now a gentle whistle. Soon even that died away to silence. The distant throb of the diesels powering the generators could be felt, rather than heard.

Zof looked silently at the others. They seemed

satisfied. So, the *Stalin* would sail after all. Then, of course, it started to hit home: yes, the ship really would sail. They would steal it. They would cruise the high seas. They would stop peacefully cruising ships, terrify and rob them, and retire wealthy beyond their dreams. As the reality struck home, Zof looked at the determined face of Kelley, the worried face of Harvey and the inevitably smiling but blank face of the fat Pine. The adrenalin began to flow. This isn't some crazy story, he thought. This is going to happen. This is real. Zof would have been less than human if he hadn't started to have second thoughts about the enterprise at this stage. However much Kelley and the others seemed blissfully confident of the whole business, his own sense of reality kept knocking him back. Yakov, you have got to be stark, staring out of your mind: stop this madness now. Tell them they're crazy. Throw them all out. Call the police. Get off the ship and go back to the Navy.

And then another and greater reality hit him. Call the police? There weren't any to call, unless you bribed them. Go back to the Navy? What Navy? Go and sit in his shabby office, wait for papers that never arrive, call Moscow on the phone except the phone doesn't actually work any more? Inspect his crew? He'd never find them again; they would starve. Yes, he was crazy to go on this trip. He knew he was crazy; but he would be even crazier to go back to nothing, to sitting alone waiting for a call that would never, ever come. Yakov, my friend, you have two options. Starve, or go down fighting. And when you put it that way, there was of course no contest.

Kelley, Harvey and Pine started to leave the engine room. Zof said nothing, but followed them silently. It was the moment, for Yakov Zof, of no return. He had started over the precipice, seen the depths before him and coldly and – at least to him – quite logically, decided to jump.

*

The arsenal occupied several hectares of the military port. It was contained inside a razor-wire-topped fence and an inner 12 foot breeze-block wall. Inside the enclosure, forty squat windowless buildings, all absolutely identical, were laid out in straight rows and lines like a chess board. Each building had a flat roof, from which sprouted small chimneys and ventilation shafts. The low level of the buildings was deceptive; they were actually five stories high, except that four of the stories went downwards, deep into the ground. They were supposed to be proof against internal explosions, each building acting as a containment room in case an accident set off the contents.

The theory had been put to the test eight years ago in Northern Siberia, when a similar arsenal suffered a small fire in one of the buildings which set off the contents in a massive fireball. Had the concrete been up to the original specification, it might have worked. As it was, the concrete was mostly sand and the reinforcement was rusted through, due to the inferior steel that had been used. The whole arsenal disappeared in a colossal flash; the Kremlin only found out about it when an agitated US military attaché in Moscow drove round at high speed twenty minutes later and demanded to know why the Russians had recommenced nuclear testing.

Maybe this was why the arsenal at Vladivostok was still guarded. Zof had already squared the five youths who notionally belonged to the KGB but, like everyone else, had been forgotten at pay time. He'd made sure they received a good share of the $100 bills that Kelley kept doling out in handfuls. Now it was time to earn their pay.

As he approached them, the two guards on duty looked up from their chessboard and sprang to their feet. Neither of them was properly dressed, but Zof decided to ignore the breach. There was little point in telling them to wear uniform when the ones they had were threadbare and unlikely to be replaced.

'Good morning, Captain,' they said almost in unison. They didn't know if they should salute, but decided to just the same.

'Good morning,' replied Zof. They'd been happy enough to take the cash to keep quiet about the preparations on the ship. Now he had to convince them to go a little further. He wondered what their training would do. 'I need to get inside building six,' he said, as casually as he could manage.

Building six was where, according to the old records he'd managed to dig out, the big 22-inch shells were stored; hopefully these were in good condition.

'Yes, Captain. I'll take you there,' said one of the youths, a short, stout twenty-year-old with glasses, without a moment's hesitation.

The training had crumbled. They'd been taught to defend the arsenal against all comers, at any cost, from anyone, even Navy Captains. Zof couldn't help but feel angry, but he swallowed it.

As he followed the stout guard through the gate into the compound where the squat concrete bunkers lay silent in the morning sun, Zof could see that the concrete was coming away from the corners of the buildings in big chunks, exposing the rusting reinforcing rods inside. On some of the buildings, wide cracks had split through the outer walls. It made him uncomfortable as he walked down the wide alleyways alongside each bunker; he knew what was inside them.

Building six was at the farthest corner of the

compound. The youth led Zof around the back of the blockhouse, where there was a set of tall steel doors, once covered in black pitch as a protection against the salt air but now rusty and streaked. The doors didn't look as though they'd been opened in years. The guard produced a small winch handle with special notches cut in it, which he pushed into a two-inch hole in the door. It engaged, he started to turn, there was a squealing as the mechanism was forced into action. The youth kept winding on the handle. Slowly, the door began to travel sideways along a set of rusty rails set into the floor at the base of the door opening, until it had almost disappeared into the cracking concrete wall.

There was a flight of steps leading down into the damp-smelling gloom. Zof was instantly worried. If the inside of the bunker was damp, it certainly wouldn't have helped preserve the explosive in the shells in good condition.

The youth tried a steel-cased light switch but nothing happened. For one appalling moment Zof thought he might flick a lighter to show the way, but instead, to Zof's relief, he produced a small torch. They moved carefully down the steps still lit by the shady daylight until, at the sixth step, it was too gloomy to see any further. Already he could feel the dampness of the place. The young guard flicked on the feeble beam of the torch, then they went carefully down another two, three, four steps. There was now water underfoot; Zof could hear the gentle slap as his shoe touched the dripping step. After twelve steps they reached the bottom; now water slopped an inch deep across the floor. There was another steel door; it was conventionally hinged, and Zof and the guard pulled it open. Another flight of steps appeared.

According to the old record book, the shells were

stored on levels one, two and three. There were supposed to be 200 shells on each level: the bottom listed as high explosive, the next level armour-piercing, and the third, uppermost level a 'shotgun' projectile that would fragment at a pre-set height and burst into a shower of incendiary splinters, designed to bring down aircraft.

Zof had talked over the armaments with Harvey and Kelley. All they needed was something to make some big bangs, and 'frighten the shit out of anyone who wanted to fight us', in Kelley's words. There didn't seem much point in taking the incendiary shells. The armour-piercing shells seemed redundant as well, but Zof wasn't the sort of Captain to go to sea without having cover for every eventuality. You never could tell what might be needed, he told himself. The old ship would take 900 shells in total; he decided to load 200 armour-piercing and 200 high-explosive shells. That should be enough for anything.

They were now on the bottom level where the HE projectiles were stored. Zof opened another steel door at the bottom of the staircase, and they were paddling in a foot of stinking black water. The guard shone the torch into the gloom. There, looking like huge bottles in a wine cellar, lay rack after rack of dull grey shells, massive lumps of machined steel weighing nearly four tons each, the biggest shells ever manufactured. Zof splashed along the racks; each one was full. The shells hadn't been touched since ... when, the early fifties? They looked in good condition, all the same. The grey steel had a sheen. He ran a finger over a shell, and felt a slimy layer of oil that had been sprayed on them fifty years ago to protect them. His finger left a shiny streak that gleamed in the dim light of the torch.

But what was the explosive inside them like? Had fifty years of dampness ruined the charge of trinitroanisole? Short of letting off a shell, which Zof was not planning to do, there was no way of finding out until they got to sea. He prayed the stuff remained stable, too. Old explosives were notorious for being delicate. The newer electrically-detonated material like baratol could be thrown on a fire and still wouldn't go off. He'd have to trust to some god or other. Maybe Kishkov's God would watch over them, he thought wryly. So far the old man's luck had held remarkably well.

Zof carried on down the aisles of racks to the centre of the bunker where he came to the ammunition lift. But the rusted cage was sitting at an angle in the shaft, and coiled on top of it lay the rusted remains of several steel cables, long ago severed. It looked as though it had fallen. Zof had seen enough. The main problem would be lifting the shells out – that, and hoping the TNA inside them was stable enough not to blow them and half of Vladivostok to pieces as they did.

*

It took a day to rig up lifting gear. Zof's small team of engineers found chains and a couple of cranes. They used the big crane to lift a smaller one to the roof, then positioned the crane over the shaft and ran the heavy chains down the five stories until they reached bottom.

Each level had a hand-operated pulley-and-chain system which, after a liberal coating of oil, was back in working order. And each level had several shell dollies, big carts designed to haul the shells to the lift.

Zof had gathered together a small group of men for the task. He had chosen each one carefully. They were all men without families. He explained the dangers of the job to each man and told him why he was chosen.

They could refuse if they wanted to; not a single man did. He warned Kelley and Harvey to stay away, too. For himself, he kept a close eye on the whole operation, staying with the team as they slowly manhandled each shell down on the dolly, pulled them to the lift shaft, and hauled them one at a time up the shaft to the roof, where the bigger crane swung them down on to a relay of flatbed trucks where they were driven, very carefully, to the quay. A diesel-powered landing craft had been pressed into service. Loaded with sixteen shells at a time, stacked on end like bottles in a crate, the tender laboured through the harbour towards the *Stalin*, the oily water two inches below its gunwales.

Zof only allowed the tender to run at the end of each day and night, when the crew shift changed. He wanted as many men as possible out of the area when the shells were being moved. One evening, the tender had tied up alongside the ship and the ship's crane had hauled several shells on board. The fifth shell was coming over the guard-rail heading for the after turret when there was the sickening sound of a length of chain running loose. Zof was standing next to the crane, keeping an eye on the operation. He failed to notice that the chain holding the shell through its lifting hook had not been properly secured. He'd already yelled at a young seaman earlier for not doing it correctly: it required a knack to get the hook to latch securely.

The shell was seven or eight feet above the deck when the chain slipped and the shell fell like a rock, base first, to the teak-laid deck. Zof instinctively ducked, waiting for the blast. The shell splintered into the teak deck, smashing the crumbling wood into dust beneath it. There was a hollow clang as the armour plate beneath the deck rang like a bell under the impact. The shell slowly toppled over, rolled gently down the deck, crushed a six-foot length of stanchion and guard-rail like cooked spaghetti, and dropped into the sea below them. Zof waited for the blast. None came. After a minute, a large foul-smelling bubble erupted to the surface with a belch as the shell burrowed into the thick sludge of the harbour floor. And there it rested.

Zof breathed again. The TNA was stable enough to take a knock like that. In which case, he thought, at least the ship wouldn't disappear in a ball of flame the first time they hit some rough weather.

After that, everyone was more careful and the loading proceeded smoothly. The shells were swung from the tender down the loading hatch into the magazines beneath each turret. Kishkov had all the shipboard systems working well, and the shells slid smoothly down the lifts into the circular rack deep inside the vessel, where they were protected by the thickest layer of armour plate in the ship, not just around the sides but across the bottom as well, in case a mine or torpedo went off near them. Kishkov had studied the pictures of the *Hood* exploding. It was clear that a shell from the *Bismarck* had penetrated the main magazine; he made sure the same could never happen to his ship.

The cordite charges were kept in a separate magazine for the same reason. The shells for the *Stalin* were just the projectiles; bags of cordite had to be rammed in after the shell to act as the propellant. These were far more easily obtained than the original shells, though Zof had to get most of the crew's wives and girlfriends sewing up 22-inch silk bags to hold the cordite: they never found out what these were for.

After the magazines were loaded, each of three turrets had to be filled with shells. In racks around the barbette, several decks below the turret itself, a holding stock of thirty shells was kept to make sure the guns could maintain the maximum rate of fire without waiting for shells to come up from the magazine. In action, the gun-crews drew from the holding stock, while the magazine-crews replenished the stock as it was depleted. One by one, the dull steel shells were neatly slotted into the custom-made racks that kept them secure.

Zof had managed to move his planned 400 shells from the bunker into the ship's magazines. Limited to just the late evening and early morning, it had taken nearly two weeks to complete the loading.

And then, in the eighth week, just as everything was running smoothly as far as Zof was concerned, the crisis hit.

With just four days to go, Kishkov, deep below in the bowels of the ship, was completing his last inspection tour. What he saw didn't exactly please him, but at least it all looked as though it would work. Just . . .

Handfuls of new white and grey electrical cable hung in tresses from passageway deckheads, often held in place by lengths of rope tied to old pipework. New pipework had been needed for the fuel system. The old pipes, once Kishkov had got to them, hidden beneath floors and bulkheads, were solid with caked oil that had turned almost to coal over fifty years. It wasn't worth replacing so Zof's engineers, to Kishkov's fury, simply ran new steel piping straight from the tanks to the boiler feed systems. Almost every plumber in Vladivostok had been taken out of action for two weeks; there were now a lot of well-off plumbers in the city. The job was botched, according to Kishkov's standards, but it undeniably worked.

His last call was in the turbine room, where the massive shafts were connected to the turbines by huge gearboxes. They had needed a lot of work, and

Zhadanov had kept him away from the crew; one of them was the young mechanic that Kishkov had yelled at weeks earlier.

Kishkov looked carefully at the massive main gearwheel. He shook his head sadly and turned to walk back up to the deck. The faintest flicker of a smile might have been noticed had the light not been so gloomy.

He met Zof and the others on the foredeck, beneath the massive forward guns that stretched out over their heads like great felled oaks. Kelley was anxious; his time frame was running out. If he couldn't move in four days' time his whole schedule was ruined. 'Well?' he demanded, when all of them were together.

Zof looked at Kishkov. The old man spat on the teak deck, still splintered and filthy. 'The main reduction gear. Hopeless. It will fail. They've welded the gear to the shaft. It's a bad weld; it will come apart the moment you put load on it. They didn't consult me, you see.'

'Is this true, Zof?' asked Kelley.

'I have no idea, my friend. If it is, it will be done properly and your ship will sail on time. Leave it to me,' and he stormed off looking for Zhadanov.

The two of them ordered the covers of the big gearbox removed. It was one of four. Kishkov was right. The huge gearwheel, six feet in diameter, had been taken out for repairs and had to be cut away from the shaft; originally it had been a single casting, to take the massive load of the huge propeller thrashing in the sea. To replace it, they had to weld it back to the shaft, and the welding looked rough.

'What do you think, Yuri?' asked Zof.

'Sorry, Yakov, I should have checked. It's pretty hopeless. It will have to come out and get re-done. It's a huge job. Got to take a week.'

'Not four days?'

'Not a hope.'

Zof thought for a moment. 'Yuri, get your best welders and best mechanics down here in one hour. Can you do that?'

'Sure,' said Zhadanov.

An hour later fourteen men in filthy overalls, all of whom looked exhausted, were standing next to the gearbox, with Zof standing in front of them.

'Zhadanov here tells me that this gear has to come off and get re-welded. He tells me it will take a week. I know Yuri well. He's always pessimistic, he's too nice. The fact is, you have forty-eight hours to finish the job, and to do it brilliantly. I want you to remember a few things. First of all, the money. If we don't do the job in forty-eight hours, the whole project is wrecked. Second, I want you to remember that you're Russian sailors. You are the best in the world. Nobody can do what you can do. And last, I want you to remember me: Yakov Zof. If you're not doing this for the money and you're not doing it for Russia, then I hope you're doing it for me. That's it, men. Forty-eight hours for a job that should take twice as long. And done to the highest standards. I know you can do it. Does anybody disagree?'

Zhadanov suppressed a smile. Nobody said a word. 'Get on with it, then, get on with it!' he yelled, and the group groaned, smiled and got stuck in.

'Yakov, I don't know how you get away with it,' muttered Zhadanov. Zof just smiled and left them to it.

*

'Well, Comrade Chief Designer?' asked Zof as Kishkov emerged from the engine room two days later.

The old man scowled. 'The job is done, Comrade Captain, the job is done. That much, at least,' he replied grudgingly.

'Which means what?' asked Kelley, exasperated at the delay and at his lack of understanding. In two days' time the ship had to sail, and these fucking Russians were still arguing.

'Is this ship ready to sail or not?' demanded Harvey.

'Perhaps. It's hard to tell,' Kishkov sulked.

Zof put his arm around the old man. It was not a friendly gesture. 'Comrade Chief Designer, you are being modest. You can tell immedi–ately if the ship is ready to go. You have looked carefully at the work, and I believe you are very happy with it now. Isn't that the case?'

Kishkov tried to smile but he couldn't manage it. 'Comrade Captain, I have looked at the work, yes. It is a miracle that your men completed it so quickly.'

'And the quality of the work, Comrade Chief Designer? The quality?'

'Yes. It is good. I would have to say it is fine,' said Kishkov, every word crawling painfully from his lips as Zof's powerful arm squeezed his narrow shoulders.

'Fine, Comrade Chief Designer?'

'Yes, Comrade Captain. Fine. Good. Excellent, in fact.'

'And you're now happy with the ship?'

'Yes, Comrade Captain. Happy. Very happy.'

'There,' said Zof, releasing the old man. 'You have a happy Chief Designer. Very happy.' He lit a cigarette. 'Your ship is ready. She is armed, fuelled and crewed. We can raise steam and catch the high tide the day after tomorrow. It's at four-thirty on that morning, just as it's getting light, so our departure will be happily discreet. Do we go or not?'

Kelley looked at Harvey. Harvey nodded. Pine, as usual, took no part other than smiling in the background. Kelley was delighted. The schedule was perfect. He looked up and down the length of the ship. Cables and hoses still snaked across the deck in tangles. Groups of men were still busily tightening, hammering, cutting. A thin skein of black smoke drifted lazily up from the huge funnel, twisting into loops as a high breeze caught it.

'We go, of course,' said Kelley finally.

Zof, like the ship, had come back to life in the two months since they started. Today he wore a new uniform, the one he had ordered the day after he met Kelley and Harvey at the Imperial. There was a look in his eye that had not been there since he watched the Berlin Wall being vandalised in full view of the police. Zof was a Captain again, and he had a ship to command. He turned abruptly on his heel and walked back down the ship to where several flights of ladders would take him up to the bridge. Zhadanov was waiting; as Zof approached, the engineer grasped the gleaming brass ship's bell and gave it three smart rings – the signal universally recognised throughout the Navy as indicating that the Commander of the ship has come aboard. Zof grinned at Zhadanov. Behind him were the other bay-chay commanders, all saluting.

The *Stalin* had a Captain and was ready for sea.

8

A little under three weeks earlier, exactly on the schedule that Tariq had worked out, two other ships had gone through their preparations for departure.

At Brest, the vast natural harbour on the north-west coast of France, a 5,000-ton freighter looking not very different from every other tramp on the seas except for being unusually clean, with a dark yellow hull and sleek black funnel, was finishing its loading in a quiet corner of the commercial docks. The *Madelaine* was almost brand new, out of the yards in Korea just a year ago, and – also unusually for a run-of-the-mill freighter – was equipped with some of the latest electronics and navigation gear. She was an expensive and well-looked-after ship and, surrounded by battered and rust-streaked tramps that hadn't seen a coat of paint on their topsides since they were launched, she looked like a fashion model standing nervously in the middle of a crowd of down-and-outs.

It was early evening and harsh yellow lamps were lighting up the ship and the quayside as she finished loading her cargo of glassware, bound for Japan where French crystal was extraordinarily expensive. She was due out of harbour the next morning, and the last container of glassware was being craned carefully into the hold.

As the slightly battered container disappeared

inside the freighter, an unmarked Renault light truck drove slowly down the quay, went carefully round the big crane and stopped at the end of the ship near the crew gangway. Six large men emerged from the back, each carrying a small wooden box. They hurried up the gangplank while another five men stood around at the foot, smoking and talking in the still evening air. The six men shortly returned empty-handed, and went to the back of the truck again to collect another small wooden box each. Twenty boxes were carried on to the ship like this. After the last box had gone aboard, one of the men handed a sheet to the Captain, Legret, who waited at the bottom of the gangplank. Legret signed it and handed it back.

'Bon voyage, Captain,' said one of them, and walked back down to the truck, where one of his colleagues was on the mobile telephone to the office, telling them to report to Lloyd's that the cargo of eighty gold bars was safely delivered and was now the responsibility of Captain Legret of the *Madelaine*. Their duties over, they all got quietly back into the van and drove away into the deepening night to their families and dinner.

At the same time, a little further north at Southampton, the *Ocean Queen* was, like the *Madelaine*, completing preparations prior to sailing. The *Ocean Queen* was like an hotel on water; the ship was over 1,000 feet long, and towering above the sleek blue hull rose half a dozen glassed-in decks. Launched just a year past, she was owned by an American hotel chain, crewed by Philippinos, run by British officers because passengers preferred them, and went to sea under the flag of Liberia, a small African country that made a significant part of her national income from arranging ships' registration papers with the minimum of fuss and no questions at all.

The *Ocean Queen*'s cargo was just as delicate as the

French ship's: not glassware but several hundred wealthy passengers of assorted nationalities who had booked on one of the *Ocean Queen's* vastly expensive round-the-world cruises. Unlike the *Madelaine*, which had loaded unnoticed in silence, the *Ocean Queen* was a blaze of light and noise as passengers boarded, supplies were brought on, streamers were streamed and all the celebrations beloved of rich widows and widowers were ritually carried out in the damp night air of Southampton's Ocean Dock. Amongst the noise and bustle, nobody noticed a dark blue Ford truck with no name draw up next to the crew gangplank, and a small group of casually dressed men unload boxes identical to those which, moments before, had also disappeared inside the *Madelaine*.

This time there were thirty-two small wooden boxes, each one carried carefully on board by hand, watched over by a small knot of nervous men. The same signing ceremony was gone through, this time with the ship's purser, Reginald Goodall. Added to the boxes, now locked away in the strongroom below the cargo deck, was also a worn brown leather briefcase.

Like their colleagues in France that night, the bearers and guards of the boxes and the briefcase returned to their small truck and immediately called in to the office, who were waiting for the call. They reported that 128 gold bars and uncut diamonds worth $10 million were safely aboard the *Ocean Queen* and no longer their responsibility. They then drove off down to the pub.

Once the messages had been carefully noted in triplicate, each security firm's office then sent coded telexes to Lloyd's of London, for the attention of Barber Ross Underwriters who took the main risk for covering the shipments while in transit. It was vital for them to record the exact time when the responsibility for the bullion and diamonds passed from the security company to the ship's Captain. The point at which one underwriter's risk ended and another's commenced made the precise time worth millions of pounds.

'Iron Ore loaded *Madelaine* 21.38 tonight. Waybill 770/981. Signed off Captain Legret. Amtrak, Brest', read the first telex to arrive.

'Cutlery Waybill BS140667 loaded *Ocean Queen*. Signed for 20.46. Regards Brinks Soton', read the next telex. Both chattered out on a telex sitting in a darkened room, and the printed roll of paper gathered in folds behind the machine.

The next morning at Lloyd's, scanning through the night's telexes, Snell the office junior tore off the two messages and handed them to Stanley Price. 'You'll want these then, Pricey,' he called cheerily and wandered off down the corridor whistling.

Price read the telexes carefully and looked at the calendar on his wall. It was from the Ben Line shipping company and showed an attractive photograph of one of their freighters ploughing through an improbably blue sea. The *Madelaine* would be in the South China Sea in 26 days' time. The *Ocean Queen* was scheduled to call at Bombay, Singapore, Hong Kong and then Tokyo. Her gold and diamond cargo was to be unloaded in Hong Kong, and she would be docking there in 29 days' time. Ten million dollars' worth of diamonds and over $20 million of gold bullion between the two ships. He waited until lunchtime when the girls went off shopping and tapped out another telex on the machine.

'You have two substantial claims ready for processing. One 26 days' time, one 28 days' time. Claims will be in area discussed. Regards Price Lloyd's.' It was addressed 'Personal' for Mr Able, Imperial Hotel, Vladivostok, and turned up in the message box at the hotel an hour after Price hit the transmit key.

*

And half a world away, back in the Pacific but 6,000 miles further south than the *Stalin*, Captain James Crawford sat uneasily next to his executive officer, Lieutenant Commander Slatter, on the desk of the USS *Jackson* – anchored just outside Auckland harbour in New Zealand. The sun was beating down, the band was playing, and the locals had mounted some kind of war dance on the foredeck. Crawford sourly supposed it was some kind of entertainment. The *Jackson* was the newest ship in the US Navy, the pride of the Fleet, and here he was sitting through yet another goddamn goodwill visit. He'd trailed half-way round the Pacific and was getting heartily fed up with the whole thing. Crawford didn't regard himself as an outstanding diplomat; but as is the way with the military, that was the job that needed doing and Crawford, like it or not, had to get on with it. At least, he thought, this was almost the last such visit and he was looking forward to getting to Hong Kong and then back to Pearl, which would give him the chance for a few exercises to wake the crew up, and also to see the back of Slatter, who had already suggested a transfer which Crawford enthusiastically supported. Slatter was young, academically brilliant, black, pushy and clearly destined for the top; none of which greatly endeared him to Crawford, for whom the *Jackson* was probably his last sea command. And the fact that Crawford didn't like him made Slatter equally put out to be on board.

Crawford watched the Maori warriors finish their war dance. The ceremonies were over. He quickly shook hands with the assorted dignitaries, made sure the Ambassador was happy and had a drink in her hand, and then quietly disappeared to his cabin leaving Slatter to mop up. Tomorrow they would sail, and he couldn't wait to get back to normality.

*

Harvey returned to the hotel the morning before they sailed and as usual asked for the mail and messages. There were none for him but two for room 409, Kelley's room. He offered to drop them off, and the clerk happily handed both of them over. One was addressed to Able; it was probably from Price, assumed Harvey. He was the only other person who would call Kelley by his *nom de guerre*. But the other was much more puzzling: it was addressed to Kelley by his real name.

Now, thought Harvey as he closed his hotel-room door behind him, who would be dropping off messages addressed to Kelley by name? The envelope was not one that the hotel used for messages so it must have come from outside. It wasn't anyone on the ship, that was for sure; they would have spoken to Kelley directly.

This worried him. He took a shower to try to wash off the now permanent sickly-sweet smell of fuel oil, and to get the black grime out from under his nails. It still worried him as he towelled himself dry. He sat down on the bed and picked the envelope up again. It was not well sealed; the envelope was poor quality. It must be from that nutter Feliks, Zof's brother. What did he want? More money?

What the hell. He pulled gently on the flap, and with just a little encouragement it lifted cleanly from the gum. There was a single sheet of the same poor paper inside, which he lifted out carefully and unfolded.

'Kelley, urgent you contact me tonight. Same place. 11. T', was all it said. The message was printed in capitals, badly formed, written by someone who was unused to writing. Harvey was puzzled, worried and upset all at the same time. What on earth was Kelley up to? He refolded the note, slipped it back in the envelope, moistened an unused part of the gum with a licked finger, and then got dressed. He pushed both messages under Kelley's door and went downstairs.

*

Harvey went to bed early, at ten to eleven. Their habit had been to stay in the bar until midnight. He told Kelley he wanted an early start, and Kelley bid him good-night in a good mood. They would sail in the morning. Everything was coming right.

Harvey walked to the lifts and stabbed at the call button. He casually looked around – the lobby was empty. Instead of waiting for the lift, he moved quietly into the adjacent stairway, closing the door softly behind him. He walked down a flight to the basement, then found the exit door that led out to a service ramp at the back of the hotel. It was dark and, as usual, sultry and airless. He walked quickly around the corner to where he would have a view of the front courtyard, and was just in time to catch a glimpse of Kelley walking across it. He waited until the American had reached the other side of the road and then he sprinted after him, staying in the pools of blackness between the lights. Kelley was still in view; he turned a corner and walked down an unlit alleyway. Harvey followed, still keeping a distance.

Harvey lost sight of Kelley in the darkness. Then there was the blink of a pair of feeble headlamps at the end of the dark alleyway, a pause, then the uncertain clunk of a badly made door closing. An engine stuttered into life. Harvey backed away to the end of the alley to remain hidden as the car whined forward, accelerating noisily. He pressed himself back into a doorway. The car drove past, entering the dim pool of light cast by one of the few working street-lamps. He could see Kelley clearly in the passenger seat. But who was the dark, bearded driver who stared intently ahead as he drove past?

*

The *Stalin* slipped her mooring chains and manoeuvred slowly out of harbour. Zof had no choice but to move the great ship without tugs; she was moored out in the deeper part of the harbour with plenty of clear water around her and he had little problem in carefully backing her off the mooring buoy. He'd waited until the tide had started to slacken off nearing the top, and the currents in the harbour were hardly enough to shift a rowing boat let alone the massive bulk of the ship.

Even at that hour, the departure was noticed by a few early-morning people, the cleaners and the sweepers and the fishermen, who remarked on what a fine sight it was; and – in the same way that a burglar can walk into a house in broad daylight and walk out with TVs, stereos and even furniture without passers-by thinking anything was amiss – not a soul who admired *Stalin*'s departure had the slightest thought of reporting the fact to anyone. Kelley had walked out of houses and offices carrying all sorts of things before; he knew this was probably the safest part of the operation. He suggested that Zof have crew members standing around on the deck so that they could wave cheerily to anyone who spotted them.

What Zof couldn't see was the figure of his brother Feliks leaning on a railing on the quayside, watching the great ship silently starting to move. He couldn't see the boiling resentment on his face, as Feliks realised the whole scam really was taking place with his snotty brother Yakov in the driving seat, making all the money no doubt, while he was left behind with a few handfuls of $100 bills for all his trouble. Feliks was far from happy.

Having backed away from the buoy, Zof turned the big ship in more or less its own length, as Kishkov had promised him it would, by putting his port propellers slowly ahead and his starboard propellers slowly astern. Pushed on one side and pulled on the other, the 75,000 tons of ship revolved gently on its own central axis. Once it had nearly completed the turn, Zof ordered all engines dead slow ahead and brought his new command up to a gentle five knots. He watched the bow of the great ship move slowly starboard in response to gentle rudder to clear the breakwater at the harbour entrance.

The scale of the *Stalin* was so vast that instead of the ship moving, it felt as though the harbour wall and the city of Vladivostok behind it was moving instead. The illusion was surprisingly strong, even to Zof's eye. It was just as well that the huge naval harbour was now deserted, he thought. Moving a ship this size through anything other than an empty harbour would not have been easy.

'Give me another ten revolutions port outer,' Zof called into the cracked bakelite handset that connected him with the engine room. The engine telegraphs, though working, were just not quick enough for the tricky manoeuvring required without benefit of tugs.

Zof was slowly passing the breakwater and, once past, he needed to turn the ship again to aim her at the open sea.

There was a gentle change in the distant vibrations under their feet as the steam pressure to the turbine driving the outer port shaft was increased. The extra power applied to one side of the ship pushed the bow around a little faster. Zof was completing his turn. Once past the end of the harbour wall, he ordered both outer engines dead slow ahead and centred his rudder. It took a good minute before the ship responded and began to creep gently forward, now in a straight line, by which time the stern, several hundred feet behind them on the bridge, left the harbour wall clear.

Now Zof faced the clear Pacific, and he could hardly wait to get going. The *Stalin* throbbed gently underneath his feet. He had never sailed on a ship this big before, let alone commanded it. It was a magnificent sensation, almost sexual in its intensity. But, as ever, his face remained impassive and totally professional. He looked as though he was taking a row-boat out.

As the ship moved slowly forward, he carefully watched the changing depth on the depth sounder. Like most of the equipment on the compass bridge it was an antique, displaying the depth beneath the hull on a large rapidly-rotating dial that briefly flashed to indicate a certain depth. Although it was old, it served the job well enough. The indicated depth remained steady at 45 feet, uncomfortably close to the draught of the *Stalin* at 32 feet, but Zof was leaving as the tide was still just rising and it wouldn't get less. He allowed the giant vessel to amble slowly ahead, barely making a ripple in the water, until he cleared the harbour. The sounder began to show a steadily increasing depth. Once he had 100 feet beneath him, a couple of miles out, he finally ordered his two outer engines up to half speed.

Deep in the engine room big cast-brass valves were opened, and soon the ship began to vibrate noticeably as the boilers delivered superheated steam down the two-foot-wide tubes into the spinning blades of the turbines. As the valves were opened wider, the steam pressure slowly increased and the blades spun faster and faster, whining with the power. Even then the two huge turbines were only delivering a small part of their total power. Connected to the whirling steel spindles of the turbines, the immense gearboxes reduced the speed but not the power to the gleaming steel shafts, horizontal pillars a yard across, which connected to the massive manganese bronze propellers that thrashed the Pacific Ocean to a foam and steadily pushed the 75,000 tons of the *Stalin* faster and faster through the water. A crisp bow wave began to form and then break over the bulge of the bow – Kishkov had copied the idea directly from *Yamoto*, the first ship in the world to have the bulge that reduced hull resistance. Underneath the hull, years of seaweed, slime and molluscs began to be torn away by the increasing flow of the water.

Slowly the huge ship powered its way through the calm sea, building up speed to reach ten knots, where it stayed. Zof called the engine room again. Kishkov was sitting there, watching over Zhadanov and irritating the hell out of him. 'How's it all looking?' asked Zof.

'No problem, Captain,' replied Zhadanov, now reverting to the formal title that he always used when at sea with Yakov. 'Even the old man looks happy. She's running like clockwork. Want some more?'

Zof wanted more. He'd been impressed with the ship before. Now, this was the real test. The *Stalin* felt good beneath his feet – like a powerful animal waiting to be let off the leash. Zof was starting to come to life.

The madness of the enterprise was forgotten; now he was the Captain, and here was his ship, ready to respond to his commands. In front of him was the open sea, blue and calm. He took a deep breath. Still he remained cold and professional to anyone watching him. Inside, the feeling that Christmas had come early began to grow stronger.

'Let's work up to three-quarter revolutions on the outers and bring the inners up to half power, if you're happy?' Zof replied to his engineering commander. There was nothing in his voice to betray his feeling of excitement, but then Zhadanov felt exactly the same way. Probably everybody on the ship did, but nobody was going to show it.

The vessel began to vibrate once more. The bow wave, which had been a sedate foam, now started to curl away cleanly from the sharp bow of the ship. The wake at the stern turned from a gentle line tracing the progress of the ship into a boiling mass of churned water. With the outer turbines running up towards full power, the two inner turbines began to rotate under the pressure of the scalding steam. Their massive propellers, until now just a drag on the ship, started to add their horsepower to the outer shafts. Thick black smoke began to pour from the single, yellow-starred funnel as the old boilers roared through the thick oil and fifty years of deposits and grease began to burn off in the fierce heat. Great mats of seaweed and their colonies of inhabitants, which had resisted the initial movement of the water beneath the ship, were now ripping off in sheets. Freed of the drag, the hull pulled forward at a steadily increasing speed.

'Twenty knots!' shouted Zof on the bridge. He coughed and tried and suppress a grin.

'Holy shit,' said Kelley loudly, having never really

believed the old ship would move, let alone at this kind of speed. Harvey was equally impressed. Both of them were glued to the front windows of the bridge and had trouble concealing their excitement.

The old ship groaned and shook. Over fifty years, various parts had become slack. Rubber door and window seals were perishing. Bolts that were meant to be tight had become loose. The *Stalin* began to quiver as the old fittings started to shake with the increasing shuddering of the ship. Kishkov, who sat in the glassed-in control booth of the engine room, was looking relaxed in spite of the shaking going on around him. The hull had been constructed using electric arc welding, one of the first ships in the world to be built this way. He had heard of some Japanese ships having weld failures, so he simply doubled his welds to be on the safe side. Whatever else might fall off, at least the hull would stay in one piece.

'Zhadanov, if you're still happy, let's bring the outers to full power and the inners to three-quarters. Let's see what old Comrade *Stalin* can do,' said Zof down the telephone, still managing to sound calm and collected.

Zhadanov and his crew, still under the watchful eye of Kishkov, opened the steam valves even more and increased the fuel flow to the boilers to keep the steam at maximum pressure. A few joints were opening in some of the supplementary pipework, but nothing that couldn't be quickly patched. Zhadanov was becoming increasingly impressed with the sheer quality of the *Stalin's* construction. It was unusual in Russian ships, he thought sadly.

Zhadanov wiped his hands on his overalls as he passed by Kishkov, still sitting in his glass-framed booth. The old man had opened the door to let in the smell and the sound of the engine room. 'You did a good job, comrade!' he yelled at Kishkov above the din of the whirling shafts and the shrill whine of the turbines. Kishkov nodded silently and kept his eyes fixed on the big steam pressure gauges as they climbed slowly upwards.

With her outer turbines now spinning near their limits and the inner turbines coming up to three-quarters power, *Stalin* stopped shuddering and the sheer inertia of tons of rotating steel smoothed out the vibrations. Now powering ahead, more like a racehorse than a complaining donkey, the great ship split the water aside and threw an enormous wash out behind her that spread quickly across the otherwise flat sea as she thundered past.

If Zof could have punched the air with joy he would have done. Instead, he clasped his hands firmly behind his back and kept reminding himself that he was Yakov Zof, Captain First Class, and senior commanders in the Russian Navy do not go around yelling with joy.

Ten miles off the coast, two men in a small wooden fishing-boat were enjoying a peaceful if not very productive morning in the bright early sunshine. One of them happened to turn lazily around and with a sudden shock was greeted by the sight of the *Stalin* pounding along almost directly at them, a line of thick black smoke spreading out behind her from the boilers still clearing out the residues of fifty years. She grew alarmingly in size, far more quickly than they expected, and in a matter of minutes from first seeing her she roared past them a quarter of a mile away, travelling at an extraordinary speed. It took less than a minute for the first wave of the ship's mountainous wash to hit them. They held on in sheer terror as their tiny boat lurched violently around as several big seas slammed into it, their original astonishment now turned to raging anger as they screamed abuse at the madman on the ship. With a rumble like thunder, *Stalin* passed by and sped on into the distance.

She reached 28 knots before Kishkov finally waved his hands at Zhadanov. 'Enough, enough. Let her get her breath first,' he screeched, barely able to make himself heard above the howl of the turbines. Zhadanov ordered his crew to shut down the valves once more, and slowly *Stalin* calmed down and settled back to a sedate 20 knots. It was still an impressive sight for a ship the length of several football fields, though having left the two fishermen far behind there was no one on the sea to admire it.

She was now about twenty miles off the coast, and the grey smudge of Vladivostok receded quickly behind her, the distant mountains of the Sikhote Alin dotting the far horizon. The Pacific was calm that morning, a gentle swell rolling up from the south that didn't even move *Stalin* in her tracks. The sky was blue and a few scattered patches of white cloud suggested to Zof that the weather was at least settled. The sea turned from the pale blue of inshore water to the deeper and deeper green of the deep sea. Clear of the coast, Zof brought her round once more to face the south-east, as *Stalin* cleaved through the clear water into the Sea of Japan and then southwards to the narrow waters of the Korean Straits, nearly 700 miles distant. Yakov Zof was a happy man.

*

Feliks was beating at Ryzov's door, and Ryzov was yelling at him to keep quiet from behind it. Ryzov was grappling with the locks in an effort to get them opened, but it was early in the day and the locks were many and complicated. Ryzov occupied the post of honorary Consul for the British as well as for the Scandinavian countries, mainly to look after visiting seamen though tourists were becoming more common these days. When he finally shot the last bolt and hauled open the thick door, the sight of Feliks Zof standing there was infinitely depressing. The man had a habit of trying to sell so-called intelligence.

'Feliks, it's a bit early even for you. What the hell do you want this time?'

'Let me in and I'll tell you. Got any coffee?'

Feliks pushed in and made for Ryzov's small kitchen. He'd been here several times before.

Ryzov made two cups of Nescafé, a luxury in Russia sent to him by some of his shipping contacts, because shipping was his real business. Feliks remained silent until the coffee was served. Ryzov wrapped his dressing gown around him and sat down.

'So?'

'So. I've got something big for you this time. Very big. Your contacts in London will find this very, very valuable. It's the best intelligence I've ever been able to offer you, Aleks.'

'For God's sake, Feliks. I don't have any intelligence contacts. I keep telling you this.'

'Sure, sure, Aleks. I know. But it's good intelligence all the same.'

'If it's good, go to the Americans. They're the ones who want the intelligence, not me.'

Feliks was silent. He wasn't going to say this to Aleks, but he'd spent the previous half-hour trying to rouse the American Consul, and had been physically thrown off the premises. Feliks' reputation as a peddler of dubious intelligence was too much to take at this time of the morning.

'Listen, Aleks. You want to write this down? Never mind. It's all about the *Stalin*. The battleship in the docks? Guess what, Aleks. It left port just two hours ago. I saw it myself. And you know why?'

'Do tell,' said Aleks, resigned.

'Listen, Aleks, sure I'll tell. No problem. How about ten grand?'

'Get lost, Feliks. Don't waste my time.'

Feliks decided to tell Ryzov the bare facts. If he wanted more, which he was sure he would, he'd have to pay. Trade samples, he'd read it was called. So Feliks Zof outlined the story of Harvey and Kelley and Kishkov and the rest of it. Ryzov sat and listened, and when Feliks had finished more or less pushed him out of the door and told him he'd be in touch. Feliks wandered off to the bar; he didn't notice the dark, bearded man reading a newspaper on a bench opposite Ryzov's house, but then, why would he?

Once Feliks had disappeared, Ryzov wrote up the story on one side of a sheet of paper. Well, it sounded unlikely, but he was paid for anything interesting and so he spent the next hour coding up the story so that it looked like shipping code, and faxed it on an open line to the office of Pacific and Eastern Freight – which was nothing more than a number in Vauxhall Cross, the ugly modern building over the river from Westminster that houses the British Secret Intelligence Service. There it lay for half a day until it was routinely collected, routinely decoded and passed, eventually, to Stanley Dalby, a minor operative in the spy establishment whose job it was to collate information from their various public sources in the Pacific Rim. To Dalby, it would have been just another nutty story; the problem was so many people were trying to sell intelligence that half the stories coming in were about the imminent collapse of Western civilisation and the sounding of the Last Trump. Dalby was used to throwing out what looked like gold and Ryzov's story, heavily stamped with the Consul's cynicism about Feliks Zof, was about to head into the shredder with the rest of them when he wondered for a moment.

There was McEwan, he suddenly thought. Lindsey McEwan was an old friend from university days, a Navy man now stationed at Northwood and crazy about old battleships. Also, fortunately, an intelligence man too. Dalby gave him a ring, told him the strange tale, and McEwan sounded interested. Dalby sent him a copy of Ryzov's story and drafted a signal back to Ryzov to find out more. Offer Feliks five hundred; he'll take it.

McEwan was a fresh-faced, keen young officer who had fast-tracked through the Royal Navy since leaving Cambridge, where to his and his family's astonishment he gained a brilliant first in Naval History. Northwood, the NATO naval command centre in the leafy suburbs of London, was his first home posting for some time and he found it hopelessly dull. Dalby's mention of battleships caught his attention. He'd done his final thesis on the strategic importance of Second World War battleships. The whole story of the mighty dinosaurs of the naval world was fascinating. He knew the great battleships well: the *King George V*, the *Tirpitz* and the *Bismarck*, America's *Iowa*-class ships, the *Yamato* and of course the biggest and mightiest of them all: the great *Stalin*, one of the few battleships to survive along with the *Iowa* vessels to the present day.

Dalby's note was interesting. Was it true? And if it was, why would anyone want it? He tried to pick up any collateral information from the Americans but, as he suspected, nothing featured in the daily digests: that part of Russia was considered very uninteresting and Langley had better things to do. Nothing from the Russians, either. But that didn't surprise him. As an intelligence service, they were a mess. Eventually McEwan arranged a meeting with Maddox, his Admiral.

'What's this about, McEwan?'

'Very odd story, sir. We've had a report that someone has sailed off in the *Stalin*. From Vladivostok. It seems that an American and an Englishman are on board. I don't have much more information, but the ship is armed.'

'Remind me. What exactly is the *Stalin*?'

'Battleship, sir. Built in the Forties. Biggest one ever built. It's been laid up since then and used as a training ship. Quite famous in its day, sir.'

'And where does this story come from, McEwan?'

'Our Consul in Vladivostok, sir. Had it from a small-time crook name of Feliks Zof.' McEwan handed over Ryzov's note which, given Ryzov's pungent comments about Feliks Zof, was not a good move.

Maddox briefly scanned the note, then looked hard at McEwan. He was a new boy, after all; hadn't been at Northwood very long. The trouble with these youngsters, thought Maddox, was that they were bright and keen and had too little to do. So they got caught up in nonsense like this. Maddox stood up and moved to the door. You couldn't be too hard on him.

'Thanks, McEwan. I'll bear it in mind. Now, look, I've got a couple of Italians waiting to see me, so if you'll excuse me . . .'

McEwan flushed red and mumbled his apologies and quickly left the room. Shit.

*

While the *Stalin* was still completing her preparations to sail, the *Madelaine* had steamed slowly across Biscay, running as usual into the teeth of a full-blown gale that heaped the grey Atlantic waters into slowly marching mountains of foam-flecked sea. But the *Madelaine* rolled easily with each wave as she headed steadily south, the skies slowly clearing and the seas steadily less violent as the coast of northern Spain approached. She left Corunna to port and started down the coast of Portugal. By now the seas were subsiding, the sun was shining and the warm waters of the Mediterranean were beckoning. A few miles north of Lisbon, the *Ocean Queen* passed about five miles off her starboard side, providing a welcome point of interest for the small crew. The *Ocean Queen* was steaming at her cruising speed of 26 knots compared with the *Madelaine*'s 15 knots and was an impressive sight as the polished blue hull and the towering glass superstructure sliced through the blue seas. She had left Southampton the day after the *Madelaine* left Brest, and even the force 9 gale in Biscay hadn't slowed her down. From the high, enclosed decks of the passenger quarters, the gale that had buffeted the *Madelaine* had seemed like a gentle breeze.

Two days from Southampton, and a few hours after passing the *Madelaine*, the *Ocean Queen* docked at Gibraltar for her first major stop. The *Madelaine* laboured on behind her and passed by Gibraltar, as Captain Legret continued his uneventful voyage towards the grubby port of Livorno on the coast of Italy, his first port of call, due six days after clearing Brest.

As their contracts demanded, each ship reported – by telex under commercial code – their exact arrival times and expected departure times back to Lloyd's, where Stanley Price duly noted the information and in turn telexed it, under their own prearranged code system, to Kelley in Vladivostok. It was the last message that Price would be able to send by ordinary telex, and it was the last message that Kelley picked up as he left the hotel, paying his bill by a real but nevertheless fictitious American Express Gold card. He read the telex quickly. As he boarded the *Stalin*, he knew at least that the expedition would have its bait.

The target ships would stay over for at least twenty-four hours. They, or rather their agents, had to telex their exact moment of departure, again to Lloyd's, and again the information went to Stanley Price's desk. Just as he left the hotel, Kelley had sent a single-word telex to Price, who now had to take a little walk. He wandered unnoticed out of the building with his briefcase and caught a cab. Fifteen minutes later he checked in at the Tower Thistle Hotel, where he'd already booked a room on the top floor. Once he reached the room, he carefully locked it behind it and opened the heavy briefcase he'd been carrying.

There were three grey plastic boxes, all carrying the Sony logo. He opened the first box, which looked like a laptop computer except that the screen was missing. Instead, above the keyboard was a narrow, pale blue strip, a screen for just one line of type. The next box was almost completely featureless other than a plug socket, into which Price pushed the cable running from the keyboard. A tiny LED glowed green as he connected up the power; another small LED, beneath which was the single world READY, remained unlit. The last box contained what looked like a wedge of tinfoil; Price fanned out the wedge and it turned into a dish about two feet in diameter. He slotted the dish into a hole on top of the second box which supported it upright, and then he inserted a small stick with a silver cube on the end into the centre of the dish.

The satellite telex was now ready. He entered a user code and a destination code, hit the enter key, and waited. After ten seconds, the red LED suddenly glowed on and the screen bore the words: CONNECTED. Price tapped out a brief message, each character jumping into position on the line as he slowly and hesitantly pecked out the letters. Once he had finished, he waited for the reply – which duly arrived. Price then carefully unplugged the equipment, disassembled it, packed it back in the case and returned downstairs to the lobby where he left the key and departed. They'd made him pay for the room in advance: he had paid cash, and called himself Morris.

*

The communications and navigation equipment on board *Stalin* belonged in a museum. Harvey had not seen so many valves since Japanese hi-fi manufacturers decided to go back to them instead of transistors for expensive and fashionable stereo sets. The trouble was, most of the equipment on board the ship simply didn't work. He presumed it had once; but the valves and other components had long since succumbed to the sea air. But it was a simple enough matter to equip *Stalin* with electronic systems that made Kishkov wide-eyed in wonder. They simply flew over to Japan, bought the kit at a marine shop for less than $20,000, flew it back and rigged it up, though getting it to work with the oddities of the current from the old generators was not easy. There was a powerful colour radar, VHF and SSB radio systems, a satellite navigation system and a satellite telex system, all contained in boxes little bigger than beer twelve-packs. The total power consumed by all of them was less than three of the valves on the antique radar system which sat grandly but uselessly at the back of the bridge.

The screen of the *Stalin's* new satellite telex system beeped as Price's message started to come in. The time delay between Price's finger hitting a key and the corresponding character appearing on the screen on board the ship was something in the order of two seconds, which was all the time it took for the stream of data bits to squirt upwards from his machine to a satellite resting low in the southern sky, where the faint signal was received, amplified several hundred times and then re-broadcast downwards from an antenna facing eastward, where it was collected in the equivalent dish on Harvey's machine and bounced into the receiver sitting at the focus of the dish:

Ocean Queen confirmed clearing Gib 14.40 today. *Madelaine* reported on time clearing Livorno. Schedule stands. How's Uncle Joe? Regards Price.

Harvey sent his reply which appeared on Price's screen with the same two-second time delay, though Harvey's typing was a great deal slower even than Price's inexpert fingers, and the characters blinked out on Price's narrow blue screen with agonising slowness.

Uncle Joe looking good so far. No problem with your schedule. Confirm schedule next stops. Kelley sends his regards. Harvey.

The *Madelaine* and the *Ocean Queen* would now start to leapfrog each other through the Mediterranean, down through the Suez Canal and into the heat of the Red Sea, the *Ocean Queen* racing eagerly from port to port while the *Madelaine* trudged slowly and steadily onwards. As they reached down across the Indian Ocean *Stalin* had left Vladivostok and was gliding slowly through the calm seas south and east of Japan, unseen and invisible as Zof kept the ship well clear of the shipping lanes and the fishing grounds. The *Ocean Queen* had called at Bombay while the *Madelaine* doggedly ploughed through the southern seas, heading steadily for Singapore. It didn't take the cruise ship long to catch up with the freighter and pass it once more as it too headed for Singapore, while *Stalin* opened up her engines and began to race southwards through the Sea of Japan. From being half a world away from each other, the liner and the freighter were now drawing steadily closer to the Pacific and the long reach of the great battleship.

9

Zof called it 'working up' the ship, and he wanted to take his time. They were cruising in a wide arc, taking them away from the coast of China and closer to the northern Japanese islands to give themselves plenty of sea room. After a couple of days Kishkov pronounced himself happy with the engines, though Zhadanov had been run ragged by the old man's demands to fix this and fix that and on one occasion had become perilously close to threatening to hit him, but he held his tongue and attended to the loose bolt that Kishkov was nagging him about.

Now, deep in the middle of the Sea of Japan with no land within hundreds of miles, it was time to try out the big guns which had never once been fired. Kishkov assured Zof and the others that they would perform perfectly; both Kelley and Harvey were less relaxed and wanted to make sure they were working before they went into action. Zof's main concern was the ordnance. He'd been worried all along by the condition of the explosive inside the shells. They seemed stable enough, at least. But would they actually explode when detonated? It was not that Zof imagined having to use them in anger; the piracy plan seemed simple enough. Any ship seeing the *Stalin* coming up on them would be crazy to do anything other than – what was the phrase Kelley kept using? – 'co-operate fully'. But Zof's training would not let him rest until he knew the ship he was commanding would at least be capable of defending herself in a scrap.

So it was that each of them watched the test with very different interests in mind.

Zof gave Morin, his bay-chay two commander, his instructions. Morin turned his crew out; he chose the forward of the two forward turrets for the test. Watched by a fussing Kishkov, the dull grey block of armoured steel responded smoothly to the electric motors that rotated the 1,000-ton turret within the barbette on newly greased roller bearings. The brass and steel hydraulic rams that operated the elevation of the guns worked equally smoothly. Kishkov had the big turret rotated this way and that and the three massive guns pushed up and down several times to get (as he said) the old joints nice and loose.

The breech door of the chosen centre gun, looking like the door to a bank vault, was silently swung open by two fat pistons. Three decks below, deep in the thickly armoured magazine, a crane gripped a huge four-ton shell by a hook in its blunt nose and swung it on to a lift. The lift moved noiselessly upwards and came to rest opposite the open breech of the central barrel. The lift then tipped slowly forward until the big shell rested horizontally, pointing at the open breech. Behind the shell, now exposed by the hinged lift, a gleaming hydraulic ram hissed forward and effortlessly pushed the shell into the breech, the gas seal rings around the shell fitting it firmly and tightly into place. The lift flipped back into an upright position and swiftly descended back down the dark shaft.

From a floor below the shell room, a fat charge of cordite propellant in a silk sack was next on to the lift. It was elevated to the open breech, where the same ram inserted it snugly behind the shell. The loading was now complete. The big breech door swung quickly closed. Hydraulic pumps whirred gently as the huge gun lifted quickly to an elevation of 20 degrees. This would give the shot a range of 12 miles, which Zof and Kishkov had chosen because it was well within the visible horizon and Kelley and Harvey could more easily judge the effects.

'Gun number 2 ready,' said Morin confidently, a couple of minutes after the loading sequence had first started. The first time they tried it, back in Vladivostok, it had taken five minutes of fumbling, and Kishkov yelled at them that the system was designed to get off a complete salvo of three shots every thirty-two seconds. He assumed they would improve with practice; but it was beyond him why such idiots found such a brilliantly designed system so difficult to operate smoothly.

They had taken up position on the highest flag bridge to give the best view and distance. Zof had ordered the ship back to five knots; he nodded when the speed had reduced. Harvey told Morin to give the order to fire.

Kishkov had warned them, but what happened next still took all of them by surprise. None of them, not even Morin, had ever seen such a massive gun fire before, and the effects were devastating.

Almost in slow motion, the giant barrel shrank back within the turret as the cordite ignited. It had almost reached the end of its travel when from the muzzle billowed a sheet of red flame, followed by a brilliant, blinding burst of white flame, then an eruption of pink smoke as if a gigantic steam engine had just exploded. Harvey was astonished to catch a brief glimpse of the shell itself – streaking through the flame and smoke and hurtling outwards towards the distant horizon – as the huge barrel bounced against its recoil stops and began to travel forward again, steam and smoke still pouring from the mouth of the gun. The sound, even in the flag bridge – a good 300 feet distant from the gun – was not only deafening but also physically painful: it was like a big hand suddenly gripping their chests as the pressure blast travelled across them. As the gun fired, the ship, which had been travelling steadily forward at five knots, suddenly paused, almost stopping briefly. The gun had been facing midships – dead forward – and the power of the shot rammed the 75,000 tons of ship astern and momentarily slowed it in its tracks. The engines whined and then resumed their note as the screws bit back into the water and the ship shook itself like a wet dog before resuming its passage.

'Fuck,' said Harvey, amazed.

'Jesus Christ,' said Kelley at exactly the same time.

'Mother of God,' murmured Zof and Morin in unison.

Even Pine, who had been smiling at Kishkov from the back of the bridge and who looked, as usual, uninterested in the whole thing, was sufficiently moved to whistle appreciatively through his bad teeth.

Kishkov beamed. He rocked a little on his feet and his wrinkled hands clenched and unclenched rapidly. The rest of them watched for the shot to fall. The shell was clearly visible, even though it was travelling at something over 1,000 miles per hour. The vast bulk and speed of it left a distinct contrail-like mark as the heat of its passing condensed the water out of the steamy atmosphere. It arced gracefully over, started to race down and plunged into the sea, where a sudden, distant white fountain erupted in complete silence to mark where, to Zof's relief, the high-explosive TNA had detonated on contact with the sea 12 miles away. The sound reached them as the waterspout was falling back into the warm waters, a dull thud that seemed to echo from one side of the horizon to the other.

Zof nodded, more to himself in satisfaction than to the old man's confidence in his armaments. He'd need Morin to train up the crews to improve the speed, but other than that he was happy with the gunnery of his new command. He'd never been on a ship with such armaments before. Missile cruisers gave you nothing like the same sense of raw power, he thought. Computers, tracking screens and a crew that were more scientist than sailor were all very well, but when you had guns the size of tree trunks pointing at your opponent, there was a very definite feeling of power at your fingertips. Having seen what the guns could do, he could understand Kelley's point about frightening the life out of the prey. Madness this might be, he told himself, but at least he had something to give him some comfort if things started to go wrong. Nine of the biggest guns ever built gave one a certain feeling of confidence.

Stalin was now ready for action for the first time in fifty years.

*

The *Madelaine* had docked to take on fuel at Singapore, pouring enough diesel into the tanks deep below her waterline to take her on the final leg of her journey to Tokyo. She was on a crowded fuelling quay in the heart of the busy port, and the shipping line's agent had difficulty finding her. Eventually he spotted the familiar yellow hull and black funnel, and walked up the gangplank to find Legret, the master, to check on the timetable. These Lloyd's contracts were a pain in the arse, he told himself. On a normal voyage, a few days here or there was no trouble. With these people, not only did you have to constantly report every movement of the bloody ship but you picked up a penalty payment every hour it ran late. They paid well, he presumed, but it took a lot of extra work. She had kept to her original schedule like clockwork for the whole journey so far, and there seemed little reason to think that she would now start running late. It was just as well, for Lloyd's wouldn't use the line for bullion shipments unless they were completely reliable. The last thing they wanted was ships wandering aimlessly around the oceans loaded with their gold, and no idea when they were likely to hit port.

The *Ocean Queen* had made Singapore days earlier and was already completing her preparations to leave. Blake, the Captain, had no need for extra incentives to keep to time. Every moment was precious. His passengers wouldn't thank him for any delay, and neither would his owners. The hourly bill for running the *Ocean Queen* ran into tens of thousands of dollars. Even just a few hours' delay would have those people in Chicago jumping up and down. Having been running cruise ships for more years than he cared to remember, he made sure that everything ran to a precise schedule. Captain Hugh Henry Blake was a plump, friendly-looking man who added consciously to the bluff sea-dog image by sporting what he liked to call a 'full set', the old naval term for a complete beard. With his white uniform and cap, replete with slightly more gold braid than he was technically entitled to, he looked every inch the Captain of the *Ocean Queen*, which was exactly why the owners had hired him in the first place.

But God help anyone who fell foul of Blake. Although an affable, jolly sort of English sea captain to his passengers, he was a feared if respected tyrant on his bridge.

A young female clerk from the owner's local agent, charged with the responsibility of telexing Lloyd's to confirm the ship's movements – the contract was the same for the *Ocean Queen* as for the *Madelaine* – called up Blake on a private VHF channel and demanded to know, a little too officiously in Blake's opinion, if the ship would leave on time. The clerk's face grew pale as Blake gave her his reply, then her face went suddenly red. She didn't say a word, but gently replaced the handset as if it were hot to the touch. The clerk was Chinese and hadn't heard most of the expressions used by Blake before, but it was clear enough what they meant.

The offices telexed their information to Price, who duly departed from his office with his large black briefcase. This time he headed for the Caledonian Hotel in the Euston Road, where once again he contacted the *Stalin*. It would be Price's last message. After it was sent, instead of returning to Lloyd's, he caught a train to Liverpool. The big black case was dropped from a window as the train was doing over 100 mph and it smashed to unrecognisable fragments. From Liverpool, Price caught the ferry to Dublin, where he boarded a Delta flight to Santiago. He sat in first class, ordered a bottle of Dom Perignon, and happily raised a glass to his old friend Jeremy Harvey.

*

Harvey watched the message come in. Once the characters had finished appearing on the screen, he pressed the print key and the machine briefly buzzed, then delivered a hard copy of Price's message. He went to Zof and together they pulled out the charts of the South China Sea.

By Friday morning the *Ocean Queen* would have reached a position about 400 miles south of Hong

Kong, out in deep water where little if any other shipping would be. The *Madelaine* would be running a little earlier, and by Thursday morning would be about 300 miles north and west of the same point, giving plenty of time for *Stalin* to cover the distance between the two.

The only question was where *Stalin* would be. Zof expertly laid off the courses of all three ships, using a soft black pencil and a set of wartime solid brass parallel rules that he'd found in the navigator's room. He drew three lines and ended each one with a thick black cross. The first line was the *Ocean Queen*; the second, the French freighter; the third represented their own proposed track. With a grunt, Zof marked off the final cross exactly on top of the *Madelaine*'s position. They'd have to keep running at 20 knots, well within her capabilities. Even Kishkov would be happy.

Stalin would be waiting.

*

Exactly on time, the *Ocean Queen* quietly lifted her two massive anchors and gently, so as not to disturb any of the still-sleeping passengers, started her slow, stately journey through the roads out into the Straits, where she began a slow turn north that would take her up past what was once called Indo-China across the Bay of Tonkin and into the South China Sea towards Hong Kong.

On the bridge in the early morning tropical heat, the first officer, George Holland, was carefully navigating the ship through the narrow, crowded waters. One of the worst problems for the *Ocean Queen* was rubberneckers – the crowd of small boats that congregated around her whenever she entered or left a port, packed with sightseers. Holland was keeping an eye on several flashy and perilously overloaded cabin cruisers that were dashing around her; cutting under her bow where they became invisible; he could run one run down without even feeling it.

Attwood, the radio officer, came out of his wood-panelled radio room on to the spacious, airy bridge, carrying a sheet of flimsy yellow telex paper. 'Sorry, George, but there's a typhoon warning just come up.'

'Oh, terrific. Just what we need. When's it due?'

'Next twenty-four hours, I'm afraid. Flash just came through from the HK typhoon spotters. Doesn't look too good.'

'OK. Better call the old man to the bridge while I get us out of here without sinking one of these stupid buggers.'

Once called from his comfortable suite on B deck, Blake strode on to the bridge just five minutes later. The moment he came through the door the atmosphere on the bridge noticeably stiffened.

He rapidly scanned the report from Hong Kong, where what started as an outpost of the British Meteorological Office, and was now a commercial joint venture with the People's Republic of China, maintained a centre dedicated to spotting and tracking the ten or twenty tropical hurricanes that skirted the coast of China each year.

Typhoons are hurricanes – the name is different in the Pacific from the Caribbean. But the effects are the same. A deepening depression, usually born over the hot tropical latitudes, begins to rotate more and more swiftly, fed with energy from the moist, hot tropical air, building up angry 100 mph-plus winds around the spiral arms with an eerily calm centre, the eye. They invariably head northwards, regularly drenching Hong Kong, before spending themselves out in the wastes of the Pacific. Each one has a name for ease of reference. In the Caribbean, hurricanes are traditionally given feminine names. In the Pacific, the tradition is for men's names, running in strict alphabetical order. The last one, two months previously, was Typhoon Charlie. This new storm was therefore a 'D' – Typhoon Donald, as a wit in the Hong Kong typhoon centre had already christened it.

Donald was a nasty storm, but a small one. Instead of being spread over 500 miles of sea, Donald measured just 200 miles from edge to edge. But the winds in the circular arms of the storm were being predicted at 120 mph-plus. It was due in the Bay of Tonkin tomorrow morning, and would move north along Typhoon Alley to edge past Hong Kong just as the *Ocean Queen* was due. It didn't take Blake long to figure out that if he stuck to his course, he would end up directly in the worst part of the storm.

It was not the safety of the ship that worried him. Typhoons blew fiercely and whipped up a nasty-looking sea, and the ship would rock around. But there was no length to the sea, so instead of the moving mountains of water that the Atlantic would throw at you, tropical typhoons gave you a short, nasty and very bumpy ride for a few hours, then cleared and left you alone. Even so, he didn't relish the thought of sitting on his own at an empty dinner table while the rest of the passengers were either too terrified or too sick to leave their cabins. He suspected the cargo of rich widows would not greatly appreciate the experience, and neither would the owners back in Chicago much like the letters of complaint. It wasn't the kind of thing that was meant to happen on luxury cruises, and Blake had been running this sort of voyage long enough to realise that he'd have to change plans.

Once Holland had calmly conned his way out around the rubberneckers without sinking any of them and made his way into clear water, Blake and he worked out a new course that would make them a few hours late into Hong Kong but would mean that they missed the trailing edge of the storm by some miles. The seas would still be rough in the wake of the typhoon, but nowhere near as bad as in the storm itself, and he was prepared to risk a few heaving stomachs amongst his delicate charges for a couple of hours to ensure he reached Hong Kong on at least the right day, even if he was ten or eleven hours late.

'We'll not tell the passengers yet, Holland, I think.'

'No, Captain.'

'Best not to get them all worked up. We'll wait until it starts to brew up, then we'll tell them there's a bit of a blow. I think we'll tell them the new arrival time in the middle of it. By then they'll be in no mood to bother too much. Let HK harbourmaster know, would you?'

'Yes, sir.'

'OK, Holland, carry on your watch. Time for breakfast for me,' and Hugh Henry Blake breezed off the bridge. The crew immediately relaxed.

*

The *Madelaine* had left immediately after finishing her refuelling. Legret saw the same typhoon forecast, but unlike Blake decided to tough it out. Without passengers to worry about, he was happy that the ship and crew could take the storm. Legret reckoned it would be over him and gone within six hours anyway, and to change course now would make him at least two days late at Tokyo. He told the crew to prepare for rough weather, and they began the task of double-securing the containers of glassware in the holds. Of all the cargoes to take into a typhoon, thought Legret, I would have to end up with a cargo of cut glass. He ordered extra packing put around the containers, just in case.

On *Stalin*, Zof had no such detailed forecast available. They had equipped themselves with a Navtex receiver, a small printer that provided weather and navigation warnings, but it was mainly for coastal and fishing use. He glanced over it and noted a typhoon warning, but the information was vague and it was difficult to see where it would be in relation to them. Zof wondered if he should call up Hong Kong for more information. The trouble was, they'd have to give a call sign before they got the forecast, and of course *Stalin* had no call sign – or none they would want to give.

Zof decided he could do without. He'd been through typhoons before; the safest place after all was at sea, for a ship. And given the size of the *Stalin*, he suspected it would be nothing more than a good test of the ship's handling. In truth, he quite enjoyed a bit of rough weather. And with his pirates on board, it would keep them in their places. There was nothing like the look on the face of someone unused to the ocean when you were ploughing through fifty-foot seas to make a professional sailor feel good. His only real worry was that the ship itself was still sound enough to take the weather. But from what he'd seen so far he wasn't too concerned.

'Comrade Chief Designer, I take it you'll be happy with this ship in a blow?'

The old man flared. 'Comrade Captain, I'd be happy with this ship in hell.'

*

Stalin was steaming south at 20 knots. Heading north-west, the *Ocean Queen* cruised along at 26 knots. The *Madelaine* steamed steadily at 15 knots, some several hundred miles ahead of her, on a more northerly course.

There were still hundreds of miles of sea between them, and in the slowly narrowing gap the blue sky steadily darkened and towering cumulus clouds began to build as the cold front moving ahead of typhoon Donald freshened the sultry tropical air. The deep blue sea that had been gently rolling under the fierce sun took on a grey hue as the clouds began to build up, and the sun became hazier and hazier and then blinked out behind a thick bank. The wind, which had been a gentle whisper from the south, backed to the west and began tugging at the smooth sea. Sharp gusts skittered across the surface, gathering the water up into ripples which were caught by another gust and turned into wavelets. The wavelets in turn were pushed into bigger waves by the steadier, stronger wind that soon replaced the gusts; and the waves were heaped slowly higher and higher as the wind continued to increase. Soon the wavetops were being torn off by the wind, leaving a sea now grey, boisterous and glinting with white horses from horizon to horizon, where just a few hours earlier had been the calm, deep blue of the Pacific.

Then the rain started. First came big, fat drops that puckered the surface of the building sea. Then as the outer edges of the spiralling arms of the typhoon approached, the drops were replaced by fitful lashes of torrential rain that reduced visibility to about 500 yards, then suddenly cleared again to reveal the awesome sight of the now angry sea and the lowering, dense black clouds, before blotting out the scene once more, like curtains being closed.

10

The spray lashed at the bridge windows as though it were a sandstorm, rattling and chattering against the thick glass in fitful gusts. The wipers were sliding back and forth at maximum speed but still the view that Zof had of the bow of the *Stalin* was intermittent. As the bow plunged into each wave, it disappeared in an explosion of white foam that whipped back across the ship in the screaming wind, and grey and green water swept across the foredeck where the spray deflector just forward of the first gun turret cleaved the sea away before it ran down the wide decks.

Kelley, Harvey and Pine had all come up to the bridge when the weather started to worsen. Kishkov had also arrived. The old man was clearly enjoying the ride and had positioned himself right in front of the windows, bracing himself against the movement between the bulkhead and an engine telegraph.

'How the hell are we supposed to find the ship in the middle of all this crap?' asked Kelley. He was not happy with the storm for other reasons. Kelley was far from being a natural sailor.

Zof looked happy with the change in the weather. 'Kelley, this is just the weather we want. The storm will cover us perfectly. No one will expect us, and no one will see us go.' Secretly he was amused by the American's obvious discomfort. Once Zof had been nervous about the sea too, even as a sailor. Rough weather and the rolling of a ship used to leave him sweating, silently and secretly, with fear. It was cured when he found himself in the deep South Atlantic, just a few hundred miles from the icecap, one winter afternoon when the wind started to rise and turned the already heavy sea into an awesome procession of water mountains marching down on them. The ship didn't just roll; it turned beam-end to beam-end, or at least it felt like that, and nobody could stand up. Even the Commander ended up sitting on the deck, braced between a bulkhead and the column holding the helm, hanging on for dear life as for twelve hours the ship was at the mercy of the sea. Nobody could eat. Nobody could do anything except hang on. He had sweated the fear out of himself to a point where at the height of the raging storm he started singing, though no one else would join in. The ship stayed afloat and the storm finally blew over. He had discovered that the ship can usually take more than the crew, and ever since then the ocean held no fear. It was a lesson the rest of them had yet to learn.

'Zof, how the hell are we supposed to board a ship in this?' asked Harvey, mystified by Zof's confidence.

'Easy, my friends. We just wait for the eye of the storm. We're pretty near it now. Find the ship, track it, wait for the storm to subside, do the job, and we'll be off again just as the storm is blowing up once more.'

'How are you so damn certain we're near the eye?'

'I was born on the Pacific coast. We are used to this sort of thing. Once the wind is howling like this, you know you're more or less in the middle of the track of the storm, which means the eye is heading in this direction.'

'How long do we get in the eye?'

'Two, maybe three hours, maybe less. This is a bad

wind, so it's probably a small storm, which gives you a small eye. You see, Comrade Kishkov's God is smiling on us. Maybe He sent this storm to protect us,' laughed Zof, looking at the anxious faces of Kelley and Harvey. Even Pine looked slightly apprehensive at the gathering weather.

'You're sure this is going to work, Zof?' asked Kelley.

'No, Mr Kelley, I'm not sure this is going to work at all. But the weather is the least of our problems. The ship will take five storms like this without even pausing. Don't worry, Kelley. You are safe here. But you're going to have to decide what to do very quickly,' said Zof.

'Why?' asked Kelley, looking even more worried, much to Zof's amusement.

'There is a signal on the radar that could be our ship. She's just come in at forty-eight miles. Look!'

Zof had been staring down the hood of the Furuno radar set they had installed at Vladivostok. Switched to its maximum range, the colour screen was speckled with tiny dots like snow that changed every time the scanner, sweeping round, refreshed the image. It was picking up clutter from the rain and from the tops of the waves. He had been fiddling with the clutter rejection control to try and tune out the mess, and had suddenly picked up a stronger blip on the very edge of the screen. The image kept vanishing, but every third or fourth sweep it glinted back into view.

'New course; steer 205 degrees,' commanded Zof, and the helmsman brought the bow of the ship towards the radar signal. They had been keeping 30 degrees or so off the wind to meet the steep waves at an angle, lessening the buffeting. Now on the new heading the angry seas were meeting them head-on. The mighty ship ploughed on but now shuddered every time they rammed headfirst into a steep sea. The visibility worsened with the spray and the rain sluicing across the bridge windows in driving streams.

'Would you like me to slow down, perhaps?' Zof asked no one in particular, gripping an overhead grab-rail as the ship slammed and crashed through the storm.

Kelley and Harvey conferred. Though he was still worried about the storm, there was simply no alternative, Kelley said, looking pale. They had to trust Zof's instinct about the eye. It was now or never. They must keep to the schedule, whatever happened. Harvey was surprised at Kelley's determination but assumed he knew what he was doing.

'Carry on. We'll go for it,' said Harvey to Zof finally, in Russian, as he tightened his grip on a handrail.

*

The *Madelaine* was steaming through the same weather, but had the seas marching up behind her. Each wave picked up her stern, shook her around, then swept away leaving the bow trailing down the back of the receding wave. As each new wave caught her, she would speed up as she almost surfed down the wave, then just as quickly slow as the bow rose. The young helmsman, Pascal, was struggling to keep a steady course through the grim sea, winding the wheel one way and then the other to try to counter the heaving ship. He was pale and his hands gripped the wheel tightly, and he swallowed frequently, trying to disguise the awful seasickness that had started to overtake him.

Legret sat at the back of the bridge watching the digits of the electronic compass flicker, reading ten degrees off course one way, then ten degrees off course the other as the bow slewed round. What the hell, thought Legret. He's young and he'll have to learn.

Leave for him for half an hour until he finds the rhythm of the waves.

The *Madelaine*, being much smaller than *Stalin*, had the benefit of being able to ride with the steep waves rather than having to smash through them. The movement was wilder, but the ship was drier and there was less crashing as each new wave passed them by to recede into the rain-swept gloom ahead of them. And, of course, Legret had the benefit of the weather pictures which his computer screen picked up every two minutes from a satellite high overhead, beamed direct from Hong Kong.

Plotted on to the image of the storm, the *Madelaine* sat squarely in the rotating spiral that formed the leading edge. This was where the wind was strongest, and he'd already noted a gust that peaked at 70 knots, well up to typhoon standards. As each updated view of the storm arrived on his screen, Legret could see that the storm was travelling north at about 30 knots. Within two hours the eye would be over them, leaving, he reckoned, a gap of about a couple of hours until the spiral arm of the trailing edge of the storm, with the winds coming from the opposite direction, began to build up. They'd be clear of the trailing edge by nightfall, and calm would return to the wildly twisting *Madelaine*.

'For heaven's sake, Pascal!' yelled Legret to the grey-faced youth when the ship gave a particularly violent lurch and the digits on the compass skittered a full 30 degrees off course. Pascal panicked and hauled on the wheel to pull the bow round but over-corrected, and the ship began to lean dangerously as the sea behind started to shove the stern around, across the face of the approaching waves. This was the start of one of the most dangerous conditions a ship can face – broaching, when a following sea spins the ship beam to the wave, then the sheer steepness of the wave topples the ship over to a capsize.

Legret leapt from his seat and pushed the young helmsman out of the way, grabbing the wheel from him. He held the wheel as he waited for the bow to come back down into the trough, then start to rise up again. Using the wheel more gently, he combined the rudder at the stern with the pressure of the sea on the bow to bring the vessel back on to a course that kept the seas neatly under the stern. The ship stopped heeling and the violent motion began to calm.

'Pascal, why don't you just watch the radar for a while?' Legret gave him a less demanding job, hoping to take his mind off his seasickness. The last thing Legret was worrying about was meeting another ship in the middle of this murk; nobody else would be crazy enough to be out in weather like this. But Pascal was the nephew of a friend who ran the dockyard and this was his first deep-sea voyage. He couldn't be too hard on the poor lad. 'Tell me if you see anything,' Legret suggested encouragingly.

A relieved Pascal pulled himself hand over hand along the bridge console to the radar set where he settled his face into the viewing hood. His stomach felt as though someone had cut a hole out of it, and his head was spinning. He was less than convinced, at this exact moment, that he was truly destined for a life at sea.

The screen was a mess of clutter from the rain and the wavetops, but unlike the amateur set on the *Stalin*, the *Madelaine* had one of the latest Raytheon commercial sets with software that could, by itself, distinguish actual radar images from irrelevant ones. The computer simply compared images that moved each time the antenna swept round with images that didn't move quite so much. Images that were irregular and moved a lot, such as waves and rain, it simply ignored. Images that were more regular, such as ships, it displayed. Pascal flicked the clutter switch that brought the software into action. Immediately the screen went blank as the computer took away the clutter.

But on the top edge of the circular screen a distinct orange blot remained. As he watched the blot fade and then brighten each time the antenna refreshed the screen, it moved fractionally towards the screen centre. It was at the very edge of the radar's range but was clearly moving towards them.

At over 40 miles away it hardly posed a threat, and as Pascal, brought up on computer games, loved playing with the complicated controls on the radar set, he kept silent and watched the blip strengthen. After a few minutes the Raytheon's computer would be able to plot the bearing and speed of the target, showing it as a line on the screen pointing along the course the computer calculated it was taking. It could then automatically watch it and sound an audible alarm if it entered a 'guard sector' that Pascal could set up. This was better than most computer games, thought Pascal, as he quickly flicked the switches that brought the guard zone system into operation: this was for real.

The computer waited until it had enough data on the blip, still the only one on the screen. Once it thought it had enough, it projected a line across the screen which Pascal noted missed the centre, their own position, by ten miles. The figures '16' appeared beside the blip as the computer calculated the speed of the target. They wouldn't even see it in this weather, thought Pascal. Every twenty seconds, the computer recalculated the course and speed. The second time it worked out the plot, the line came to within eight miles of the *Madelaine*'s position. The speed increased to 17. The third time, the line was within five miles and the speed 18. The fourth time, the line was a mile off and the target ship indicated as having a speed of 20 knots.

With a shock, Pascal saw the line cut right through the screen centre and the speed remain at 20 knots. The blip started flashing as the computer warned that the target would enter the guard zone and posed a collision threat. In the two minutes it had taken for the system to plot the positions, both ships had moved a mile closer to each other. According to the screen, they would meet in one hour and twenty minutes.

Pascal looked up from the screen. 'Captain, sir, there's a ship on the screen and it looks as though it's heading for us,' he said hesitantly, uncertain that he should be saying anything.

'Thank you, Pascal. Keep an eye on it, there's a good lad,' replied Legret, thankful the boy seemed to have something to occupy him.

Pascal didn't know if he should tell the Captain about the computer's collision prediction or not. The Captain didn't seem to be in quite the mood just yet, so he thought he ought to remain quiet. He turned back to the hood and started playing with more of the electronic tricks. The Raytheon had a target size function, where it could attempt to calculate how big the target was. Pascal hit the button. After blinking 'wait' for ten seconds, the numeral '20' beside the target was joined by another numeral '290', indicating that the radar calculated the length of the ship at an astonishing 290 metres, which Pascal assumed was the computer's first guess that it would shortly correct. Such a ship could only be a supertanker, and supertankers didn't go ploughing stormy seas at anything like 20 knots.

The numerals did change. First they dropped back to 260, then to 220. But then, as the data became more and more reliable, the size began to increase, stabilising at 280 metres, just under 1,000 feet long.

Pascal plucked up his courage to speak again. 'Captain sir, the ship is very big and travelling at twenty knots.'

'Thank you, Pascal. That's one hell of a ship, huh?' smiled Legret. 'How far off is it? I don't suppose we'll see it in this muck.' He humoured Pascal. There was no way the boy was right.

'Captain, sir, it's about forty miles off still. But, Captain . . .'

'Yes, Pascal?'

'. . . it seems to be coming right at us.'

'Oh, well, I wouldn't worry, Pascal. It's miles off yet. If it doesn't change bearing at twenty miles, let me know. Good work, though, Pascal, good work.'

Legret spun the wheel as a particularly large wave hoisted the stern skywards with surprising speed. The *Madelaine* paused briefly as the wave ran under her midships leaving the bow high out of the water, then crashed back into the trough sending a bow wave across the decks of the heaving freighter. Behind her, the sky had a ragged streak of light growing in it.

*

Zof, heading southwards, could now see the eye of the storm clearly. He had been right. The last of the cloud mass that made up the leading edge spiral was visible on the horizon, a curving line of dark, almost black cloud, with a clearer, brighter patch beyond it. Every few moments the view disappeared behind the sheet of spray blowing off the bow.

'Target's about thirty miles off. We'll close in about an hour,' called Harvey, who had his face buried in the radar viewing hood.

'Looks like Zof was right about the storm,' said Kelley.

'We should get the crew ready now. We won't have long,' warned Harvey.

'OK, Harvey. What do we say? "General Quarters" – isn't that what they say in the movies?'

Harvey asked Zof to get his crew ready. It was a moment Zof had been looking forward to. He ordered the combat stations alarm sounded, pairs of rings in quick succession from the ship's bell system, broadcast over the public address system, which they had managed to get working using the original valve amplifier. The clanging echoed and dinned around every corner of the ship, drowning out the howling wind. Within moments the passageways came alive with running men, all heading for their prearranged positions as part of their various bay-chay, using both sides of the ship instead of keeping to the port side – it was an ancient Russian naval tradition that the starboard side of the ship was used by officers only, a tradition that had survived even the Revolution.

It looked like chaos. But almost as soon as it started, the men had vanished to their combat stations and a tense silence fell over the ship.

The forward main turret was manned, as were two side anti-aircraft turrets. Another party stood by the crane that would lower the new Zodiac inflatable over the side. The small boarding crew, to be led by Harvey and Pine, started to get into foul-weather clothing. Pine was having some difficulty in struggling into a jacket that was too small for him.

The crew in the forward turret went through the process of loading a round in the centre gun.

By the time Zof was satisfied that the crew were in position, the ships were just 20 miles apart.

*

Pascal was still watching the radar screen; the bearing line connecting the orange blot to the centre of the screen remained unchanged, as did the speed and size numerals.

He had selected the range rings display, where at five-mile intervals faint circles spread out like ripples from the screen centre. The blot was now approaching the fourth circle out.

'Er, excuse me, Captain, sir?'

'Yes, Pascal. What is it now?'

'That ship. It's still heading right for us.'

'And the distance, Pascal?'

'Now twenty miles, Captain, sir.'

The raging seas were showing signs of dropping now, as the skies above them were starting to clear.

'OK, Pascal, come and take the wheel again. Keep it steady, though, steady. Don't wind the wheel like you were hauling in a fish. Feel the movement of the ship and don't try to force it, OK?'

'Yes, Captain,' said Pascal as he pulled himself back across the bridge against the still energetic rocking.

Legret peered down the hood at the screen, and was impressed with the way Pascal had set the system up. It was something he still had to look in the instruction book to achieve. There was the other ship, just as Pascal had said. He wasn't sure he believed the computer's plot, so he silently watched the progress of the image for a full three minutes. By then, even from his own calculation it was obvious the ship was heading for them and showing no sign of changing course. In this situation Legret wouldn't normally worry about changing course until much closer. But in weather like this he wanted plenty of sea room. The storm made his ship come to a new heading more slowly than usual.

'Pascal, come ten degrees starboard,' he called, still with his eyes at the viewing hood.

When approaching each other on a collision course, ships are required to take early avoiding action. They must pass port-to-port. Legret had ordered a textbook

manoeuvre, making a sufficiently big course
correction to be noticed by the other skipper so that
he made his intentions clear. The *Madelaine*'s motion
worsened as the bow came round, but Legret judged
the sea to be reasonable enough to take the new
course. He watched the bearing line from the target
vessel slowly move to the left of the screen centre.

Then he swore and looked at the blip more closely.

The target had seen his action and was changing its
course too. But instead of widening the gap, the ship
had turned in quite the wrong direction and the
bearing line closed up again, shifting slowly across the
screen to connect once more with the dot at the
centre that represented *Madelaine*'s position.

The ship was following him, and bearing down.

Legret reached for the handset of the VHF radio
and in his thick Normandy-accented English he called
the other ship.

'Vessel on my bow, this is *Madelaine*, *Madelaine*,
over.'

He released the talk-button on the handset and
waited for the ship to respond. There was just the
steady hiss of the carrier wave. At 20 miles, the other
ship was well within radio range and surely could see
him on radar.

He waited half a minute and then tried again.
'Vessel on my bow, this is merchant ship *Madelaine*. If
you can hear me, you are on a collision course with
me, I repeat, you are on a collision course with me. I
will be altering course ten degrees to starboard in one
minute. I will expect you to do the same, over.'

Again there was nothing except the carrier signal.
Legret let one minute pass and then ordered Pascal to
turn the bow another 10 degrees to the right. He
watched the radar screen as the turn was completed,
finding it difficult to hold his face to the viewing hood

in the even more violent motion of the ship. Once again, the bearing line shifted slowly to the left of the centre of the screen as the *Madelaine* took up her new course. And to Legret's absolute fury, the bearing line slowly came back again as the target ship altered its course in response.

He grabbed the VHF again. 'Vessel on my bow, you are endangering my ship, I repeat you are endangering my ship. Your intentions appear to be deliberate. What the hell are you playing at?'

No reply. Legret considered the situation. Either the vessel was steered by a fool who didn't know about the port-to-port rules of the road, or for some reason was actually trying to make contact with him and the radio wasn't working. But it was such a huge ship. He assumed the first explanation; after all, there were dozens of huge ships on the high seas steered by idiots who hadn't even qualified for a swimming certificate.

'Come to port twenty degrees,' he ordered Pascal. By going in the opposite direction he could prove the point one way or another.

The motion of the ship calmed again as the stern once more faced the following, and by now reducing, waves. He watched the radar, and Legret shook his head in disbelief as the approaching ship also changed course to maintain the collision heading. The second explanation was by now the only reasonable one. The vessel must have a problem and had no means of communication available.

'Vessel on my bow, this is *Madelaine*. You are maintaining a collision course. I assume you are in need of assistance. I will maintain this heading but reduce speed until I see you visual. If you require me to stop and render assistance, please signal by horn or light. Over.'

Legret now peered from the wheelhouse window

in the direction of the strange ship. The cloud ahead formed a thick, low black mass, but already above him the sky was clearing and the sun began to blink through rips in the cloud. The sea sparkled in the sudden bursts of sunshine, but was still an angry green streaked with white foam, and still heaved and rolled. The other ship was now 15 miles away, which would normally put it just within visual range. But the cloud ahead was still releasing sheets of rain that obscured the horizon. Legret would have to wait to let it clear.

*

Zof followed the twists and turns of the *Madelaine* on his radar screen with some apprehension. It was like hunting a fox. Legret's angry voice over the VHF, which Zof had been monitoring, added to the spirit of the chase. As a professional, Zof actually felt for the Captain of the freighter. He knew how worried he was feeling, and probably how angry he was getting. Here was a strange ship, behaving in a very unseamanlike way. Zof hated doing it, in truth. The ship was a civilian not a naval vessel, and the Captain would find it difficult to cope, especially in this weather. But he knew the ship wasn't going to come to any harm, and he could understand Kelley's point about frightening them into submission. It felt strange and uncomfortable, all the same. Here he was, going into the piracy business for the first time, and already he was getting cold feet. Yakov, for Christ's sake, if you're going to be a pirate you might as well start acting like a good one. This is what you do now. You're not some high-flown Captain any more. You're just a pirate. Now stop feeling soft and act the bloody part. He straightened up from the small radar screen and pushed himself back to the chase.

As the *Madelaine* slowed, he ordered 30 knots to close the gap faster. The huge turbines responded almost instantly, and the massive ship shouldered aside the waves as it began to thunder through the boiling sea in a cloud of spray that flew up above even the highest point of the towering superstructure.

'Now, gentlemen, I think we should follow the naval tradition and hoist our battle standard.' Harvey pulled a large flag from under a locker and handed it to Zof. Zof opened a section of it, and looked at Harvey.

'Not this!' he said.

'What else, Zof? We're just pirates, after all.'

'Fly the Red Banner,' he demanded.

'Zof, for Christ's sake! Let them think the worst. Frighten the life out of them or they'll give you trouble,' insisted Harvey.

Zof didn't like it. But then, Harvey was right. They were, after all, just pirates. He summoned a crewman who had the unenviable job of climbing up to the yards that reached up towards the superstructure. In the driving wind and rain he attached the flag and ran it up. Unlike Zof, he couldn't help but smile when he saw what it was.

*

Through the binoculars, Legret saw an indistinct white cloud fading in and out of view on the horizon where the ship should have been. It emerged from sheets of distant rain, then disappeared again. Each time it emerged it looked bigger. Then it stayed visible for a few seconds, and he saw that the cloud rose and fell; it was spray breaking on something in the distance.

Then, as the spray subsided before blossoming upwards again, he saw a grey tower briefly appear. Suddenly a glint of sunlight caught the ship and he momentarily saw the outline of the superstructure of what was clearly a naval vessel.

'Shit!' he said to himself. A warship. Now what the hell was this all about? A navy exercise? A patrol?

Stalin now began to emerge from the rain and the murk, and though its bow was buried in spray its shape was clear to Legret. He watched in awestruck amazement as the huge ship ploughed at extraordinary speed through the boiling seas. His first officer, Mouret, had now joined them on the bridge, equally astonished by the sight.

Still *Stalin* maintained an unswerving collision course.

Legret warned the engine room to stand by for maximum power. He held his course, hoping that at some point the mighty ship would show signs of slowing.

'Do you think we should put out a message to the coastguard, Captain?' asked Mouret, looking nervous.

'Not yet. Let's see what happens. Anyway, Mouret, I doubt we're within range.'

Stalin closed mile after mile. Twenty minutes later the ship was now clearly visible, just three miles off. The spray was lessening as the seas dropped, and the sun had started to shine brightly. Then at two miles, to Legret's relief, the charging beast began to visibly slow and the spray reduced to a crisp bow wave, then dropped even more as the bulbous bow settled back into the water. As the huge ship slowly started to turn, the awesome length of the vessel began to reveal itself. The radar's computer had been right all along.

Slowly and calmly, the great ship turned broadside on to the *Madelaine* as though to block its path. Legret brought his own ship to a halt, awed by the spectacle. As the *Madelaine* lay there, rocking in the waves, the huge forward gun turret on the warship slowly rotated towards them. As though in slow motion, the three huge muzzles tracked round and, as they did so, the centre gun gently moved downwards until it came to rest with the gun pointing directly at the *Madelaine*'s bridge.

Legret snatched at the VHF once again. 'What the hell are you playing at? You're behaving like pirates.'

Mouret, who had been watching *Stalin* through the binoculars, nudged Legret and pointed to the crosstrees of the huge warship. Legret lifted his own glasses and focused them on the flapping black flag that Mouret was silently pointing at.

'Mother of Christ!' murmured Legret under his breath. Rattling in the strong wind, a skull and crossbones flew from the high mast.

11

'Right first time, Captain,' burst a voice from the VHF. It had a coarse American accent. 'Now, if you gentlemen on the *Madelaine* haven't already noticed, we have several very big guns pointing directly at you. We'd be very happy if you didn't make any calls on your radio. If you do, we'll have to drop a shell or two in your direction. Am I making myself clear?'

Legret growled down the VHF handset. 'You are joking, I take it?'

'Joking, Captain? Oh dear,' returned the voice, and then there was a long silence. Then the big gun pointing directly at the *Madelaine* began to move slowly upwards. It appeared to be pointing at the top of the *Madelaine*'s mast when it stopped. Suddenly, the huge barrel lurched back into the turret and a spout of brilliant white flame flashed from the gun. Legret could hear a screech as the four-ton shell raced overhead. He blinked after the brilliant flash and ran out on to the deck to see if his ship had been hit. It was intact, but in the distance there was a dull thud and a huge column of spray climbed into the sky and then fell slowly back.

'There now, Captain. That's how serious we are. The next shot will blow your little ship into tin cans. Now listen. A boarding party will approach. Let down a gangway or a ladder when you see them. They will give you instructions when they arrive. We'll remain here, and our guns are still loaded.'

Zof was far from happy. He didn't like the chase; he didn't like flying Kelley's bizarre flag; he least of all liked opening fire on an unarmed ship. He had told Kelley as much, but the American just laughed.

'Shit, Zof, some kind of pirate you're making. You tell me a nice way to rob these people, we'll do it. Listen, I spent my life stealing things. Guess what? People don't like it. You go in soft, people start fighting you. They put up resistance. Then you got two choices. Quit, or get the thing back under control with some blood and guts. Now, you want the nasty way, Zof? This way all they get is scared, not hurt. You want people hurt?'

Zof had to control his anger at the American. He didn't like his patronising lessons in crime. But however angry he felt, he had to go along with Kelley. Of course he was right. This was the only way to do it. It didn't mean that Zof had to like it, but, he told himself, this was now his job and, if it was going to be done, it had to be done properly. That's what he would expect of himself. That's what his crew would expect. He had led them into this; he could hardly go soft on them now. Not cool, calm, collected Zof. He hated doing it. But nobody would know. Not yet, anyway.

A tiny orange inflatable containing six men was lowered into the heaving sea from the side-deck of the *Stalin*. The vast bulk of the warship created a lee, and the inflatable skipped across the distance between the ships in minutes. The boarding party clambered up the rope rescue net that Legret had put out; even Pine managed to haul his massive bulk up the netting as though he was 100 lbs lighter. They pushed their way quickly up to the bridge where a very wet Harvey faced a shocked Captain Legret.

'Good morning, Captain. Sorry about all the fuss. Please listen carefully to what I ask you to do. So long as you obey my instructions without question, neither you nor your ship will come to any harm. If you don't, I and my men are quite prepared to use weapons. Mr Charlie here,' said Harvey, referring to Pine by his alias, 'has already served several years in prison for assault.'

Frighten the punters first. Pine smiled happily at Legret, nodded, and hefted the stubby Heckler and Koch sub-machine gun he was carrying.

Legret's heart was thumping. He could feel his dry lips throb with each beat, and his breath was coming in short stabs. Nevertheless he stared Harvey in the eye. 'Sir, I am Captain of this ship. You are committing an act of piracy. I demand you leave immediately.' He actually felt worse for having said it.

'Mr Charlie, would you be so kind?' said Harvey quietly to Pine. Pine walked happily up to Legret, putting the gun into his left hand. He smiled broadly at the Frenchman, who didn't know what to do. Why is this fat man grinning at me like an idiot? While Pine was still smiling, the Frenchman found out. The fat man barely moved, but now there was a sound of air softly sighing out of a body and Legret dropped to the deck, his legs having collapsed under him like a slaughtered cow. Pine walked calmly back to Harvey while Legret lay twisting on the floor, fighting for breath. After a few seconds he was noisily sick.

Mouret and Pascal stood rooted to the spot. Neither of them was capable of uttering a word. Pine's deliberate display of brutal, unhurried force and the smile on his face while he did it had exactly the effect that Harvey wanted. In real life most people never saw violence like that, and it froze the life out of them when it happened in front of their eyes.

Harvey walked over and helped Legret to his feet.

He was wiping snot and vomit from his flour-white face on to the sleeve of his Captain's jacket, and was taking deep, slow breaths. Harvey guided him towards a chair and sat him down heavily. 'My apologies, Captain. You see, we mean exactly what we say. Now if you and your crew follow my instructions to the letter, everything will be fine. How are you feeling?'

Legret stared up at Harvey. Still unable to talk, he shrugged his shoulders in resignation.

'Good. Thank you, Captain. I presume this gentle-man is your first officer?' he asked, indicating Mouret. Legret nodded, passing his sleeve across his mouth again and gagging.

'Your name?'

'Mouret.'

'How many crew do you have, Mouret?'

'Ten.'

'Get them all to the bridge. Now.'

Mouret spoke nervously into the internal phone. 'They are coming. It will take a few moments,' he replied as he put the phone down.

'Fine. I'll wait.' Pine, Harvey and the four Russian sailors positioned themselves in each corner of the bridge. It took five minutes for all the crew to arrive, looking confused and worried. Most of them were Algerians. As each one came on to the bridge, Pine cursorily searched them and pushed them into a corner.

Once all ten were on the bridge, Harvey told the still pale Legret to instruct them to obey orders. Slowly and painfully, Legret did as he was told.

'Good, Captain. Now, you and I will go outside, and Mr Charlie and his colleagues will remain with your crew.' Harvey led Legret out of the bridge, down the ladders and on to the drenched deck. The sun was out now, and the wind had died down to fitful gusts.

Stalin lay ahead of the rolling *Madelaine* like a low grey island.

'Captain, you have on this ship a cargo of gold bars. I imagine they are in a strongroom or safe, which is probably in one of the cargo holds. You have exactly three minutes to take me to that safe and open it. If you have not done so by the time the three minutes are up, I will speak to Mr Charlie on my radio and instruct him to break both the legs of your first officer. If you have still not done so by the end of another minute, Mr Charlie will repeat that act of violence on your young friend. And for every other minute that goes by, the same will happen to another member of your crew. Do you understand?' Harvey was banking on the threat of violence to get Legret to move without thinking about it. Let a victim think and he will start to fight back. Instant, blind obedience was easiest; and for that you needed a very frightened man.

'OK, OK,' murmured Legret. All he wanted now was for these maniacs to get off his ship. He led Harvey down a series of passageways and ladders until they arrived at a locked watertight door. Legret pulled out a set of keys, rapidly opened it, and they entered a small, damp cargo hold that was completely empty apart from a large steel box welded to the hold floor. Legret hurriedly produced another set of keys, selected one, and inserted it into the big keyhole of the steel box. He pushed down on the handle, tugged on the door which opened with a squeal, and stood away to let Harvey see inside. Neatly stacked on top of each other were twenty small wooden boxes, each holding four gold bars. Eighty bars, calculated Harvey quickly, maybe worth ten grand each. Eight million pounds, English money, he thought. He grinned.

He had taken just two minutes and eight seconds to get to the gold.

Harvey called Pine down to the hold on the hand-held VHF. The fat man carefully locked the crew on the bridge, having torn out the cables to the radio equipment, and joined Harvey in the hold together with the two Russians. They worked quickly and efficiently bringing the cases up to the deck. Alongside the *Madelaine*, another, larger boat had joined the inflatable. The cases were lowered carefully into this larger craft, which then powered back across the choppy sea toward the waiting battleship.

Pine and Russians got back into the inflatable.

'Goodbye, Captain. And thanks,' said Harvey cheerily as he waved farewell to an angry Legret and disappeared down the boarding ladder. Legret leaned against the deckhouse bulkhead as he watched the inflatable disappear across the chop. His stomach was sending waves of pain around his body and he still felt sick; but above all he felt an overwhelming fury at the calm and precise assault on his ship and his cargo.

The whole robbery had taken under one hour; it had netted Harvey and the crew of the *Stalin* something in the region of $12 million. Piracy was clearly a paying proposition, thought Harvey as the spray continued to drench him. And this was just the start. He had to admit, the thing was going much better than he had thought it would when Kelley first suggested the idea so many months back. He had thought Kelley was mad when he came up with it, but the American seemed determined.

Now, with the first of the gold safely off the target ship, what could go wrong?

As if to spoil his first flush of success, the image of Kelley driving past him in the darkness of Vladivostok suddenly swam back into view. Shit. So, what the hell was he up to? The inflatable crashed through a rogue wave and Harvey ducked a cascade of spray, blinding him with warm salty water. It was time to see Kelley, just as soon as he could. Harvey was nervous about tackling the American. But now, with a boat full of gold, his confidence was quickly rising.

Zof felt a powerful sense of relief, too. It had seemed easier than he thought. The robbery had happened, the crew was back with the proceeds and nobody appeared to be hurt. So far, so good. They were now somewhat richer than when they started. Zof knew his crew would be feeling this even more powerfully than he was, and it gave him confidence. So, Yakov, your career as a pirate has now officially started. You are a full-time criminal, now to be hunted on the high seas for ever, but you're still here and you're still breathing and you're still in command. It works, he told himself, not without some amazement: it really does work.

*

The rough weather of the last few hours had taken its toll on the wealthy widows sailing on the *Ocean Queen*. Of the eleven invited to dine that evening with the Captain, three had already called off formally, and Blake was surprised to see the five who had finally made it. Although he'd missed the worst of the weather by re-routing his course, it was still heavier than he would have liked. He had no option with his new course but to take a beam sea, and even with the stabilisers out the ship had developed a steady, slow side-to-side roll which, although gentle, was just the sort of regular movement to set off everyone's stomach.

'And how are you enjoying our little storm?' asked Captain Blake, turning away from a woman with the fixed smirk of someone having recently enjoyed a facelift and attempting to engage a rather attractive forty-something-year-old with black hair.

'A bit rough, Captain. But it doesn't appear to have made much difference to the ship. We seem to be maintaining speed,' said the woman, who thoroughly disliked the Captain's patronising way. A senior executive of a large oil company who was only going by *Ocean Queen* because a friend had persuaded her, she was not exactly enjoying the experience, and Blake's wealthy-widow bedside manner didn't do much for her.

Blake was no fool; he caught the edge in her voice right away and stopped playing the bluff old sea captain. 'Well, the storm is a bit worse than I expected, to be honest. I think we might be a bit late in Hong Kong. I've been trying to skirt our way around a full-blown typhoon to the north of us, so I think we'll be tying up a few hours behind schedule.'

The woman was on a tight schedule and needed to make Hong Kong on time. 'A typhoon? I hope it doesn't make us too late, Captain?' she replied.

'Well, we had to make quite a detour, I'm afraid. It would have been very uncomfortable otherwise. We went a couple of hundred miles off course to make sure we missed the worst of it. But we put on a bit of extra power and we'll reach Hong Kong with no trouble. Maybe just a few hours late, nothing to worry about.'

'Off course? By very much?' demanded the woman, still thinking about her schedule.

'Quite a way,' laughed Blake, beaming. 'We're miles from where we would have been. Otherwise we'd be bouncing around like a cork in a bottle. Now, that really would have put everyone off their dinners, eh ladies?' He resumed his professional attentions to the rest of the party. The sun-tanned, skin-stretched women on the table giggled like schoolgirls, and the dark-haired woman scowled. Her temper was far from improved by the slow, methodical rocking of the ship. If she missed her appointment, she'd sue.

But as far as Blake was concerned, so long as the *Ocean Queen* docked within a few hours of the appointed time, no one would mind that the ship was several hundred miles away from the position she should have been in. No one, that is, except Yakov Zof.

*

Harvey had planned to get hold of Kelley the moment he returned to the ship. Somehow, in the excitement of unloading the gold, the confrontation lost its appeal. Zof's crew gathered around to watch the boxes come on board.

'How much?' said one young man to an older officer, awe in his eyes.

'Millions, boy, millions,' replied the older man, smiling. This really was going to work.

And then, when the gold had been safely stowed, Zof was on deck again getting his crew back to work. The next target was waiting, he shouted. Good work. No time to waste. Back to your jobs. The great ship got down to business once more, and Harvey had to bide his time.

It was nearly three hours after the *Ocean Queen* failed to show up where she should have been that they started to worry. In fact, as far as Kelley was concerned, there was now some cause for panic. He wanted to know where the fuck the ship had gone and had Zof screwed it all up? Zof re-checked his calculations. Not a chance. According to Price's information, they should have seen the big liner well before now. There wasn't even a glimmer on the radar screen.

Kelley was agitated. Harvey wanted to know what the big deal was. The *Ocean Queen* had to be around somewhere. What the hell was the big hurry? It was something else he found strange. If it took too long to reach her, Kelley patiently explained, Legret would have had ample time to reach land and to contact the authorities, who in turn would be able to warn the liner. Legret knew the rough position of the *Stalin*, too. The *Ocean Queen* would be able to stay out of their way, and who knows what the authorities would then throw at them? They couldn't afford the delay, Kelley said. Now Harvey understood. He and Zof went to the chart table to figure out what had happened.

It was Zof who reasoned it through. 'Listen to me, Harvey. If you were the Captain of a big cruise ship and you heard about a typhoon, you'd do one of two things, right?' argued Zof.

Harvey wasn't following.

'I'll tell you. You could stay in port. This is a bad idea: your passengers will eat and drink themselves silly and this costs you a fortune. Or you could carry on. The problem is your passengers now spend the next five hours throwing up over the guard-rails. This does not do the reputation of your fine ship a lot of good either. So you skirt your way around the edge. You stay as best you can out of the storm, but still keeping pretty near to time. Now, if I was Captain of the *Ocean Queen*, look – here's where I would be going,' and Zof traced a line well to the south that was hundreds of miles away from where they were heading.

'That's miles off, Zof. Are you sure?' Harvey asked.

'Sure? You always want certainties, my friend. No, I'm not sure. All I can say is that if it was me, that's what I would have done.'

'We'll never get there in time.'

'No problem. Look. If we could sustain thirty knots, we would be there in thirty hours. That would give the Frenchman only five or six hours to make a port, maybe Macao, at the very outside. We'll have intercepted and be on our way just as he's telling his story to anyone he can find to listen,' said Zof. He'd already ordered the ship to increase its revolutions so as to gain more speed and narrow the gap between the two ships. Kishkov, down in the engine room, was already watching the steam pressure rising on the boilers and wondering if the fifty-year-old system would stand the extra strain. He was giving Zhadanov another headache, too.

Harvey explained the idea to Kelley, who swore loudly but then began to calm down. All of them knew that either they went for the *Ocean Queen* as quickly as possible or got out now. It had to be worth a try. Even if Legret contacted the authorities quickly, Kelley knew the reaction of the police would be to spend their time asking detailed questions first, which of course gave the bad guys plenty of time to get away.

Then what would happen? The coast stations would put out a warning, of course, but if you were the Captain of a ship and heard that a small French freighter had been robbed by a Second World War battleship, what would your reaction be? Kelley suggested that most of them would believe that the Frenchman had done it himself. It didn't seem unreasonable.

The turbines whined and the shafts shuddered as the great ship began to pick up speed. The seas were now dropping as they moved nearer and nearer the eye. Soon the wind and the seas would pick up again as the trailing edge of the typhoon struck; but at 30 knots or more, the ship would cleave through the storm waves as though they were just ripples on a pond.

Kelley had retired to his cabin. He lay on his bunk with a bottle of Scotch near to hand, and thought the thing through very carefully. Now they would be well out of the position he had assumed they would be in, which meant that the *Jackson* would be many miles further away than he wanted. He needed twenty-four hours clear with the *Ocean Queen,* but with the *Jackson* being – as he thought – so far away, he'd have to wait maybe days for the damn ship to turn up. It was a wait he couldn't afford. So, when the *Ocean Queen* put out the distress call, he needed to make sure the *Jackson* didn't just turn around and sail to the *Ocean Queen's* position; now he needed them to break their necks to get there. He didn't have the time to hang around. The hold-up needed some extra drama to turn *Ocean Queen's* current predicament as a ship just having been robbed into a vessel suffering a full-scale emergency. And then an idea occurred to him: one that would bring the Americans running to the rescue of their ship. He smiled, as he thought about it some more and wondered if it would work. He'd need to get Harvey and Zof on side. And on top of that he'd have to get hold of Harvey, when he had the chance, to give him the full story. Frankly, the Englishman still worried him. He had a feeling that he was going to be a problem when the time came. Maybe Tariq had been right all along.

*

Up from the south the *Jackson* was steaming steadily towards the edge of the typhoon, but was still hundreds of miles off. Slatter was on the bridge when the warning came through; Crawford had gone to his cabin. He decided to call the old man up just in case. He hoped he was asleep when he punched the dial to connect him to his cabin.

'Crawford here,' said Crawford instantly. He rarely napped, especially when Slatter had command of his ship. It made him uneasy.

'Sorry to disturb you, sir. Typhoon warning to the north. Still twelve hours away, but I thought you'd like to know,' said Slatter.

'Thank you. Where's the storm centre?'

Slatter told him. It was still nearly 500 miles away. Crawford was in no hurry. Their well-publicised schedule meant that they weren't due in Hong Kong for a week. He was supposed to treat his new ship gently; iron out the bugs. He told Slatter to slow down to around ten knots. That way, the storm would be long gone before they got there.

And in the normal course of events, the *Ocean Queen* would have been hundreds of miles away.

But Blake had altered course. And now Crawford was slowing down. Kelley's plan was to have at least twenty-four hours clear with the *Ocean Queen* before the *Jackson* could get anywhere near. He didn't know it, but his plan wasn't going to work. The *Ocean Queen* and the *Jackson* were slowly closing on each other. Zof's guess about the new course of the *Ocean Queen* was right; the problem was that the *Jackson* would by then be much too close for comfort.

*

Legret was still feeling a dull pain where Pine had punched him. He was in a dimly lit storeroom below the bridge, and his anger began to subside slightly as the power indicator light on the MF radio lit up. It was the extra set that Lloyd's insisted on as part of the bullion contract. He was surprised that the pirates hadn't known about it; they seemed to have so much other inside information. But that was the least of his troubles. He'd never used the set before and didn't have the slightest idea how it worked. He'd had to ask Pascal down to get it working for him.

It had taken Pascal just moments to turn the set on

and tune it to the international distress frequency. The MF set had a much longer range than the VHF. Legret picked up the handset, and soon his distress call was being picked up by several ships, several ground stations and a small, gold-foil-covered satellite in high geo-stationary orbit 24,000 miles above the Equator.

12

Cheltenham, a peaceful English country town sleeping timelessly in the gentle hills of the Cotswolds, has several modest claims to fame. Middle-class girls of aspiring families go to be educated at the genteel, ladies-only college. The older generation, just as middle class, retreat from the noise of industrial Birmingham to retire to faded but still elegant Regency town houses. And once a year, when the daffodils nod in the manicured front gardens, 100,000 heavy-drinking Irishmen arrive from the ferry to spend three days with the blue-bloods at one of English horse-racing's greatest festivals.

That's what the tourist brochure mentions. What it doesn't say is that Cheltenham is also home to the greatest concentration of spies in Western Europe.

Just outside the historic town centre, on an anonymous site off the busy ring road, lies a jumble of buildings and huts that looks like an out-of-town industrial estate that's seen better days. Its studied ordinariness is given away on a closer look: razor-wire coils looped on top of a twelve-foot-high fence; an unusually large number of bored security guards; and, only just visible from the ring road behind a three-storey brick and glass office block, a bristling collection of large and small satellite dishes and aerials, pointing in every direction, up and down, and one huge one facing directly upwards like a monstrous birdbath.

This is the Government Communications Headquarters, GCHQ, the eavesdropping centre for most of the Western world. Not a fax, phone call, telex, data link, radio or TV transmission is sent without someone at GCHQ listening carefully to it. Someone. Or more usually, something.

Spies in the electronic age rarely indulge in cloak-and-dagger theatricals. Most of them aren't even inside the country they're supposed to be spying on. The typical British spies are not glamorous James Bond types, but poorly paid civil servants more interested in the clerical grade they will achieve in their next promotion than the temperature of a Martini. They live for the most part in pleasant Cotswold stone semi-detached houses on small estates and go shopping at the local supermarket on Saturday. Their daily work consists of ensuring that the real spies, the giant computers which fill locked and guarded rooms in the anonymous GCHQ buildings, have done their jobs properly. This necessitates the filling in of a bewilderingly large number of forms, either to tell the computers what to do next or to report to someone, somewhere, what the computers have discovered. Most of it is meaningless routine.

So it was that in Maureen Sweeney's life there were no great secrets or espionage treasures. Even if there were, she would never be able to recognise one. Her daily task as one of the thousands of civil servants at GCHQ was to collate on to a form the number of occurrences of certain words that the computers, in listening to the airwaves and phone lines, detected. She did this by scrolling through a computer screen and copying down the information by hand. A project to do this by computer had come to grief last year when the software, two years late, had completely failed to work in practice. For now, the daily task continued.

Her screen was connected to a large IBM 3090 mainframe computer, a machine so vast it was plumbed into a water supply to cool the endless racks of microprocessors. The computer was cumbersome and rated by technical people as very old-fashioned. Ageing as it was, it still had one huge advantage: the machine could process a huge amount of simple data extraordinarily quickly. As a result of this, for the last seven years it had been given a simple task.

It listened ...

Through the forest of dishes and aerials outside, it sampled the frequencies of satellites and radio stations all over the world. It listened to every single telephone call that was sent through satellites. It listened to every radio station, from South London mini-cabs to supposedly secure Pentagon frequencies. It was connected via British Telecom into every telephone exchange in the country. It was hooked into every mobile telephone cellular station. And, by a special arrangement with the Americans, it was connected to just about every telephone line and radio frequency in America too. When somebody, some-where, made a call, the IBM machine would be listening to that call, however secure the caller imagined the conversation to be.

With that volume of traffic, it was impossible for even that mighty computer to listen in detail. Instead, it simply waited until certain words were used. Once it heard such a word, it automatically recorded the whole message and at the end of its working day reported the fact to Maureen Sweeney, who in turn drew up the daily KO (keyword occurrence) report which was sent somewhere that she didn't even know about. She had no idea what the actual keywords were

– she used numbers instead; whoever the report went to had their own keys to decipher it.

The selected keywords were an odd collection, numbering several thousand. They included the obvious, like names of Government ministers, but also added their known nicknames as well, just in case a bit of scandal was hitting the airwaves. They included a variety of words to do with terrorism and organised crime, plus a good handful of scientific words. There were financial words, too, as Governments took an increasing interest in the activity of speculators. Sometimes the Bank of England would be informed that the pound was about to come under pressure and so could intervene early on in the process. They never knew quite where the information came from, but it was always reliable.

That day, among the millions of words it processed at lightning speed, the IBM machine had heard two words it had been told to take an interest in. 'Pirate' had been on the system for some time: it was a developing problem in Asia and in the Caribbean. The other keyword was 'Battleship', which had been used for many years to turn on the computer to eavesdrop on the conversations of any passing naval traffic. It was a rarely used word these days, but nobody had got round to cleaning it off the system.

Legret had used his hidden MF radio to send two other messages besides his general distress call. First, he raised the mainland Chinese coastguard and with some difficulty got them to understand what had happened. His French accent didn't help their limited understanding of English. And just as Kelley had thought, they disbelieved him anyway. Nevertheless, he extracted a promise from them that they'd relay the message to the Hong Kong and Macao authorities. Then he sent a second message, this time to Lloyd's in

London employing a pre-agreed low-level word code for security. He regretted to inform them that their gold was now aboard a pirate battleship, and was this covered by the insurance? If the bloody Chinese wouldn't take him seriously, he was damn sure the Lloyd's people would.

Unknown to Legret, all of his messages would be taken seriously. When he was painfully explaining to the Chinese about the robbery, the IBM machine at Cheltenham was sniffing the oriental airwaves for anything of interest when the word 'Piracy' caught its attention. In a fraction of a second it plucked the signal out of the ether and sent the message to one of its banks of discs for later analysis. Seconds later it heard another keyword, 'Battleship', and so recorded the message again. Each word had a value. 'Battleship' didn't rate highly, mainly because it was so old. 'Piracy' had a higher value, but still was not enough to set off any alarm bells.

The machine was more interested in the second, supposedly private, message it picked up from the *Madelaine*. Lloyd's commercial code had long since been broken; it took one of GCHQ's less talented code-breakers a spare afternoon. Even so, the computer was programmed to give any such coded message a high priority – even if the keywords were themselves not very interesting. On the simple basis that anything in code was bound to be more interesting just because somebody wanted to keep it secret, it was worth more points on the intelligence scale of things. The machine decoded the message as it went, and the fact that the keywords then appeared in the decoded message made them doubly interesting. The machine still didn't set off any bells, but gave Legret's second transmission a score that suggested somebody ought to take a look at it.

As Maureen Sweeney idly noted towards the end of the day when she compiled the report, the combined value of the two messages pushed them towards the top of her list for that day by quite a wide margin. They were only numbers to her, but a high score like that was just a little bit out of the ordinary. As she had been instructed, she told the computer to print off the messages for circulation to those who were cleared to get them. Her work was then duly complete. She placed the report in her 'out' tray, put on her coat and caught the bus home in time to catch *Eastenders*. She had no idea of the train of events that she had unwittingly set off.

*

In spite of the priority it had received, it was still another twelve hours before anyone took any notice; and even then it wouldn't have happened if Lindsey McEwan, still stationed at Northwood, hadn't had other reasons for finding the message startling.

Each morning he arrived just before eight, reviewed the intelligence reports which had never contained anything even remotely interesting, scribbled a note to his Admiral digesting the reports, and then spent the rest of the day trying to find something useful to do. He had coped with this for several months and was seriously thinking of packing it all in. The truth was, the defence cuts of the last few years had left more officers than there were ships to use them on. He'd be lucky, he thought, if he ever saw a boat bigger than his Mirror dinghy again.

As usual that morning, he threw his coat on to a small, worn leather sofa, slumped down in the uncomfortable chair and picked up the flimsies that were the intelligence reports. He scanned quickly over the material and immediately sat bolt upright.

What made the hair at the back of his neck rise was the conversation he'd had with Stanley Dalby from Vauxhall two months ago. That crazy story about the *Stalin*. Nobody was interested in it then, and McEwan was forced to let it drop.

Legret's first message to the Chinese coastguard caught his eye first:

This is the French freighter *Madelaine*. I am reporting an attack by pirates 1100 hours today. The pirates were from large old-fashioned Russian battleship, identity unknown. Position 132.10.29E, 23.14.04N. A valuable cargo was stolen. I am now heading for the coast. Can you please send assistance once my ship is in helicopter range. I have requested any vessel in the area to maintain watch and assist.

McEwan ignored the banter between the Frenchman and the Chinese coastguard. Even the computer transcription – GCHQ had long ago cracked the problem of getting computers to write down speech, but insisted it remained a secret – couldn't follow half the rest of the conversation. He checked the time when the message was sent: it was now about eighteen hours ago.

The next flimsy was more interesting still. It was Legret's secret message to Lloyds. Decoded, it read:

Madelaine attacked by pirates. Ship was very large old battleship, believed Russian. Pirates boarded and knew of gold. All boxes removed. No other interest. Am contacting nearest coastguard. Expect to make HK about 24 hours. Arrange to meet.

He scanned the rest of the rubbish and pushed it to a corner of his desk. Nothing was half so interesting as this little story. What on earth was an old Russian battleship doing out on the South China Sea? Was it Dalby's strange tale about the *Stalin*? Was it a crew mutiny? At last, something interesting was happening in Lindsay McEwan's life. He carefully placed the two flimsies in a fresh buff folder, then got on the phone and demanded to see the old man within the hour. The Admiral's secretary was a fussy little officer called Owl who wanted to know what was so urgent that it couldn't wait. McEwan refused to tell him, but promised personally to come over and strangle the man unless he got his appointment. Owl got him into the Admiral's diary in exactly 58 minutes' time.

*

The *Stalin* was thundering through the slowly calming seas westwards, towards Hong Kong and the steadily cruising *Ocean Queen*, some 150 miles further away. Deep in the engine room, Kishkov watched the steam pressure rising. The old pipes were still holding. At 30 knots he smiled to himself and allowed the engine-room crew to increase pressure even more. Slowly the needles on the pressure gauges crept upwards and the great turbines spun even faster. The ship's log indicated 34 knots when the needles came uncomfortably close to the red line: 75,000 tons of ship was now travelling at nearly 40 miles an hour.

The *Madelaine* was well away, far over the horizon, steaming as quickly as she could towards the mainland. *Stalin* had left her hundreds of miles behind. In around three hours, if Zof was right in his guess about the cruise ship's captain, they would see the *Ocean Queen* on the horizon. Zof scanned the horizon through the streaming bridge windows with a pair of battered Japanese binoculars, then walked to the radar set, then back to the bridge window again. The distant horizon was empty. He was the kind of man who made clear, firm decisions in public and then spent the rest of the time worrying in private if he'd really done the right thing. Of course, he kept telling himself, even if he was right, he still wouldn't see the ship, not for a while yet. The *Ocean Queen's* Captain, surely, would have the sense to alter course as Zof expected him to. Surely...

He had convinced himself that he was right. He kept telling himself he was. If he was wrong, for all he knew he could be heading in the opposite bloody direction. Zof kept his eyes fixed to the binoculars and carried on confidently scanning the horizon. But both the distant horizon and the radar screen remained obstinately blank.

*

On the *Ocean Queen's* bridge, Blake was still puzzling over a message from the Hong Kong coastguard relating the strange tale of the *Madelaine* when Attwood, the radio officer, called him from the radio room.

'Captain, we've received a coded message from Lloyd's. Will you come down for it?'

Blake went down to the radio room where Goodall, the purser, met him. Between them they were the only people who could de-code the telegram.

Once the message was rendered into plain language, Blake looked more concerned at the *Madelaine's* story. It confirmed the robbery but this time mentioned the gold, which Legret's public message had remained silent about it. It warned Blake that it looked as though the pirate ship had inside information – but failed, of course, to mention Price's disappearance. The message went on to say that if they knew about the gold on the *Madelaine* they almost certainly knew about the even more valuable shipment on the *Ocean Queen*. It warned Blake to be careful. The two men looked concerned and went back to the bridge and to the chart table. Blake checked back over the timings and the positions.

'It looks a long way off, Captain,' commented Goodall once the positions had been plotted.

Blake looked at the distance between his current position and the *Madelaine*'s at the time of the hold-up. It was close, but nowhere near close enough for any ship, surely, to be able to close the gap. Not before they made the protection of the territorial waters of Hong Kong, anyway. On top of which, *Ocean Queen* was well off her scheduled position: if the pirate ship had inside knowledge about her position, they'd be over 100 miles further to the north. There was over 150 miles separating the two positions.

'What's an old ship like that going to do? Fifteen knots top?' Blake asked Goodall, somewhat rhetorically. 'Say twenty knots worst case. That gives us seven hours to get to somewhere near HK. If we pile it on we should be there in six or seven easily', he continued, still staring at the two small pencil circles that he had drawn on the chart to indicate the position of the two ships.

'I can't imagine it doing twenty knots, Captain', said Goodall.

'Me neither. Anyway, we'll pile it on, Goodall, just in case. We'll be in Hong Kong long before anything could happen. Cable Lloyds, would you?' They turned the light off over the chart table and Goodall went off to tell the insurers, while Blake went back to the bridge and ordered the engine room to increase revolutions to the maximum. Bugger the fuel, he thought.

Stalin, crashing urgently through the seas with her machinery shrieking, was now a little over 120 miles away, just three hours distant. Although he wasn't certain of it, Zof had convinced himself that the course he was following in his mind's eye was a more or less direct line to the *Ocean Queen*.

What he didn't know, and neither did Kelley, was that if he continued that line southward by several hundred miles, it would meet with the *Jackson*, lazily cruising in the still calm waters beyond the effects of the typhoon but slowly closing the gap hour after hour. The drama of the pirate raid on the *Madelaine* hadn't reached the *Jackson*; they only monitored military channels unless they were within 100 miles of the coast, and nothing, yet, had hit them.

*

After McEwan had booked his appointment, he called through to GCHQ. It took him some time to get hold of somebody who could do what he wanted. After the fifth transfer he spoke to a supervisor. By now he was irritated. 'I want two keywords put on a higher priority. "Pirate" and "Battleship". Anything pops up, I want reports immediately. Can you do that?'

'I should think so, sir. No trouble. It will take about a week. Is that OK?'

'A week is hopeless. This is urgent, man. I want it done within the next five minutes.'

'I'll need proper authorisation, sir. Grade 2 or above,' said the man apologetically. Grade 2 meant Admirals, amongst others.

He'd need some help. 'I'll be back,' said McEwan threateningly.

'Yes, sir,' replied the smug voice. Not even McEwan, who was used to getting his own way in most things, could buck the system. He slammed the phone down and called Owl. He told Owl, who was easily scared, exactly what he wanted done. The man sounded worried. McEwan explained that he was about to see Maddox and he would tell him that Owl had held up vital intelligence. He gave him five minutes. Six minutes later GCHQ called him with a screen reference number for the secure e-mail network. He called it up, smiled to himself, and printed it off just as Rear-Admiral Charlie Maddox, head of Naval Intelligence, was buzzing through to McEwan that he was ready to see him.

'OK, McEwan, what's the fuss?' asked Maddox once McEwan had settled into the big armchair in front of the antique desk.

'Well, it's hard to say, sir, really. Strange sort of story. These are intercepts from yesterday about a French ship off HK getting raided by pirates.' He handed the buff folder across to Maddox who slowly read through the first message.

'Happens every day out there. Hardly headline stuff, McEwan.'

'Yes, sir, but this one was carrying gold bullion, and the pirates appeared to be from an old Russian battleship. The second message is also rather interesting. It was sent in commercial code to Lloyd's of London.'

Maddox turned the flimsy over to read the second message. His bushy eyebrows raised themselves very slightly as he read the brief document. 'What sort of battleship? Do you have a name?' he asked McEwan, looking directly at him very suddenly.

McEwan almost blushed. He had mentioned the *Stalin* report to Maddox two months ago, and Maddox had politely thrown him out of his office. He hated to remind the Admiral, so he didn't.

'Don't yet know, sir', responded McEwan diplomatically.

'Then these messages came through just now,' as he handed over the message that had just arrived, Lloyds' warning to Blake. 'Apparently *Ocean Queen* is close by with a similar cargo of gold. Lloyd's have warned them to be careful. They think the pirates have inside knowledge somehow, and they suspect *Ocean Queen* might be a target.'

'*Ocean Queen*?'

'A new cruise liner sir. Big one. British crew. American-owned. Left Southampton a few weeks back. Lloyd's use the scheduled liners for gold shipments. Supposed to be safer than aircraft. Full of rich widows and what-have-you. Quite a few hundred of them.'

'Good lord.'

'Yes, sir. That was my reaction, too.'

'Where's *Ocean Queen* now?'

'I've plotted it here. You can see that *Ocean Queen* is well away from the French ship's reported position. She'll be in HK long before the ship that got the Frenchman could get anywhere near her.'

'But you don't know what sort of battleship?'

'Not yet. The message don't give a name. I've got some contacts in HK intelligence. I'll get them to have a chat with the Frenchman.'

'Well, do it quickly, McEwan. We could have a major problem here.'

'How so, sir? Something would have to be bloody fast to catch the *Ocean Queen* before it made HK.'

Now it was Maddox's turn to look sheepish. 'That's the problem, McEwan. Three weeks ago Russian Naval Intelligence reported the *Stalin* had disappeared. Your little story a while back was not nonsense after all. Bloody great ship. You should know it, McEwan, you're supposed to be the expert on these things, I hear. By all accounts it was, and still is, the biggest warship ever built: 75,000 tons, bloody big guns and armoured to the tops. Oh, and about the fastest, too. 35 knots top whack.'

So. There was the confirmation. It really was the *Stalin*, out raiding at sea, after all these years.

'Could this be the ship, McEwan? The damn thing is supposed to be fifty years old. I can't imagine how they got it running again.'

'I suppose it's possible, sir. The Americans hung on to their *Iowa*-class battleships which were built at the same time. They're still in good working order. I heard that *Stalin* was well looked after, too. The story that nobody wanted to break up a ship with Joe Stalin's name on it, at least not when he was alive. It was kept in service as a static training ship. If it was well looked after, it wouldn't take that much work to get it going.'

'How well do you know this ship, McEwan?'

'She was one of several that I studied, sir. I mean, I've never seen her and the commies were pretty secretive about it. Why?'

'Might prove useful, McEwan. Now, if it is this ship, we'd better get hold of the *Ocean Queen* and get some warning to her. Trouble is there's bugger all we can do. I shouldn't think we've got much down that way. What flag is *Ocean Queen* under?'

'Liberia. But she's owned by some bunch in Chicago and she's crewed by Brits. I suppose everyone's going to be interested in her.'

'Sounds that way. I'll have to get Whitehall to let me talk to Ray Bell at the Pentagon. I should think Vauxhall Cross has sent Langley the story anyway. And I suppose Whitehall will want them to run the show, as usual. In any event, maybe I can prevail on our lords and masters to let you in there somehow, McEwan. There can't be many people who know much about these old ships, after all. Besides, we've got some of our people on board, haven't we? We need to wave the flag and all that. I'll see if we can get you in as liaison. Impress them with what you know. Can you do that? Keep your pyjamas packed. Oh, and you'd better let your chums in Hong Kong know what's up. Get them to talk to the *Ocean Queen* and warn them. Tell them we're trying to drum up some help. That's all. Oh, by the way?'

'Yes, sir?'

'Sorry. Should have listened.'

'Thank you, sir,' said McEwan as Maddox was picking up the phone to talk to his political masters. Within several hours the ministry had spoken to Downing Street, Downing Street had spoken to Grosvenor Square, Washington had considered, and sent back the reply that thanked them for the information and said they'd be happy to allow Maddox to speak directly to Ray Bell at the Pentagon – who, they made clear, was now in charge of the whole thing. They had taken over the developing operation without even blinking.

As he left Maddox's office, McEwan walked thoughtfully back to his own sparse room. He could have let himself get angry at his superior's decision to ignore the original report, but even he had thought it a strange story at the time and didn't really push it. When he got back to his desk, he let Hong Kong know the full story and asked them to contact the *Ocean Queen* direct.

Then he decided to call Dalby over at Vauxhall.

'Stanley, how are you, old son?' asked McEwan in his friendliest tones.

'Terrific, McEwan. What do you want? You only use that tone of voice when you need something.'

'Let me buy you a decent lunch. How about Sheekey's? Today?' McEwan knew the call was monitored and made sure he didn't say what he was after. He knew Dalby would get the message, just by the urgency of the request.

'OK. Today. But you're paying,' replied Dalby, sounding resigned.

'See you at one.'

They met at a small table at the restaurant, hidden down a small alley off the Charing Cross Road. McEwan was eager, Dalby restrained.

'So? How's the spy world these days?' asked McEwan once they'd started on a bottle of Sancerre.

'Still in business, McEwan, for Christ's sake. What's the deal?' asked Dalby testily.

'You remember that story you wanted to sell me a couple of months back? About the old Russian battleship?'

'Ah, that story. It's come alive, then. Knew it would.'

'Can you give me a bit more?'

'More? As I recall, you were bloody sniffy about it at the time. Thought you'd like the tale. Heard no more.'

'Sorry. Didn't seem very big at the time. I mean, I tried the old man but he didn't want to buy it either. Look, we all make mistakes, for heaven's sake.'

'Sure, no problem. We find out, tell you boys, get ignored. No skin off my nose, old son. Cheers.'

McEwan waited while he put down his glass. 'OK. I'm grovelling. Now, unless you want to pick up the bill, would you mind being so very kind and telling me the whole story? All the details this time?'

Dalby looked mournful. He was enjoying McEwan's discomfort.

'So?' asked McEwan again. Dalby was pushing his luck.

'So. When was it? A couple of months ago or so? Anyway, our Consul in Vladivostok put us in touch with a guy called Zof, Feliks Zof. He'd been hammering on the American Consul's door with a story about some people who wanted to steal a big ship. This character is well known in the town as a drunk, a crook, a drug-dealer and various other kinds of shit. He seems to make a habit of selling so-called intelligence so anyone who'll buy it. Not to put too fine a point on it, he's becoming something of a debased currency so the Yanks told him to fuck off.'

'Brilliant.'

'Come on, McEwan. It's hardly the most reliable source, is it? Anyway, this Zof charges in to see our man and tells him the full story. Some foreigners, no names, are offering silly money to get *Stalin* back into commission. He reckons his brother, name of Yakov, who is a shit-hot sea Captain etcetera etcetera, goes for the deal. Then they get hold of some old guy, Kishkov, who was supposed to have designed the thing in the first place. This was the gist of the story. Cough up ten grand in dollar bills and the rest is all yours.'

'Then what?'

'What do you think? Some drunk asks for ten grand for some crazy story about old men and ships? What would you do? We told him to fuck off as well.'

'No follow-up? No questions?'

'Not much. Offered him five hundred and he gave us a bit more.'

'I didn't see any more reports.'

'Sorry, McEwan. That was it. Hardly worth circulating, but I gave you the gist of it when I called you, just the story.'

'What happened?'

'We heard a couple of days after that Feliks' body had been washed up on a beach south of the city. Shot in the head. Probably some gangland killing or other, but it makes you think, doesn't it? Maybe there was something to it after all,' said Dalby mournfully. Then, to McEwan's surprise, he rooted around in a document case and produced a sheet of paper that contained the original cable which the Consul in Vladivostok had sent together with the brief follow-up, all five hundred dollars worth. It wasn't as Dalby had said, much, but it added a little. He handed it over to McEwan, who scanned it quickly. It gave a little information on the two Russians. And the people who wanted the ship in the first place.

McEwan was surprised that Dalby had thought to bring the cable with him. 'How come you knew that I was going to ask you this, anyway?' he asked.

'We're not stupid, McEwan. The whole bloody thing blew up this morning with some Cheltenham stuff coming through and your man Maddox yelling blue murder at the boss for not picking it up, closely followed by loud noises from across the water. I just got back from the bollocking when you called. I didn't think you wanted to talk to me about football,' said Dalby, still looking mournful.

McEwan ignored Dalby's explanation and re-read the signal. It mentioned Zof and Kishkov, and Kelley and Harvey. 'Zof I've never heard of. But Kishkov I have. I would have thought he was dead by now. Well, well,' and they ordered the second bottle and talked about Julie, a well-known – in more ways than one – young lady who made herself very popular during their last year at Cambridge.

While McEwan was lunching, Maddox had untangled the red tape and finally been allowed to talk directly to Chief of Naval Operations Ray Bell, the man in the Pentagon who ran the US Navy. Maddox desperately wanted McEwan in there to keep an eye on things, but knew better than to do it directly. He simply told the story, told him about the liner, gave him enough to scare the shit out of him about the *Stalin*, and asked if he could think of anything. Bell listened carefully, and Maddox could tell that he thought somebody was joking. But he promised to look into it urgently. Maddox hung up the secure link. He knew the Americans well, he respected their professionalism and their skills. Right now, Bell would be talking to his intelligence people. And if McEwan was right, Bell would find out soon enough that they knew just about nothing about the *Stalin*; while Maddox had been careful to ensure that Bell understood that McEwan knew everything.

Bell, just as Maddox had thought, managed to find out virtually nothing about the story. But Langley had reported the robbery separately, via their own monitoring, and within half an hour Bell had talked to Billy Ross, Chairman of the Joint Chiefs, and Ross had agreed to help out. The Air Force offered a couple of planes out of Futenma on Okinawa to go take a look. Bell also asked his own staff to send the nearest warship. It was Crawford, on the *Jackson*, who minutes later received the coded message.

*

Half an hour after McEwan had called Hong Kong, Blake was called again by Attwood from the radio room.

'I've got the HK Naval Assistant on the radio. He needs to talk to you urgently and in private,' said Attwood softly over the internal phone. Blake came down from the bridge and picked up the handset of the satellite-linked radio. The line kept fading so Blake resorted to shouting, though it made no difference.

'Captain Blake, Chisholm here, sir. I'm on the naval intelligence staff at the Hong Kong embassy. Call your head office if you need confirmation. It will take an hour to go through the process and this is an urgent call, but it's up to you.'

'Yes, Mr Chisholm. What can I do for you?'

'Thank you, Captain. I understand you had a message recently about some gold pirates? From Lloyd's?'

'Now how the bloody hell did you know about that?'

'Sorry, Captain. Let's just say that it came to our attention. You know how these things are, sir, I'm sure.'

'Don't worry, Chisholm. What's up?'

'What's up is that we're pretty sure these pirates are after you.'

'That's what we were told. We've got it under control, Chisholm. We're well away from the reported position and we'll be making HK pretty soon. They're too far away to catch up.'

'That's the problem, Captain. We think there's a risk they may be able to catch you up. We understand that the pirate ship is a very fast old Russian battleship called *Stalin* that was stolen about three weeks ago. It can do about 35 knots – just about the fastest big ship in the world, by all accounts. They could be catching up, you see. That's what we wanted to tell you.'

Blake did a rapid calculation in his head and looked at his watch. He swore under his breath. If Chisholm was right, the pirates could be as close as an hour away. He worked it out again and came up with exactly the same answer. Even though he had increased speed to his maximum 28 knots, he would still be miles away from Hong Kong – around 200 miles at least.

'Good God, man, they might be just an hour away,' he said eventually.

'That's what we calculated, too, Captain.'

'Well, Chisholm. Looks like you're going to need to get us some protection out here. I've got a lot of people on this ship.'

'Yes, Captain. Unfortunately, we don't have anything even close.'

'Nothing?' shouted Blake, incredulously. 'Not even in HK?'

'Sorry, Captain. We had HMS *Cardiff* in here yesterday, but she sailed off southwards. She's over a day away from you by now. Apart from that the cupboard is bare, I'm afraid. The Chinese don't let us have too many warships around these days, you see.'

'Well, Chisholm, you're going to have to think of something.'

'We're on the case, Captain. I gather your owners are Americans. We've spoken to the American military and they're looking at the problem right now. They're talking about sending out a couple of planes from Okinawa. Sorry it's a long way off, but it's the nearest they can find.'

A long way? thought Blake. It would take hours, for God's sake. 'Nothing else, Chisholm? There must be something, for Christ's sake?'

'Well, yes, Captain. Our friends have also volunteered a missile cruiser. Apparently she's been alerted and she's supposed to be heading towards you. She's called *Jackson* but she's a long way off. ETA is about seven or eight hours, maybe more with this storm going through.'

'Bloody hell, Chisholm! That's not a lot of good. What am I supposed to do?'

'We're doing everything we can, Captain. I'm sorry.'

There was a pause as Blake calmed down a little. 'OK, it's not your fault. We'll keep a watch and increase speed. I'll come back if anything develops.'

Blake stormed back on to the bridge. He called together the officers and crew who were there and briefed them on the situation. There was a stunned silence. There was nothing they could do if attacked.

'But look on the bright side. That ship is fifty years old and almost certainly can't make that speed any more. We'll increase speed to maximum, and I'm pretty sure we can get within range of HK before anything happens. Get on with it, but we'll have half-hour shifts on continuous radar watch, please. Call the engineers and ask them for everything they can give us.'

In their cabins, the passengers felt the gentle vibration of he engines increase noticeably, and the ship began to shudder a little as the *Ocean Queen* started to force its way urgently through the heaving seas.

*

From the Futenma Air Force Base on the island of Okinawa, two USAF F-15 Eagles screamed into the sky, lighting their afterburners that pushed them even faster into the cloud-laden sky. They punched through the cloud base with such speed that a brief hole was left in the low grey murk to mark their passing. It took just four minutes after take-off for the aircraft to reach 30,000 feet where the sun blazed in a deep blue sky. The pilots turned the afterburners off and the two sleek aircraft settled back to cruise at a sub-sonic and fuel-efficient 600 knots.

Two hundred miles to the south, the *Jackson* was coming round to a new course and increasing speed as well. When the Pentagon had contacted him, it took Crawford just moments to work out the relative positions. He smiled when he realised how close he was. Having spent the last two months trailing around the ports of the western Pacific, being nice to the local dignitaries and even nicer to the press, he was frankly fed-up with it. Now, the thought of a real mission cheered him up, even if it was coming to the rescue of a bunch of rich widows on a cruise liner. This story about an old Russian battleship intrigued him greatly; he was sure they'd got their facts wrong; but if they were right, it was like going to a turkey shoot. A fifty-year-old veteran without missiles versus the most modern ship in the US Navy? Crawford could hardly wait. He ordered the new course. The weather looked grim to the north, which sharpened his sense of excitement even more. At 25 knots, more or less flat out for the *Jackson*, he'd make the position within eight hours. He just hoped he wouldn't be too late to see the action.

Back at Northwood, all McEwan could do was sit back and watch the situation develop, relying on GCHQ to update him if anything happened. He thought of getting through direct to Blake on the radio, but decided for now that it would probably only worry the poor bastard even more if the Navy started wanting to know what was going on all the time. The one thing Maddox couldn't get the bloody Yanks to provide him with was satellite photographs of the area. Ever since the Falklands, where US satellite reconnaissance had been crucial, the Americans had become leery of letting the Brits into the spectacular technology that was now available. They never did trust them not to leak it all to the Russians.

Failing any other intelligence, McEwan called an old friend of his in Hong Kong, who happened to have good connections with the local spooks. Could he get hold of the Frenchman? Find out more about the raid? Any helpful information? He was promised immediate action. So McEwan sat at his desk and waited. He'd heard about the *Jackson* and the planes. He knew where the *Ocean Queen* was. The only mystery right now was exactly where the *Stalin* was located.

He had an unpleasant feeling that it wouldn't be too long before she made her presence known.

13

The pilot of the F-15 felt he was suspended, motionless, over an endless sea of lumpy, dull grey cloud, bowed into a huge curve from horizon to horizon. The hurricane had long since passed, but its remains sat over half the South China Sea obscuring the view almost completely. There could have been 100 ships down there and they couldn't see a damn thing. They had tried looking under the cloud, but at 2,000 feet they were still in the murk and the winds at lower altitudes were gusty and sharp, and tossed the fighters around like corks bobbing on water. They quickly climbed back up to a comfortable cruising height.

Even the ground search radar was proving useless. It gave a clear picture over hard ground, but all that happened when it looked down at the choppy sea was that anything down there simply got lost in the mush of confusing reflections from wavetops and rain. The radar screen looked like a blizzard of snow.

'Futenma AFB, this is Batman One,' called the lead pilot back to his base.

'Go ahead, Batman One.'

'Yeah, Futenma. Listen, we can't see a damn thing. The base is way less than 2 zero and it's pretty gusty down there and the radar's snowed out. Can you get me a satellite fix?'

'Negative, Batman One. I'm told there's nothing in

your area.' Otherwise, dumbass, we'd have given it to you; the controller's thought was left unsaid.

The network of spy satellites hadn't been re-routed to cover the area, and they weren't about to do that just for some unconfirmed story about a pirate ship. In any case, even with cameras that could resolve images a metre across from 180 miles up in the air, they still needed clear air – only infra-red or radar could penetrate the cloud cover, and the storm would have rendered them nearly as useless as the F-15's system.

The pilot snapped off the radio in disgust. This goddamn goose-chase was a pain. It was clear that finding *Stalin* was a lost cause. They'd already used a lot of their fuel radius and their loitering time was beginning to run out.

There was only one thing they could do now, he decided: find the *Ocean Queen* instead and make contact. At least they knew where the ship was. He punched the coordinates of *Ocean Queen's* last reported position into the navigation system and added a bit of compensation to make up for the movement of the ship since then. He switched on the autopilot, the computer rapidly calculated the best course to rendezvous with the liner and brought the aircraft gently round to a new course towards the *Ocean Queen*. He ordered the auto-throttle to maintain 400 knots; the lower speed would save some fuel, and he figured this would give him the maximum loitering time once he made contact with the ship.

*

Zof's radar picked up the *Ocean Queen* at 45 miles out. Mounted nearly 200 feet up on the central tower, *Stalin's* small radar set had the benefit of height which gave it an extra few miles' range over the *Ocean Queen's* more powerful, but lower, radar system. The semi-professional set would have missed a smaller target; but the *Ocean Queen*, at over 1,000 feet long, was about the biggest radar target that could be presented; the high, angular superstructure was a mass of sharp corners that couldn't have been designed better as a massive radar reflector.

Zof called Harvey over to look at the hazy blip on the edge of the screen. Harvey fiddled with the gain and tuning controls to see if he could get a clearer image. With the *Stalin* running at 34 knots and the *Ocean Queen* at 28 away from them, the *Stalin* was closing at 6 knots, making the blip a little over six hours away. If it was the liner, they would have it in sight sooner than that. They watched the indistinct blip slowly become more solid, and it crept gradually inwards towards the centre of the screen. At this range it was impossible to tell anything about it.

'It's big,' said Zof. 'It could be our ship,' after another hour had passed. So. He had been right after all. Thank God for that, at least.

Harvey went over to Kelley, who was lounging at the back of the bridge. 'Kelley, it looks as though it could be our ship coming up.'

Kelley looked at his watch and nodded. 'How long before we get there?'

'Four, maybe five hours,' Harvey replied.

'Any sign they've spotted us?' Harvey asked the same question of Zof.

'Impossible to say. It's holding a steady course and speed. I'm sure they'll pick us up on radar soon if they haven't already. I suspect they will just carry on at the moment', replied Zof. Once again, his private thoughts were split: on one hand, he had now committed himself and his crew to piracy. There was no going back and, if he was going to do it, he would make damn sure he did it well. But on the other hand here he was, a massive armed warship, about to threaten an unarmed vessel carrying hundreds, maybe thousands, of innocent passengers who would in no way be prepared for this. He felt most of all for the Captain and the crew. But then, here was a job that had to be done, and done well.

Kelley stood up and smiled. 'Well, here we go again. What do we say? Action stations or something? Let's get on with it.'

Zof ignored Kelley's comments. He certainly didn't intend to treat it as an order. He waited another three hours as the distance slowly closed between the ships before picking up the handset and calmly ordering his crew to their battle stations. There was no urgency, just a quiet professionalism as the crews went to their appointed places. The *Stalin* was getting ready for battle once more.

*

'Captain, radar target bearing 120 degrees at forty miles. Quite a solid signal,' sang out George Holland, the *Ocean Queen*'s first officer.

The bridge became suddenly silent and tense. Blake visibly stiffened and went across to the screen. The *Ocean Queen*'s radar screen was nearly two feet across, and what it lacked in height compared with *Stalin*'s, it more than made up for with clarity. At the edge of the screen was a sharp and large echo, steadily heading directly for them. Even though the *Ocean Queen* was heading away from the battleship, the gap between them was closing steadily at six and a half sea miles every hour.

'Speed?' asked Blake.

Holland tapped a couple of keys. Instantly the software calculated the speed and displayed it next to the target. It read '33'; the final '3' flickered rapidly between 2 and 6 as the system recalculated the target's speed every half-second.

It could only be *Stalin*. Nothing else could travel that fast. At that speed, Blake quickly figured, it was a little less than an hour away. Hong Kong was still hundreds of miles off. They hadn't a hope in hell. Blake straightened up from the radar screen and went back to his Captain's chair, where he called Chisholm, the Hong Kong naval man.

'Chisholm, your ship has found us, I'm afraid.'

There was a brief silence on the line. 'Thanks for letting us know, Captain. I'm sorry there's not more we can do,' Chisholm responded mournfully.

'Not half as sorry as we are. Any news? Where are those bloody Americans? Late as usual, I suppose?'

'They must be near you by now. Do you have 320 decimal 8 on UHF? It's the USAF frequency.'

Blake leaned across and asked Attwood, the radio officer, who nodded.

'I do. I'll yell for the cavalry then.'

'That's the best we can sort out at the moment. We really are trying everything we can think of, Captain.'

'Thanks, Chisholm.'

'Sorry, Captain. Take care. I mean, give them the gold if that's want they want. No need for heroics or anything.'

'Don't worry, Chisholm. I'll have the gold gift-wrapped and waiting. Stand by on this channel, OK?'

'OK, Captain. Good luck.'

Blake put the handset down and looked grimly out of the bridge window into the overcast seascape. Somewhere out there *Stalin* was heading straight for them.

*

The pilot of the F-15 was staring into the radar screen in the hope of detecting something recognisable in the snow that glittered across the miniature green disc. He twisted the gain and clutter controls to see if he could tune out the muck, but it wouldn't clear unless he turned the clutter control to maximum, which then wiped everything out. It was hopeless. He flicked the set to stand-by and the screen went blank; he'd try again when he got closer. According to his navigation system he was somewhere near the *Ocean Queen*. But even with the latest electronic positioning systems, he was beginning to feel that he'd have to collide with the funnel on the ship before he'd find it. His UHF radio squawked; then through the headphones came the plummy voice of Captain Blake.

'United States warplane, this is *Ocean Queen*, do you read me?'

Breathing a sigh of relief, the pilot flicked a switch. 'Yeah, *Ocean Queen*, this is US warplane Batman One. Go ahead, sir.'

'Warplane, this is *Ocean Queen*, we have the pirate ship on radar and it appears to be heading directly for us. Are you in position to render assistance?'

'I think so, *Ocean Queen*. Visibility is poor. Give me your precise position and the bearing of the pirate ship.'

Blake read the latitude and longitude position over to the F-15, and gave him the bearing and distance of the pursuing ship.

There was a pause while the pilot worked out the positions on his navigation computer. Then the UHF set burst back into life: 'Roger, *Ocean Queen*. We're very close. I'll come down through the cloud cover and take a look. Stand by on this frequency, Batman One out.'

Blake put the handset down. 'Batman indeed,' he snorted, but all the same felt a growing sense of relief. At least there was someone out there.

The F-15 pilot flicked his radio back to the air-to-air frequency. 'Skulski, I'm going to try downstairs and see if I get a visual. Hang on up here for me and circle.'

'Roger, One.'

He eased the throttle gently back. As the air speed dropped the aircraft slowly lost height, the altimeter lazily unrolling the digits. He soon sank into the billowing grey cotton wool that was the cloud top. The sun blinked out as the cloud enveloped him. As he sank down through the murk, the wind gained strength, and the aircraft began to shudder and lurch as though it were straining through a grey woolly undergrowth. The cloud grew denser and blacker. Soon, the rain began to rattle on the cockpit canopy like sand in a storm. It came in fitful attacks, desultory one second, angry and loud the next. The lower the aircraft dropped, the darker the cloud became and the more violent the buffeting from the wind. He left the radar on stand-by; there didn't seem much point in trying it out until he was clear of the weather.

The altimeter was reading less than 1,000 feet when suddenly the F-15 dropped out of the cloud base and visibility instantly returned. He was descending quickly now, over 30 feet every second. Suddenly his breath froze in his throat.

It was not the sudden release into light from the wet cotton-wool of the cloud, nor the sight of the *Ocean Queen* steaming majestically across the spray-flecked sea. What made his mouth drop open with astonishment was suddenly seeing the *Stalin*, about 500 yards away, powering at full speed through the green seas, heading directly for him as the aircraft descended towards the sea.

'Oh, shit!' he yelled. His fighter-pilot's instincts quickly took control. He yanked the stick away and pushed violently on the rudder to turn away from the rapidly closing ship, and at the same time rammed the throttle lever forward as far as he could.

The plane had descended from the cloud base doing 180 knots, about as slow as it could go without falling out of the sky. Trying to turn quickly at low speed was not an ideal manoeuvre. The manual stated clearly that you needed at least 250 knots before pulling tight turns. The plane shuddered and complained loudly. The General Electric turbofan engines, each one normally happy to deliver 50,000 pounds of raw, kerosene-scented power, were also complaining at being forced to go from near-idle to full power in one burst. The extra fuel flooded into the combustion chambers but, without its normal diet of high-pressure air ramming into it, the fuel burned badly and the engines coughed and stuttered before slowly winding themselves up to produce the power that was now so urgently asked of them.

The pilot had little option other than to point the nose down in order to gain speed, to get the plane and the engine to respond. To do this he found himself aiming squarely at the top of the *Stalin's* fast-approaching mast. There wasn't time to think. There wasn't time for anything other than a muttered prayer.

*

Zof, Harvey and Kelley were all staring out of the bridge window straining to catch the first glimpse of the *Ocean Queen*. The radar showed her just 20 miles away. The weather was clearing and the view to the distant horizon was crisp, though above them an unbroken layer of thick cloud still revolved slowly around the storm centre now hundreds of miles past them.

Zof was scanning the horizon with his old Nikon

glasses, a present from Polina from way back when he first joined the Pacific fleet. The top of the ship should be visible any moment now. Harvey was next to him. His eyes moved slowly from one side of a small sector of horizon to the other.

There, shimmering and dancing just above the crisp line of the horizon, was a squat smudge that could have been anything at all but looked, to Harvey, like the top of a funnel.

'There!' Harvey pointed.

Zof brought his glasses round slowly, travelling along the horizon. The smudge danced into view. Seen through 15 miles of humid air, it literally rippled. But the ripple stayed in the same place long enough for Zof to know that it was something other than an atmospheric trick.

'I think that's your ship,' he said quietly in Russian. Only Harvey heard him. 'We'll be on her in just over two hours. Shall I alert the crew? They're all in place.'

'I think so, Captain.'

Zof lifted the handset of the internal PA system and was just about to speak when he went silent. He was looking out from the bridge window. What he saw made him stop dead – and then he shouted something that even Harvey couldn't catch, bursting across the PA system. Loosely translated, he told his crew they might like to think about taking cover as the bastards were coming in.

Harvey and the others saw the F-15 at the same time and instinctively got ready to duck. It dropped out of the clouds and didn't look like stopping: it loomed larger and larger in seconds. At the very last moment it looked as though it was going over the top of them, but then dived down towards the *Stalin*. Suddenly it banked and with a scream it flashed over them, missing the mast by what looked like inches. Everyone on the bridge had actually ducked as it roared over; they straightened up as it passed and watched it from the side windows. The aircraft was banking hard and a wing-tip was close to the water. It curved elegantly off and began to gain height as it flew away and upwards, thin black smoke from the exhaust trailing across the sea's surface.

'Jesus! What in the name of hell was that?' demanded Kelley.

'United States Air Force. An F-15. Looks like they're on to us, Kelley,' replied Harvey quietly.

Zof was already calmly sending out his orders. As the F-15 curled away he knew it would come back. He hadn't expected action; but now he saw the aircraft he quickly ran through in his mind what he would expect it to do. His years of training operated rapidly. The aircraft, if it was going to attack, would go through an almost routine procedure. On a modern ship, Zof's response would have been almost as routine: deploy electronic counter-measures; arm the SAMs; acquire the aircraft on the tracking radar. It would be a battle between electronic chips; the fastest one would win. And, at least in this area, Russian technology was every bit as good as the West's.

But he had no electronic counter-measures; no SAMs; no radar other than the fishing-boat kit the American had insisted he instal. Worse than useless. But then ... he ordered the ship's bell to ring the double alarm signal, and Morin ordered his crews on to the AA guns mounted in the grey steel blisters that ran up the sides of the central tower. He had two types: the 40 mm machine guns and the 110 mm guns that fired shrapnel which would down anything within 100 feet of where it exploded. Zof felt strangely confident in the old ship's defences. He watched the now-distant aircraft with interest rather than concern.

*

The F-15's pilot breathed again as the rev. counter spun upwards and the aircraft rapidly gained height. He levelled off at 1,500 feet and went into a slow circle to give himself time to think. First he called his wingman, circling above at 15,000 feet, to join him on the deck. Then he called his base.

'Futenma, Batman One.'

'Go ahead, Batman.'

'Listen, buddy, I found your goddamn pirate ship. She's about the biggest mother I ever seen. Now you want to tell me what the hell I'm supposed to do about it?'

'Roger, Batman. I'll get back to you on that.'

'You do that. But listen. I got twenty minutes' loiter out here. Then we're coming back, whatever. You read me?'

There was no reply. Firth, the controller at Futenma, was calling his commander who, in turn was trying to get through to the Pentagon, who already realised that the only person who knew much about the ancient ship was on the other side of the world. An underling of Bell's got through to McEwan quickly.

'We found your ship.' 'Your' ship noted McEwan with a wry smile. They're in charge, but it's my ship. 'Our guy's only got twenty minutes. Any ideas before we go in?' he demanded of McEwan.

McEwan knew full well that the aircraft would be useless against the massive armour of the *Stalin*. He also worried about the anti-aircraft fire power of the big ship. What it lacked in technology it made up for in sheer muscle.

'Best to keep pretty clear, I think. Just let them know you're there. Maybe that will be enough to put them off. That old ship packs a pretty powerful punch. Tell your men to be careful,' advised McEwan.

'Listen, McEwan. These are a couple of the best airplanes ever built. They could blow any ship out the water, and some pile of Russian junk is no problem. We'll do more than put them off. We'll scare shit out of them.'

'They're your planes. But for heaven's sake, be careful. That ship's more dangerous than it looks.'

'Yeah, sure. Thanks for the help. Don't worry. I'll let you know.' The line went dead. McEwan started to worry.

Firth's voice burst into the pilot's headphones a few moments later. 'Batman One. Orders are to scare shit out of them. Beat 'em up a few times to scare them away. Got that?'

The pilot shrugged but didn't comment. He only had another fifteen minutes or so. His wingman had joined him. Together they turned to face *Stalin* and opened up the throttles to go screaming in towards the ship, low, fast and menacing.

*

Zof watched the two aircraft turn and begin their approach. They were dropping down to skim the waves; the classic manoeuvre of an aircraft coming in to attack, using the low altitude to confuse the opposing radar they imagined was detecting them. The aircraft were clearly visible to the gun crews, and they aimed their 40 mm twin machine guns and 110 mm guns directly at the fast-approaching F-15s, centring them in the old-fashioned visual sights.

Zof remained impassive. Inside, he was wondering how the hell this old ship would stand up to the attack. Every nerve was screaming at him to take action: get a radar plot, arm the SAMs, shoot them out of the sky. It was straightforward enough. But he could do nothing except wait and see what they would do, and then see if he could scare them off by old-fashioned gunfire. The theory that the *Stalin* was effectively invulnerable to modern weapons sounded fine on dry land; out here, when the bastards were attacking, it felt different. A whole lot different. So, he simply stood there and waited, trying to instil a sense of confidence he didn't really feel into the rest of the crew. He had to trust to Morin's abilities; that's what the man was there for. Now he had to do his job.

Morin, the gunnery bay-chay commander, had already spoken to his gun-crews and they knew what they had to do. Let them approach. Stay easy. Let them come in. You've nothing to worry about. Steady. Let them get nearer and nearer ... every man on the guns could almost hear Morin's calm voice telling them to wait until the last possible moment.

The planes were almost upon them. 'NOW!' seemed to shout Morin. Every man on the guns let rip. A sparkling, stuttering barrage of machine-gun shells and high-explosive shells burst out to meet the incoming aircraft. Kelley was getting to ready to duck. Surely it was too late? The planes were much too close.

As a matter of course, each F-15 pilot had engaged his EDS, engagement defence system. It rapidly scanned all the frequencies that hostile gun and missile guidance radars would transmit on. Within milliseconds of detecting any radar locking on to the aircraft, the system would sound a warning buzzer in the pilot's ear to take evading action, and then, having tracked the signal back to its source, would first fire flares to distract a heat-seeking missile and second, a Revenger missile targeted onto offending radar. The missile would accelerate to supersonic speed within a couple of seconds and fly down the track of the radar emission, blowing the radar into dust. All this would take place within a few seconds. Virtually foolproof, no fighter pilot would dream of going into action without it turned on. It was the ultimate defence.

The EDS system on each F-15 quickly scanned the frequencies. It flashed up and down the spectrum. All it heard was the burble of stars and sunspots; as far as it was concerned, the horizon was empty. The last thing it was built to detect was Second World War large-calibre machine guns aimed by eye, which were now pointing directly at the aircraft as they howled in at a couple of hundred feet above the sea. The system couldn't detect the gunners aiming at them, and certainly couldn't detect the shells as they arced out across the sea with a stream of tracer. But the lead pilot could. As he neared the ship, the guns suddenly glittered, and he saw the tracer coming towards him. It was about the last thing he expected. He was trained to face heat-seeking missiles, not crude, low-tech machine-gun fire that had been superseded as anti-aircraft equipment twenty years ago. His instincts told him to turn away, to try to evade the stream of bullets. He hauled the aircraft into a tight turn, which was about the worst thing he could have done.

Any Second World War fighter pilot would have told him to carry right on in, opening up with everything he had to scare the hell out of the gunners and stop them firing. Nose on, he was a tiny target for the guns and his chances of being hit were minimal. But his modern training simply didn't allow that manoeuvre. The aircraft groaned under the g-forces of the turn as the tiny profile of the F-15 facing the gunners suddenly grew as it presented its wings and underbelly to the oncoming gunners on the *Stalin*.

The men aiming the guns turned all their fire on the leading F-15 as it turned. It was like a turkey shoot. Even though they had only a few seconds before it moved out of range, the big, fat target they were suddenly presented with could have been hit by a blind man. Shell after shell ripped home through the flimsy alloy shell of the aircraft. At least twenty shells found the target. The bigger HE shells exploded in dark flowers of shrapnel that burst across the sky.

Skulski, the pilot of the second F-15 and still a distance behind the leader, watched in horror as the tracer danced around the stricken aircraft. In a split second, lines of thin smoke trailing from the leading aircraft were etched across the sky, curving away, following the desperate turn. And another split second later there was a silent blossoming of red and orange, like a new rose bursting open, then a smudge of black cloud, then tiny white flecks on the distant sea as the debris drifted like snow from the place where the F-15 had been a few seconds before.

'Christ almighty,' muttered Skulski as he flew the second F-15 out of harm's way into a wide circle. His heart was pounding and he quickly gathered his thoughts. He knew that man; that same morning they had been laughing and joking in the sunshine. Now there was nothing. Not even a fucking parachute. It took just half a second for the red, raw, bloody anger to rise in his mind. He flicked on the arming switches for the four AS9 missiles loaded under his wings and turned to face *Stalin* once more. There was hard revenge in his eyes.

The AS9s were the American equivalents of the French Exocet missiles, but smaller. Launched from an aircraft, they dropped to within 20 feet of the sea surface and then homed in by radar on the target ship. They rarely missed. And they never, ever missed a target as big as the *Stalin*. The missiles would race in too fast for defensive action and blast huge holes in any ship they encountered within seconds of being fired. They were deadly weapons, feared by any naval commander.

The computerised weapon system took over once armed. In milliseconds it identified the target, asked for confirmation from Skulski which it rapidly received, then loaded the target's image into each missile's computer. It then bleeped in his headphones to tell him that the four missiles were locked on to the target. He pressed the launch button, and one after the other all four missiles silently left the wing pylons and then, igniting, streaked away across the wavetops towards *Stalin*. Long before he came within range of the machine gunners, he had sent the missiles on their way and circled back to watch his revenge take its inevitable course.

Each missile 'saw' *Stalin* on its radar system. As they came closer, they subtly changed course to aim for a central point ten feet above the waterline. This, the designers had found, was the best place to strike home. The idea was that the missile would penetrate the outer skin on the ship and then explode inside where it would wreak total havoc, destroying systems and fatally crippling the ship. The explosive charge was not massive, but bursting inside a modern lightweight missile cruiser packed with electronics it was more than enough to complete its task.

The first missile struck. But instead of encountering a thin outer skin it rammed itself headfirst into over two feet of laminated armour plate. It exploded, left a smear on the side of the ship, frightened the life out of the gunnery crews and left a few small marks on the armour plate. The other three, striking home in more or less the same place in quick succession, had an equally negligible effect on the veteran battleship. They didn't even slow down its progress through the water.

On board, Zof watched the events with some surprise. The downing of the first aircraft was remarkably simple; the theory about the *Stalin*'s defence would now, however, be really tested. He ducked as he saw the missiles launched, but by now was feeling a lot more confident in the old ship's ability to take the punishment. He therefore watched the second F-15's attack against the old-fashioned armour with some interest. The others, even Pine, had flung themselves to the floor when the first F-15 came into attack, dusted themselves off when it was downed, then repeated the process when the second aircraft launched its rockets.

Zof fought every instinct and stayed standing. There was a moment when he thought he might have to get down on the deck with the rest of them; but he managed to resist the overwhelming impulse.

After the shock of the exploding missiles had subsided and everyone on the bridged realised that they were not merely unharmed but essentially unaffected, there were sheepish grins and even a yell or two of delight.

'How about that!' said Kelley, looking relieved as the second F-15 curled away in the sky and disappeared from view into the cloud base.

They watched for a minute or two, but the attacker showed no sign of coming back for another try.

'It must be low on fuel. It probably flew in from a land base – they're not carrier aircraft. I don't think it will be back very soon. But we must now get our task over quickly,' said Zof.

'How long have we got?' Kelley asked.

'Perhaps an hour. Perhaps less,' replied the Captain. The ship had comfortably absorbed everything, so far, the Americans could throw at it. He knew they would be back for more; and he knew now that he would probably be facing a major battle in the not-too-distant future. He didn't think that he would be allowed to get away with what they had just done. Right now admirals, generals and governments would be rousing themselves. He had more than tweaked their tails. But Zof knew long ago that he had crossed his particular Rubicon. Somehow, now that he knew a fight was coming, he felt better; it was what he was trained for and what he knew. And given the performance of the ship so far, his confidence in escaping was growing every minute. But for now he was just a pirate. He had a job to get on with and he wanted it over as quickly as he could.

In an hour or less, as he told Kelley, nothing was really going to happen. The two F-15s were ground-based aircraft; that meant there were no carriers within range. And presumably no warships, either, or none that would be there quickly. Zof knew more than most that the ocean was a huge place to hide in, even with the most sophisticated tracking satellites in the world. He knew he would have plenty of time to get the operation over with, and then get away, to hide in the vastness of the ocean and prepare himself for the inevitable. Zof felt, as he had never quite done before, a growing certainty in the success of the operation.

'An hour? That's enough. Let's get on with it,' replied Kelley, who clearly had little idea of the hornets' nest he had just kicked over. What the hell, thought Zof, and started issuing the orders in a soft but penetrating voice that made the crew move with a determined sense of purpose. Kelley, full of optimism, felt the engines shudder as the revolutions increased, and the great ship leaned gently as it turned on to a new course towards the *Ocean Queen*.

*

As they left Zof on the bridge, Kelley whispered to Harvey to meet him down in his cabin. 'Keep it quiet,' he said, and walked off. Harvey gave him a minute, then followed him. He tapped softly on the cabin door, opened it and found the American sprawled out on the bunk. Kelley jumped up.

'Hi, kid. Come in. Drink?'

'No thanks,' said Harvey. Not that he didn't; he just thought he should keep a clear head. He wondered what Kelley wanted. Whatever it was, Harvey had his own agenda too: he knew he had to bring up the subject of Kelley's secret meeting back in Vladivostok. Kelley always made him nervous, more so when that mad bastard Pine was around. But now Pine was nowhere to be seen. He had to nerve himself for the confrontation; but he would let Kelley go first. 'What was it you wanted?' he asked.

'I need your advice,' started Kelley. The American wanted to start selling Harvey the idea that had struck him while thinking about a way to slow down the liner; he thought he needed to allow more time to let the *Jackson* catch up. 'The thing is,' he continued, 'I'm worried about that liner. I mean, how fast can it go?'

'*Ocean Queen*? God knows, Kelley. I should think it's fast. Twenty-five knots, maybe more,' replied Harvey.

'That's what I thought; that's our problem. I think it could get help too quickly. We need more time to make sure we get away, so we want to find a way of slowing it down. Not hurting anyone, just disabling it. You know about these things. How about we blow the rudder off with a torpedo? Would it work?'

'Christ, Kelley, are you crazy? You could sink the thing,' replied Harvey, suddenly taken aback by this new idea. Piracy was one thing. Drowning 2,000 people was something else.

Kelley looked crestfallen. 'Too dangerous, huh?'

'Fucking right, Kelley.'

'We could do it very carefully, just enough to stop

them going anywhere. What do you think? I mean, what happens if that ship gets to within distance of the coast within a few hours? Remember, we're nowhere near where we thought we would be. We banked on plenty of time to get away. It's getting tight, kid, too tight for comfort,' said Kelley, drawing close to the Englishman.

Harvey found himself back in a corner. Kelley was right, of course. But exploding torpedoes under a cruise liner seemed a very dangerous way of doing it. On the other hand, he didn't really have much of an alternative.

'What does Zof say?' he asked eventually.

'Yeah, good idea. We'll ask Zof. He'll know,' smiled Kelley. From the look on his face, the conversation appeared to be over, but Harvey knew this would be his last chance. His heart was thumping. He had to take it. Now or never.

'Listen, Kelley, there's something I wanted to raise with you,' Harvey started nervously.

The American looked coldly at him. 'Sure, fire away.'

'That last night in Vladivostok?'

'What about it?'

'The thing is, Kelley − I saw you, you see. You left the hotel late at night; you drove past me with some character at the wheel: Arab-looking. Some meeting or other. I mean, what exactly is going on here?' His heart was beating furiously now.

Kelley stayed silent; he just looked at Harvey. He hadn't expected this, of all things. There was a narrowness in his eyes that Harvey had never seen before, and he didn't like it.

'Well?' demanded Harvey, after an uncomfortable pause.

'Sit down,' said Kelley, a note of menace in his voice that Harvey didn't fail to spot as he sat. Kelley's mind was racing now. Better get it over with, he thought. Get it over with, get the thing finished. He should have listened to Tariq.

'I'm sorry you found out like this.'

'What are you on about, Kelley?' asked Harvey, now worried.

'I was going to tell you, maybe in a few days. But I guess I should tell you now. Listen, kid, this piracy thing?'

'Yes?'

'Well, it's not quite what it seems.'

'What the fuck is it, then?'

'It's a deal I struck. That guy you saw me with? He's the representative of a certain Middle-Eastern state. I've been commissioned, I suppose you could say, to help them acquire a particular cargo from a particular ship which will very soon be on its way here.'

'I don't believe this, Kelley,' said Harvey.

'Oh, you'd better believe it, Harvey, you'd better believe it. Listen, kid, you're gonna be richer than you thought. Much, much richer. These people are paying cash into secret Swiss accounts, a hundred million clean, untraceable dollars. Far more than the gold. Didn't you ever think how we were going to launder that stuff? We'd have to have sold it to those Indian crooks for maybe twenty cents on the dollar to get rid of it. Sorry, Harvey, that's a fools' game. Leave the gold to these stupid commies upstairs. This way you get hard cash, no questions. Fifty million dollars. No tax. How about that?' Kelley's face was flushed with enthusiasm.

'And what do we have to do for this?' Harvey asked.

'We rob *Ocean Queen*. Disable the thing. Hang around over the horizon. *Ocean Queen* puts out a distress call, if she hasn't already. Everyone gets upset, particularly the Americans who own the damn thing. There's a US ship called *Jackson* around a day's sail away. That's why the timing had to be right. The *Jackson*'s carrying nuclear warheads. We wait until it arrives, hold it up. She won't give us any trouble. That's why we needed a ship like this. We lift the warheads, scoot down to the Monte Bello Islands, where these guys are waiting, choppers and all, and off we go, dropped off at the nearest friendly port. It's gonna work, Harvey. You'll be seriously rich.'

Harvey remained silent, in no position to argue. It occurred to him that Kelley was crazy.

'You think I'm crazy?' laughed Kelley. 'I'm not crazy, Harvey. This is my chance of a lifetime. Yours too. Think about it. We've got a major power on our side, helping out. It can't go wrong.'

'Who? Who's behind this?' Harvey demanded.

'You don't want to know. A certain Middle-Eastern state that would very much like to lay its hands on nuclear weapons and would be even happier to poke Uncle Sam in the eye at the same time. That's all you need to know.'

'Who, exactly?' asked Harvey incredulously.

'I didn't say, Harvey. Don't ask. Now listen, you with us or not? I mean, it's quite important.'

'If I'm not?'

'Hey, no problem. We'll drop you off near some island with a load of gold. I like you, Harvey. Trust me. It's your choice,' said Kelley.

But Harvey knew it wasn't. Not at all.

'Sure. Thanks for letting me know,' he said, unconvinced.

Kelley decided to take that as a 'Yes'. 'You made the right choice. Now, we got a lot of work coming up. You OK?' he asked, putting his arm firmly round the Englishman's shoulder.

'I'm fine. Thanks, Kelley,' said Harvey as he opened the door.

'Sure, kid. No problem,' Kelley said as Harvey closed the door behind him.

Kelley waited until Harvey had gone, then went to find Pine. He was in the officers' mess, eating. Kelley beckoned him away from the table and they went, unnoticed, into an empty room where Kelley closed the door behind them. He had a little job for him to do, said Kelley. The fat man's eyes gleamed and his smile broadened.

14

The ship's PA system chimed three delicate notes, and Blake's deep, reassuring voice boomed out. 'Ladies and gentlemen, this is Captain Blake speaking. Can I have your attention for a moment? If you look out on the starboard side ... that's the right-hand side if you're facing forwards ... of the ship, you'll see quite a large battleship heading towards us ...'

Hundreds of heads on the starboard side of the ship looked out of the windows and saw *Stalin* in the distance. Wealthy parents pointed out the ship to their children: 'Look at the big ship'. Wealthy widows were less interested; most glanced up briefly, then carried on reading magazines and sipping coffee.

'... and we're going to rendezvous with this ship in about ten minutes. They'll be sending a party across, and we'll be delayed for a short time while we help them out with a problem or two. I hope this won't inconvenience anyone. We're still on schedule for Hong Kong for later this evening. Thank you very much, ladies and gentlemen.'

Blake flicked off the PA system. After all, there was no point in scaring the passengers as the ship drew steadily closer. They hadn't contacted him yet, but he wanted to make sure the passengers were well settled long before anything happened. Now, he simply wanted the pirates to take the cargo of gold and get off his ship quickly. There was no point in putting up a show, even if he had been in a position to do so. All he could do now was watch the *Stalin* ploughing on towards him through the bridge windows. He didn't have very long to wait.

'*Ocean Queen*, this is warship *Stalin*,' burst Harvey's voice through the VHF speaker on the bridge. Zof declined to speak directly to the *Ocean Queen*. He wasn't a pirate, just a seaman, so he told Harvey. Besides, they'll like your English voice.

There was a long pause before the replay came back. Blake was surprised by the English public-school accent coming over the loudspeaker. This was supposed to be a Russian ship. '*Stalin*, this is *Ocean Queen*', replied Blake evenly.

'*Ocean Queen*, good afternoon, sir. I'm sorry about this interruption to your voyage. As we approach, would you be so kind as to come into the wind and stop your engines. We intend to board you. We are armed and we will not hesitate to use force if you do not follow our instructions exactly.' Harvey's rounded English voice sounded calm and confident.

'*Stalin*, *Ocean Queen*. I understand your instructions and I will be complying peacefully with them. You do of course understand that you are committing an act of piracy on the high seas for which the penalty is death?' Chisholm had told him to add the legal warning, just for effect. Blake didn't feel very convinced as he did so.

'Yes, thank you, *Ocean Queen*. We understand exactly what we're doing,' came Harvey's reply, heavy with irony. 'Thank you for your co-operation. My RIB will come to your starboard side. Have a boarding ladder ready down to sea-level please. We are monitoring your radio transmissions and I suggest that you make no further calls unless in response to us. Please confirm.'

Blake paused. Whoever he was, he seemed to know what he was doing. 'Yes, *Stalin*, we confirm.'

'Thank you. You can start bringing your ship to a stop now. We will be with you shortly.' The hiss of the carrier wave stopped abruptly as Harvey released the transmit switch.

Blake ordered all engines to stop. As the power ran down, the elegant liner slowed in the sea, the crisp bow wave dropping away from the sharp stem and the foaming wake calming to a gentle ripple behind the stern. Left to itself, the ship slowly began to respond to the pressure of the wind and ponderously turned beam on to the fitful gusts of the remains of the hurricane. On the starboard side, down which the crew were now lowering a boarding ladder, it was sheltered from the wind by the bulk of the sheer blue walls of the *Ocean Queen*'s massive hull, creating a calm lake of water disturbed only by a gentle swell.

The inflatable drew alongside and Harvey and Pine, leading six other Russian seamen armed with old but operational Kalashnikovs, stepped calmly up the boarding ladder, followed by Zof.

Zof had insisted on coming. He wanted to see *Ocean Queen*, he wanted to see exactly what was going on. Something inside him told him he should meet, face to face, the Captain of the ship he was hi-jacking on the high seas. Perhaps it was a guilt thing. Perhaps he didn't want to be a thief in the night. He just knew he couldn't stand by on the bridge of the *Stalin*. But he would stay in the background and remain anonymous. He'd changed out of his uniform and was wearing overalls. Being hi-jacked was bad enough for the *Ocean Queen*; he guessed that being boarded by a Russian Navy Captain in full uniform would be too much.

Kelley had objected loudly when Zof told him he was going. With what the American had in mind, this was the last thing he wanted. 'Too dangerous', he had said. 'You're needed here.' Any excuse he could think of. But Zof snorted and went anyway, leaving an anxious-looking Kelley behind on the ship. Kelley couldn't very well change his plans now; the whole thing was too complicated, and Zof's presence couldn't be allowed to ruin it. He grabbed Pine just as they were leaving.

'Pine, just be careful, you hear?' he hissed. The fat man smiled vacantly. This was no longer such a good idea, Kelley thought. But he had no alternative, and this would be the best chance he would get. One way or another, Harvey wouldn't be coming back to the *Stalin*. He'd just have to take the chance with Zof.

A pale and nervous seaman, under orders from Blake, led the party quickly up to the bridge where Blake and the rest of the *Ocean Queen*'s senior officers were gathered, sullen and apprehensive.

Harvey approached Blake, who stood slightly ahead of the quietly waiting group of officers. Zof stood in the background with the rest of the crew, watching the unfolding drama. 'Good afternoon, Captain. My name is Baker, and this is Mr Charlie. As you can see, we are armed and so are our friends here. Let me just reassure you, gentlemen, all of us are quite happy to use physical violence at the slightest excuse. Isn't that right, Mr Charlie?'

Zof felt angry. Here he was, just one of the pirates; but watching these people in action was making it all very different. It was so far away from how Zof had been brought up; a lifetime of duty, patriotism, honour and god knows what else ... now he was just one of a gang engaged in a seedy robbery. Everything inside him urged him to step in and take control of the situation, order these thugs off ... but, of course, he had to just stand there and watch. The command was clearly in someone else's hands. For the first time in his life, at least on board a ship, he felt powerless and weak.

Pine went through the well-rehearsed process of frightening the life out of the victims to ensure their unquestioning co-operation. It avoided so much trouble later. He calmly walked up to Holland, the first officer, who was taller than Pine by a good head; but the slow, deliberate walk and the fixed smile that Pine employed was, as it was meant to be, totally unnerving. Holland stood rooted to the spot and visibly stiffened as Pine slowly approached and stopped directly in front of him. As he looked nervously down at the fat, powerful man, there was a total silence on the bridge.

Pine, looking Holland steadily in the eye, and smiling broadly, slowly reached out and grasped Holland's testicles. Holland gasped, not so much with pain as at the sheer outrage. The pain came next. Pine gripped harder and harder, and began to twist. But he did it with a deliberate, arrogant slowness, and he started to giggle eerily, high-pitched like a girl. Holland started to gasp and groan. He grasped Pine's hand, but gently, fearful of causing further pain. Pine squeezed harder; Holland slowly sank to his knees. Pine maintained his grip and stooped down with his victim, still smiling, still giggling.

Zof was appalled. Just watching the cold, calculating violence of the fat American was bad enough. But in spite of everything that Kelley had told him about frightening people to avoid trouble later, he could not bring himself to put up with this. He was seriously thinking about doing something when Blake jumped forward instead: 'For God's sake, man, there's no need for ...', but he stopped in mid-sentence. Pine, without releasing his grip on Holland's testicles, turned to look at Blake with one of the most evil expressions that Blake had ever seen. The smile had gone; the look alone was enough to stop him. Pine returned his attention to Holland. He squeezed even harder and Holland yelped – then he suddenly let go, smiled broadly, patted Holland on the side of the face and returned to stand next to Harvey.

Zof held his breath. Pine was a lunatic. He knew that if he intervened Pine would turn on him; this worried him little, but then, of course, the whole thing would break up into chaos. He had to keep reminding himself he was just a pirate, just a pirate. Get on with the job and stop bleating, for God's sake, he kept telling himself. Get it done, and done quickly, and get off the ship and get away from here. He clenched his fists into tight balls and stood exactly where he was.

Holland stayed on his knees, his face white and his hands clutching at his groin. Zof watched the scene with awed fascination. Now he began to understand. He didn't like it, but Pine had reduced them to frightened, compliant sheep, ready to do anything. Maybe it was better this way.

'That was Mr Charlie in one of his better moods. He can be far more unpleasant. Now, all you need to do is follow my instructions quickly and without question,' Harvey explained in a reasonable, even friendly tone of voice. He shot a glance at Zof: don't meddle, don't get upset – this is how we do things. Harvey felt uncomfortable from the sheer presence of the man, not that it seemed to worry that animal Pine in the slightest.

Blake stepped forward. 'Look, you obviously know what you came for. I'm perfectly happy to let you have the gold. I want no more violence,' he stated quietly. He didn't want to be seen as a threat, he kept his voice down and his hands clasped meekly in front of him. But inside he was raging. Without any thought of the consequences to himself he could happily have gone up to Pine and slit his throat. But his first concern was his crew and his passengers. He had to keep his fury under complete control.

Now it was Harvey's turn to feel uncomfortable. He looked at Blake. Something was wrong here, he thought. 'How exactly do you know what we've come for?'

'It's all over the airwaves, man. You robbed a French ship. I presume it was you?'

Harvey stayed silent. So, that explained the air attack. How the hell did that French freighter get to port so quickly? They couldn't have got a call out – the radio was smashed. There was no time to think it through. Now he wanted to work even faster and get out of the area. Zof quickly reached the same conclusion. If their presence was now being widely broadcast, they were starting to run out of time. The last thing Zof wanted was to endanger his own ship, and especially his crew.

'Very well, Captain. Listen carefully. You'll take Mr Charlie here, together with three of these gentlemen' – he nodded at the surly Russians – 'down to where you're keeping the gold, together with thirty-three members of your crew. Under the supervision of my friends here, thirty-two members of your crew will each carry one of the boxes down to the RIB moored at the boarding platform. It will be necessary to make two or three trips back to our ship, so your crewmen will form an orderly queue and wait. My men will conceal their weapons so as not to arouse the suspicions of your passengers. Make sure your crew co-operate. The thirty-third man will collect the briefcase of diamonds and bring it to me here on the bridge. Is that clear?'

'Perfectly,' replied Blake icily. They knew every detail, for Christ's sake.

'Very well, Captain. Please proceed.'

Blake spoke to his crew and issued the orders. Under the supervision of Goodall, the purser, the party was assembled, taken down to the strongroom and then, one by one, each wooden box was lifted by a crew member and carried up several flights of ladders to the door that led on deck to the boarding ladder. Once the RIB had fifteen boxes in it, one of the Russians stopped the queue of crewmen, untied the RIB and slowly motored the heavy cargo across the sheltered stretch of water to *Stalin*, where an equal number of crewmen were waiting to carry each box off the boat.

Harvey and Zof silently watched the operation proceed. The RIB returned after twenty minutes to collect the balance of the cargo, and the process was repeated. After an hour all thirty-two boxes, each containing four ingots of solid gold, were safely aboard the pirate ship. The RIB tied up alongside the *Ocean Queen* for the last time, waiting to take Harvey, Zof and the men back again.

Up on the bridge, Blake and the rest of his officers stood in an anxious group. They had remained silent throughout the robbery. The Russians and Pine had just returned, together with a very quiet Goodall who was clutching a worn brown leather briefcase. As they walked in, Holland glanced nervously at Pine who ignored him and went to the front of the bridge where he leaned cheerfully against the window with arms folded, gazing idly at the group. It reminded Zof of a sheepdog staring at a flock of nervous sheep.

Harvey held out his hand, and Goodall passed over the briefcase. Inside was a thick black velvet pouch secured by a leather drawstring which he pulled apart and having looked inside, he invited Zof to take a look as well. The heap of uncut diamonds, some large and some small, looked like a handful of crushed ice. He was surprised how small a pile it was, given that Kelley assured him that it was worth $10 million. He drew the drawstring tight and dropped the bag back into the briefcase.

'Thank you, Captain. That appears to be all. We appreciate your co-operation. Just one last thing. Who's the radio officer?'

Attwood stepped hesitantly forward. 'That's me,' he said nervously. As Pine walked up to stand next to him, the crazy smile had come back.

'A moment of your time. The radio room, please,' requested Harvey, politely and softly. The mere presence of Pine made Attwood extremely helpful and co-operative.

Attwood led Harvey and Pine down a short flight of ladders from the bridge into the room where the main communication systems were located. On *Stalin* the radio room was huge, filled with veteran Russian radio equipment, valves, huge dials, rheostats with three-inch-diameter control knobs, all bolted into green steel cabinets that must have weighed tons. The *Ocean Queen's* radio room was small, quiet and comfortably furnished with thick carpet. A small rack in one corner held the radio and satellite communication systems that provided multi-channel links with the outside world. The biggest items of equipment were the two colour PCs that ran most of the systems.

'Where's the power supply?' asked Harvey.

Mystified, Attwood opened a door in a bulkhead locker. A small grey box with a single red light was located inside; several grey and red cables were connected to the box. The function of the power supply was to connect the fussy electronics with the power system of the ship. The system, like any mains system, was subject to power surges, so the job of the box was to smooth out the voltage and supply it with a steady, regular current that wouldn't upset the delicate microprocessors in the communications systems. Kelley had told him to go straight for this unit. This, he said, was the quickest way to disable the ship's ability to communicate. Once that was gone, Kelley had carefully explained, then the whole system was dead and couldn't be re-started. He went to some length to ensure that Harvey understood this: it was vital to make sure the ship couldn't communicate. He seemed to know an unusual amount about the ship's communications systems; he explained that the information had come from Price. Obviously, the insurers needed to know about these things, he said.

Kelley told Attwood to turn off the mains, which he did. The PCs blipped, whirred briefly and then died. The tiny red light on the power supply unit slowly faded to darkness. Harvey then took the Kalashnikov that Pine was holding and smashed the butt of the rifle into the small metal box with as much force as he could muster, but still failed to break it. The unit had a dent but remained whole.

'Shit. Get that thing out of there,' ordered Harvey. Attwood hastily reached in, unscrewed four butterfly nuts and pulled the unit out, detaching the plugs from the back. Harvey pushed from the room carrying the unit, walked out to the wingbridge and flung the small box over the side into the green water below. He came back smiling.

'There now, Captain, we're finished. Thank you for being so very helpful. Until we depart, kindly remain here on the bridge with your officers.'

Blake nodded. Harvey turned to go and Zof, still keeping silent, followed him. His fury had not abated one inch, but now, having seen the operation go so well, he just wanted to get off the ship as quickly as he could, and return to some sanity and the reassurance of his own ship and his own crew. He would do something about that fat bastard when he got back. Pine turned round as they left the bridge and winked at Blake, giving him a wide grin, then turned and followed Harvey and Zof.

They hurried down the deck, through a door, down four flights of ladders to reach the exterior door that led to the gangway and the RIB. A few surprised-looking passengers stood back nervously as the group hurried past them.

The gangway consisted of two flights of steps with a landing about half-way down, and another landing at the water's surface where the RIB was tied. Zof's five crewmen went down first, followed by Harvey, Zof and Pine who held back to bring up the rear. Harvey presumed this was to cover their escape, though there was no threat from either the crew or the passengers. The three of them had reached the first landing when Pine suddenly grunted out.

'Harvey!'

It was loud enough to carry, and Harvey turned. Pine, smiling as ever, was holding a Browning 8mm automatic, pointing it directly at Harvey's face as he turned. Pine fired three shots, following Harvey's head down as he collapsed. The first shot hit him on the side of the chin; he didn't make a sound, but his legs simply gave way beneath him. The second shot struck him in the cheek, snapping his head to one side with a jerk as he fell. The third hit him just below the throat, at the moment he slumped on to the landing grating.

Zof stared at the scene with utter astonishment. He gaped at Harvey's slumped body pumping red blood from three gaping wounds. He looked back up at Pine who was calmly holding the gun. The acrid smell of the gunpowder was still in the air. He found it difficult to speak, the sense of shock overwhelmed him.

'What in the name of heaven...?' he demanded, regaining his power of speech after a shocked silence that must have lasted no longer than a few seconds but which felt like minutes. 'You just shot Harvey,' he added, obviously but with disbelief.

'Don't get outta your box. I had orders,' grunted Pine, looking down at the inert body of the Englishman.

'Orders? Whose orders? Are you crazy, you fat American shit?' bellowed Zof – now, suddenly getting angry. His accent made his words sound sharper as he bore down on Pine, menacing and powerful. Even Pine was worried by the big Russian and hefted the Browning in his hand, getting ready to use it if needed.

'Listen, keep away, OK?' Pine grunted back hoarsely, menace in his voice. 'I had orders to get rid of Harvey from Kelley. He was a danger, I don't know why. Take it up with Kelley. Now get us out of here or we're all in the shit, you included. Move!'

Zof stared at Pine for a moment. The fat man wasn't smiling any more. 'Jesus', he muttered in Russian, and glared at Pine as he stepped over the body which was leaking blood that audibly dripped into the still water ten feet below the grating. There was no point in doing anything yet. Pine was right. Get off the ship quickly. Then he'd get Kelley. And Pine. In shocked fury, Zof silently followed Pine down the ladder to the RIB which rocked as the fat man got in. There was a sullen, angry mood settling on everyone in the small inflatable as they cast off and headed towards the battleship. No dared speak to Pine, still unsmiling, and Zof sat angrily in the stern of the boat. He had rarely felt an anger so powerful; but, as usual, he kept it under strict control.

*

'Did you order your man to kill Harvey?' demanded
Zof furiously when he reached the bridge. He had
marched straight off the RIB, pushing everyone out of
the way, Pine included, to find Kelley. His crew
watched him storm past in awed fascination. Zof in
this mood was deadly.

Kelley looked at him coolly. 'I had to.'

'You had to? You *had* to? Your fat pig made a meal of
the robbery, Kelley, and then went on to shoot your
man in cold blood. Now, my friend, you will explain
exactly what is going on here before I call my men
together and have you and that fat goblin thrown in
the damn sea.'

'Calm down, Zof. I had to have Harvey silenced. He
was going to give us away.'

'What do you mean, give us away. To whom?'

Kelley had worked out history while the others
were away on the liner; he thought it sounded pretty
good. He was certain that Zof wouldn't go for the real
thing, so he would sell him a different story, wait until
he was close to the *Jackson*, then order Pine to sort out
the troublesome Russian. This he would do by taking a
few hostages, Zhadanov for one. Zof would do anything to protect his crew. He'd let him go once they'd
scuttled the ship. In the meantime, there didn't seem
any point in creating trouble just yet. Or so he hoped.
The problem was, thought Kelley, that Zof didn't seem
as stupid as Tariq had insisted he was. The story that
his agents had picked up around the Vladivostok
dockyard was that Zof was pretty crazy, sitting in that
office all day. But he didn't seem at all crazy now: far
from it. Kelley hoped he'd buy the story but he wasn't
very convinced, not now he started telling it: 'I'm
pretty sure he was a plant from Lloyd's. An agent of
the insurance people in London,' he added helpfully.

Just as Kelley had thought, Zof didn't look convinced. 'How do you know this?'

'I don't. Not for certain. But a few things over the last month only add up if Harvey was working for them. Look how rapidly we got the information on the shipping movements, for instance. You can't tell me that Price could have beaten their goddamn security so easily. Look how that dumb fighter found us so quickly; how the French ship got a message out so easily. Sorry, Zof, but I think Harvey was giving the game away.'

'Kelley, that's not much to go on. Not much to kill a man for,' growled Zof threateningly.

The Russian wasn't buying this sit, thought Kelley. But he had to carry on now.

'Maybe. But there were other things, long before we met you. Strange trips, like he would disappear for a few days. He was too damn straight as well, you know that? Listen, Zof, trust me. I got a feeling about the kid. Anyhow, you really want to take the risk?'

But something still wasn't making sense to Zof. Kelley had just mentioned the *Madelaine*'s distress message, but he wasn't on the *Ocean Queen* when Blake first told them about it; there was no way Kelley could have known. 'How do you know about the *Madelaine*'s message? We only just found out about that,' Zof pressed.

Kelley paused briefly. 'Right. Pine told me over the VHF – while you were collecting the gold. I told him to report anything suspicious. That was the final straw. I told him to sort Harvey out quickly, before he could get us into more trouble.'

Zof didn't like it and, what was more, he didn't believe it. But he wasn't sure. Kelley's story seemed strange, but it had a ring of truth about it. And if he was telling the truth, Zof couldn't very well do anything. So he was stuck; right now, he couldn't afford to take the risk. Not for himself, not for his crew. Kelley was right. Zof was in no position to take the risk. Not yet.

Zof went quiet. Kelley's argument was getting more compelling. He didn't like the way it had been done, and Kelley should have warned him. But if the American was right, maybe it was the only thing to do. Zof still didn't trust the man, but for now he'd have to let it rest. 'So, my friend. Now what the hell do we do? If you're right, they're on to us anyway.'

Kelley turned and looked out of the bridge window at the *Ocean Queen*, lying motionless in the water a few hundred feet away.

'There's only one thing we can do. We'll have to disable that ship. If Harvey warned them, they'll expect the *Ocean Queen* to be making best speed for Hong Kong.'

'So why would disabling help?' asked Zof, puzzled now.

'Simple. The authorities' first concern will be finding *Ocean Queen* to make sure the passengers are OK. Once she doesn't contact them or show up anywhere, they'll panic and spend their time looking for her. We'll be able to slip away while they're distracted. If we let the ship go now, they'll be able to spend more time chasing us instead of looking for the liner. All we have to do is knock out their steering gear. You can use one of the torpedoes.'

Zof arched an eyebrow. 'You want me to torpedo a civilian ship with all those people on it, Kelley? Are you mad?'

'You got a better idea, Zof? We got to disable that ship somehow. I thought you were supposed to be able to do that sort of thing? You can set the torpedo to detonate near the ship, not exactly under it. You know what you're doing. It's safe enough. They can call for help. Of course, if you'd rather take the risk ...'

'And how do they get a call out to let anyone know what's happened? Harvey disabled the radio system.'

Kelley nearly blew it and stopped for a second. He'd forgotten that minor detail. And then his years of training, of covering up corruption, came to his rescue and a story sprang fully formed into his mind.

'Hey, no problem. They must have a spare. Ship that size, for Christ's sake,' he responded.

'So why did you get Harvey to bother disabling the radio at all?'

'I told him to; otherwise he'd get suspicious. They can get a call out, no problem,' came back Kelley quickly. He knew full well that the *Ocean Queen* would get a distress call out soon enough – he'd arranged that part already; Zof would think it was the spare, of course.

'There must be a safer way than using a torpedo, for heaven's sake. Why not send a crewman over to disable the ship?'

'Because we've got to get them scared. The Americans need to think we're deadly serious to get them in a real panic. Just disabling the thing is hardly going to do that, is it? The whole point is to frighten them, not just to disable the ship. They've got to think it's about to sink.'

Zof had to concede the point. Kelley's logic was frightening but impeccable. Zof reckoned they could just about get away with it. A torpedo aimed at the back of the liner would do plenty of damage but was unlikely to sink the ship. But he wanted the liner warned. Get people forward. Get the watertight doors shut. 'OK, Kelley. We'll try it. But listen, I didn't get into this to kill people. Anything goes wrong, we go back and pick them up. No matter what. And I will give them a proper warning. You understand me?'

'Sure, Zof. No problem. Just make sure you do the job properly. They got to get distracted looking for the liner. Remember the death penalty, Zof. They fry you, or they hang you. These guys don't just shoot you quietly one morning.'

'These are British people we're robbing, Kelley. If the Brits catch us, we're safe enough.'

'Forget it, Zof.' Kelley knew his law. 'This is an American ship under a Liberian flag. They'll kill you, sure enough. And even if it is the Brits, they still keep the death penalty for piracy. That and screwing the Queen's goddamn daughter, believe it or not.'

Kelley's threats didn't greatly worry Zof. He knew that worse was already in store if they didn't make good their escape.

*

Stalin had eight underwater torpedo tubes, located at the bow, four on each side. They were built to house heavy high explosive, long-range torpedoes, but the crew was loading a modern, lightweight wire-guided torpedo that together with a dozen others had been thoughtfully collected by Zof before they departed. The torpedo couldn't be fired using the normal compressed air system to drive it out into the water: it was too small to fit the tube snugly. In any case, Zof didn't like the look of the ancient compressed air plant. They would simply flood the tube and the torpedo should drive itself out under its own power.

The loading was completed. Now Zof had to get the *Stalin* into position to fire the torpedo. He ordered half-speed ahead and the wheel hard over. A burst of white foam erupted from the stern of the battleship as four huge screws bit into the water, sending it boiling to the surface. Slowly, but with gathering speed, the massive vessel began a long, lazy loop to starboard. As the ship turned, he called Blake on the VHF.

'*Ocean Queen*, this is *Stalin*. This is a warning, I repeat this is a warning. I intend to fire one torpedo at your stern to disable your vessel. I will do this in about five minutes' time. Please order your watertight doors closed and make appropriate arrangements for the safety of your passengers and crew. The detonation should not cause major damage as I will be aiming to miss your ship but to explode nearby. Do you understand this warning?' Zof released the 'transmit' switch on the handset and waited for the reply. He could imagine the chaos he was now causing.

The carrier wave suddenly cut in. Blake's voice was calm but furious. '*Stalin*, *Ocean Queen*. I have received your warning. You understand I have nearly a thousand civilians on this ship?'

The carrier wave ceased. Blake was waiting for a reply but Zof would give none. There was nothing he could say.

The carrier wave hissed again. 'Rot in hell, you bastards' said Blake, spitting out the words, then the carrier wave went silent. Zof shrugged. There was nothing more he could do. He would make sure his aim was true, at least.

It took several minutes to bring the prow of the *Stalin* round to face the *Ocean Queen*. Zof ordered the engines stopped before the prow was facing the liner. The sheer inertia of the 75,000 tons of ship meant that it continued turning; Zof had judged his manoeuvre to a nicety. Just as the stern of the *Ocean Queen* came into a direct line with the torpedo tubes at the bow of the *Stalin*, the ship became motionless. Zof asked Lavrov, the bay-chay three commander in charge of mines and torpedoes, to order the torpedo crew to fire. He had made sure Lavrov understood the importance of the shot. Don't hit the bloody ship, or I'll crucify you.

The torpedo sprang to life inside the flooded tube. The powerful electric motor wound the multi-bladed propeller up to maximum revs within a few seconds. The stubby weapon leapt forward, out into the warm Pacific water, and headed at a rapidly increasing speed towards the *Ocean Queen*.

It was fitted with a simple wire-guided steering system. A basic rudder gave about 20 degrees steerage left or right, operated from the ship. It was exactly like steering a toy boat on a lake. It ran out of range after two kilometres, but this was usually enough to position the torpedo with sufficient accuracy to do the damage intended.

It took two minutes exactly to find its way to the stern of the liner. As it approached, a simple sonar proximity fuse registered the nearing mass of the hull. Lavrov expertly guided it to miss the stern by 30 feet. At 50 feet to go, he armed the warhead. A few seconds later, as the proximity fuse detected the nearing hull, it sent an electrical signal to arm the detonator. Just two seconds later, as the hull started to recede, the fuse decided this was the nearest it would get and set off the detonator which a millisecond later ignited the main charge.

The *Ocean Queen* had a single large rudder and twin screws. The rudder and the screws were located close to each other, a deliberate design to allow the screws to exert their power against the wide blade of the rudder, thus increasing the manoeuvrability of the ship.

The warhead exploded 30 feet behind the rudder. The shock wrenched the rudder away from its supporting bearing; then tore away the bottom third completely, sending the jagged sheet of metal spinning towards the port screw. It smashed into the screw, bending three of the eight blades back on themselves and in the process twisting the bracket that held the shaft and screw assembly as it emerged from the hull. The sudden pressure on the bracket was transmitted immediately to the shaft itself, and although it was nearly three feet in diameter and machined from solid stainless steel, it too bent under the impact of the explosion and the flying rudder blade. The other screw and shaft were undamaged by the debris, but the shock was transmitted along the undamaged shaft to the main reduction gearbox inside the engine room. The gear system was in neutral but the drive gear on the shaft was lifted out of its bearing and smashed into the drive gear from the turbine, ripping several teeth from the wheel.

The hull itself remained intact, though badly bent, but the bearing that supported the rudder was dislodged from its seal through the hull, and the water began to force its way through the torn opening.

On the bridge of the *Ocean Queen*, Blake had watched *Stalin* slowly make her turn away from him, and assumed they were making their getaway. He was about to order the ship to get under way when he noticed that the battleship was continuing its turn.

'What the hell are they doing now?' he asked no one in particular as he watched the pirates.

He soon found out when Zof's warning came on the radio. He was right: there was chaos as Blake ordered the passengers and crew away from the stern and closed the doors, waiting for the blast.

They couldn't see the torpedo which was designed to run deep enough to be invisible to the target ship. As they watched the motionless battleship, they felt the sudden lurch from the stern of the ship, followed by a distant thump as the explosion broke the surface of the water. Pandemonium broke out. The atmosphere was already tense, stretched like thin wire. It wasn't panic but it was close.

*

Zof watched the explosion through binoculars. The warhead charge on these modern torpedoes was not great; he'd aimed well off, too, to make sure he didn't sink the liner. But you could never be certain. He hoped to God Lavrov was right.

He waited for the foam to subside. There didn't appear to be much visible damage, but the whole ship had heaved up from the stern and the torpedo had clearly found its mark.

'It looked close, didn't it?' said Kelley. 'I thought it would go off some way behind the ship. Let's hope the ship is OK, Zof. Like you said, we don't want any more deaths,' he added.

Zof stayed silent and carried on watching the liner. It was too far away to see the panic on board that he knew he had caused. But the *Ocean Queen* had settled back down in the water and kept an even trim, at least for now. He was pretty sure his aim was good. Time would tell. If the damage was bad, they'd find out within the next few minutes. Otherwise it could take hours.

Kelley, on the other hand, was delighted with the result. It gave him a better story than he'd dared hope. Now he had the perfect excuse for keeping Zof hanging around. According to his calculations and to Tariq's intelligence, the *Jackson* would now be at least twenty hours away, maybe more. They could sit quietly and wait for the ship to fall into the trap. It was running perfectly, thought Kelley. Nothing would go wrong now. But would Zof go for it – or would he have to be pushed?

'I hope the ship is OK, too, Kelley,' said Zof. He sounded unconvinced.

'Yeah, it should be. So, Zof, let's get away from here. Quick as we can. They'll be OK,' he suggested.

'Not yet, Kelley, not yet,' muttered Zof, looking through the binoculars. The liner was keeping a good trim, but it was too early to say exactly what had happened.

Kelley knew Zof well enough now. It was time to push the man.

'Look, Zof, we can't hang around here, OK? Leave the ship alone. They can look after themselves. We gotta get out of here, and fast. Get your crew working, for Christ's sake,' he demanded.

'Kelley, shut up, please. I will make these choices. I do not intend to leave this ship sitting here if the passengers are in danger. Maybe it's the sort of thing you do in America. In Russia, we treat people differently. Now go back to your cabin and wait,' growled Zof.

Perfect! 'Christ, Zof, you trying to get us all killed? You want to sit here for the fucking Navy to turn up?'

'I take my chances, Kelley. So do you,' said Zof, starting to get annoyed.

'We can't just wait here. Tell you what, Zof. Go over the horizon and wait out of sight. That way, we can get to help them if they need it, and if they don't we can get the hell out of it. How's that?' He prayed the stubborn Russian would fall for it. They would wait for the *Jackson* out of sight. The American would heave-to for the rescue operation, and then the *Stalin* could strike. They would be a helpless target, just the sort that Kelley preferred. And it would give him time to get Pine to sort out the little problem of what to do with Zof.

Zof paused. The American's idea was not so bad. Wait over the horizon. If no help showed up within, say, twelve hours, he could always go back and get them. They'd hear them coming from miles off, of course, on the radio. They'd be yelling themselves hoarse. It took Zof about a second to work all this out; he had a capacity to change his mind with lightning speed when a better idea came up.

He put down his binoculars. 'Very well, Kelley. Over the horizon. You should have joined the Navy. You'd have been good,' smiled the Russian thinly, and gave the orders to start up the ship. Kelley smiled too, but it wasn't in appreciation of Zof's comment.

The *Stalin* got under way again. Zof brought her up to 5 knots and very slowly steamed away from the *Ocean Queen*. At ten miles off, he brought the ship to a halt once more. He and Kelley watched the *Ocean Queen* intently through binoculars.

'It looks a bit down in the stern to me,' said Kelley after a while. 'I couldn't be sure, of course.'

Zof examined the stern. It was difficult to tell, but he thought it might look a bit low, now that Kelley mentioned it.

'It's difficult to get it precise, Kelley. My crew didn't exactly have a lot of time for training, you know,' replied the Russian.

'So, Zof, you were right to wait. Just in case,' said Kelley. Zof stayed silent and carried on watching the stern of the huge liner through the glasses, the same battered old Nikons he'd had for years.

The sullen silence was shattered a moment later as the bridge door was thrown open. Kishkov had burst into the room ...

His watery eyes were shining with rage, and there was a look on his face of overwhelming anger. Zof and Kelley turned in astonishment at the sight of the angry old man. He had gripped the sides of the bridge doorway and was screaming a stream of Russian, jabbing his finger at all of them again and again.

'What's up with him, for God's sake?' asked Kelley from the side of his mouth, not wanting to antagonise the crazed old man. He couldn't understand a word he was screaming at them.

Zof found it difficult to pick up the sense of the Russian's gibbering. He was almost incoherent and was speaking in an accent Zof wasn't used to. He listened carefully for a few moments, trying to pick a few words out of the stream of anger.

While Kishkov continued raving, Zof whispered a running translation into Kelley's ear. 'He's upset that we torpedoed the *Ocean Queen*. He says it's murder. He wants nothing to do with murderers. He asks God to curse me, you, the ship, *Stalin*, the Russians and just about everyone else. As Chief Designer, he's ordering me to put out boats to rescue the *Ocean Queen* passengers. Then he's taking over the ship. Then you must pray for forgiveness. Apparently God will strike us down shortly,' relayed Zof.

Kelley looked incredulously at Zof. 'Do we need this? Tell the old fool to fuck off.'

'Kelley, my friend, I do not think that is the best way to handle the situation. Let me talk to him', said Zof. He went up to the old man and took his arm. Kishkov was shaking with rage – and then Zof caught a wave of vodka fumes that stung the back of his throat. It was difficult to tell if he was completely drunk or not. He guided Kishkov towards a chair on the bridge and managed to get him to sit down, though he was still muttering.

Zof spoke to him gently and firmly. The ageing designer seemed to listen as Kelley watched suspiciously from near the wheel. After several minutes the old man was visibly calmer; he was nodding his head and starting to smile. It was like an upset child being calmed down by a parent.

'What on earth did you say to him?' asked Kelley when Zof stood up and left Kishkov blowing his nose.

'I told him we will leave the scene, but we will maintain a radio watch. I explained my plan. This makes sense to him. Now he feels a lot better. I think our friend here has enjoyed a little too much vodka down in the engine room. But now he is fine.'

This was all Kelley needed. He'd just got Zof where he wanted him, and now the old man was playing up. These fucking Russians were all crazy. Now he'd have to get Pine to take care of Kishkov, too. This was starting to get complicated. What the hell. At least the rest of it was going to plan.

Leaving Kishkov quietly sitting, Zof could resume the task of getting the ship out of sight. He issued the orders to his bay-chay commanders, explaining exactly what his plan was. Knowing his crew would not be able to leave the stricken liner either, he explained the need to escape and the need to keep watch, and they were satisfied.

The battleship shuddered into life as the turbines began to spin and the four huge screws once more bit into the water.

15

When Skulski, the pilot of the second F-15, relayed the
story of the downing of the aircraft by the *Stalin* to
his controller at Futenma Air Force base, it set off a
train of events that moved with the speed of a
tornado. What started as a slightly more than routine
recon. mission had turned into open warfare. Stage by
stage – but at the kind of speed which only the
American war machine can work at once roused – the
temperature of the incident increased.

Within hours the Chairman of the Joint Chiefs of
Staff, General Billy Ross, had called his senior staff to
an emergency meeting to see what they were going to
do about this presumptuous Russian pirate. The
meeting was scheduled for 5 o'clock Eastern Time, just
as Zof would be moving *Stalin* to its stand-off position
to await the fate of the luxury liner it had so recently
disabled.

In advance of the meeting, Chief of Naval
Operations Ray Bell, in charge of the US Navy and one
of the Chiefs whom Billy Ross had summoned, had
been speaking again to Maddox at Northwood, the
man whose call to him earlier that day had started this
whole horrible mess. Much as he hated to admit it, he
needed Maddox's help, and fast.

Apart from what Maddox had told him, Bell had
managed to discover very little more from his own

intelligence about just how powerful *Stalin* might be. There didn't seem to be anyone on his staff who knew much about the ship at all, other than it was big and very fast, in its day. He needed to know more. And quickly. And Maddox had mentioned some guy who seemed to have the answers.

Military and diplomatic etiquette demanded that he should go through all the usual channels; this would take about a week. Bell was not the sort of person to stand on ceremony. Maddox already had the clearance to talk directly to him; he didn't see any reason why he shouldn't talk directly to Maddox. Ross told him to go ahead. Five minutes after that, Bell was through to Northwood on the secure landlines.

'Charlie, how you doing?' asked Bell. The two men had met several times before on various exercises and NATO thrashes. This was the second conversation within a few hours and they dropped the titles.

'Very well, thank you, Ray. I gather you've had a bit of a problem with this little scrap in the South China Sea. I hope you'll pass our condolences on to the family of your young airman. I think he was very brave,' said Maddox.

'Thanks, Charlie. Between you and me, I think he kind of gave it away. A guy in a plane like that shouldn't have been shot down by some Russian heap of antique iron, know what I mean? I guess my guys should have listened to your man there a bit better. But I appreciate your thoughts. Listen, Charlie, our senior people are getting together later today to take a look at this thing. We got a good ship pretty near, the *Jackson*, but I don't want to send it in until I know more about what exactly is going on here. I guess we could do with your guy ... what's his name? ...'

'McEwan?'

'That's him. Can you get him over here? He seems to

know something about this Russian battleship. We're a bit hazy on it on this side, I'm sorry to say.'

'He certainly does, Ray. Studied the things at University, can you believe? Tells me he knows as much about them as anyone alive. God knows, he seems to know what he's talking about. I'll get him on a plane to you right away. Commercial, I'm afraid. Bit restricted on planes, these days.'

'Hey, Charlie, no problem. We can help out with that. I can have an SR71 ready to go at Fairford within the hour. That might speed things up a little.'

'Thank you, Ray. I'm sure it would. And Ray, keep me in touch, would you? I gather we have some of our people on the liner they're after. I'd appreciate you watching our interests. I mean, I'm sure you will.'

'Charlie, relax. I'll let you know everything we're doing, OK? Take care.'

Maddox put down the scrambler phone and looked up at McEwan. There was a look of satisfaction on his face. 'That solves a problem or two. I think they're rather desperate for you, McEwan. You've got less than an hour to get out to Fairford. A Blackbird is warming up. You'll be at Andrews in under two hours, and the Pentagon half an hour after that. They don't know a bloody thing about your ship, McEwan. Just stick with it and report direct to me via the embassy when you can. Look after our interests, for heaven's sake.'

McEwan couldn't think of anything to say as he hurried out of the room. Maddox watched him depart, deeply sadden by his own impotence and envious of the raw power of the Americans, but pleased all the same that he'd managed to keep a man centre stage, if nothing else. Oxfordshire to the Pentagon in 2 hours, he reflected. If he left Fairford for London at the same time as McEwan was taking off, he'd still be stuck on the M25 while McEwan was walking through the bloody front door of the Pentagon. The best he could have done to get McEwan there would have been an economy ticket on the next BA flight to Washington.

*

Crawford on the *Jackson* was getting the full story. The attack by the F-15; the downing of the aircraft; the robbery and then the torpedoing. All this was happening just 100 miles to the north; much as he wanted to charge in, he knew full well that he needed to take stock of the situation. Bell's staff at the Pentagon ordered him to slow down, too. This Russian ship was an unknown quality: they weren't going to let their newest ship charge in blind.

Crawford sat in his cabin fuming. After months at sea playing at diplomats, here was some action, but nobody could tell him a thing about this Russian antique and he had no idea what he was likely to face. How bad could it be, he thought to himself? A fifty-year-old ship crewed by a bunch of dissidents? But the Chief had ordered him to stand off until they knew more about it, and stand off he would. Slatter, irritating as always, was getting gung-ho, which in Crawford's book was the worse thing a USN officer could be. A bit of serious action would teach him. It was sad, he mused, that they would be up against an enemy who didn't stand a hope in hell and would probably give up the moment *Jackson* looked serious. Still, Slatter would learn something.

*

The five most powerful men in the world were gathering in a secure conference room inside the gloomy Pentagon building. The vast five-sided block built in the 1930s, by the same General Leslie Groves who went on to master-mind the building of the first atomic bomb, had the same sense of gloom and foreboding as the first nuclear device.

General Billy Ross, Chairman of the Joint Chiefs, was sitting drinking coffee at the head of the table as the other four assembled.

Abe Brinkley – the small, neat and fussy head of the CIA – was first into the room, punctual and eager as ever. He was a politician and therefore disliked as a matter of principle by everyone, including Ross. Even if he wasn't a politician, he would still have been disliked. He wore his ambitions like the rest of them would wear a row of medals on parade.

Brinkley was followed in by Air Force chief Martin Prendergast, a big, overweight man whose skin gleamed with sweat even on a cold day.

Then came Spencer Boggs of the Marines, with his famous crew-cut and his trademark scarred face – claimed by the press (and not contradicted by Boggs) to be a Vietnam war wound, but in reality the result of an enthusiastic tackle in a college football game – who marched in five minutes later.

Ray Bell, the relaxed Navy Chief, ambled in last, the only one wearing casual clothes. He was supposed to be taking a day's leave, but he'd been in his office most of the time since the incident blew up; he'd be damned if he was going to struggle into uniform. Pentagon staffers were not surprised to see him in jeans and battered sneakers. Bell was never the most conventional military man in the place.

The big rosewood doors were pushed closed behind them by two armed Marine guards. The meeting was about to start. Like all such meetings, the proceedings were carefully taped to produce the minutes afterwards. Ross started as usual by announcing the date, the time and those present in a low monotone, looking directly at the slim microphone in front of him.

He finished, paused and then went in for the kill. Ross hated wasting time on meetings.

'Ray, this is a major fuck-up and the President's people are screaming blue murder. I need to get back quickly and I want a plan. You want to start?' he asked without further preamble. The transcribers would later edit the comments so that the minutes would read that 'the Chairman stated that the President was concerned over reported events and he asked the meeting for urgent plans to be prepared.'

Chief of Naval Operations Raymond Carver Bell grinned. He liked the tough, no-nonsense approach of Billy Ross, the black kid from the East side who had hauled himself up to become (short of the President), the most powerful man on earth.

'OK, Billy. Here's what we know so far. I guess you other guys can fill in some more details. This ship, *Stalin*, disappeared from Vladivostok naval yard a week or so back. Nobody, by all accounts, noted a damn thing until some time later. Eventually the Kremlin airheads figured it out, and the event appeared in intelligence reports but, frankly, no one took any notice. It didn't seem much of an issue at the time. Then yesterday we got a call from the Brits saying the *Ocean Queen* liner was about to be robbed by pirates, namely this ship. The liner is one of our ships, by the way, but Liberian registered. Sorry, Billy, but our guys weren't too excited, you know? It was a pretty crazy story. Anyhow, Martin here very kindly sent a couple of F-15s out of Futenma just to help out.'

'And the rest we know,' commented Ross sharply. 'This is bad news, Martin. The President is fuming and the press won't be far behind. He wants to know how a fifty-year-old pile of crap shoots down one of our guys and leaves the other one kissing his ass. He also wants to know how come someone steals a 75,000 ton battleship and our intelligence services say damn all about it.'

'That's not fair, General. We issued reports,' bristled Abe Brinkley of the CIA.

'Hey, come on, Abe. I re-read those reports on the way over. Let me quote: "Unconfirmed reports suggest battleship *Stalin* taken over by disaffected crew and stolen from Navy yard. *Stalin* is fifty-year-old battleship probably in unseaworthy condition. No further information available" – buried on page eighteen, Billy, page eighteen of a routine intelligence report. I mean, where's the sense of priority?' asked Bell, looking angrily at the small intelligence chief. The room's dislike of the man could almost be felt.

'No one knows much about the ship, not even your Navy Int. guys, Ray. Ask them, maybe. Frankly, it was not considered a major target. We got plenty of things going on that we need to keep an eye on. Museum exhibits we got little call for,' responded Abe Brinkley, his sleek features looking smug behind the wire glasses.

'The Brits sent some story over, didn't they? Recently?' asked Bell quietly.

'Sure. Uncorroborated. Hearsay. Junk intelligence. You want me to circulate stuff like that without clearing it? Do I look stupid?' responded Brinkley, not looking very comfortable.

'Well, Ray. I guess we've all got the problem now. Do you know anything about this ship? Any idea how we got caught with our pants round our ankles?' Ross asked.

Ray Bell looked uncomfortable. 'Billy, like Abe's people, that ship was not on our list of interesting targets either. I've been trying to rake up some information for the past few hours, but we don't have anyone with any real idea. The only person who seems to know anything about it is a Brit, I'm afraid.'

'A Brit, Ray? What Brit is this?' asked Ross sharply.

'Sorry, Billy. I hadn't managed to tell you. One of Charlie Maddox's staff, a lieutenant called McEwan. He claims to be an expert on these old ships; says he knows a fair bit about the *Stalin*. I'm having him flown over by Blackbird. He should have landed by now. I thought he might be helpful, before we rush into anything?'

The five other men stared at the Admiral. The idea of inviting an outsider to join them, and a Brit at that, was distinctly uncomfortable. The five most powerful men in the world were backed up by vast intelligence resources costing hundreds of millions of dollars, including the most advanced technology in the world. Bringing in an outsider rendered each man's intelligence budget open to question.

'We need a Brit, Billy, do we?' asked Spencer Boggs, the Marine chief. He looked evenly at Ross, his Army superior, quietly putting Ross on the defensive.

'Looks like no one else has got much to offer, Spencer,' said Martin Prendergast acidly. He turned to Ross at the head of the table: 'Billy, I don't want to lose any more men.'

'Well, Spencer, let's hear what our British friend has to say. No harm in it,' replied Billy Ross with a wry smile. 'Where's your man now, Ray?'

Ray Bell picked up the phone on the mahogany table in front of him. He spoke a few short sentences, then replaced the handset. 'He just got off the helo. He'll be here in five minutes.'

'Great, Ray. Let's take a comfort break and back in ten,' said Ross, getting to his feet. The rest of them immediately stood up. Some made calls, others went to the washroom. The two Marine sentries carefully picked up the single sheet of notepaper that each was allowed and, doodled on or not, placed it in a sealed metal container for secure destruction, replacing it with a single clean sheet.

*

McEwan arrived at the Pentagon reeking of kerosene and in a state of pleasant shock. He had grabbed a Navy driver to take him out to Fairford, where he had been waved through the security cordon like a five-star general. The SR71 Blackbird, sleek and powerful, was waiting on a distant area of tarmac, the two huge engines slowly whistling to themselves on idle. He was handed a helmet and a g-suit, which he struggled into, and then bodily lifted over the wing stub into the rear seat by two big ground crew. The pilot was already strapped in, visor down, completely oblivious to McEwan's presence.

The moment that McEwan had settled into the tiny cockpit and connected up his oxygen hose, the perspex canopy descended, shutting him into the aircraft. The engines roared into life, and the Blackbird bumped its way over the tarmac to the end of the runway. It sat there for half a minute. Then without warning, the engines flared, the aircraft leapt forward and raced down the runway and within twenty seconds was airborne. They climbed at speed into the sky above Oxfordshire, reached 60,000 feet, levelled out and rocketed out across the Atlantic at 2,200 mph. They touched down at Andrews Air Force Base, just outside Washington, exactly one hour and forty minutes later.

The sweet smell of jet fuel was overpowering throughout the flight. He found out later that the SR71 was notorious for leaking fuel; its two huge jets used so much that most of the plane was a giant fuel tank that seeped kerosene from the day it was made.

The plane thundered down the runway hauling twin drogue chutes. As it pulled up to a sharp halt, the canopy was already opening. McEwan was pulled out of his seat and hustled into the back of a grey Chevrolet van that accelerated back down the runway where a big helicopter was waiting, the twin rotors already lazily turning. He was pushed on to the helicopter less than two hours after leaving Fairford. The Pentagon building was just 12 miles away.

Now, at the main entrance to the Pentagon, he was being carefully frisked and photographed by the crew-cut Marines who, in surly silence, looked after the security of the rambling, awesome building. Once given clearance, he was escorted at speed down seemingly endless corridors, turning this way and that, past the curious glances at his now crumpled Royal Navy uniform that still reeked of kerosene, to meet the CNO, Ray Bell, who was waiting outside the JCS conference room.

His escort, one of Bell's staff, introduced them formally. 'Lieutenant McEwan, Royal Navy, Admiral Bell, Chief of Naval Operations.'

'Good to see you, Lieutenant. You're Maddox's expert, so he tells me?'

'Yes, sir. Pleased to meet you,' replied McEwan, who if he was taken aback by the Chief of Naval Operation's jeans and sneakers certainly wasn't going to show it. He saluted smartly, and then shook the outstretched hand.

'Good trip?'

'Extraordinary, sir, thank you.'

'Good planes, those things. Smell like shit, but they're fast.'

'I had noticed,' grinned McEwan.

'So, Charlie Maddox says you know all about this Russian ship?'

'Yes, sir. Well, a little. I did my thesis on Second World War battleships and sort of kept an interest since.

Stalin was the biggest and best, sir. She was something of a special subject, you see.'

'Sure, McEwan. So you can tell my people all about the ship? I mean, armaments, tactics and so forth?'

'Oh yes, sir. No problem. I can also brief you on the pirates themselves. We've found out a little bit about them.'

'Reliable sources?' Bell wasn't going to admit that his own people were still struggling to get anything.

'I know some people in Hong Kong. They were able to talk to the Frenchman, who was robbed by the pirates first. We managed to get a name. We're tracing down the connections now. Also we found out something about the Russians on the ship. Maybe your people can help?'

'Listen, just tell us everything you can and we'll figure it out from there. You ready?'

'Absolutely, sir.'

Bell led McEwan back into the conference room. The others saw him enter and resumed their seats. Billy Ross waited for the group to settle.

'OK, Ray, maybe you'd like to introduce your friend here?' started Ross, settling back into his chair.

'Sure. This is Lieutenant McEwan of the British Navy ...'

'Royal Navy, sir,' interrupted McEwan in a soft voice.

'Pardon me?' said Bell, surprised by the interruption.

'Royal Navy, sir. We don't call it the British Navy; we call it the Royal Navy. Tradition and all that, if it's all the same to you, sir.'

Spencer Boggs was trying to keep a straight face. The others were also trying to keep smiles under control.

'Sure, McEwan. Royal Navy, not British Navy. Sorry about that,' said Bell acidly.

'That's quite all right sir. Common enough mistake,' McEwan replied. Boggs snorted loudly.

'OK. The lieutenant here is something of an expert on Second World War battleships and knows something about this *Stalin* ship, so he tells me. Also he will update us on the pirates themselves, about which I gather we now know something. It's all yours, McEwan,' said Bell, and left McEwan to it.

'Yes, sir. Thank you. I don't know how much you know about *Stalin*?' McEwan started.

'Just assume we know nothing, son,' growled Ross. It was close to the truth, but McEwan wouldn't know that.

'Yes, sir. Well, the *Stalin* was, and still is, the biggest, fastest and most powerful warship ever built. She was originally commissioned to counter the threat of the Japanese and American heavy battleships being built at the time. In particular, she was meant to outrun and outgun the *Yamoto*. You will recall that your own Navy put paid to that particular ship towards the end of the last War.'

Bell and the others nodded wisely. Nobody had the slightest inkling of the fate of the *Yamoto*, but everyone was happy to pretend that they did.

'However, the *Stalin* never actually entered active service, of course. She was just completing her sea trials when the atomic bomb entered service instead ...' Ross smiled at the polite euphemism for Hiroshima '... and the Soviet leadership's resources were devoted to other ends. She was mothballed and tied up at Vladivostok, where she was built. Right up to the collapse, she was used as a training ship, so she was kept in good condition, even though I don't think she was ever modernised. Up until a couple of years ago that's what she was doing, then we sort of lost sight of her after that. The collapse of the Soviet Union hit the Pacific

Fleet pretty hard, being so far away from Moscow. Whole crews simply walked off ship, mainly as a result of not being paid for over a year. That part of Vladivostok was pretty dependent on the Navy for local jobs, so feeling ran rather high when years of secure employment just vanished.'

'What do we know about the guys who took this thing?' asked Ross.

'A little. We know something about the Russians on board – and a bit about the others.'

'There are others?' asked Abe Brinkley of the CIA, not managing to hide his surprise. He'd automatically assumed the pirates were disaffected Russians.

'One of the leaders appears to be, er, British. Our people interviewed the Captain of the French ship once he reached Hong Kong. Apparently there were two of them, calling themselves Baker and Charlie. The Frenchman reckoned that Baker was definitely English; he claims he recognised the accent. Charlie was a particularly nasty character, by all accounts. We're assuming they're cover names, of course. Able, Baker, Charlie: the old phonetic alphabet. We assume there's an Able somewhere, but our Frenchman didn't get to see him.'

'If they're Brits, maybe you should send out your British Navy to help us with the problem, Lieutenant' commented Prendergast of the Air Force, heavy with sarcasm. Ross shot him a glance that was clearly meant to keep him quiet.

'Carry on, son,' growled Ross.

'Yes, sir. The motive appears to be purely financial. The French ship was carrying a substantial quantity of bullion; so is – or probably was, by now – the *Ocean Queen*. We think there is inside information being passed across. As I left, we heard from Lloyd's that one of their people, called Stanley Price, has vanished. They think it might be him.'

'So what about these Russians?' asked Brinkley.

'Yes, sir, the Russians. A chap called Yakov Zof appears to be the main character, sir. Bit of a local hero, well-known in the Navy by all accounts, and not at all happy about his new masters, and really rather cheesed off about not being paid for some time. He's quite good, so my sources tell me. Outstanding, actually. They also seem to have found the original designer of the *Stalin*, name of Kishkov. Quite famous in his day. We had no idea he was still alive, but he seems to have survived incarceration by Stalin and appears to be on board the ship. He's 82 but still active, and mad as a hatter according to our reports. Apparently he changed from being a Stalinist to a religious maniac during his time in the camps. Not surprising, I suppose.'

Brinkley was quietly furious that the British officer seemed to have a better grip on intelligence coming out of Russia than his whole organisation.

'What are your sources here, exactly? What's your collateral?' asked Brinkley, hoping his annoyance wouldn't show.

'We were lucky enough to have an inside source. Quite reliable, too, by all accounts,' replied McEwan, trying to look nonchalant about the precious intelligence that Dalby had passed on, and being very careful not to mention the fact that Brinkley's own people had told Zof's brother to get lost. Clearly Brinkley hadn't heard about Feliks' efforts to sell the story.

Brinkley didn't follow up the question. McEwan wasn't going to reveal his sources, that was for sure. There was a pause in the meeting, as though it wanted time to take a breath. Boggs broke the pensive silence. 'So these guys are pretty serious? Basically, Billy, we got ourselves a bunch of Brit and Russki pirates cruising the Pacific stealing just about anything they can get their hands on, headed up by some shit-hot Navy Captain,' said Boggs. 'They already shot down one of our guys. Looks like the US Cavalry has to come to the rescue before anyone else gets hurt.'

'I guess that's more or less right,' replied Ross, looking at McEwan.

'That being the case, I don't see what option we have but to get Ray's people in there hard. A full-scale strike now should solve the problem. This is a fifty-year-old ship we're taking on here, Billy. It's not asking a lot just to go in and take the thing out.' Spencer Boggs never saw any point in beating about the bush.

Bell nodded. 'I've got the *Jackson* standing by about four hours' steaming away south of the scene. You give me the word, I'll send them in. She's my newest ship. Turkey-shoot stuff, Billy, no problem.'

'Makes sense,' replied Ross. 'I mean, the *Jackson* and a bit of back-up from the Air Force should easily be enough to stop this thing. Hell, with all the technology we've got, we should be able to track it down and sort these characters out within a few hours. I don't see the big problem.' He was looking at McEwan.

'I really don't think it will be that simple, sir,' murmured McEwan, finally responding to Ross's stare.

'How come, son? You're talking about the biggest Navy and Air Force in the world against one beat-up vintage warship that probably doesn't even have radar. You're talking target practice, son, not rocket science. The *Jackson* is the newest ship in the Navy. It could blow a fleet of Second World War battleships out of the goddamn water and get home in time for lunch.'

The Americans' faith in technology was like a religion, thought McEwan. 'I still think it's going to be difficult. Look what happened to your aircraft, sir, with all due respect.'

'That was just bad flying, McEwan. The guy we sent didn't think he was about to be shot at. It was just sloppy. And some good luck for *Stalin*,' commented Martin Prendergast, still sensitive about carrying the first casualty around the table.

'I don't think so. You see, your pilot would have had his IFF and target warning systems switched on. I think he'd be relying on that to warn of an impending attack. He'd be expecting to get locked on by the enemy radar and use that as his first warning, right?' said McEwan.

'Right,' admitted Prendergast. 'Standard procedure. Textbook stuff. What's the problem?'

'The problem is, sir, there's no weapons guidance radar on the *Stalin*. No IFF, no high technology to detect. Your pilot was waiting to get locked on to them, but there was nothing there to lock on to him.'

'So no warning, eh, son?' nodded Ross, seeing which way McEwan was going.

'That's right, sir. No warning. In fact, for modern detection systems that mainly rely on radar and radio emissions, *Stalin* is as effectively cloaked as a Stealth fighter.'

'But now we know what to expect,' Bell came in, 'all we have to do is find them and blow them away.'

'Admiral, think what happened with the missile fired from the F-15. I grant you she has no modern defences against missiles; but what she has got is over two feet of armour plate. This stuff was designed to absorb the kinetic energy of an 18 inch shell hitting it square on. The fact is, gentlemen, I don't know of any modern HE missile that can deliver anything like that energy. Modern weapons are designed to penetrate the lightweight hulls of our present-day ships and explode inside them. Your best missiles are just going to bounce off *Stalin*.'

'So we torpedo it. Our modern torpedoes can hit a boat in a bathtub from miles off.'

'Same problem, Admiral. *Stalin* was built with extraordinary underwater protection. By all accounts, Comrade Kishkov was paranoid about submarine attacks. *Stalin* has got a triple bottom with an armour layer and a honeycomb structure throughout the bottom half of the ship. A modern torpedo will do very little to it.'

'Not if we hit the steering gear. That's what finally got the *Bismarck*. We can send in a torpedo and blow the sterngear right off.'

'I'm afraid our friend Kishkov was ahead of the Germans in that respect. He put the propellers in tunnels so they're almost surrounded by armour plate. The rudders are massive things and are contained inside cages that will detonate a torpedo before anything gets near them. On top of that, he had chains hung all around the sterngear to act as first line of defence, and extended the bilge keels aft to provide solid side protection. You'd be lucky to blow the rudders off. And even if you managed it, he can still steer on his props which are almost untouchable. It's the same problem, sir – modern torpedoes simply don't carry the explosive power to get through all that protection. A modern lightweight hull will fold up if it's hit; but this thing just ignores them.'

'Come on, McEwan. A modern torpedo carries a massive charge. You're not telling me that this old heap won't even notice one?'

'More or less, sir. Remember that these old ships were designed to absorb massive blows of kinetic energy – sudden explosions concentrated in a very small area. Modern warheads are too diffuse. The designers today are after speed and stealth, so warheads are small and accuracy is all-important. The

Stalin was built to take hits from torpedoes three times the size of anything we use today, and still carry on sailing.'

'Now hang on, son,' said Ross, getting irritated. 'What you're telling us is that ship is unsinkable. I don't buy that. No ship ever built is that powerful.'

'I agree, General. The problem is one of technology. Our modern-day technology is deadly, but not against the brute force of something like *Stalin*. We had the weapons fifty years ago, no problem. But not today. And if you did press home an attack anyway, what ship could stand up to 22 inch shells raining down on them? Modern ships have no armour. Their only defence is to track incoming missiles and either dodge them with radar deception or shoot them down in mid-air. Sorry, General, but you can't fool four tons of high-explosive shell into going somewhere else. And you certainly can't shoot the bugger out of the air, either. Excuse the language, sir.'

There was a silence while each of the chiefs thought through what McEwan was telling them. Ross leaned back in his big leather chair and chewed vigorously on the end of a dark blue pencil that had 'Joint Chiefs of Staff' gold-embossed in large letters down one side; they vanished at such a rate as souvenirs that a new box was opened every morning. 'OK, son, if you're right, we got ourselves a biggish problem here. I'm not sure I want to tell the President that a Russian battleship is going to steam around the high seas until kingdom come, and there's nothing we can do about it. You got any bright ideas?'

McEwan looked around the faces staring expectantly at him. 'Well, sir, I do have one idea, but I'm not sure you'll like it very much,' he replied.

'Try us, son,' growled Ross.

'*Stalin* was built to counter the threat from various

battleships in the forties...it was designed to be bigger, faster and better armed than any of them. You can imagine the Politburo's paranoia about not being beaten by the West. We Brits had the *King George V*-class. The Japs had the *Yamoto*-class. You, of course, had the *Iowa*-class – the *Iowa* itself, then the *New Jersey*, the *Wisconsin* and the *Missouri*. You may recall that all the *Iowa*-class ships were finished rather late in the War. In fact you were still building two more, the *Illinois* and the *Kentucky*, when peace was declared. I gather the last two were finally scrapped in the Fifties, still unfinished, I believe.'

'OK, McEwan. Is this a goddamn history lesson or are you about to go through the idea that I think you're driving at?' interrupted Ray Bell.

McEwan grinned. 'Probably, sir. Shall I continue?'

Ross waved his hand to McEwan to carry on.

'As I said, the last two *Iowa*-class ships are no longer with us. But as you are aware, all four of the others have survived, still on the active service list in Pearl Harbour. You'll remember they all saw service in the Korean War, and the Vietnam War as well. In the early Eighties all four were modernised with guided weapons and Cruise missiles in response to the nuclear *Kirov* battleships of Russia.'

The four veteran battleships had not only survived fifty years of changing technology but fifty years of political arguments too. This was helped by the fact that the *Missouri* was one of the most famous ships in the fleet: on August 14, 1945, the then new battleship, moored in Tokyo Harbour, was the setting for General MacArthur to accept the surrender of the Japanese. Whenever a President or Congress wanted cuts, the old ships came out at the top of the list, but somehow the Navy had fought them off. They were currently something of a sore point: in theory the ships were still in active service, and were maintained as such, but Congress was blasting away at them as usual and, to pacify them, they had been left in a state of suspense, carefully looked after but crewless. This made them look a lot cheaper to run, even though the crews had only been dispersed around Pearl and most of them considered themselves still on the battleships. The politics would resolve themselves within the next few months, but as things stood Bell knew that the ships would probably have to be mothballed. Now, here was a chance for them. He knew exactly what the Englishman was about to suggest and was delighted; Washington had agreed to bring him over here, for Christ's sake – they had better damn well listen to what he had to say.

There was a longish silence. Eventually, Ross asked the inevitable question when it was clear that McEwan was certainly not going to take them any further. 'So what's the idea, McEwan?' he asked softly. Everyone else around the table knew exactly what McEwan was about to suggest, and the rest of them were secretly as delighted as Bell.

McEwan looked at the gathering. He could feel them willing him on.

'The idea is quite simple, gentlemen. Any one of the *Iowa*-class would be a reasonable match for *Stalin*. Two should be more than a fair fight. I suggest you get the *Iowa* and the *Missouri* out of Pearl as quickly as you can and send them after *Stalin*.'

All six nodded sagely at the suggestion. After a polite pause, Billy Ross turned to Admiral Bell. 'Ray, how long it's going to take to get these ships going? I mean, if we agree with Lieutenant McEwan's idea here?'

'I think it's a pretty good idea, Billy. No problem. As I'm sure the Lieutenant is more than aware, both ships he mentioned are currently only just in service. The crews are on leave, but we can get them back fast enough. Give me some time to get them provisioned and crewed and I reckon we'll be taking pot-shots at Uncle Joe Stalin within ten days. How's that sound, Billy?'

Ross looked around the table. All the chiefs were nodding quietly.

'OK, McEwan. Sounds like an idea. Now, if you would be so kind, perhaps we can have a moment on our own?'

McEwan was being thrown out. If the American military were going to war, they didn't want to discuss it in front of an Englishman. It took less than five minutes' discussion for them to agree that the Englishman's idea was not only workable but the only real option they had. The decision taken, Bell left the meeting to get his staff together to draw up the detailed plans. The *Iowa* and the *Missouri* would go to war. But Bell wanted to leave nothing to chance. He understood McEwan's strategy well: fight obsolete technology with obsolete technology. But just in case – just in case – he ordered his staff to get the carrier battle group led by the massive *Independence* under way as his back-up option. Overwhelming force was the latest Pentagon fashion; there was no more overwhelming force in the world than those two large battleships with a carrier group in the background.

16

Blake had got his stricken liner under a degree of control. The biggest problem following the torpedo strike had been the passengers – seconds after the explosion, panic reigned. The crew began to anticipate a disaster; some had gone to the lifeboats to get them prepared. Blake sent his first officer, George Holland, to see what the damage looked like; then he went on the PA system. His rich voice was as full of confidence and calm as his years as a liner Captain could make it. He described the explosion as an 'unfortunate little incident which we're having a quick look at. Everything appears normal up here on the bridge, but we'll have a look anyway,' which soon had the effect of calming everyone's stretched nerves. Crewmen looked sheepish and returned from the boat stations; one or two wealthy widows untied the lifejackets they had managed to find and laughed, but it was a strained, nervous laughter.

The Captain's calm voice hid the sharp tension on the bridge. The wheel had gone completely dead. Electronically linked to the rudder steering hydraulics, a single red light gleamed on the small indicator board on top of the wheel, indicating that the helm was not functioning. The chief engineer reported the damage to the shafts and gearboxes moments later. It quickly became clear that the great liner had no means of propulsion, no means of steering. What was not at all clear was if she was now taking on water; and if so, how much.

Holland reached the last-but-one watertight bulkhead at the stern of the *Ocean Queen* as Blake started a walkabout on the main deck, calming the passengers by strolling nonchalantly around, beaming at the worried faces he came across, telling them there was absolutely nothing to worry about and everything was completely normal. What the passengers couldn't see was the handheld VHF in his jacket pocket tuned to Holland's matching set.

The first officer was worried. He quickly discovered there was no power behind the watertight door. He tried the light switch to take a look through the small spyhole in the door, but nothing happened; he couldn't see a thing. The emergency circuit wasn't working, either. So, figured Holland, this meant one of two things; either the explosion had damaged the electrical circuits in the compartments ahead of him, or else, more worryingly, there was so much water behind the closed steel door that the lights had shorted out.

The trouble was, the only way of finding out was by hand-cranking the door upwards – it was less a door, more a solid steel shutter – and seeing if anything came out. Even if there was a lot of water behind the door, Holland was pretty confident that he could close it again by cranking it back down. He unlatched the two clasps that a few minutes ago had electrically locked the door under the emergency command from the bridge. They lifted smoothly. Holland then started turning the red-painted handle. It was geared, so that the door moved slowly even though he was winding the handle with some vigour.

The door sat inside a lip; even though it moved

slowly upwards, the lip maintained the seal for the first six inches of travel. Holland cranked away but nothing came through. He cranked faster, getting irritated with the slow gearing. The dull ache in his groin from Pine's vicious assault flared up with the effort.

With a bang that made Holland literally jump, a jet of solid water exploded from beneath the door and arced across the compartment to crash against the opposite bulkhead with unbelievable force. Holland threw himself against the bulkhead next to the door, staring in horror at the gushing sea-water; already an inch of water was sloshing round his feet. He started hauling on the winch handle again, this time in the opposite direction, but the sheer pressure of the inrushing water was powerful enough to act as an almost solid bed, holding the heavy steel door clear of its seating against its own weight.

Holland grappled for the VHF and switched it on, but all that came over the speaker was the hiss of static. There were too many steel bulkheads between him and Blake to let the signal through.

He yelled a swear-word as loudly as he could in frustration. The echoes bounced around the steel compartment and mingled with the din of the crashing water. Like a spell, the inrush suddenly eased; it stopped hosing against the far bulkhead and started pouring more gently into the growing pool of water on the floor. The pressure of the water was falling rapidly, and within moments it had stopped completely. Holland now knew what had happened. The ship had started a slow roll. The watertight door was offset to one side of the ship; so when he had opened it, the water behind was backed up on that side. As the *Ocean Queen* rolled slowly back, so the water sloshed away to the other side. In a few moments, it would come back up again.

He wound the handle rapidly and the door clicked shut back in its seat. There wasn't that much water behind it, after all. He must have caught it just at the moment in the roll when it was at its deepest.

Holland made his way back through the ship, keeping the VHF turned on until the hiss finally subsided and he caught a clear signal. He reported to Blake the moment he could get through.

Blake had returned to the bridge and was waiting for Attwood, his radio officer, to report back to him on the damage to the radio system. He didn't hold out too much hope of getting it working again. The pirates appeared to know what they were doing and seemed to have smashed the system beyond repair.

However, he listened to Holland's report with a growing sense of relief. Had the damage been ship-threatening, the water intake would have been worse. As it was, the flooding seemed limited to the two after compartments, which the vessel could easily take. He might be powerless and unsteerable, but at least his ship was going to stay afloat under him. He immediately picked up the PA microphone and broadcast yet another reassuring message.

Attwood was waiting to see him when he put the microphone down.

'Any chance, Sparks?' Blake asked. He still insisted on using the old-fashioned slang name for the radio officer.

'Well, yes, actually, there is,' replied Attwood with a surprised tone to his voice.

'I thought they smashed the radio up.'

'No, not really. All a bit odd, actually, sir. They didn't touch the equipment itself, just the main power supply box.'

'Isn't that serious?'

'Well, a bit, sir. I mean, I'm going to have to hot-wire

the radio into the mains supply. The computers won't work because the voltage is all wrong for them, but the main radio system should operate without any real trouble.'

'Bloody careless of them, Sparks. Get on with it, then. Give me a yell when you've got something.'

'Give me a few minutes, Captain. No problem.'

Blake knew nothing about radios and power supply boxes. He assumed the pirates had just got it wrong. Attwood, on the other hand, thought it was very curious indeed. The power supply unit was an anonymous-looking box, whereas the radio system and computers were much more obvious. Why would a bunch of thugs choose to take out one of the most obscure components in the whole rig? Especially the one that was probably the most easily repairable? Attwood got to work with pliers and lengths of wire. He stripped the mains cable of the radio unit back to bare wire, did the same with the ship's mains, joined the two together with a terminal block, wrapped several turns of black insulating tape around the connection and turned the mains back on. It took two minutes.

The radio system had its own internal computer that remembered the frequencies for a whole range of stations around the world, and kept the signal stable even if the frequency wobbled a little – which they all did. The spiky current direct from the ship's generators instantly disabled the computer, as Attwood had thought it probably would. But that only meant the radio had to be tuned by hand. He twisted the dial until it reached the international distress frequency and called Blake.

When Blake came down into the radio room, he looked surprised at sight of the radio set with its glowing digits.

'It's tuned to 2182kHz. I think it's working. The

signal might fade in and out a bit, but otherwise it seems OK', said Attwood.

Blake pressed the switch on the handset that engaged the transmitter.

Mayday, Mayday, Mayday, this is *Ocean Queen, Ocean Queen*. My position is 18 degrees nineteen point two minutes North, 117 degrees twelve point nine minutes East, repeat, 18.19.02 North, 117.12.09 East. I am disabled and taking on water. Request immediate assistance. Over.

He released the transmit switch. Would anyone answer?

Several stations picked up the Mayday call. The nearest INMARSAT satellite, tuned automatically to the distress frequency, relayed the message to four different coastguard organisations: China, Hong Kong, the Philippines and Japan. The ever-vigilant computers at Cheltenham, now instructed to listen for – among other things – the keywords 'Ocean Queen', alerted their minders within a second of Blake replacing the handset. Via Langley, Blake's message would take only a few minutes to be pushed, as a handwritten scribble, into Abe Brinkley's hand at the Pentagon.

Some nearby ships heard the call, too. A few battered freighters, still recovering from the effects of the passing typhoon, noted the message and hoped a bigger, faster ship would help, but in the meantime started to plot a course for the stricken liner as they were required to do by law. The Japanese supertanker *Komosuru*, low in the water with crude oil from the Gulf, radioed an offer of assistance within a few moments. She was cruising at 12 knots and was 90 miles away. Blake gratefully accepted the offer – she would be big enough to take off the 2,000 passengers and crew, if he needed to abandon ship.

And the USS *Jackson*, already steaming towards the *Ocean Queen* picked up the signal as well. Captain James Crawford looked at the message that his radio officer had transcribed, worked out the position in his head, and told the officer to reply:

Ocean Queen from USS *Jackson*. Your Mayday received. Am making 28 knots towards you, ETA 4 hours. Is your vessel seaworthy for that time?

The message was flashed back to the *Ocean Queen* where Attwood, having spoken briefly to the Captain, replied:

USS *Jackson* from *Ocean Queen*. Yes, we are shipping water but we are fine for now. Our steering and propulsion systems are damaged and out of service. If the situation worsens we will let you know. All other stations please note that USS *Jackson* and MV *Komosuru* are proceeding and no further assistance is required.

Several freighter captains, listening to the interchange with some relief, altered course back again. And Crawford insisted with his engine room that another few knots were perfectly possible. He got back on the secure line to the Pentagon with the news. Surely to God this would speed things up?

The slim-hulled, fast cruiser sliced easily through the waves. *Jackson* was one of the newest *President*-class missile cruisers; she bristled with high technology and was armed with ship-to-ship and ship-to-air missiles that could shoot down a seagull from 20 miles away on a moonless night in thick fog.

But her main role was as an anti-submarine ship: her task was to track nuclear submarines and kill them. For this she was armed with 20 small nuclear depth charges, each one of 5 kilotons – mini-nukes they called them, as the warhead had a quarter the power of the Hiroshima blast – but which would easily cripple any vessel within a two-mile radius of the explosion. The blast was deadly to any close-by submarine: the underwater shock-wave would literally burst the boat apart at the seams.

The *Jackson* was in fact the supreme example of the late twentieth-century warship. And it was now racing at high speed towards the *Stalin*, the last flowering of a technology born at the battle of Jutland eighty years earlier, lying in wait over the distant horizon.

*

Zof was listening idly to the VHF radio when the *Ocean Queen*'s distress call came on. He felt a sense of relief. He was pretty sure the aim was good, but he had worried for the Captain and crew, and the passengers; now, at least he knew all was well. He waited for any replies, but couldn't hear a thing other than the wavering hiss of static. The VHF set that Kelley had acquired lacked the sensitivity of the *Ocean Queen*'s equipment, and it couldn't pick up the distant reply from the *Jackson*. He heard the *Ocean Queen*'s subsequent response to the *Jackson*, but it gave away nothing about the position of the American ship. Because Kelley had told him so, he assumed it was miles off. He went to find the American to give him the news. Now he could stop worrying – and get the ship away.

They had spent too long here already, and he knew the Americans would be gathering their forces.

Aircraft might already be on the way, though he suspected they would be re-thinking their strategy after the failure of the F-15s, and this would take them some time. But time was starting to run out. The vast wastes of the ocean were beckoning, and he wanted to lose himself in its comforting emptiness.

Kelley was in the Admiral's rest room several flights below the bridge, designed to be a haven of peace and comfort from the cares of command, a place where the senior officers could share a bottle or two of vodka in some peace. When the ship had been finished fifty years ago, it was a luxurious wood-panelled retreat reminiscent of a dacha in the woods outside Moscow. Now the carpet had gone and the wood panelling, left to the excesses of baking Vladivostok summers and numbing winters, was splitting and rotting. Kelley had turned it into his own private retreat and had found, from somewhere, a deckchair in which he was lazily sprawled as Zof walked in.

'Hi, Zof. Come in. Sit down. Want a drink?'

'Thank you, Kelley. Too early for me,' replied Zof. He lit a cigarette instead, and the musty cabin filled with the reek of the tobacco. 'The liner, Kelley. They got their call out. He put out a Mayday asking for immediate assistance.'

'See? I told you not to worry. Any reply?'

'A tanker, *Komosuru*. Oh, and the USS *Jackson*. According to the *Ocean Queen*, her steering gear is wrecked and she has no propulsion, but otherwise her master is happy. Coming from a ship like that, I should think the message will be half-way round the world. Now I feel much happier, my friend. We can get out of here, before the Americans arrive. The ship is fine. I think we can go.'

'Hey, relax, Zof. It will take them hours to get here.

Anyway, look how we coped with that crazy plane. Didn't stand a chance.'

Zof looked at the stocky American with some surprise. 'Kelley, I wonder if perhaps you are becoming stupid,' he growled. 'We would be crazy to sit here waiting for everyone to arrive.'

'Zof, it was you who wanted to hang about; remember? So we are. There's no sense in running yet. What happens if the *Ocean Queen* starts taking on water in the meantime? A lot can happen while we're waiting. We should stay around a bit longer.'

'Kelley, my friend, the ship will be fine. We don't need to stay here. We have to get out – and now, I think.' What was the matter with the man, thought Zof. What about the American ship heading for them? Kelley didn't seem worried about it; the truth was, he wasn't. According to Kelley's plan, the *Jackson* was still many, many miles away.

'Do I detect some nervousness, Captain Zof?' asked Kelley, stressing 'Captain' as sarcastically as he could. 'Listen, you getting worried?'

It was not the right thing to say to Zof. But Kelley knew that. 'Yes, Kelley, I think so. We have just completed two of the biggest acts of piracy on the high seas. We are carrying several million dollars' worth of gold and diamonds. We have killed a man in cold blood and we have shot down an American warplane. We are sailing around on a stolen ship. Kelley, I think you are full of shit. We go, right now.' Zof was getting angry.

Kelley hadn't seen the big man roused before. Others had; they would never have spoken to Zof the way Kelley did. 'Hey, calm down, Zof. Have a drink.'

The big Russian walked calmly over to Kelley, who was still sitting in the deckchair. He seized the American by his shirt and jerked him violently to his feet. While Kelley was still wondering what had happened, Zof struck him across the face with his open hand so that Kelley's face whipped to one side. Kelley was too shocked to retaliate – too shocked, and too awed by the overpowering presence of the man.

Zof grabbed Kelley by the shirt again and pushed his face into the American's. Their noses almost touched.

'Kelley, you never *ever* speak to me like this again, you understand? You are speaking total shit. I am not some kind of idiot. Something is going on. Why was Harvey shot? I do not believe your story. Why are we waiting around here for the world to find us? Kelley, you will be so kind as to tell me what is happening here before I break your little shit neck. Understand?' And with every word that Zof spoke, he shook Kelley so that the American was nodding.

'For Christ's sake, Zof,' he croaked.

'Do you understand?' Zof demanded.

'Yeah, for Christ's sake. Now put me down.'

Zof wasn't quite finished. He released his grip on Kelley's shirt so that the man could breathe but held him at the back of the neck in a powerful vice of a grip that felt to Kelley as though he was going to snap his backbone. 'Don't mess with me. You get one chance to tell me what's going on. Any more shit and I will become very angry.' He loosed his hold on Kelley's neck and pushed the American away. Then he sat down and folded his arms, looking intently at Kelley.

Kelley backed away, massaging his bruised spine as best he could. Zof's grip had left red weals down the back of his neck. Where the fuck was Pine? What the hell. Zof wouldn't be put off by the fat man anyway. There was no point in spinning a story to the Russian, not now. He had to tell the truth, otherwise the whole plan would get shot to pieces. Could he get Zof on his side? Could he at least get him to live with the deal? He didn't see what options he had. Maybe he could buy some time. He had thought Zof swallowed the whole of the original story; but obviously he hadn't believed a fucking word of it.

Kelley took a mouthful of vodka. 'OK, Zof. Here's the deal. The real deal,' and he started to tell the truth.

*

McEwan had been escorted to some kind of hospitality room by one of Bell's staff officers, Lewry. He still felt uncomfortable after his sudden trip over the Atlantic, and the offer of a cup of strong American coffee was welcome. Lewry was Bell's intelligence chief and was interested in McEwan's knowledge of the *Stalin*.

'You seem to have got quite a handle on this Russian ship, Lieutenant,' asked Lewry in a friendly off-the-cuff kind of way.

McEwan wasn't going to fall for it. He was just as interested in discovering exactly why his presence there seemed so important to the Americans, and why their own intelligence appeared so light.

'Oh, well, they were always something of a hobby of mine. Fascinating things,' he commented guardedly.

There was a silence, both men looking down at their cups of coffee. McEwan decided to break it. 'I was wondering about your own information on the *Stalin*. You seem a little, if you don't mind me saying, hazy?'

Lewry thought it was better to be open with the Englishman. It might encourage him to tell him more about his sources.

'Well, I guess we are a little, Lieutenant. Fifty-year-old ships don't belong on our intelligence network. We can call up data on every commissioned warship in the world in seconds, and get full specifications if we want them. But Second World War battleships? Listen, Lieutenant, that's history, not intelligence.'

'Tactics?'

'What can I tell you? Same problem. We've got experts on every known type of naval warfare on the staff. When the old man wanted someone who knew about Russian battleships, no way. Like I said, you're dealing with history here, not warfare.'

Lewry's reference to history made McEwan ask the next question, which was obvious to him as a historian but probably not to a professional military man.

'What about intelligence archives? There must be some reference to this ship?'

'Nothing, apart from the odd comment about training problems in the early Eighties. We went right back, right through the old microfiche records.'

'How far?' asked McEwan.

'How far? Sixties, Seventies. We don't go back beyond that.'

'Nothing from the War years? The Thirties and Forties?'

'Now you really are talking history, Lieutenant. That stuff's buried down in the basement archive somewhere. I can't see what use it would be.'

'I think it could be a lot of use. When I was researching this subject my own sources were reasonable but limited. When it was being built, the *Stalin* must have been a serious target for US intelligence services during the period. Your people certainly knew of its existence. The one thing I need is detailed information on the construction of the ship. If it was a target, then the chances are your archives will hold some details.'

The thought had never occurred to Lewry; it wouldn't have. With the most sophisticated intelligence database in the world, why would anyone go grubbing around in the archives looking for material from the Thirties, for heaven's sake?

'Any chance of taking a look?' asked McEwan.

Lewry would have to go back to see Bell soon. He didn't see any harm in the Englishman indulging his passion for history while he was here. McEwan might even find out something useful, and maybe he'd be a bit more open about his sources when he came back.

'Sure. No problem,' said Lewry. He scribbled out a brief note and left the Englishman in the hands of one of his junior officers, who took him down long corridors and dim staircases deep in the bowels of the Pentagon. For McEwan, as a historian, it was the chance of a lifetime. What he really needed was to discover some weakness, some structural mistake in Kishkov's work, that would provide an opportunity for an attacker. But just looking at old intelligence on Soviet battleships would be fascinating enough.

The archives were on the first level of the huge basement that ran around three sides of the five-sided building. An insignificant door, bearing the anonymous sign 'A4', was the main entrance to the repository of some of the greatest military secrets of the past. For years, historians, academics and politicians had been trying to get that door opened. The Freedom of Information Act made access easier. All the sensitive stuff had long ago been transferred to the electronic systems. But with the reticence that only the professional military mind can display, a whole department was involved in sorting through even ancient papers that someone had requested, deciding if they were sufficiently unembarrassing to release and, if they were, which bits were to be blanked out. Unbelievably, this blanking process was done by hand and thick black marker pen.

The archivist was a hunched, thin man who wore tinted glasses and whose hands fluttered constantly. McEwan's escort handed him over, together with the note from Lewry requesting that McEwan be given access to the archives. The archivist read the note carefully, looking sourly at it as though it were contaminated with something.

'I'm going to have to check this, sir.' He picked up the phone and rang Bell's office. The call confirmed that McEwan was to be given the run of the place, though it was clear from the archivist's expression that letting an Englishman loose was not what he would allow but, what the hell, the boss said so.

'Soviet battleships, 1944 and 1945?' said the archivist in response to McEwan's request. 'You'll do best in aisle 156, section 8, shelves 1, 2 and 3. That's our Soviet naval intelligence for that time. Then try aisle 221, section 12, shelves 4 and 5. That's copies of Allied intelligence reports, same subject. Any problems, call 111 on the phone system and you'll get to me. Oh, and by the way, sir, we have TV monitoring on every aisle. Place the material you want in the trolleys you'll find provided, call 171 on the phone and an orderly will take your material to the nearest reading room. Do you understand?'

McEwan nodded, impressed. The man had quoted him the aisle, section and even shelf numbers from memory. He mumbled his thanks and set off in the direction the archivist had pointed him towards. On either side of him stretched the numbered aisles, each a couple of hundred yards long. They were lined with metal racking rising to the roof, twenty feet high. Packing the shelves were cardboard boxes in various colours and of various ages. The sheer quantity of information was staggering.

He passed aisle after aisle, heading slowly towards

156. It took him a full ten minutes to reach the right number. He turned into it. Each aisle was divided into sections. At section 8 was a small cardboard sign: 'US Nat.Int.Reps. May 44, October 45. USSR.' According to the archivist, the bottom three shelves held the material McEwan was looking for.

He started pulling out the box files. The first few were Northern Fleet and of no interest; but half-way down the first shelf he found the first mentions of the Pacific Fleet. Six files later he struck gold: there were three box files devoted to the *Stalin*, each one crammed with thick documents. He closed the files and tossed them into one of the trolleys that were conveniently left in the corridor. He carried on searching but only came across one other reference, which was also tossed into the trolley. Like a supermarket shopper, McEwan then pushed his trolley off to aisle 221 and searched the other suggested shelves. These were reports from other countries' intelligence services that were copied to the US through the embassies. He discovered only one reference, and he was delighted to note that it was from the Royal Navy; that file joined the others in the trolley.

He called for the orderly as instructed. After an unreasonable wait a bored Marine turned up and led him back down the aisle to a glass-fronted reading room, pushing the trolley for him as McEwan trailed behind. The Marine locked him into the room, together with the trolley, and took up position outside the door, staring inwards with hands clasped behind his back. A closed-circuit TV pointed at McEwan from a corner of the room as he reopened the boxes, laid the material out in front of him and started inspecting his haul.

The amount of information the Americans had on

the *Stalin* was extraordinary. Laying their hands on it, McEwan thought, must have cost the lives or sanity of more than several dedicated agents in an era when, before electronic surveillance, men and women had to actually get there, on the ground.

And here it was, locked away in the ancient archives; it was treated simply as historical material rather than intelligence, and Navy Intelligence as well as the CIA used electronic database systems containing only recent material. No one had ever imagined that intelligence would ever be required on a fifty-year-old ship, so it was never loaded. McEwan knew full well that they would have found their way here eventually; but his historian's instincts had guided him that much faster.

Several of the documents were technical appraisals of the ship, clearly based on expert knowledge but written within the Pentagon. Other files were even more extraordinary. One contained high-quality photographs of most of the vessel, including pictures from inside the gun turrets; others were reports of sea trials. He opened the slimmest one and extracted the only reference, a single sheet of yellow paper reporting that *Stalin* had been officially taken out of service. It was dated September 1945, just a few weeks after Hiroshima.

He then turned with some anticipation to the last file, containing copies of the Royal Navy material. There was a document containing another technical assessment of the ship, but he found it only repeated much of what the American reports said. He was about to put the document away when he noticed a thick wad of paper glued inside the back of the buff cover. When he unfolded it, it opened outwards seven times and then once vertically, like a huge map. To McEwan's eternal joy, it was a detailed cross-section of the entire ship, right down to the specifications of the armour plate. He was poring over this treasure, utterly absorbed, when the glum Marine opened the door.

'General Ross wants you back upstairs right away, urgent, sir.'

'Can you get copies of this to me upstairs?' asked McEwan, holding out the diagram.

'I'll have to check, sir. Yes, I suppose so,' said the Marine noncommittally.

McEwan started the long walk back, smiling to himself. At least he now knew he could discover his enemy's strengths; therefore it wouldn't take him long, he reasoned, to discover his enemy's weaknesses.

*

Harvey was not dead. But he was about as close as anyone could get to it. Once the raiding party had departed, he was carried off the ladder to the sick-bay where the ship's doctor managed to staunch the flow of blood and get a plasma drip into him. The blood loss was massive and his blood pressure was hovering just above the danger point. Harvey was hanging on by a thread, and he couldn't be in worse hands.

Doctor James Seymour had just graduated from medical school and was taking a working holiday on the *Ocean Queen*, where he expected to treat nothing worse than seasickness and hangovers, which had until then been his main employment. Major gunshot wounds were way out of his experience; he was far from happy.

Seymour had managed to get Harvey's blood pressure stable and the heartbeat became steadier. He checked again on the pulse, then set off to the bridge to get the Captain's advice. He'd just left the sick-bay when the torpedo went off. The next twenty minutes were spent between making sure Harvey was all right and calming down the hundreds of passengers, and some of the crew, who seemed to look on him as some kind of ministering angel – mainly because he was wearing a white coat with a stethoscope around his neck. He hadn't the foggiest idea what had happened but assured everyone that everything was fine. Eventually he reached the bridge. The Captain listened briefly about Harvey.

'I'm sorry, Doc, not much I can do. The ship's buggered and we're waiting for a tow, but they won't be here for another couple of hours. Is it urgent?'

'Frankly, Captain, yes. I haven't really treated anyone like this before. He could hang on for hours or days. He's reasonably stable now, but the blood pressure is low and anything we can do here is very limited. If you can get some help it would be very useful.'

Blake was not happy to go out of his way for one of the pirates, but realised that if they could keep him alive he might have some useful information. He got back on the radio to raise Crawford on the *Jackson*. Crawford listened and then offered to fly his surgeon out on a helicopter. Greatly relieved, Seymour went back to his patient and waited nervously in the bleak, white room.

*

'Listen, Zof, how much do you think we've got so far?' said Kelley, once he'd calmed down enough to be able to answer the Russian's demands for an explanation. Starting with the money, as he had with Harvey, seemed the best place to begin.

'Gold and diamonds? A very great deal. More than enough. But why do you ask? Exactly how does this affect whatever you are trying to do here?' replied Zof, still sitting with arms folded, waiting for the full story.

'Sure, we got plenty. Maybe twenty million dollars' worth, OK? The problem, my good Captain, is down to some basic capitalist economics.'

'Explain. I am listening,' said Zof. The big Russian stared at Kelley, who felt it was like being watched by a bear.

'The problem is that we got to get rid of the stuff. Turn it into liquid cash. And guess what? We don't just walk into the nearest branch of the Moscow Narodny bank and make a deposit. The stuff's hot. We got to find someone to take it off us. The Indians will do that. Trouble is, Zof, the best we'll get is ten cents on the dollar. Maybe less.'

Zof smiled. 'So, my friend, it sounds as though you have a problem. Once I've paid off my men, it seems to me that you have very little left for yourself.'

'Don't kid yourself, Zof. Our twenty million bucks ain't going to be worth more than maybe two million. You share that out among your men, you gotta split it, what, four hundred fucking ways? Each man gets shit, Zof. Five grand. That's less than half your guys picked up when you took them to dinner. And they gotta wait, maybe months. It's kid's stuff.'

Zof was starting to get angry. If Kelley had put him and his men through all this just to end up with $5,000 a man, he would have a real problem on his hands.

'My friend, if that is the case, then you have some explaining to do.' There was a warning tone in Zof's voice that Kelley couldn't miss.

'I know, I know. Listen to me, OK? There's a much bigger deal. Lots more money. But it's different. You ready for this, Zof?'

'Try me, Kelley. Try me.'

Kelley sat down opposite Zof. Maybe the big guy was going for the story. Might as well carry on. 'How does ten million US dollars in hard cash transferred to a Swiss bank account in your name sound? Plus another thirty million for the crew in cash. Seventy-five thousand bucks a man if you want to split it democratically. Plus genuine passports and full papers for any country you name. Real cash. No deals. No risks. All above-board, and no need to wait to spend it. More of it than you'd ever see if you spent the next century pirating your way around the world.'

Zof just carried on looking at Kelley. He raised his eyebrows but did nothing else.

Shit. He's making this hard work. 'So, Zof, what's worth this kind of money? You want to know this, maybe?' He wanted to get the man to say something. Anything.

Zof paused; he uncrossed his arms. 'This is a good question. I am sure you are about to tell me. Please continue.'

Kelley saw that Zof wasn't going to play the game. What the hell. Slowly and in detail he spelled out the whole deal with Tariq, A to Z. The warheads. The *Ocean Queen* as bait. The *Madelaine*, to provide them with just enough information to get them interested. How the radio on the *Ocean Queen* was left busted but easily repairable so that they could send the message. The real reason why he wanted to stay where he was, so he could intercept the *Jackson* and complete the deal. Zof sat silent, just listening, giving nothing away.

Eventually Kelley simply ran out of things to say. He stopped talking and returned Zof's unflinching gaze. Say something, for Christ's sake, you Russian bastard!

Suddenly Zof stood up. He paced across the cabin, then turned to Kelley. 'How, my friend, do you propose to deal with the American ship and the whole American Navy? Have you thought of this?'

Welcome on board, thought Kelley to himself. He's going for it. 'You have a touching faith in the power of the Americans, Zof. This ship is effectively invulnerable. You of all people can understand that. None of these crappy little warships can do us any real damage. You've seen the effect of the warplanes, too. The weapons are not up to it. The only thing they can do is nuke us, and I really doubt that they'll do that when they think they can catch us, which they can't. Listen Zof, it's going to work. We wait for the *Jackson* to turn up, we intercept. Even if they try anything we'll be fine. We can use the *Ocean Queen* as a hostage if things get bad; then the *Jackson* is forced to give up. They won't send any more aircraft because of what happened last time. We get our men aboard the *Jackson*, knock out the communications. We offload the warheads, then we get away with at least twelve hours' leeway before any other ship gets near.'

'And then?'

'High speed down to the Monte Bello Islands where our friends will be waiting. We'll offload the cargo and collect the cash within thirty-six hours. Then we're away. I've arranged helicopters to get us to the mainland.'

'What happens after then? We'll be hunted around the world. The Americans will not take this lightly.'

'Come on, Zof. Do you think the Americans know our identities, for a start? And in any event, publicity is the last thing they'll want. Having just lost a shipload of nukes, they're going to want to keep things quiet. Wouldn't you?'

'Where did poor bloody Harvey fit into all this?'

'Poor bloody Harvey? Listen, Zof, the guy had found out about the plan. There was no way he could be trusted. Harvey's trouble is that he had a pretty narrow view of the world: he did not like the idea one bit, so I had to get Pine to silence him. That, or we'd all be up shit creek. Me. You. Crazy Kishkov. All your goddamn crew as well, Zof. I had no choice.'

Zof was still pacing the room.

'So, Zof. You in or out?' asked Kelley. It was the same question he'd put to Harvey.

There was another infuriating pause. Zof finally stopped pacing and, extraordinarily, started laughing. It was not a false laugh but a genuine overflow of mirth, coming from deep inside the man. Kelley was by now beginning to panic and wondered if he should try to get out of the cabin to find Pine. Tears were streaming down Zof's face as Kelley slowly got up and started to edge towards the door.

Zof saw him and put his hand on his arm, gentler now but still firm. 'Kelley, my good, good friend, please sit down. I'm sorry. I should take this more seriously. It's just that here I am, the great Russian sea captain, taking up a new career in piracy, an honest living so my brother would say, to make some real money. And now what do I find? I'm back to fighting the Americans for a living, but this time I'm stealing nuclear warheads to hand over to a madman whose only ambition is to do what we should have done years ago, which is teach the Americans a lesson. Kelley, this to me, I am afraid to tell you, is very, very funny.'

Zof was wiping his face with his sleeve. In truth, he felt a huge sense of relief. Now he knew the real story, a whole lot of things made sense. Frankly, he didn't think they had a hope in hell, but he buried that thought deep inside himself. No one else could know that. He had to keep fighting, no matter what happened now.

'So, Zof? Are you with me or not?' demanded Kelley, refusing to share in the humour.

Zof's face suddenly darkened. He jabbed a finger into Kelley's chest and kept it there, pushing a little each time he spoke. 'Listen to me, Kelley. I do not give one piece of shit for your plan. You are mad, and so are the rest of them. But I will help you. You know why? It's not the money. I want none of what you will get for the warheads. Share it among the crew. They deserve it. I will help because I want to beat shit out of the Americans. I will help you because there will never be another chance to win the last fight. Listen to me well. I will command your ship and I will show the Americans what we are made of. As for my crew, they can make up their own minds. I'll tell them at the right time. I'll get you towards your Islands, and then I'll make my own way from there.'

'For nothing, Zof? Not a penny?'

'For my crew, Kelley. For Russia. For the service. Don't insult me by offering me money.'

'OK, Zof. It's your party. I guess that's what we'd call a deal.'

'That's exactly what it is.' Zof had just stood up to go when, wailing from the loudspeaker mounted on the bulkhead, came the sound of the ship's general alarm. Someone on the bridge had hit the panic button. Zof looked at Kelley.

'Hey, nothing to do with me,' said Kelley defensively.

As both of them ran to the bridge, the whole ship was swarming. Men were rushing about the passageways, but didn't know what to do. The alarm had been sounded but no orders issued. Zof pushed his way past the men, shouting at them to calm down as he did so.

He burst on to the bridge, where he'd left Morin in charge.

'Morin, what the hell's going on?'

'Thank Christ you're here, Captain. Look! On the radar. Another ship just come into sight, forty miles off.'

'So?'

'Over the radio, Captain. We just heard them. Talking to the *Ocean Queen*. It's an American warship, Captain. It's called *Jackson*.'

The ship had finally come into range. Zof looked at Kelley. The *Jackson* was supposed to be hundreds of miles away. Now it was virtually on the horizon.

'Oh, shit!' muttered Kelley.

The adrenalin surged into Zof's veins. It was like waking up from a deep sleep. The enemy was here. Time for action. He buried his fears even deeper, issued his orders in a commanding, confident voice and got his ship ready for action once again.

17

Commander Warren Cleveland actually stood to attention when the call from Admiral Bell was connected. It was unusual for anything interesting like this to happen in Cleveland's military life. A Navy man since leaving high school, he was a talented administrator rather than a seaman, and forty years of quiet, dedicated paper-pushing had given him his last, sought-after post as Base Commander at Pearl Harbor, a role where the most demanding task was supervising the arrival of visiting naval dignitaries and looking after them around the night-spots of Honolulu – of which there were many, all personally known to Cleveland.

He arrived at his desk at his normal hour of 10 a.m. to be greeted by his flustered secretary, who told him that the Pentagon had been trying to contact him since nine. They were going ballistic.

'The Pentagon? *The* Pentagon?' said Cleveland, panicking.

'That's what they said.'

'Jesus! Why didn't you tell me, for chrissake? Who at the Pentagon?'

'Your car phone was switched off. Apparently. An Admiral Bell, they said. it was very urgent.'

'Bell? Jesus Christ.'

'Who's Bell?'

'Bell, my dear, only happens to be the Admiral in charge of the entire goddamn Navy. The boss. The top dog. Call them now, tell them I was in an urgent meeting. You've tracked me down and here I am.'

Cleveland went back to his office and waited for the phone to ring. That's when he stood to attention. It was highly unusual for an Admiral to talk directly to a Commander like Cleveland; normally the Admiral's staff would formulate the plan and then communicate it down the line for execution. Bell's staff had been working on the sequence of events necessary to get the old ships out and running, but he decided to talk to Cleveland anyway. It was a major breach of etiquette and tradition, and his staff would go crazy, but Bell was never the kind of officer who cared much for the conventional way of doing things, and in any event he wanted Cleveland to move like a scalded cat.

'Commander? I've been trying to contact you for over an hour. Where the hell were you?' started Bell.

'Yessir. Sorry, sir. I was . . .'

'Never mind, Cleveland. Listen. I've got an urgent task for you. I'm calling personally because I want this done without fail and you're the top man. You've heard about the Russian battleship that downed one of our planes? We're going after the sonofabitch.' Cleveland had heard; the story had gone round before the Pentagon managed to get a lid on the rest of the tale, including the robbery of the *Ocean Queen*. Bell went on to frighten the life out of Cleveland by telling him that he wanted crews assembled, fuel organised, technicians briefed – and the *Iowa* and *Missouri* ready for sea as soon as physically possible, and in any event no later than three days from today. They could provision and arm the ship as much as possible, and then RAS – replenish at sea – to collect the rest of their supplies and take on the fuel load. Bell wanted the RAS ships – huge floating warehouses and fuel bunkers – out of port first tide tomorrow, so that they would have a good start on the battleships. He had his two best Captains flying out now to take over each ship; both had served on them before. Everything was moving. Orders were on their way. He just wanted Cleveland's firm assurance that it could be done. Any problems with that, Commander?

Cleveland was dumbfounded, but he wouldn't have dared say no. Forty years sailing a desk had taught him that you never refused a senior officer, least of all your Admiral, even if he was talking total horseshit. Least of all someone as ruthless as Bell. Cleveland kept his doubts to himself. In truth, if anyone could do what Bell was asking, it was probably Warren Cleveland. Logistical problems like this were something he actually enjoyed; it was the talent that had taken him to the top of his particular branch. Thinking about it, he found he quite relished the challenge. And in any event, getting the Russian that had shot down an American flyer was a pretty good incentive.

'Yessir, Admiral Bell. I'll get on to it right now. Leave it to me.'

'Good man, Cleveland. By the way, I said three days. Let's see if we can do it in forty-eight hours.'

'Yessir. Thank you,' replied Cleveland, but Bell had already put the phone down.

Oh shit, thought Warren Cleveland. Oh shit.

Within half an hour he had his eight senior officers standing around him next to the gangplank of the *Iowa*, moored up in a secure corner of the yard, with the *Missouri* berthed alongside. He already had a list in his head of the tasks which needed to be accomplished. Now he rattled them off. His personnel officer had to round up the crew; both ships maintained a skeleton complement of 100 men each, mainly for maintenance duties. Most of the rest of the crew were on leave on the islands or were hanging around other ships; with Bell's backing from the top, he would have to round them all up. There would be plenty of bitching but no refusals, not when they knew what the mission was. His fuelling officer would get as much fuel oil as possible into the bunkers within the next few hours, and would organise the RAS once the *Iowa* and *Missouri* had sailed.

His weapons officer was given the job of getting the main armament ready. The orders from Bell's staff had come through; strangely, thought the man, the list included HE shells for the big guns but no missiles, the most common weapon carried on board these day. He asked Cleveland if this was correct; don't ask stupid questions, he was told sharply.

As far as getting the ships themselves ready to sail, Cleveland knew he'd just have to take a few shortcuts. The maintenance crews had kept both vessels in a near sea-ready state. He'd get his engineering people in to check out as much as possible, but he wasn't expecting to find any problems; he told his engineering officer not to worry. If a fault was serious enough to sink the ship, maybe he should let everyone know. Otherwise leave it alone.

After he'd briefed them, he sprang the timing on them: 48 hours. They all swore. Cleveland just held up his hands and told them to get on with it. Orders from the Pentagon. You want a transfer to Alaska? Remember our flyer downed by these Russians? Pull your goddamn fingers out.

Cleveland started to warm to his task. Within a few hours the two ships were swarming with men, the lights were coming on as the generators got started, black smoke poured from first one funnel, then the other, as the huge diesel engines lumbered into life.

The *Iowa* and the *Missouri* were virtually identical. They represented the latest American naval thinking during the Second War, and thus shared with *Stalin* many similar characteristics. But they were lighter, smaller, less well armoured than *Stalin*. The Americans took the Washington Treaty, which limited the size of capital ships between the wars, more seriously than either the Russians or the Japanese. Both ships sported three turrets each containing two 16-inch guns, plus the usual assortment of lighter armaments; both could make 28 knots, a few knots slower than *Stalin*. Though powerfully armoured, both were designed to absorb shell hits from other 16-inch guns rather than the massive 22-inch shells *Stalin* could hurl.

McEwan was familiar with the shortcomings of the *Iowa*-class ships, especially compared with *Stalin*. That was why he was so keen to dig out the old records of the *Stalin*, to see what the weak points were. But they had advantages, too. The *Iowa* vessels were more manoeuvrable, to start with. With less weight and bulk to shift, an *Iowa* could not quite dodge and dart, but *Stalin* was a ponderous beast by comparison. And although slower, an *Iowa* could reach 28 knots a great deal quicker than *Stalin* could achieve 15 knots.

The rate of fire was better with the American ships, as well. It took time to shift the four-ton 22-inch shells around inside *Stalin*, time to load, time to fire, time to clear the breech. For every huge shell *Stalin* fired, an *Iowa* could fire three.

And with the latest gunnery radar controlling the guns, the accuracy of the ship's gunfire would be greatly ahead of the *Stalin*'s; McEwan was pretty sure that the Russians wouldn't have installed new radar on a training ship that would never leave port. It was too expensive.

McEwan didn't find it difficult to persuade Bell to send him out to Pearl Harbor, particularly with Whitehall putting pressure on Washington to keep a Royal Navy man with the task force, even if only for liaison purposes. There was a British national on board the Russian ship, after all. He had a copy of the plans of the *Stalin* from the archives, and spent the uncomfortable twelve-hour flight to Honolulu looking through them very slowly, taking in Kishkov's ideas plate by plate, rivet by rivet. As he scrutinised the plan, with its spidery mass of lines and measurements, he spent an increasing amount of time looking at the stern section of the massive ship. It displayed the internal structure, showing the bulkheads, the decks and even the detail of the armour-plating, the thickness, and how it was bonded to the rest of the ship. It took time to follow each line on the drawing, but McEwan slowly realised that the way the armour-plating around the stern section had been arranged was different from the rest of the ship. It was hard to be sure but there appeared to be, he thought wryly, a very literal chink in Kishkov's armour.

*

The *Jackson* was now just 40 miles from the stricken liner. Crawford was sitting on his bridge in tropical whites when his executive officer told him they were now within helicopter range. He ordered his surgeon on to the helicopter with a supply of blood plasma and watched from the back of the bridge as the matt-grey chopper lifted delicately off the deck at the rear of the ship, hovered for a moment, then curled gracefully away, its exhaust smoke visible as a twist of black against the boiling white surf from the wake of the speeding vessel.

'*Ocean Queen*, this is USS *Jackson*', called Crawford over the MF radio.

Blake answered almost instantly. 'Good afternoon, *Jackson*. Nice to hear from you.'

'And you, sir. I thought you'd like to know that we have just despatched our helo for you with our surgeon on board. I guess they should be with you in around fifteen minutes. He'll call you when visual for landing instructions. How's your ship?'

'Still disabled but otherwise fine.'

'And *Stalin*? The pirate ship?'

'Long gone, sir. Headed off south at a hell of a lick. Do you have any plans for it?'

'If I could catch the bastards I would, Captain. I would very happily blow them out of the water. As it is, I think we should sort out your problems first,' replied Crawford.

'Good idea. I'll look forward to seeing you soon.'

'Affirmative, Captain. Our ETA with you is about two hours from now. Our surgeon will probably stay with the casualty unless it looks very bad. *Jackson* out.'

Crawford hung up the handset. Further along the bridge, his radar officer glanced occasionally at the navigation radar which was set, as usual when cruising, at 16 miles range. Next to her was the big circular screen of the OTH (over-the-horizon) radar; a far more powerful set that could 'see' over the physical horizon by bouncing waves off the ionosphere. In wartime or on active duty, the set would be switched on – an operator would then have seen a clear blip from the massive bulk of the *Stalin*, standing off over the horizon about 50 miles from where the *Ocean Queen* drifted gently in the Pacific swell. As it was, the set stayed off, nothing showed on the screen, and the operator spent most of her time gazing at the far horizon thinking lustful thoughts about the engineering officer with whom she had lately been conducting a steamy affair.

Like a bear lurking at the back of a dark cave, *Stalin* crouched silently below the horizon, barely moving, not making a sound. The trap had turned round. Now the hunter was about to become the hunted.

*

The helicopter's rotor forced a solid gush of air down on to the foredeck of the *Ocean Queen* that was deflected by the steel plating and billowed down the deck, flicking long-forgotten drinks cans and unnoticed shreds of waste paper – undisturbed until now even by tropical typhoons – in a whirl up into the air and out across the sea. Small puddles of sea-water lurking in hidden recesses were blasted out in long rivulets that, after a few minutes, made the foredeck look as though it had been raining.

The pilot was carefully judging his landing on the make-shift heli-pad, trying to miss the obstruction of the forward signal mast and the two large anchor winches. His whipping rotor was clearing the mast by what looked like about three feet. He held the hover at full power for another few seconds while he checked his landing clearance. Satisfied that he would just make it, he lowered the collective lever. The whining jet engine immediately subsided, and the helicopter felt as though it was dropping the last ten feet like a falling stone. The door was opened and the surgeon, Weiner, gratefully got his feet on to the ship's deck.

Weiner was older, wiser and a great deal sourer than the eager young medic who was greeting him. On top of which, he was not at all happy to be wrenched off a nice comfortable ship, least of all by helicopter, because some snotty kid couldn't fix a bullet wound.

'Hi, I'm Doctor James Seymour,' grinned the young man with a wide smile like a puppy, holding out his paw in greeting.

Weiner glowered at him. He didn't look old enough even to have started medical school. 'Sure, son. Where's the casualty?'

'Oh, right. Absolutely. I'll take you there right now.'

'You do that.'

On the way down to Harvey, Weiner quizzed Seymour to establish the patient's condition. They went through the double doors to the sick bay. It took Weiner ten seconds to realise that unless Harvey got some whole blood inside him he was likely to go into shock.

'Have you blood-typed, son?'

'Oh, no, not really. Not got the kit, you see.'

Weiner pulled out his blood-typing set-up and within a couple of minutes established the blood group as the usual O.

'What blood group are you, son?'

'"O". Why?'

'Any diseases? AIDS? Hepatitis?'

'Good lord, no.'

'Sleeve up, then, son. You may be crap as a doctor, but I guess your blood's as good as anyone's.'

*

Within half an hour colour had started to return to Harvey's face and his blood pressure, though still low, was at least within the bounds of the living rather than the dead. Seymour, on the other hand, looked distinctly green, having given up a pint and a half of his blood and watched it seep slowly into Harvey. On his eventual return to dry land, he would give up medicine and become an estate agent.

Now Seymour was left watching over the patient by

Weiner, who had retired to Seymour's cabin to get something to eat. He was watching his patient carefully, wondering if the blood pressure would get any better, when Harvey suddenly opened his eyes wide and leaned up on one elbow. He reached out for Seymour and clutched him violently by the sleeve.

'Where's Kelley? Where's the Americans?' he rasped through his damaged throat, his glazed eyes focusing just enough to make out Seymour's now alarmed face.

'Easy, easy,' replied Seymour, taken aback by his previously inert patient's sudden recovery and violent awakening. This was all he needed. He thought of rushing off to grab Weiner, but Harvey clutched his arm even more urgently.

'They're waiting ... for Americans', said Harvey, suddenly lucid. He tried to sit up and started wagging his finger in the air. 'Bait ... they're waiting ... get the warheads ... ask Kelley', and then he slumped back on to the pillow, eyes closed, breathing quickly.

Seymour took his pulse. It was weak and fluttering. Slowly Harvey's colour returned and the heart rate steadied. What on earth was all that about? Seymour asked himself as he watched Harvey slip into a deeper sleep. Americans? Waiting for them? Something told him that this was not a piece of information that Weiner should have first. Seymour went to the bridge to track down Blake urgently.

'Captain, our pirate friend is looking a bit better. Actually, he said a couple of things. Quite interesting, really. Thought you might want to know.'

Blake's initial irritation at being waylaid by the young doctor suddenly turned to interest. 'What's he said?'

'He woke up for a second or two and raved on about warheads, Americans and waiting, something like that.'

'Bastard's full of bullets, Doc. Bound to say some crazy things.'

Attwood was nearby and overheard the conversation. 'What did he mean by waiting, Seymour?' asked the radio officer, now interested.

'Not sure, sir. He passed out a few seconds later. Something about bait, I thought he said. I couldn't see the fishing connection at all, sir.'

'Fishing?'

'You know, bait for fishing?'

'Oh, I see.' said Attwood. Seymour really was not very bright; best to leave him in blissful ignorance. 'Thanks, Seymour. Better get back to your patient. We're pretty busy up here.'

'Yes, sir,' said Seymour sheepishly and left the bridge. He never knew how important his message was.

Once the young man had gone. Attwood took Blake to one side and spoke quietly to him. 'This bait thing, sir. It's a bit worrying. It kind of makes some sense about that business with the busted radio.'

'Why?'

'It was a funny way to go about busting the radio. I mean, if you wanted to smash a radio, you'd just kick it in – the unit itself, something obvious. Instead, these people went for the power supply box, which is pretty technical.'

'Maybe they thought it was quicker?'

'Maybe. But that would suggest they knew what the power supply box actually was. And if they knew that, they'd know enough to realise that it could easily be by-passed and the radio reconnected. They'd know it would take about ten minutes to jury-rig a bypass circuit. Enough time to get away, but leaving the radio still operational. Crazy, isn't it?' finished Attwood doubtfully.

'So what are you leading to, exactly?'

Attwood looked embarrassed. 'Well, maybe they *wanted* us to make a distress call. Maybe they wanted to use us as bait of some kind. Our pirate seems to know something about it. Perhaps he was trying to warn us. Maybe that's why he was shot.'

'Sounds a bit bloody far-fetched, Attwood. Bait for what, for heaven's sake?'

'I really don't know sir. Perhaps they're trying to use us to lure another ship so they can rob it? Maybe it's hostages? I really have no idea, I'm afraid.'

Blake didn't really go for Attwood's theory. What on earth could the *Ocean Queen* be bait for? And anyway, the pirate ship was long gone. But Blake was not the sort of man to hang around if there was a point to prove or to disprove. And, in any event, he rather liked the idea of giving this pirate a hard time. He still remembered that appalling fat ape of a man and what he did to Holland. He strode down to the sick bay with Attwood following on behind, flung open the doors and found Seymour dozing in one of the chairs. Harvey was still out cold on the bed, but looked reasonably alive. Weiner was nowhere to be seen.

Seymour jumped up with a start as the captain barged in.

'Wake him up, please, Doctor. We need to talk to him urgently.'

'He's very sick, Captain. I'm not sure I should . . .'

'Sorry, Doctor. Has to be done. Maybe you should get the American chap in?'

'Oh. Right. OK, I'll get him.'

Weiner calmly walked into the room a minute later, followed by the nervous Seymour. The surgeon was still chewing on something. Attwood hoped to God it wasn't chewing-gum; Blake had a thing about chewing-gum. But no Captain of any ship – no

Admiral, if it came to it – had ever worried Weiner. Usually, it was the other way round.

'I hear you want our patient woken up. It's impossible,' said Weiner flatly, pointedly declining to use the Captain's formal title.

Blake wasn't going to be pushed around, least of all by an American.

'Is that so? You see, my colleague here thinks your ship might be in considerable danger if it gets any nearer. We think this man here knows all about it. I thought we should have a word with him, to be on the safe side. Or would it be easier to wait a few hours until your ship gets here? Would you like me to speak to Captain Crawford?' Blake glared at the surgeon.

Weiner looked sourly at Blake, then he rummaged in his case and injected Harvey with a small syringe full of a pink liquid. 'You've got five minutes at best,' he said and sat down next to the patient.

They waited for two or three minutes for the drug to take hold. The Englishman's breathing began to quicken and a flush of colour stole over his cheeks. The eyelids fluttered several times, then Harvey opened his eyes suddenly; there was a wild look to them as he looked at Blake.

Blake leaned over the staring face. 'Can you hear me?' he asked in the loud, slow voice that Englishmen of a certain generation use for talking to foreigners, or to children. 'Can you hear me?' he repeated, more loudly this time, not getting any response from the man.

Harvey slowly moved his head up and down. He kept licking his lips to try to moisten them.

Blake didn't feel a great deal of sympathy. Not after this man had held up his ship; not after he had robbed it; not after what the evil fat bastard did to Holland. 'Baker, listen, I want some answers from you,' he said.

'Not Baker,' whispered Harvey.

'You called yourself Baker,' said Blake.

'Not Baker. Harvey. Real name.'

'OK, Mr Harvey. You robbed my ship and now you're talking about Americans and bait. What exactly is going on?' demanded Blake.

At the mention of Americans, Weiner started to take more interest.

'Listen to me very carefully.' Harvey's croaking voice sounded urgent and he pushed himself up on his elbows. He swallowed several times to get some moisture into his dry mouth; the bullet wound in his throat made it difficult to talk. Weiner didn't move a muscle to give him water as he listened, transfixed, to the emerging story. 'He doesn't want the gold at all … this is all a trap. They disabled you as bait. There's an American warship nearby coming to help. It's carrying nuclear weapons … he's going to take the warheads … that's what he really came for. I found out and wouldn't have any part of it. That's why he had me shot … they meant to kill me. Are the Americans here yet? You've got to get them away. He's waiting.'

Weiner stood up. 'Sure we are, Mr Harvey. Right here. Right in the middle of the goddamn trap. Who is this "he" exactly?'

'Kelley … Michael Kelley. American. Thought he was just after the money, you see … seemed like a good scam. Pine is the thug. He's the one who shot me. Zof's running the ship. He knows nothing about the nuclear business.'

'And who wants the warheads, Mr Harvey? Who's paying for all this?'

'That's why I wanted out when I discovered.'

'Who is it?' demanded Weiner, getting angry.

'I'm not sure. But they're paying millions. Kelley delivers them to the Monte Bello Islands somewhere near Australia, then gets flown out. I was only after the money. I wanted nothing to do with this mess,' and Harvey slumped back on to his pillow, beads of sweat glistening on his pale face. His eyes were drifting closed; the drug was beginning to wear off.

'Jesus Christ,' murmured Weiner. 'I need to get hold of my ship right now,' he said quietly to Blake.

'Of course. We'll get you to a radio right away.' The three of them left Harvey with an astonished-looking Seymour. Harvey was unconscious again, breathing fitfully, sweat running in dribbles down the side of his face.

'Your patient was remarkably lucid, Doctor,' remarked Attwood to Weiner as they hurried along to the radio room.

'I should think so. Gave him a shot of pethidine. Great for waking up the dead and getting the truth out of them. Whether he survives or not is another question. Frankly, I don't give a damn.'

*

Weiner's call to Crawford was fractionally too late. A few minutes earlier and Crawford could have stopped his ship and remained invisible. As it was, the *Jackson* had just appeared at the outer edge of the *Stalin*'s small radar set.

Zof called Kelley over and pointed out the blip.

'Kelley, they're here. Look.'

Kelley watched the tiny orange blip on the 24-mile ring of the radar screen. He studied it intently for a full minute as Zof ordered his ship to start up and the crews to go to action stations. There was a smell of sweat and excitement in the air. The bridge crew visibly stiffened as Zof barked out a series of orders to get the ship into a state of readiness where it could take on one of the most technologically advanced warships in the world. Their series of victories, first over the American aircraft and then over the *Ocean Queen* had given the whole crew a sense of triumph and an undeniable sense of danger. All of them knew they were in it up to their necks; most of them would have done it anyway for the money. But now they realised they had tweaked the tail of the lion, and the lion would bite back. They went about the task of preparing for the confrontation with a grim determination to win at all costs.

'It's stopped,' said Kelley quietly, in the midst of the bustle of the bridge. He had been peering at the screen: the blip remained motionless on the 24-mile ring. 'Have they seen us?' he asked.

'Maybe. But why stop?' replied Zof, mystified. 'You're sure it's stopped?'

'It's stopped. Do you see it moving?'

Zof looked at the screen as Kelley stood aside and watched the blip for a full minute. There was no sign of movement. The *Jackson* had found them hours earlier than they had expected; but Zof wasn't going to let that make any difference. Whatever was happening, it was time to act. He turned away from the screen and got on the ancient PA system: his voice echoed around the ship, now silent as the crew listened carefully to their Captain's orders. Zof had thought carefully about how to explain the real purpose of the mission to the crew. He would let them into his confidence slowly, he decided.

'In an hour or so we will probably be engaging in some action with an American missile cruiser. It is very close to us and it is coming to the rescue of the liner. You don't need me to explain the danger this poses to us all,' he explained.

'Sounds like real action this time,' said a twenty-year-old seaman nervously to a friend, as they listened to Zof's voice. They were crouched inside one of the gun turrets.

'Don't worry, kid,' said the other man, who was older and had sailed with Zof before. 'It's Zof. He knows what he's doing. He'll sort them out, you'll see. Always got a plan, that guy.'

'I intend to engage the Americans quickly, and I am sure we can persuade them to surrender. I think once they see what they are up against they won't risk being taken to pieces. Then I plan to send a boarding party over. The ship is carrying some small nuclear warheads. I think it will be excellent protection for us to relieve these Americans of their cargo. Call it insurance. Then we'll leave them to explain their sudden loss to their masters. Now, get to your battle stations,' finished Zof, and the click on the PA told the crew he had finished.

'Told you, kid,' said the older man. 'Imagine the looks on their faces in America when they hear we've walked off with their warheads. It's going to be like stealing sweets from a baby,' he smiled as they started preparing the turret for action.

Zof had much the same idea in mind. And now, for the first time in his career, he was readying his ship for action against the real enemy. Not an exercise this time, the real thing. He found himself enjoying the experience.

The *Stalin* began to come to life again: the gentle trembling of the ship as the idling turbines increased their speed, then a pronounced shudder as the steam pressure was raised to start the vessel moving. The four enormous screws turned slowly as a windmill to begin with, then speeded up to bite into the warm Pacific water like helicopter blades, slicing through the sea and shoving the bulk of the steel monster forward with every beat.

As the ship made her way ahead and gained speed, Zof ordered the helm swung round. Without much forward motion to start with, the great vessel was reluctant to answer the swinging rudder; but as the speed built, so did the turn. A creamy foam appeared at the stern, a tumbling bow wave grew at the prow, and the ship began to heel gently into the increasingly tight turn as *Stalin* turned to face the *Jackson* some 24 miles away. Once *Stalin* had laboriously built up speed, the two ships were less than one hour apart.

*

Crawford had brought the *Jackson* to a stop minutes after Blake's message had reached him. He ordered the engines full astern and the slim, elegant ship shuddered, slowed and finally came to a halt in the water. Crawford had already established contact with the Pentagon. Bell had been found, and – as Zof and Kelley were staring at the stationary radar blip on their screens, wondering why she had stopped – Crawford was talking directly to him. At the same time, the *Jackson*'s radar officer, alarmed by the sudden stopping of the ship, thought she should switch her radar to a longer range than the 16 miles she was using. This was a standing order in emergency situations, though no one had bothered to tell her what the emergency was all about. As the picture changed to display the 24-mile radius, she spotted a distinct blip at the edge of the screen. She watched it for a few moments. Displaying a heading and speed next to the blip, the radar system detected the start-up of the *Stalin* and the change of heading. She watched with surprise as the blip gained speed and turned slowly to a heading aimed directly towards them.

She turned to the Captain, who was engaged in a serious-looking conversation on the red security radio. He looked preoccupied, and she thought it best to wait. Crawford on a good day was not a friendly man. On a bad day he showed a particular dislike of female officers. This looked a bad moment in a bad day, and she was not going to tempt an outburst.

Crawford put down the handset, and she approached. 'Large radar contact at twenty-four miles, sir, closing on a reciprocal bearing. It's now at fifteen knots, sir, and building.' The *Stalin* was heading straight for them.

She had clearly chosen the wrong moment. Crawford, having just come off the line to Bell and his staff at the Pentagon and agreed that the best plan would be to stay clear of the Russian until help arrived, now discovered that what was almost certainly the *Stalin* was instead heading directly for him, at a speed that would close them in around an hour. Crawford swore loudly and violently, glared at the hapless female, and ordered all engines full ahead and the ship to action stations.

The rules of engagement were being made up as they went along. Nobody had expected this situation, and as yet the Pentagon planners had not had time to figure out what to do. It was approaching a wartime situation in which the commander on the spot had a great deal more latitude that would have normally been the case. In any event, if it was the *Stalin* bearing down on him, and Crawford was certain that it was, the overriding orders were to ensure the safety of the ship, and in this case the safety of the nuclear warheads he was carrying. It was here that Crawford made his mistake, though any officer in the United States Navy would have done exactly the same. The *Stalin* was a fifty-year-old warship with a scratch crew, probably untrained, devoid of any modern weaponry, coming face to face with a warship that carried more firepower than a whole fleet of Second World War battleships, and the ability to deliver that firepower with near-absolute accuracy.

Bell had, of course, warned him of McEwan's theories on the virtual invincibility of the Russian, but years of training made Crawford utterly convinced that his ship was many times more powerful than the Russian could ever be. Without any hesitation, Crawford reached a simple and obvious conclusion: there was no way the Russian posed a real threat. In that case, logically, the best protection for his ship, his crew and his cargo was to go in on the attack. The Russian would simply back away; or, if it came to a fight, would surrender ignominiously. If these crazy Russians thought they could steal his cargo, they were in for the surprise of their lives.

The ship shuddered again as the engines powered up once more, and the passageways sprang into noisy life as the crew moved expertly to their action stations. Whatever Zof and the crew of the *Stalin* had in mind, Crawford was not about to play ball.

18

The black speck on the horizon was slowly getting bigger. As Crawford watched it through his binoculars, it shimmered in the distance like a mirage. Drawn out to one side of the distant ship, the wind pulled a crisp black line of oily smoke from the *Stalin's* funnel. The approaching battleship was heading directly for him.

He had got his own ship under way as quickly as he could and was managing 26 knots, and *Stalin* was thundering along at over 32 knots if the radar was to be believed. At that closing speed, they would meet in under half an hour.

Crawford was a Captain of the old school. He hated females on his ship; he hated all the political correctness that was running uncontrolled through the armed forces. He had joined the Navy for action, not for playing at diplomats or managers. But however strongly he felt about these things, he remained a cold, hard, rational commander who would die rather than risk his men. Once he had got his ship under way to confront the Russian, he contacted the Pentagon to expl in his actions. Bell's staff exploded, and moments ll himself came back on the line.

ord, that ship is deadly. There's no way you it on.'

ral, if your information about her speed

is correct, there's no way I can outrun her, not now. My ship is already in danger. We're ready to take her on.'

There was a pause. Bell knew his man was right. His staff, listening on speakers, looked at each other, then at the Chief, and nodded. Maybe McEwan was wrong. Maybe the old ship would give up the moment they saw *Jackson* was not going to be bullied. It had to be worth a try.

The *Stalin* was now becoming visible as a larger smudge dancing in the warm air on the distant horizon. As far as Crawford was concerned, there was no way he could simply give in without at least trying. And if it didn't work, he couldn't see that he would lose that much. If it was his cargo they were after, then his cargo would become the hostage. They sure as hell wouldn't dare sink him. It was the kind of hand that Crawford enjoyed playing.

Exactly the same point had occurred to Bell and his staff. If they were after the warheads, the pirates were not going to sink the *Jackson*. Bell had several hurried conversations with Ross, who was in the situation room as the drama unfolded. If necessary, let the pirates have the warheads. They knew where the ship was; it couldn't get away. The *Stalin* would be tracked across the oceans and then, when the time was right, would be brought to heel with little trouble. Ross nodded. Bell nodded in turn. One of his staff officers took up the dialogue with Crawford.

'OK, Captain. CNO agrees your plan. But if the Russian doesn't get scared off, orders are to surrender peacefully and let them have the cargo.'

'Yes, sir,' replied Crawford, and put the handset down.

He called over Slatter, his XO. Slatter stood smartly to attention in front of Crawford, forcing the Captain to physically look up at him, which Crawford alwa hated. Crawford ran through his plan. Slatter and he rarely saw eye to eye, almost as a matter of principle; their deep dislike was mutual. Slatter listened carefully to the Captain's plan. He would follow the Pentagon's orders. Almost . . .

'I sure as hell am not going to let the bastards walk all over us, Slatter. The Pentagon tells me to surrender unless they take fright straight away. Keep out of trouble. Direct orders,' said Crawford.

'Better obey them, then, sir' responded Slatter.

'Sure, Mr Slatter. I'll obey them. But first I'm going to knock five kinds of shit out of them. I do not propose to give up that easily. We'll put up a fight first. It may frighten them off, it may not. But they're going to know that the USS *Jackson* does not just turn over and wave its goddamn legs in the air. Now I want to make sure you understand. You're the XO. In theory you can stop me. I'm disobeying orders. I should surrender if they don't get scared off. You can arrest me and take over the command. What would you like to do? Surrender or kick their Russian asses to hell?'

Slatter's face broke into a wide grin. Crawford was usually the cautious one, and Slatter was delighted with the plan. As far as he was concerned, abject surrender was unthinkable. A heap of Russian junk was steaming down on them, and not a missile to its name. It was too good an opportunity to miss. The old enemy was just trying it on. They didn't stand a chance.

For the first time in his tour on the *Jackson*, Slatter was right behind his Captain. 'Let's go to war – sir,' he re____d, but this time the 'sir' was said with respect.

____ two men went back inside the bridge and

____ operation.

____ make ready the 402 system and stand by,'

'402 aye, sir,' called the weapons officer. He turned to his array of screens and keypads and started arming the 402 system, the Navy's latest weapon, otherwise known unofficially as the 'Kamikaze'.

The weapon was so new that it had only just finished trials, and the *Jackson* was the only ship in the Navy fitted with the system. The Navy had been mightily impressed with the performance of Air Force laser-guided weapons in the Gulf War and wanted something of equal accuracy. It would be handy, reasoned Naval staff, to have a low-power weapon capable of delivering a surgical blow with extreme accuracy. Navy men gazed with wonder at the video footage of Air Force smart bombs popping through windows and down chimneys. Guided by lasers aimed from aircraft circling overhead, the bombs had, literally, 'brains' – they could follow the laser beam and strike their targets with astonishing accuracy. Or so the manufacturer claimed anyway. And the Navy wanted something just like it to shoot at ships.

The problem was that a ship would find it difficult laser-marking the target to guide the weapon with the required degree of accuracy. Either you had to get very close, which was impossible, or else you had to be in the air. Putting up a marker plane or chopper might work, but it made the whole thing more cumbersome. Besides, not every ship would have access to an aircraft. Was there a way of guiding a weapon with pinpoint accuracy, without the need for a marker aircraft, from a ship, alone?

An engineer at Raytheon came up with the answer, inspired by watching his teenage son donning a virtual-reality helmet to play a computer game. The 'Kamikaze' consisted of a small missile in two parts. The first part contained a camera, a computer and very sensitive position-sensing device. The second part carried the warhead.

The target was first acquired using normal radar. Then the 'Kamikaze' system was fired, aimed in the general direction of the target. Only the first section of the missile was launched at this point: it travelled slowly, around 100 mph. It was also very small; little bigger than a large seagull, powered by a compressed gas engine that gave it a range of 20 miles. The size of the missile made it impossible to detect on radar: it was just too small to register, so there was little chance of shooting it down even though it travelled slowly. It was equally invisible to the human eye, at least until it was closing in. And then, of course, it was too late.

The camera in the nose of the missile relayed a high-quality digital colour picture back to the operator, who saw the image inside a VR helmet which allowed him to guide the first part of the system to the selected target. The view in the VR helmet was frighteningly realistic. Operators had a genuine feeling of diving down on to a ship and flinched when the missile was about to connect. They couldn't help themselves. The system's unofficial 'Kamikaze' name was given to it the first day it was tried.

The rest of the system was automatic. The second part of the missile, containing the warhead, was launched a moment before the first section impacted. Following the position information relayed by the leading missile, the warhead was propelled towards the target at a speed in excess of the speed of sound. It co___ ___red the image it saw with the recorded image ___ ___tted from the leading part to make fine ___ ___ts – to allow for the movement of the target ___ ___mple.

___ at very high speed. And in trials, it

achieved extraordinary accuracy. Crawford had watched an operator carefully guide the tiny leading drone into a window four feet square on a test tower rigged on a barge at the test site. Around five seconds later the warhead carrier roared through the window without even touching the sides. The Navy ordered as many as Raytheon could make, and the *Jackson* was the first ship in the fleet to be equipped with the 402.

Right now, the weapons officer was carefully selecting the blip of the *Stalin* as the target for the 402.

'402 target acquired and locked, sir.'

'Thank you, Weapons. Stand by,' replied Slatter, waiting for the final go-ahead from Crawford. *Stalin* by now was much clearer on the horizon, steaming relentlessly toward them at maximum speed, about 15 miles away and closing as the big ship's superior speed narrowed the gap.

Crawford's plan was, in essence, to make the bet both ways. Although *Stalin* was a formidable ship, it was manned by ordinary people. In fact, he reasoned, they weren't even ordinary by Navy standards: from what little he had learned from Bell, they were a ragtag bunch of dissidents and street crooks, or so it sounded to him, and he reasoned their morale would be pretty flaky. In other words, the men were the weakest part of this ship.

Following the F-15 attack and the raid on the *Madelaine* and the *Ocean Queen*, they probably felt pretty pleased with themselves. So, explained Crawford to Slatter, they had to be given a quick lesson that messing with the *Jackson* was not going to be a near roll-over. 'Frighten the shit out of them,' was Crawford's exact expression, said with a broad grin, unwittingly reflecting Kelley's identical strategy.

They'd pop a 402 round through the bridge windows of the *Stalin*. It wouldn't be enough to disable the ship or even affect it greatly, but it would frighten the shit out of the commander and crew; very probably might even kill one or two of the ringleaders if they got lucky. What did Slatter think?

'What happens if it doesn't work?' Slatter asked.

'Don't see how it can fail, Slatter. We're not going to miss, are we?' replied Crawford.

'Maybe not. But *if* it doesn't work?' persisted Slatter.

'Hell, Slatter, we just stop and hand over the nukes, for Christ's sake. But I'll be damned if we don't put up at least some resistance. If it fails we can't lose. Bell will chase the bastards around the oceans until he catches them. But you never know your luck, Mr Slatter. They might think twice.'

Slatter had conceded the point. Now he waited for Crawford's go-ahead to fire the 402 system. The Captain stood silently on the wing of the bridge looking back through his glasses at the *Stalin*.

'Mr Slatter, stop the ship and bring her round so we can all watch the fun.'

'Aye, Captain,' responded Slatter eagerly. He ordered the course change and the engines to all-stop. The *Jackson* swung around her under its own momentum even though the propellers stopped thrashing the water. In a neat manoeuvre, just as the ship had turned at right-angles to its original course, it came gently to a halt, exactly where Slatter wanted it. He prided himself on his boat-handling ability. The ship had stopped broadside on to *Stalin*, now clearly visible in the distance even without the aid of glasses.

'Very well, Mr Slatter. Open fire when you're ready,' ordered Crawford.

'Aye, sir. Opening fire now.' Slatter nodded to the weapons officer, who donned the VR helmet and got ready for the shot.

A few seconds later there was a gentle 'pop' from

the launch platform in the centre of the ship as the tiny drone was thrown into the air by a small rocket. The rocket fell away and the compressed gas engine took over. Stubby wings flicked open and the drone settled into level flight, doing a steady 100 mph, towards Stalin; it would take around five or six minutes to reach the battleship.

Inside the operator's helmet, the view was exactly what a pilot would have seen. It was probably how the real Kamikaze pilots spent their last few moments on earth, watching the selected target ship getting slowly bigger in their windscreens. The operator could see *Stalin* clearly – the digital image was electronically stabilised and even the vibration from the drone's tiny rocket motor didn't affect the picture. He moved the joystick control a little to the right and the drone responded immediately, shifting the image of the *Stalin* into the centre of the virtual 'windscreen'. He'd been told to aim for any forward-facing window on the bridge, though he wasn't yet close enough to see them.

The drone flew steadily on, maintaining a height of around 30 feet above the sea. Nobody on the *Stalin* would be able to see it, even if they knew where to look.

The operator began to see the details of the upperworks of the *Stalin*. The central citadel and funnel became clear. A few moments later and the finer details of the superstructure resolved themselves. He could clearly see the huge guns pointing directly at him. Above the turrets rose the central command tower. As the drone continued to close in, he concentrated on the central tower where the bridge had to be, delicately adjusting the joystick to keep the image central in his screen.

Now the drone was a mile away, and to allow the operator as much time as possible the tiny compressed gas engine throttled itself right back, providing just enough power to keep the drone airborne and on course but slowing the speed to 50 mph. The operator now had a little over one minute for the closing mile to sort out his target and drop the drone squarely through the bridge window.

Now the superstructure details were clear. The operator could see the bridge, a square structure that jutted out from the central tower with a line of eight square, forward-facing windows.

But then he noticed another similar structure. This one was higher than the first, but it had the same number of windows and about the same dimensions. And just as he started thinking about moving the joystick to angle the drone slightly upwards, he spotted yet a third possibility, this time at the bottom of the tower: a squat-looking structure just peering above the gun-turrets with slit windows and what looked like a solid steel casing all round it.

No. Far too small for a command bridge. He ignored it. Now he had two possibilities. The windows were growing quickly in size ... which one, for Christ's sake? Why were there two fucking bridges? Nobody had mentioned this. He swore quietly. He had seconds left. The countdown clock in the bottom of his field of vision indicated '15' to go. Which bridge? Had to be the middle. Had to be. No time. The windows were now coming up on the screen. Ten seconds. Shift the drone. Choose a window. Five seconds. Shift the drone a bit more. Centre the window. Two seconds. Centre again. One second. An astonished face staring directly at him, darkened by the glass. The face getting bigger ... the eyes suddenly widening ... the man ducking. Almost nose to nose. Then ... the image disappeared, fading gently in front of the operator's eyes to a grey field of nothing, like being plunged suddenly into fog.

The rest was completely automatic.

When the drone's main engine throttled down with a minute or so to go, the follow-up missile started its own countdown. After thirty seconds it blasted itself out of the launcher tube on the *Jackson*, the rocket motor igniting a second later, rapidly accelerating the small missile to a speed of 700 mph. As it accelerated, it received the position information from the drone as well as the video picture that it compared with its own image from the camera in the nose. It had recorded the entire flight of the drone and the tiny computer on board was busy ensuring that the flight of the missile followed the drone's exact path. As the drone smashed through the bridge window on the *Stalin* the missile was in flight, rapidly processing the image and the location with such accuracy that it even jinked very slightly at the point where the operator couldn't decide which bridge to go for, though it was travelling at such a speed by then that the movement was unnoticeable.

The computers had done their jobs well, calculating the flight times and position with extraordinary accuracy. The drone had perished smashing itself against the far end of the bridge. The main missile's tiny camera and computers annihilated themselves exactly 4.65 seconds later as the missile blasted through the smashed window and, realising it had reached its destination, detonated its warhead in a small but violent explosion which, in the confined space, ripped the inside of the bridge into flying, burning shreds of debris.

The explosion was powerful enough to kill Kelley, Zof and the rest of the crew on the bridge.

Or it would have done, it they'd been there. But the only person on that bridge was an unfortunate Russian seaman who had gone up to watch the fun, and instead had watched a tiny plane buzz towards him and smash through the window to impact itself against the far bulkhead and then, as he turned to look back out of the window, was just in time to see a missile shrieking towards him before it erupted into a brilliant orange flash, which was the last thing he ever saw.

The rest of the bridge crew, Zof and Kelley included, had retired to the armoured battle bridge with the slit windows half an hour earlier, getting ready for battle, and in particular protecting themselves from the flash of the big guns if these needed to be used.

Kelley could see the *Jackson* clearly. He wondered why it suddenly turned broadside on to him, although at that distance he couldn't see it was stopping. He called Zof over, but as he did he noticed the tiny drone winging towards them.

'What the hell is that, Zof?' asked Kelley in a tone that brought the Russian forward to peer out of one of the slit windows.

'I have no idea, Kelley, my friend,' replied Zof, still watching the drone travelling slowly towards them, 'But it looks as though it came from the *Jackson*.'

'They want to play rough by the look of things. Maybe we should have a friendly chat with the Captain.' Kelley reached for the handset of the VHF. As he plucked it from its cradle, the drone completed its journey above them, though they couldn't see it and with two feet of armour plate around them they couldn't hear it smashing itself to pieces on the upper bridge. But, 4.65 seconds later, when the missile roared in over their heads and exploded on the bridge 40 feet above them, there was a deep and ominous thump that shook the whole superstructure. They all involuntarily ducked.

Zof knew he'd taken a hit, but the explosion was not so big.

'Shit,' yelled Kelley, crouching on the floor as the reverberations of the explosion rumbled around the armoured room. Water was spraying over them from a ruptured line somewhere. As the reverberations died away, Zof was first to his feet, grabbing the microphone and ordering damage-control parties to report, then yelling at the helmsman to push the wheel right over to bring the ship round, then yelling even more loudly at the engine room to make smoke. It was a classic manoeuvre from the era before reliable radars and electronic counter-measures: hide. He was still wondering what had hit them; some kind of missile, obviously, though the blast was less than it should have been. But Zof's mind didn't waste much time on wondering. His worry was another shot hitting them.

Maintaining speed, the vast ship slewed around, leaning against the turn, the high superstructure canting over at a surprising angle, while in the engine room they reduced the air to the boilers, making the sweet oil burn poorly to produce a clinging, heavy smoke that poured out of the stack and sank towards the ocean in a dense wall that the *Stalin* flung herself into.

*

There was a whoop of delight on the bridge of the *Jackson* when the distant flash was seen on the *Stalin*'s superstructure. Crawford, watching through glasses, saw the missile hurtle directly at the bridge structure and momentarily vanish before an orange flash was clearly seen through the windows. Although he'd seen the tests, he was still amazed at the accuracy of the missile. He grinned widely as the crew of the ship, leaning over the rails, cheered.

They watched as the great ship then started to veer to one side. Presumably the helmsman had been killed and they had lost steering control. Then black smoke began to pour from the stack and *Stalin*, continuing the turn, soon vanished in the murk, though her course was still visible on the radar.

'What do you make of that, Mr Slatter?' asked Crawford, slightly taken aback by the smoke. It was an unusual manoeuvre, to say the least.

'Direct hit, Captain. I guess they're trying to hide in the smoke.'

'Don't they have radar?' asked Crawford incredulously.

The radar officer thought it was a direct question. 'Oh, yes, sir,' she quickly replied. 'But they've been transmitting on a low-power i-band. Funny signal. Bit like a fishing-boat radar.'

Stalin was now invisible in the thick black cloud.

'Even so, Captain, it makes another shot with the "Kamikaze" impossible. We'll never be able to target it in that shit, beg your pardon, sir.'

'OK, Mr Slatter. Point made. I guess we just go in after them. Make ready the Harpoons,' ordered Crawford.

'Aye, sir,' responded Slatter, giving the orders to get the Harpoon surface-to-surface missiles ready. Crawford was now spoiling for a fight. Slatter found it odd to have their usual roles reversed this way.

*

The water had stopped spraying over them. They had recovered their composure and Kelley was burning with rage. The damage-control parties reported what had happened. He couldn't believe that the *Jackson* was crazy enough to open the bidding. The whole idea was that the mighty *Stalin* would creep up on the unsuspecting *Jackson* while it was busy helping the *Ocean Queen*. They would terrorise the crew, lift the nukes, and be on their way. All that had collapsed. The *Jackson* was now not only fully aware of their existence but had opened fire first.

Zof seemed calmer. It was clear that the *Jackson* was about to have a go, the way it came in like that. It was a warship, after all. It was built to fight and that's exactly what it was doing. He'd have done the same. OK, he thought, whoever you are. You want a fight, then a fight is exactly what you're going to get. Zof had no doubt who was going to win. He'd been on ships like the American cruiser before; he knew they were a mass of advanced technologies that were brilliant against another floating computer. But against the solid steel walls of the *Stalin*, he knew it didn't stand an earthly. Come on, my friend, come on.

'Stupid bastards. Stupid, stupid, stupid,' raged Kelley to anyone who wanted to listen.

'They're coming after us, Kelley,' said Zof. 'I think we should ready our guns. It looks as though he wants a fight. It won't take him long to realise his mistake.'

'Jesus, Zof, just frighten the life out of them. Drop a few shells near him. You don't want to sink the thing,' fumed Kelley. Why on earth couldn't they behave themselves? This was going to be messier than he had thought.

Kelley was right, of course, and Zof suppressed the urge to blow the thing from the seas. But he could damn well frighten them. If I can't sink you, I will bring you to your knees. 'OK, I think, Kelley. A warning shot or two will do the trick. One of our shells could easily sink the ship if it connected. I think we can manage to convince him,' he smiled. Zof couldn't help himself. At his command he had more firepower than a whole fleet, old-fashioned as it was. The sheer terror of those huge guns was enough to make any other naval commander think twice. It was an awesome power and Zof took a professional pride, and deep down a real pleasure, in wielding such weaponry. It was crude macho stuff, and he wasn't normally subject to such idiocies. But it was impossible to resist the raw, basic thrill of it all.

Zof gave the orders and readied the ship while it was still hidden in the smoke.

The gun-crews drew six high-explosive shells from the magazine, and loaded them into the gaping 22-inch-wide breeches of the guns. Then silk sacks stuffed with propellant were pushed in after them. Gleaming stainless-steel hydraulics whispered shut the thick breech doors, each three feet thick, then turned them 24 degrees to lock them into place.

Then they waited. The fire director sat high in the superstructure with the huge optical rangefinder system, its arms stretching out 70 feet each side of the central citadel. But his view was totally obscured by the clinging smoke that surrounded the ship.

Zof waited until his gun-crews reported themselves ready. Then he ordered the *Stalin* back on to a course heading for the *Jackson*, and out of the smoke.

The ship gathered speed once again. 'Morin!' called Zof, beckoning the young officer over. He whispered in his ear and Morin nodded, then disappeared in a hurry. He ran from the bridge, back towards the ladders that led up the massive central superstructure. He climbed three sets of ladders, the thick black smoke surrounding him making his eyes water. He reached a high platform where the halyards of the signal mast ended, neatly tied off on big brass cleats. Fifty feet above him, only just visible in the murk, the skull and crossbones still flapped in the wind. He unwound the halyard and slowly pulled down the flag, then unclipped it and let it go into the wind. Like a blackened seagull, it wheeled and dived behind the ship and disappeared into the darkness. There was a locker on the platform. Morin opened it and, just as Zof had said, found what he was looking for. He clipped the new ensign on to the halyard and hauled away. It was bigger than the skull and crossbones; once the wind caught it, it rattled out into its full glory. Morin hauled on the halyard until it rose, foot by foot, to the top of the signal mast.

As the *Stalin* burst from the black smog at full speed, the proud ensign of the Soviet Navy, the Red Banner, its yellow star flapping vigorously on its blood-red background, flew defiantly from the mast. If Zof was going into battle, it would be under his colours and not like a thief in the night. The *Stalin* was now the flagship of the Pacific Fleet. The crew saw the new battle standard, and there was a pride in their eyes that most of them had thought was extinguished for ever.

Charging headlong towards its enemy, the ship threw up a curling bow wave that gleamed white against the grey hull and deep black background. Even at that speed it took time to emerge with its whole threatening length, like a long train coming out of a dark tunnel into bright daylight. The moment the murk cleared from his viewfinder, the fire director measured off the range by bringing together the two images of the approaching *Jackson*. It was just five miles, and closing. He transmitted the range and bearing to the fire control computer deep in the armoured centre of the ship.

The extraordinary electro-mechanical device, built in 1944 and copied largely from German technology in the days when Hitler and Stalin were pretending to be good friends, was the direct forerunner of the modern digital computer. The only real difference was that it was not programmable to perform different tasks. It was built solely to solve the complex differential equations that told the gunner the elevation and bearing of the guns in order to hit a target at a certain range and direction, allowing for wind-drift, air temperature, weight of shell, propellant, humidity, speed of ship and temperature of gun barrel. You simply set the various parameters on big dials, entered the range and bearing and switched on the machine. The whole machine then cranked and ground, and two large dials finally pointed to the required elevation and bearing. Compared with a modern computer it was ludicrously slow, but nevertheless gave a highly accurate solution within several seconds which no human working with pen and paper could have done, least of all in the heat of battle.

The dials were set, the readings from the fire director entered, the machine cranked and the solution transmitted to the gun-crews via large brass indicators inside the gun-turrets. The guns were raised to the appropriate elevation and swung round to the required bearing.

'Guns ready, sir,' called a seaman to Zof.

Zof looked at Kelley, who nodded.

'Fire turret one,' ordered Zof. Moments later the three huge guns roared with flickers of orange and purple, then a brilliant white flash, as the propellants ignited and hurled the bulky shells towards the *Jackson*. To avoid straining the ship, each gun was programmed to fire fractionally after the other one, leaving a gap of half a second between each detonation. The effect was to prolong the roaring and flashing into a continuous blaze of raw energy that made the entire ship shudder. The din seemed to fill the whole sky.

On the *Jackson*, all Crawford and Slatter saw was

the *Stalin* suddenly roaring out from the smoke. Then came a massive flash, brilliant even at that range. A second later, both men could actually see the shells as they flew silently towards the *Jackson*. Slatter only had time to yell 'Incoming!' before the first shell bored into the sea 500 yards off the bow and exploded in a geyser of boiling white foam that climbed 100 feet or more into the sky. Just as the water reached its height and started to fall back, the second shell exploded in the sea, this time 400 yards off the bow, then the third shell, 300 yards off. A perfectly bracketed shot. As the water collapsed, the *Jackson*, still racing forward at full speed, ran into the aftermath of the impacts. Hundreds of tons of water cascaded down on to the foredeck, then the bridge, then the centre section, before its force was spent. The effect was like ploughing into a high sea at speed, the bow of the ship ducking down under the weight of the water, shouldering into deep green sea, the vessel slowing and hesitating before the buoyancy of the bow forced her up again. She threw off the dead weight of water and started to pick up speed.

The bridge was awash. There was no time to close the doors before the shells landed, and the spray had drenched Slatter and Crawford, who had nearly been swept off the bridge by the force of water landing on them. It had sluiced through the doors and like a miniature tidal wave had flowed right through the bridge area. Electrical systems were already sparking and shorting, and the radar had gone blank.

'Everyone OK?' yelled a soaked Slatter, staring at the dazed crew on the bridge. No one was missing, no one was hurt. All of them were dazed and disorientated. Crawford, his cap missing and the white uniform sticking to him, stormed onto the bridge incandescent with fury.

'Slatter, we're going to blow those sons of bitches out of the goddamn water. What happened, for Christ's sake?'

'No idea, Captain. But our shot seemed to have stirred up the hornets' nest.'

'Damn right, Slatter. Well, I'm not giving up yet. Get a couple of forty-eights off and give those bastards a fright.'

Slatter was about to point out that it would be a waste of two perfectly good torpedoes but, looking at Crawford's furious face, decided not to get into an argument. He ordered two Mark 48 torpedoes launched, a low-technology weapon that homed accoustically and carried an impressive warhead of over a ton. Their great advantage was speed, achieving some 40 knots under water, making avoiding tactics at close range by the target vessel an almost hopeless proposition.

The 48s flew from their tubes and dropped with two loud splashes into the water, sank to 20 feet and then, 100 yards from the *Jackson*, rose back to the surface on their way towards *Stalin*, leaving clear trails in the water from the gas-powered engines.

The launch was spotted by Kelley, who was closely watching the *Jackson* for its response. He'd never seen a torpedo trial before, but even to his untrained eye it was obvious what they were. 'Torpedoes, Zof!' he yelled.

But Zof had already spotted the trails working towards them. It was exactly what he expected. But he knew what Crawford didn't, which was that it would take a lot more than even a direct hit from his two torpedoes to do any damage. Kishkov's design was too clever for that.

Even so, he calmly ordered the ship aimed directly at them, to 'comb' the trails. He still wanted to minimise the effects. And it was plain good seamanship. The manoeuvre was a classic one, often rehearsed. While the Russians used an old-fashioned guided torpedo that was subject to jamming, the Americans used a self-targeting system that was deadly but which, after years of practice against dummies, the Russians reckoned they had perfected the technique of avoiding.

The idea was first to present the narrowest target; he would have turned the ship to try to outrun them if he'd had the time, but they were simply too close, and running too fast. He maintained speed, on the basis that if he could miss them he'd then stand a chance of outrunning them on the other side if they turned to follow him, which is what they were programmed to do. If your closing speed on the torpedoes was fast enough, you went past them before they could complete their turn and, while they were turning again to follow, you could gain some distance on them. The range of the 48s was limited and they were meant to run out of power shortly after this move. That's what the textbook said, anyway. Now was the chance to try it with live fish. Zof felt confident enough now to let the torpedoes smash into him broadside, but he didn't think it would do the crew's morale a great deal of good.

With a dry mouth Kelley watched the two pale lines speed towards them. There was dead silence on the bridge: only the incessant throbbing of the great ship, like a troubled heartbeat, and that was felt more than heard.

Zof remained perfectly calm and positioned his ship well. At a closing speed of 70 knots the first torpedo 'heard' the ship clearly, but was confused by the length. The noise of the *Stalin's* bulbous bow shouldering at speed through the water caught its acoustic attention but, as soon as it did, the thrashing of the four propellers seemed more important and it decided to alter course again. By that time the ship was roaring past at speed and the sound was coming from everywhere, confusing the aiming system. The torpedo started to wander, and by then the ship was past. It turned to follow, but the turn slowed it down and it began to fall behind.

The second torpedo was luckier. It suffered from the same confusion, but *Stalin* was closer. It was knocked off course by the bow wave, and the water pressure kicked the stern of the torpedo away, shoving the nose in towards *Stalin*, while the torpedo's momentum pushed it straight into the ship's side where a simple contact fuse detonated the ton of explosive right alongside the hull.

The huge ship felt as though it had leapt into the air. The torpedo had exploded against an armour belt and the armour absorbed the huge power of the blast, coming away in small flakes, splitting slightly down a seam but remaining unbreached. Having absorbed the blow, the armour belt than transmitted much of the energy to the rest of the ship, and the shock was like sitting inside a metal room with someone beating on the outside with a sledgehammer. Loose fittings came away, even inside the engine room. Pipes burst, electrical connections failed, some high-pressure steamlines ripped out of a fitting, badly scalding two crew members.

Zof knew by some instinct that the damage was slight, but called for damage-control reports once the echoes of the hammering explosion died away. Kelley had rushed from the armoured bridge to the deck outside to see what damage had been done, but nothing was visible. The remaining torpedo exploded some distance behind them, having given up the chase.

Confident he was in the clear, Zof now ordered his
ship to dead slow, and turned the bow away from the
side of the explosion in case water was being forced
into a hole by the movement of the vessel. It was more
textbook than a real worry. The *Jackson* too looked as
though it was stopping, now just four miles away,
clearly visible on the horizon. Like Zof, it was waiting
to see what damage it had done.

The damage-control parties quickly reported to Zof.
Their report was welcome, and he turned to Kelley.
'Well, our old ship really is tough. A bit of water
through a burst seam, but nothing we can't control.
I'm beginning to think we really are invulnerable.
Missiles, torpedoes, aircraft – and we're still in the
game. Now, let's sort out this little American insect
once and for all.'

Zof had spent a lifetime in training for this
moment. He savoured it, sure of his position in the
game, knowing that he was a move or two from
checkmate. He picked up the VHF and pressed the
transmit switch.

'*Jackson*, this is *Stalin*. Listen to me and listen very
carefully. At this moment I have you targeted by six of
my 22-inch guns, each of which is loaded with high-
explosive shells. I guarantee at least three of my shells
will hit you. Any one of them will take the bottom out
of your boat. You have no defence, Captain, none at all.
In exactly sixty seconds from now I will give the order
to open fire. What will stop me is you replying on this
channel within that time with a single word. That
word, Captain, is "surrender". Now, I'm starting my
countdown. *Stalin* out.'

There was silence from the speaker as Kelley
looked at his watch, counting away the seconds.

Crawford heard the message and looked at Slatter.
They'd hit the *Stalin* with one missile and one torpedo,

and the damn thing was now telling them to surrender.

'Captain, he's right. We can keep shooting, but unless we want to nuke them I can't see what we can do. If they hit us with one of those shells we go down in seconds.'

'They're not going to sink us, Mr Slatter. They can't afford to. Not if they want the nukes,' responded Crawford angrily.

With forty-five seconds to go, Zof ordered the guns on the forward turrets to elevate as though they were being aimed. The gun-crew, with thirty seconds to go, got the big guns slowly traversed and elevated in the general direction of the *Jackson*.

Slatter and Crawford couldn't miss the movement of the guns. 'They sure as hell ain't joking, Captain. If they can't have the nukes, they might as well sink us.'

'Dammit, Slatter. Dammit,' said Crawford, consumed with frustration. He had nowhere to turn. The game had reached a stalemate and he had no cards worth playing. But Crawford was determined not to be the one to surrender.

With twenty second to go, the guns stopped moving. The speaker on the VHF set remained silent: fifteen seconds were left, and Zof looked unworried. Kelley didn't share his relaxed feelings.

'Zof, maybe they're …' started Kelley. Zof, still looking at his watch, put his fingers up to his lips to keep the American silent. There were ten seconds to go.

Five more seconds ticked away. Five were left. Four. Three. Two … the speaker burst into life.

'*Stalin*, this is United States Warship *Jackson*.'

Zof lazily picked up the handset. 'Hello, *Jackson*. This is *Stalin*. Can we help you, sir?'

'OK, *Stalin*. We surrender.' The anger in Slatter's voice was clear; even through the distorted mush of the VHF. He was as furious with Crawford for making him do it as he was with the *Stalin* for beating him. Zof grinned. The move had worked. Checkmate! Twenty years in the Navy, and he was surely the first Russian to have brought an American ship to the point of a bloodless surrender. If only the rest of them could see this. He restrained his urge to yell at the top of his voice. Calm, cool, forever the professional, he moved in for the kill.

19

The anchor, 14 tons of rusting cast-iron filled with lead shot for extra weight, plunged down from the bow of the *Stalin* and, unslowed by the water, punched its way to the muddy sea-bed 300 feet down, followed by the snaking chain, each link the size of a car. Once the chain stopped running, Zof applied gentle astern power to bed the anchor firmly to the sea bottom and lay out the chain free of tangles, ready for a quick departure. The sea-bed beneath them was shallower than most other parts of this ocean; they were lucky to find a patch that was just within the anchoring depth of the huge ship, thought Zof. Carrying nuclear warheads between two drifting ships was not his idea of fun.

Slowly the big ship swung to the anchor, moving before the wind and tide until it was broadside on, where it was balanced by the forces acting on it. Zof had calculated his final position well; once the ship stopped moving, the *Jackson*, one mile distant, was directly under all *Stalin's* guns, which Zof then trained to point menacingly at the American cruiser. On the horizon, where the water was too deep to anchor, the *Ocean Queen* gently drifted, giving her passengers a distant view of the two ships.

Crawford had already anchored the *Jackson*, as commanded by Zof. He was more worried than Zof about anchoring in deep water; his ship, less than a third the length of the *Stalin*, didn't carry as much chain and he had to run all of it out. He told Kelley he needed time to organise his anchoring and, in the twenty minutes it took to get the anchor down and the chain secured, spoke at length with Bell via a secure radio link that the *Stalin* couldn't pick up.

Zof ordered the gangway lowered to the water, and the two big inflatables were launched. The boarding party was Pine, Kelley, and a dozen of Zof's most trusted men, each of whom was armed.

This time, Zof refused Kelley's invitation to go. He'd seen Pine's methods and didn't like them. And though he would have given all the gold in the world just to see the American Captain's face, he didn't trust them one inch. There was no way of telling what they would do. He could enjoy his victory from a distance. They were going to be very, very angry. He wanted to stay with the *Stalin* just in case they needed to go into action again; more importantly, Zof knew now that he had to plan the escape of his ship in detail. The Americans were not going to take this lying down. Once the *Jackson* had given up its cargo, the *Stalin* would be a target for every American ship and aircraft within the Pacific Basin. He wanted to check out the ship; he wanted to make sure the crew were ready; he wanted to double- and triple-check the charts of the island-littered waters he would have to sail through to get south towards the Monte Bello islands; most of all, he wanted to figure out what the hell to say to the crew to explain Kelley's final mad scheme.

And there was something inside him that didn't want anything to do with stealing the nukes – not now he knew what they were meant for. Kelley had trapped him into the voyage, and now he had no option but to go along with it. But he didn't have to be confronted with every detail right under his nose. No,

Kelley, my friend, you carry out your business on your own. I will be busy enough trying to get the rest of us out of the mess I can see coming.

The boarding party trooped down the long gangway and settled in the inflatables. The Suzuki outboards started with a single pull; then both boats slipped their flimsy mooring ropes, curled away from the grey steel wall of the *Stalin* and headed across the open swell towards the *Jackson*.

Crawford and his crew watched the approach of the two inflatables, standing silently at their positions, no man moving. Few US warships had ever undergone the indignity of surrender. It felt strange, thought Slatter, to be standing idly by while two small rubber boats came up to do goodness knows what. The most advanced ship in the US Navy was now at the mercy of a handful of crazy Russians. In the background *Stalin* lay broadside on, each of the nine huge guns pointing directly at the *Jackson*. From this distance, Slatter could clearly see the black smudge on the side of the ship from the impact of the F-15s missile. The ship's sides, a layer of thick armour, looked impregnable even from a mile away. And flapping in the breeze, high above the superstructure, the Red Banner proudly flew.

The fat, grinning figure of Pine as first up the gangplank. Two very large American sailors stood sullenly close together at the top of the flight of ladders. To get off the gangplank, he would have to push past both of them. Pine stopped and looked up at the taller of the two, a heavily built hulk of over six feet, smiling innocently at the man. Then he turned round to look at Kelley, like a dog waiting for its master. Kelley nodded almost imperceptibly and Pine pushed past, turning sideways to squeeze through, muttering apologies and 'excuse me' to both sentries.

Neither moved but the fat man managed to get his bulk past and he walked a pace beyond them. Kelley waited; he knew what was coming.

Pine quietly turned and gently walked up behind the big sailor, who was now standing with his back to him. With relaxed and unhurried violence, Pine silently lifted his foot and, pausing to aim, shoved it powerfully at the sailor's backside, grunting with a short, high-pitched laugh. Surprised by the sudden push, the big man tottered forward, caught his foot on the toeguard at the entrance to the gangway and then, struggling to regain his footing, arms starting to flail, disappeared over the side of the ship. There was a muffled splash a second later.

The second guard watched his companion totter overboard in astonishment. Everyone on the ship was frightened of the big man, Pawluk, who had just disappeared over the side. No one, but no one, did that to Pawluk.

'Now, shitface, move aside and let my friends on. That's not a polite request, by the way,' whispered Pine to the remaining sailor, smiling at him. The sailor took a fraction of a second to decide to comply. Whatever; the fat guy was clearly nuts, he decided. He stood back, and leaned a little over the side, where he could see Pawluk – looking surprised as well as angry – being given a helping hand back on to the landing platform at the water's edge.

Kelley and the Russians followed Pine. Slatter, changed into a dry uniform, was waiting at the foot of the ladders leading up to the command deck and the bridge. He walked towards the party, stood crisply to attention, snapped off a sharp salute that seemed more of a challenge than a greeting and stood back, ushering the party towards the ladders.

'And who exactly are you?' asked Kelley, stopping.

Like the seaman a few moments ago, Slatter was surprised to be facing an American. 'Lieutenant Commander Slatter. Executive Officer. Welcome on board the *Jackson*. The Captain is looking forward to meeting you. Sir.'

Kelley arched an eyebrow but ignored the sarcasm. Let them get it out of their system if it made them feel better. He didn't think there would be any real trouble now. Not after Pine's little display, unplanned but not unwelcome.

'Well, Slatter; I'm looking forward to meeting your Captain. And Mr Charlie here,' replied Kelley, referring to Pine by his cover name, 'is delighted to make your acquaintance, aren't you, Mr Charlie?'

'Oh sure, delighted,' whispered Pine, eyeing up Slatter as though he were a side of beef at a slaughterhouse sale.

The party moved on up the ladders to the spacious bridge, Slatter leading the way. At the top of the ladders stood Crawford, and behind him his bridge officers.

'You the Captain?' asked Kelley, though it was an obvious question with Crawford standing in front of his men with gold braid on his sleeves and his cap and several rows of medal ribbons spread across his chest. Crawford nodded formally but remained where he was, his hands clasped behind his back.

'Captain, as of now I'm taking over your ship. My men are armed and will use force, which I really hope will not be necessary. We have a simple task to complete and I want your fullest co-operation and that of your crew. You will give the necessary orders to that effect. By the way, Captain, my ship's guns are loaded and are trained directly on you. If there is any trouble, or we fail to return, they are under strict orders to open fire. They will blow you out of the water. They then go on to sink the *Ocean Queen*. Understand?'

Crawford stared hard at Kelley. His heart thumped inside his chest, not from fear but from an extraordinary rage that many years since he had learned to control – though only at cost to his blood pressure. His face was flushing red and there was a slight but noticeable quiver in his voice. 'Very well. You have our co-operation under duress. What exactly do you require? We'd prefer to get this over with quickly,' Crawford replied, aware that although he might be able to control his anger at the humiliation, some other crew member might not be able to resist having a go themselves.

'That's just fine, Captain. You and your officers stay here on the bridge under the eyes of a couple of my men. Who's this?' he asked, indicating Slatter.

'Slatter. My XO. Executive Officer.'

'Slatter comes with us. I guess he has access to every part of the ship?'

'Not the nuclear magazine. That needs two keys,' replied Crawford.

'You have the other, I guess? Hand it over, Captain.'

Crawford paused; then he unbuttoned his shirt collar, removed his cap and lifted a chain over his head. He handed it to Slatter.

'This is it?' asked Kelley, surprised at the low security.

'This is a warship on active duty, sir. It is not normally expected that pirates walk calmly on board and carry off the warheads,' replied Crawford.

Kelley took the key and then suddenly stopped. Crawford knew they had come for the nukes: Kelley hadn't figured it out a minute ago when the Captain said that the nuke magazine needed two keys. Now it hit him between the eyes. 'How do you know we want the warheads?' asked Kelley quietly. Something was going on here.

Crawford flushed again. 'You asked for the nuke magazine key. I presumed that's what you came for.'

Kelley looked at the Captain. He wasn't sure he'd asked for the key; he wasn't sure at all. But right now, something was telling him urgently to leave it alone; get this over with fast, the nervous voice told him. It could wait until later. He didn't feel comfortable standing around on the warship, surrounded by the hostile eyes of every seaman on there. 'OK, Slatter,' said Kelley, ignoring Crawford for a moment. 'We need a party of twenty or thirty men at the magazine, and you'll need to launch your biggest boat. What's that?'

'We have a stores tender. It's forty feet long.'

'That'll do. Launch it and bring it up to the landing stage. Is there a crane there?'

'Yes.'

'Get it ready.'

Slatter walked inside the bridge and started giving the orders over the ship's public address system. His voice echoed around the *Jackson* as the crew listened in silence to the clipped tones of Slatter's instructions. He put the microphone down and, like an animal waking up and gradually getting to its feet, the ship and the crew began stirring into action, slowly at first and then with a quickening pace.

Followed by three of the Russians, Slatter led Kelley and Pine down the bridge ladders and along the outer deck, back towards the stern of the ship, then through a steel door. They followed him down three flights of ladders which led into the heart of the ship, then they were taken along a brightly lit passageway that doubled back, so now they were heading towards the bow. They turned a corner and saw a crowd of thirty seamen standing there, waiting for Slatter. Pine stiffened and levelled his sub-machine gun. The sailors were sullen and silent, and didn't move as Slatter approached.

'OK, stand back. These men are with me and we are giving them our fullest co-operation,' ordered Slatter, also feeling the tension in the air. The tight confines of the passageway smelt of sweat, even though the distant susurrus of the air-conditioning system drifted chilled air into the place. Nobody moved, so he just pushed forward. Like a school of fish they parted when he came near; then closed in behind the group. At one point they were completely surrounded and Kelley thought that Pine might go haywire; but finally, Slatter reached the door.

It was painted bright yellow with black diagonal stripes and was covered with warning signs, one of which authorised the use of 'deadly force' against trespassers. This struck Kelley as funny. Slatter punched a code on a stainless-steel keypad, then pulled down on the lever. It groaned and he pushed the door open and fumbled for the light. Fluorescent tubes blinked several times before bathing the room in a bleak blue-tinged glow. Slatter beckoned Kelley and Pine into the room, then took them down another short passageway. At the end was another door; this time completely featureless other than for a single small hole in the centre.

'How the hell do you move warheads out of here?' complained Kelley, who couldn't see how they were going to carry a couple of dozen warheads out of the narrow, twisting passageways.

'Lifts to the deck. This is personnel access only' muttered Slatter, as he pushed Cleveland's key into the central hole. There was a muffled clunk. He took the key out and inserted the one he had been carrying. Another clunk. Then a brief hiss of escaping air as the vacuum-powered door mechanism pulled the door from its seating and pushed it backwards on rails set into the bulkhead. Fluorescent tubes stuttered on again, this time automatically. The team crossed the threshold into the nuclear magazine.

The warheads were no bigger than large paint cans. Each of the two dozen devices were held on shelves by steel straps, with wire cage fronts. They looked as if made of solid stainless steel, and shone so brightly that Kelley had the bizarre thought that Crawford sent someone down every morning to polish them.

But Kelley was surprised by the size of the warheads. He knew the basic principles of atomic weapons well. Take a ball of enriched uranium 238 or plutonium, stick a small barium neutron source in the middle, wrap high explosive around the ball and set light. The high explosive compressed the ball of nuclear material to a liquid of super-critical density and the barium neutron emitter in the middle gushed high-energy particles into the liquid mass, setting off the chain reaction which produced a very big bang. The theory was simple, but the practice was tricky. You had to compress the nuclear ball uniformly from all directions at once with the high explosive charge, otherwise the molten uranium or plutonium would spurt out under the unequal pressure and you'd get, at best, the nuclear equivalent of a damp squib; at worst, you'd end spraying radioactive slush over a few hundred yards' radius.

To make it work, Kelley had assumed, you needed a lot of explosive, a lot of core material and numerous associated electronics and control devices. The pictures of bombs he'd seen looked as though they weighed tons, not pounds. The Hiroshima bomb had weighed five tons.

'They look too small. These are the warheads? I don't believe you' said Kelley.

'What do you mean, too small?' asked Slatter.

'The nukes I've seen are big. Big, big bombs, several tons. These are too small.'

'Tough shit mister. These are the only ones we've got. If you don't like them, maybe you should just get back to your Russian friends' said Slatter acidly.

Kelley grabbed Slatter by his shirt-front and pulled him towards him, while Pine lifted his sub-machine gun again, this time pushing it into Slatter's back.

'You stupid shit!' shouted Kelley into Slatter's face. 'Don't piss us about. Get us to the warheads before I blow your fucking brains out'.

'These are the fucking warheads!' Slatter shouted back with equal ferocity. 'What do you think they are, for Christ's sake?'

Kelley stood back, releasing Slatter, now feeling uncertain after the man's vehement response. He wasn't behaving like someone trying to pull a fast one.

Slatter saw the hesitation. 'You're living two decades ago, my friend. Guess what? They made them smaller, like they made everything else smaller. These are 5-kiloton warheads, each one of them. You want to look for great big bombs, feel free, my friend, but you ain't gonna find shit.'

Kelley looked at Slatter. 'Can I talk to the bridge from here?' he demanded.

'Sure. Here,' said Slatter, handing over a handset to Kelley and pushing a button.

'Bridge,' called a formal voice from the other end.

'This is your friendly pirate. I want to speak to my ship. Can you connect me with them down here?'

'Wait,' came the curt reply, and Crawford called up the *Stalin* before patching them through to Kelley.

As they waited, Slatter shrugged his shoulders and leaned against one of the shelves. Kelley looked at the gleaming canisters. 'So how do these work, anyway,

Slatter? You just chuck them in the water and run like hell?'

'Sure. Then you disappear up your own asshole,' cracked Slatter. Pine walked quietly up to Slatter and gripped his wrist, lifted his arm into the air and started twisting. Slatter yelped with pain; Pine dropped the officer's arm. 'Show some respect, you get me?' he smiled, backing off but staying close. Even Pine didn't care to antagonise the crowd of sullen sailors just outside the door.

'OK, no problem,' said Slatter in a lower voice, looking warily at Pine. 'These are just the raw warheads. You have to load them into the delivery system, in this case the Mark 8 Nuclear Depth Charge carrier. It's a kind of missile that we fire off the back. It goes off a safe distance, about five miles, then drops into the sea where a depth mechanism fires the warhead. It's supposed to kill any submarine within a mile or so of the blast.'

Kelley had wandered down the racks holding the warheads. He had no idea if Slatter was telling the truth or complete horseshit. His suspicions had already been roused by Crawford, who somehow seemed to know exactly what he'd come for. The warheads could be anything, anything at all. Tins of fucking peas, as far as he could tell. The handset whined, a rasping siren-like noise that was designed to be heard above the din of battle. Kelley lifted the handset: it was Zof.

'Zof, what the fuck does a nuclear warhead actually look like?' asked Kelley.

Zof laughed down the line. Kelley's great plan was falling apart because he didn't know how to recognise what he was trying to steal. It amused him greatly. 'Well now, my friend, that all depends.'

'Don't piss about, Zof. I'm looking at a couple of

shelves full of shiny steel cans, like – what, big paint cans. They look too small to me. I thought they'd be much bigger. Are these warheads or are these guys selling me shit?' He wished for the first time that Harvey was still alive; he would know.

'Maybe. MIRV warheads, last time I saw one, were pretty small. Not as small as you say, but then the Americans had much better technology when it came to warheads. I had heard that they had got their tactical weapons pretty small. Maybe as you describe. It's perfectly possible, Kelley' replied Zof.

'What the hell's a MIRV?'

'Multiple Independently Targeted Re-Entry Vehicle. Nuclear missiles with many warheads, Kelley.'

'These are supposed to be depth-charge warheads, Zof. Nothing to do with MIRVs.'

'They would still be small, I suppose. If they're used from a ship you would not want a very big explosion, would you? This would not be good for the ship.'

Zof's sarcasm was lost on Kelley in his anxiety. 'So I go for them, do I?'

'Your deal, Kelley, not mine. But yes, I think you are probably looking at the warheads.'

Kelley smacked down the handset on to its cradle and walked back from the far end of the magazine where Slatter was waiting. 'OK, Slatter, let's get on with it. No point hanging around. I want all of them hauled out of here and taken to the boat. Get your men working on it.'

'How do we know they ain't taken some of the stuff out?' asked Pine in his low voice. It was one of his rare intelligent comments and Kelley looked surprised, then realised that the man had a good point.

'What stuff are we going to take out?' asked Slatter, looking exasperated.

'Bits of nuclear material, fuses, I don't know. Maybe

you had a chance to take them apart so they're no
use?' responded Kelley.

'Jesus, mister. Even if we had a chance we wouldn't
know where to start. Take a look at these things, man.
They're not screwed shut, they're fuckin' welded. Look!'

Kelley inspected a canister more closely. There
didn't appear to be a lid or access point anywhere on
it. There were two multi-pin plug sockets, like SCART
sockets but bigger, and a couple more jack sockets in
the side; but other than that the shiny canister was
solid and featureless apart from the yellow stencilled
'Danger Radioactive' signs and some very long alpha-
numeric groups. There was certainly no sign of
tampering. None that Kelley could see, anyway. He'd
have to trust them.

'OK, I guess they're fine,' he conceded, having looked
carefully at several of them. He felt as though he was
buying a used car.

'Can I get this going now?' demanded Slatter.

Kelley nodded. Slatter left the magazine and
returned with five of his men. They quickly removed
the cage front and metal straps from five of the
warheads and proceeded to take out each one of them,
one warhead per man, struggling slightly under the
weight of each device. Gripping them firmly to their
chests, one after the other they carried them from the
magazine out into the passageway. There were twenty
warheads in total, and it took no longer than ten
minutes to clear them out. Kelley and Pine, backed by
the three suspicious Russians, watched carefully until
the last one was removed.

The warheads were carried to the ordnance lift to
bring them up to deck height, where the team of
sailors were waiting to retrieve their loads and carry
them down the deck. A line had already formed –
sweating sailors gripping a warhead each – down

towards the crane suspended above the supply barge that would take the warheads back to the *Stalin*.

Kelley and Pine walked quickly up the stairways, following the last sailor out of the lift room, and reached the head of the line, breathless after the climb. Kelley told Pine to watch the rear, then hurried past the line of sailors to where the first of the warheads were being loaded into a net sling suspended from the small loading crane, where they were gently lowered to the steps at water level. The ship's stores tender – a stumpy, barge-like craft with a steering position set at the stern of the open deck – sat moored and empty, waiting for the cargo.

Everyone on board, even Kelley, knew that according to the experts you couldn't set the warheads off by accident; that they had to be connected to an electrical source and even if you tossed them in a fire the worse you would get would be a smallish bang, though the radioactivity released wouldn't do you a whole lot of good. But nobody was going to trust the experts. Every man handling the warheads treated them with delicate care as they were lifted, carried and set down like babies. No man would have dared drop one; the nerves of everyone, including Kelley, would have snapped.

Slowly the first load was stowed carefully on the deck of the stores tender. The second load followed down soon after; the crane crew running it slowly to make sure nothing disturbed the precious load. It was like packing eggs.

While Kelley had gone ahead to supervise loading, Pine stayed at the rear of the queue of sailors just as back-up. The other Russians had gone ahead with Kelley, so Pine was now alone. His concentration was fixed on the slow procession in front of him, so he didn't hear Pawluk, the big sailor he'd kicked into the sea, walk up behind him, although Pawluk was a big bear of a man who couldn't walk on tiptoe without sounding like someone stamping. From that position, Pawluk with one blow of his huge fist could have done Pine real damage; as it was, he carried a baseball bat and was still shaking with rage at the humiliation he'd suffered, and this was a mistake. In his desire for revenge, he couldn't help but let Pine know that he was about to be destroyed.

'Hey, motherfucker, you wanna real fight?' he grunted before he swung the bat with violence but little accuracy at Pine's head. Pine spun round with surprising speed, still smiling, and then saw Pawluk's huge bulk behind him and the bat swinging towards his head. As his brain assimilated all three facts at once, it took him a split second to start to duck. But here Pine miscalculated, too. Pawluk's aim was so bad that if Pine hadn't moved, the baseball bat would simply have caught him on the neck. But by ducking he restored Pawluk's aim to his head and the swinging bat connected with a wet, sloshing sound on the side of Pine's face, where the blow immediately exploded three teeth from his mouth in a splash of red blood and fragments of white tooth enamel. The sub-machine gun skittered uselessly across the deck as Pine dropped to his knees in shock like a felled steer at a slaughterhouse, his face spattered in blood not just from his mouth but from the split cheek and cracked cheekbone under it. He simply knelt there, unable to even think, senseless from the awesome shock of Pawluk's swing.

Pawluk had to re-think for a second. His first blow hadn't gone where he wanted it to, and the result was therefore not instant death but instead a dangerous wounding. He stood back a moment, then decided to take another swing, this time downwards straight on to the crown of Pine's bowed and supplicant head. He started lifting the bat over his own head to get the best swing, and was poised like an executioner to deliver a blow that even from the blunt bat would have split Pine's head in half.

But the primeval fighter's instinct told the near-senseless Pine what was happening, though he was barely conscious of Pawluk's coming blow. As the bat flew downwards, Pine's dimming mind commanded his body to heave itself sideways. With a bubbling moan, he lurched away from the descending blow and threw himself to one side. The bat crashed down and rang on the deck.

Pawluk was enraged. He dropped the bat and reached out to grab Pine, who was now trying with difficulty to push himself away. Pawluk managed to lift him to his feet and swung his free fist into Pine's dribbling mouth, not once but six times, each time his great paw sloshing into the wreck of flesh and bone, mashing the damaged features into a gob of bleeding meat. Pawluk's rage began to ease at the sixth blow. The damage he had done Pine was deeply satisfying. The white scarf had turned deep red and was loose against the fat man's neck. Pawluk almost felt slightly sorry for the man as he held him upright with some difficulty – Pine's eyes were completely closed, and he didn't seem to be breathing. He released Pine from his grip and the fat body slumped to the ground like a sack of potatoes and lay there, oozing blood and looking lifeless. Pawluk thought about kicking him around a few times but now, his anger diminishing, there didn't seem much point. He turned to walk away.

This was another mistake, for Pine was still conscious. As a fighter he was used to being smashed virtually senseless. In the ring, and in countless street fights, he quickly learned that the best defence in such situations was to lie still until your opponent thought he had won. Pain meant very little to Pine, anyway. Kelley often told him he was too stupid to feel pain, and there was some truth in the idea. Through the red fog that clouded his bruised eyes, he could see Pawluk turn. This was his chance. He carefully reached inside his jacket where he kept a Smith and Wesson .38, the famous Magnum. Though he had barely enough strength to hold the piece steady, he managed to point it in the rough direction of Pawluk's retreating back and squeezed the trigger twice. The first shot caught Pawluk behind the knee and quite literally took his leg off, the bullet smashing his knee apart. The second caught him in the buttock, smashed into him with a force powerful enough to spin him round, and the big man collapsed next to the shattered remains of his lower leg which lay bleeding and twitching on the bloody, slippery deck. Pine's shaking hand now dropped the gun and the light in his eyes started to fade. A twitch of his bruised mouth looked as though a smile was passing across it, but that too drained away and the fat man drifted into oblivion.

The whole of Pawluk's attack was silent; only Pine's two shots were heard, and most of the men instinctively ducked, their nerves already keyed up by handling the warheads. Kelley spun round from watching the loading. He ran back along the deck, past the crouching sailors, to where the two limp bodies now lay.

He was appalled at the scene. Pine lay hunched against the bulkhead, the gun still in his hand, his face an unrecognisable blob of red and black. He was breathing hard and quivering. Pawluk lay on his back six or seven feet away, blood still pumping in a rhythmic pulse from his severed leg and from his back. His eyes were closed and he was the purest shade of white that Kelley had ever seen. He recognised the big sailor immediately; he glanced at the blood-splashed baseball bat lying nearby and it was clear what had happened.

Kelley had seen blood and gore before. In his days as a policeman on the streets of New York he had participated in more than one punishment beating; but had rarely seen anything so bloody.

And now, surrounded by the hostility of the ship, he felt his nerve starting to give way. The earlier battles. The deadly warheads. The sullen, grim crowd of sailors. Now this. Christ almighty! He felt a sudden compelling urge to simply get off the ship and run. But he took a deep breath and walked quickly back to the head of the line. The sailors watched him hurry back and stood aside as he passed, then turned to go and look at the scene for themselves, fascinated and horrified like spectators at a road accident.

Kelley stormed past them to Slatter who was at the loading point, wondering what was going on. 'My man's been floored by one of your gorillas, Slatter. I'm going to sort out your fucking Captain. You make sure this stuff's all loaded on the launch, then get your men out of here,' he ordered. Then he walked quickly up the bridge where Crawford and his officers were gathered in a group under the watchful eyes of the remaining Russian guards. They hadn't heard the shots.

'Crawford, one of your bastards has dropped one of my men. They're both in a bad way. Get medics down there now. Do what you like with your man, but I want mine sorted out ultra fast and stretchered down to the launch within five minutes. Got it?'

'My surgeon's on the *Ocean Queen*. We had to fly him out to treat a gunshot victim – one of your efforts, I believe.'

'Sort it, captain. Get someone down there now,' shouted Kelley nervously. In his rising unease, Crawford's news about the gunshot victim simply didn't register with him. Getting Pine, and getting off the ship, was the important issue. Just getting off the ship. Take it easy ... stay cool ... they were nearly there. The warheads were loaded; they were multimillionaires. Just a short sea trip back and they were home free.

Crawford barked orders into a handset, then followed Kelley off the bridge to see what was going on. They found Slatter on the way, coming up to meet them. He was breathing hard.

'It's Pawluk, Captain. Got shot. Looks like he had a go at the fat one,' said Slatter, ignoring Kelley's presence.

'Stupid bastard!' muttered Crawford. The two officers followed Kelley to the after deck where three paramedics were trying to sort out the mess. Two of them were working on Pawluk.

'Get them off him now! Get my man sorted,' demanded Kelley, the edge in his voice leaving no room for argument. They left Pawluk alone and started to remove Pine's bloodstained shirt and mop up the mess. Pine was breathing heavily as they swabbed away the gore. The damage was not so visible once he was cleaned up; the swelling covering his face, forcing his eyes closed, was quickly turning purple and covered up the gashes and wounds. They sprayed an antiseptic over as much of the face as was safe, protecting the eyes with pads, then covered the face with gauze wadding. One of the medics produced a hypodermic syringe and aimed it at Pine's naked arm. Kelley suspected it was morphine and knocked it from the medic's hands. Pine had a real problem with drugs, and once on them was crazy; he didn't want to risk that now.

It took four of them to lift the fat man on to a

stretcher. Slatter instructed them to carry the body down to the launch. Kelley sent a couple of his Russians to follow them, just in case. The paramedics eventually returned to see what they could do about Pawluk, which probably wasn't very much.

Kelley and the officers stopped at the top of the gangway leading to the launch. He had calmed a little now; the mission was nearly over.

'Captain, once we get away, you keep your goddamn ship at anchor, understand? Our ship goes first. Once we're over the horizon you can do what the fuck you want. The *Ocean Queen*'s going to need your assistance anyway. We've blown her rudder off and she ain't going nowhere.'

'It's the least we can do,' replied Crawford sarcastically. 'Don't worry, mister. You'll be clear to escape. But you realise you can't possibly get away with this?'

Kelley smiled at the cliché. They been telling him that all his life, and so far he'd got away with it very easily. 'Oh, I think we can, thank you, Captain, I think we can. We've managed quite well so far. You see, for all your technology, you're just no match for good old brute force. I guess you could always nuke us out of the water, of course, but nobody's really going to let you do that, are they? No, I'm sure your friends in Washington will have a crack at us, but with more of your advanced technology. We look forward to it, Captain. Tell them that, why don't you? We're looking forward to it.'

Kelley turned to go, then suddenly turned back again. Something which Crawford had said earlier suddenly popped back into his brain like a warning flag. 'Your surgeon on the *Ocean Queen*. Why was he there?' He had a terrible feeling he knew the answer.

'I gather you shot one of your own men. I had to send my surgeon over to patch him up.'

'Patch him up?'

'Yes, mister. He was in a pretty bad way. I don't suppose you care greatly, but you damn nearly killed him.'

20

McEwan was getting ready to start his presentation in the comfortable wardroom of the *Iowa*, thundering along at 28 knots, heading south-west through the warm Pacific sea, with its sister ship, the *Missouri*, keeping pace a mile behind off the starboard quarter.

Both ships had been built at the same time as *Stalin*, but the two American vessels purred and hummed through the rolling blue sea where *Stalin* had crashed and shuddered and rattled. Kept in service for much of their lives, both had been carefully and expensively maintained, equipped with every gadget and convenience that modern technology could think of. The wardroom was more like a lecture theatre. Deep, comfortable chairs were placed in rows, and a computer projector positioned at the front of the audience where, amongst the senior officers, Captain Vieques, commander of the *Iowa*, and Captain Murray of the *Missouri*, sat listening carefully to the English officer's presentation.

McEwan had started by describing the disposition of the various ships involved. Using the computer screen, he displayed a chart of the western Pacific, with Japan in the top left-hand corner, Singapore in the bottom left-hand corner, Australia across the bottom and Hawaii on the right.

First he showed the position of the *Ocean Queen*

'still drifting without power at about two knots eastwards with the tide', about 400 miles west of the Philippines, 50 miles east of the Paracel Islands and nearly 500 miles south of Hong Kong, deep in the middle of the South China Sea.

'Then here, gentlemen,' and McEwan touched the keyboard to display two red blobs, one labelled 'J' and the other labelled 'S', 'are *Stalin* and *Jackson*. Both are currently anchored in a small patch of shallow water. They're about twenty miles to the west of the *Ocean Queen*, which means the *Ocean Queen* is just about over the visible horizon. As you've already heard, the seizure of the warheads has gone off smoothly...'

'One of our men got hurt, don't forget that,' murmured Vieques in a gravelly voice from the front row.

'I'm sorry, Captain – yes, of course. That apart, the pirates have now departed from the *Jackson* and I gather Captain Crawford is awaiting instructions.'

McEwan pushed another button and a further red blob appeared on to the map, this time to the south, marked 'K'. 'The *Komosuru* is here, about two hours away at its current speed of ten knots. She was answering the distress call from the *Ocean Queen*. She's a bulk carrier...'

Vieques interrupted again. 'Carrying what, exactly?'

'Light Gulf crude. About forty thousand tons of the stuff. Not the sort of ship to have around if the bullets start flying, of course, but she's still in the picture if we need her. She's a big ship and could probably tow the *Ocean Queen*, or even take off the crew and passengers if needed. There are a few other vessels within a hundred miles or so of the scene, but frankly I suggest we keep them well away.' McEwan paused to look at is audience, who expressed no opinion one way or the other. They were waiting to see where all this was leading.

'And here,' continued McEwan, pressing another button on the keyboard which introduced two more blobs very close together, marked with an 'I' and an 'M', so the map now looked as though someone had bled over it, 'are you, *Iowa* and *Missouri*.' The 'I' and 'M' blobs were a long way off the position of the *Stalin*. The distance from Pearl Harbor to the South China Sea was the best part of 4,000 miles. Having set off 48 hours ago at their maximum speed of 28 knots, they had covered nearly 1,500 miles. It would take another three and a half days to reach the position of the *Stalin* and *Jackson*. Vieques and Murray were painfully aware of the time gap, and how it created a window in which *Stalin* could escape. A big ship is a very small object in the middle of an ocean as vast as the Pacific. Even with the best available surveillance systems, they'd be hard pushed to pick her up if she got cleanly away from the *Jackson*.

'So,' went on McEwan, 'you can now see the problem. *Stalin* is departing as we speak. The *Ocean Queen* is drifting, with a thousand people on her. We're three days' steaming away from the area. And a ship with a few thousand tons of very inflammable oil is sailing right into the middle of it all.' He paused for effect. 'Any suggestions?'

At least one officer in the audience snorted, but otherwise the room remained silent. Vieques and Murray watched McEwan carefully. To put it mildly, both men had been astonished at his presence at the start of the voyage, not least because he carried Pentagon written all over him. He was not welcomed and he was not wanted, and his British accent and manners irritated the hell out of them.

For the first few hours on board, McEwan was almost a prisoner in his cabin until summoned by Vieques. Only McEwan seemed to know much about

Stalin, and Vieques wanted to know what they were heading for in his hastily recommissioned ship. Half an hour later, Vieques was impressed with the young Englishman. His knowledge of the *Stalin* was clear, but so was his commitment to catching the pirates and also his respect for the US Navy, though to be honest even McEwan would have later confessed to gilding that lily somewhat to overcome the depressing hostility.

Within half a day, he was turned from leper into not quite hero, but perhaps more like the mascot for the ship. And it was clear even to Murray that McEwan's knowledge of the *Stalin* and of the whole sorry event was critical to their own success.

They followed his presentation carefully and, when he asked for suggestions, knew that he was being polite. Now they quietly waited for him to answer his own question.

'Fortunately, gentlemen, we know where *Stalin* is headed. The man shot on the *Ocean Queen* has proved most helpful, particularly with a little guidance from the hypodermic needle of the *Jackson's* surgeon.' There was a muffled snigger from the audience; Weiner was notorious. McEwan punched yet another button on his computer and an arrow appeared pointing at the north-west coast of Australia where a scatter of tiny blobs was identified as the Monte Bello Islands.

'These are the Monte Bello Islands. Some of you may know them as the place where we Brits tested our first atom bomb in the Fifties. Since then, they've been pretty much deserted, and they're well protected by bloody great big signs threatening immediate radioactive death, which is of course nonsense. They have the benefit of a nice deep anchorage right in the middle of the group, and the nearest human settlement is over 200 miles away. This is where *Stalin's* crew plans to hand over its cargo.'

McEwan had deliberately saved the big news until last. He figured that it would sharpen up the mood of the ship's company greatly.

Murray fell straight into the trap that McEwan had laid. 'And who exactly are these madmen going to hand over a bunch of warheads to, Lieutenant?'

'Sorry. Didn't mention that, did I? Unfortunately,' said McEwan as mournfully as he could manage, 'it's your old friend Saddam Hussein. I gather they're meant to be in Baghdad within fifteen hours of being collected. Helicopters, fast jets, desert landing-strips, all sorts of arrangements apparently. We don't have all the details, of course.'

McEwan could have burnt the Stars and Stripes in front of them and they wouldn't have noticed. Tension filled the room as each man stared at the screen, looking carefully at the distance from where *Stalin* was to where McEwan's arrow was indicating the islands, and trying to figure out how to close the gap. McEwan again anticipated the question.

'It's around 2,000 miles to the Monte Bellos. And he's going to have to go through the Indonesian islands to get there, which will slow him down. We're looking at at least four days for them to make it. Five or six days if he takes the longer route round, which I suspect he won't. If we alter course southwards' – McEwan indicated a course that, instead of sweeping them north of the Philippines, would take them south of the Marshall Islands towards New Guinea, cutting south of the island towards Timor, then across the north coast of Australia towards the Monte Bellos – 'we can get there before them. Quite comfortably, in fact. I reckon about a day to spare.'

'And then?' asked Vieques. It was the question almost everyone in the room wanted to ask. The story of the F-15's attack and the *Jackson's* apparently abject surrender was now common knowledge, even if the details of the *Jackson*'s failed missile and torpedo attack were not yet known outside the most senior officers.

'And then? That's pretty much up to you, Captain. I've looked carefully at the details of the *Stalin* and it's going to be a tough fight, no doubt. But you have advantages, although you'll be using your big guns, not missiles. You have a greater rate of fire, so you can deliver a greater tonnage of shells against *Stalin*. You have radar-directed gunnery as well, which *Stalin* doesn't, so you can keep up the fire in bad visibility, which is exactly what you'll get after a few minutes of the big guns opening up. *Stalin* depends on visual sighting, and once the visibility goes they'll have real problems. And you have greater manoeuvrability, even if *Stalin* is faster on the straight. I'm convinced we can eventually sink the ship if we catch it, and I'm pretty sure we can.'

'You make it sound easy, Lieutenant,' commented Vieques.

'Not at all sir. It will be a hard-fought battle. They'll be lobbing 22-inch shells at you, and if one connected properly your armour is simply not strong enough to bounce it off, though that depends on them getting a direct hit square on. If they hit you at an angle, my guess is that your armour will just about take it. The bigger danger is plunging fire. If a shell drops on to your deck, you've got some pretty weak places. But they can only do that from long range, so they'll have to get pretty lucky.'

'Torpedoes? Missiles?' asked Murray.

'I wouldn't bother with missiles. They simply don't carry the weight of explosive to do any real damage. I looked into dropping a smart bomb down the funnel, but the designer seemed to have a real worry about that weakness and provided a series of armoured boxes between the boilers and the smokestack. It would shake them up but, unless we could drop several tons of high explosive in one go, I suspect it won't get through.'

'But surely a torpedo attack will work?' continued Murray, unwilling to accept that any ship was so perfect or its crew so skilled that it could never be sunk.

'That's certainly more of a possibility, but Kishkov – that's the designer, by the way – was paranoid about torpedoes. He used a triple bottom, not a double, used thick armour for the outer plating, and on top of all that he created a honeycomb across the lower part of the ship that would cope with flooding even if you managed to get through the bottom. The stern gear is well protected, too. Kishkov had a big thing about protecting that part of the ship; you might do some superficial damage, but I doubt you can get through the protection.'

'So all we can do is pour shells on to them and wear them down? Is that what you're saying?' asked Vieques.

'More or less, Captain. There are two of you, after all, and you can rain a fair bit of shot on to them. I doubt *Stalin* could stand up to a sustained barrage for very long. You see, Kishkov designed it to withstand the impact of single large shells. In those days, the chances of hitting the target very accurately more than a few times were remote. With your radar gunnery you can maintain accuracy for a long period, much longer than Kishkov would have imagined possible.'

'And this ship has no weaknesses at all?' Murray asked.

'That's difficult to answer. I've been looking at some

old plans of the *Stalin*, and there is one possibility, but it's pretty much an outside one. Towards the stern of the ship the armour-plating is thinner than around the rest of the vessel. There are no critical systems at that point, so it's thin for about thirty feet, and then right around the stern section it resumes its usual thickness. Now before you get excited, "thinner" in this case means that instead of being two feet thick, it's eighteen inches. It's still pretty strong stuff.'

'So what's the possibility?' continued Murray, intrigued by the chance that the old ship might after all have a weakness.

'Well, it looks as though the designer was trying to save weight by making the armour thinner. The trouble is, it's left a sort of structural overhang. The weight of armour has made the stern of the ship very heavy: fine so long as it's supported by the water, but if we could get enough shells on to the weaker section, we might just be able to bust it off. Your radar-controlled guns can keep hitting the same place time after time. It might not work, but frankly it's the only weak part of the ship. It's got to be worth a chance.'

Vieques got up. As the senior of the two Captains, he was in overall command of the two ships. 'OK, Lieutenant. Thanks for your views. I guess we need to talk about this.' He looked at McEwan, expecting him to leave. McEwan took the hint, gathered a few papers and left the room, leaving the computer projector humming away, with the red blobs gathering in the South China Sea and the images of the two American battleships heading for the scene like the distant cavalry.

*

Kelley was worried. Once the unloading was under way and Pine in the care of the Russian naval doctor, he retreated to the bridge where he found Zof. 'Harvey is still alive, you'll be pleased to hear,' he announced.

'Well, well. So the fat goblin's efforts were not successful after all,' said Zof. He was pleased that Pine had screwed up but, like Kelley, could immediately see the danger it now put them in. If Harvey was still alive, and was talking, he could give a lot of information away.

'Sure. Something went wrong. The *Ocean Queen* called in the *Jackson*'s surgeon and he's looking after him.'

'So what can Harvey tell them?' asked Zof.

'We don't know if he's told them anything. He certainly knew what our real mission was; that much I had to give him. I think he knows our ultimate destination. We have to assume that the Americans are aware who we are, what we're doing and where we're going next,' replied Kelley with a grim expression on his face. 'Those guys on the ship knew we were after the warheads, for example. Only Harvey could have given that sort of information. I guess we're blown, Zof.'

'If they know you were after the warheads, they surely know every other part of the plan by now,' said Zof.

'Looks that way.'

It was what Zof had feared. But like a good Captain, he had assumed the worst and made his plans. Zof had spent his time well in Kelley's absence. He knew the ship was capable of a high-speed home run. Given their experience with the F-15 and the *Jackson*, he was feeling more hawkish. 'But where is the problem, Kelley? The have to catch us first. Even if they manage to, there is little they can do to stop us. We have beaten all of them so far. So why are you still worried?' In truth, Zof didn't relish the fight; he didn't even feel that confident. It was just that he knew it was inevitable, and it seemed like a good idea to start nerving everyone for it.

Like Zof, the last thing Kelley wanted was a slugging match with the US Navy. Zof's confidence gave him the distinct impression that he would almost welcome it, which of course was exactly what the Russian wanted him to feel. 'I don't know,' replied Kelley. 'I just don't like being so exposed. I'd rather have surprise on our side. Check our course for the Monte Bello Islands, then figure out the least-expected way to get there. If they're trying to track us we'll keep out of their way.'

'Kelley?'

'What?'

'Don't tell me how to run the ship, my friend,' said Zof with a note of warning in his voice. The Russian had already done what Kelley was suggesting; it was his first priority. There was nothing he found more irritating than someone telling him how to do his job, particularly when he had already done it.

'Sorry,' said Kelley. He looked at the big Russian. Perhaps he read his mind, in a moment of clarity. Perhaps he could see the inevitable battle approaching. If it did come to a fight, he needed Zof on his side. A sudden shiver of cold fear ran through him. Good God, where was this really going to end?

'OK. No problem,' said Zof. Like Kelley, he understood the sudden charge of tension. The danger was getting real. This was no longer a game, no longer a few casual acts of piracy; it was full-scale war they were both facing. They glanced briefly at each other and for a sudden moment they connected: the pride in Zof's eyes and the desperation in Kelley's. They read each other like a book; then the moment passed and they returned to their private worlds and their private fears. But together they looked at a US Navy chart of the seas, bought quite freely in a small shop in Vladivostok. Zof outlined the plan and, as he did so, Kelley started to understand the man's confidence.

It was clear that, one way or another, the whole mass of islands north of Australia formed a barrier – but they also created opportunities for shelter. Zof was convinced that the Americans would head south of the archipelago in an attempt to cut them off. He had no idea who or what would come after them, but he agreed with Kelley that somebody would be out here looking for them.

'Kelley, my friend, the fastest route is the worst one if we're being looked for. We go east of Borneo through the Celebes Sea, then down to the Sunda Islands. We can squeeze between Sumbawa and Flores, though the channel is tricky and I haven't got the faintest idea if we can make it. Then we're clear. The trouble is we're close to land for a lot of that trip, you understand? Between Borneo and Celebes we pass through a fifty-mile-wide strait. The gap between the Sunda Islands is less than three miles. And all the time we are cruising through one of the most crowded waterways in the world. It would, I think, be impossible to miss us.'

'So, Zof, what's the least likely way?'

Zof paused and looked carefully at the chart. He had been an enthusiastic chess player in his Naval Academy days. His brain had rapidly worked out a move, calculated the consequences, discarded it, looked at another move, considered those consequences too, discarded that, and kept processing routes until he was left with one where the consequences were, as far as he could see, at worse minimised and at best hardly worth worrying about.

Zof had spent half an hour going through his moves –
his end game, he called it.

'It's simple. We think the Americans know where
we're heading. It would be reasonable to assume they
think we'll get there as quickly as possible to drop off
our valuable cargo, yes? So, we do the opposite. We go
slowly. We sail eastward, towards New Guinea, then
down into the Arafura Sea north of Australia. That
keeps us off the popular routes, and keeps us slow.'

'I don't see the advantage.'

'Easy! If we're being looked for, the ships can only
come either westwards, out of the Indian Ocean, or
eastward down from Pearl Harbor. If from the Indian
Ocean, we come against them with plenty of warning.
If from Pearl, they may have passed us and we come
up behind. Either way, given that we're supposed to be
hurrying down from the north, creeping up on them
from the east is about the last thing they'll think of. It
works, Kelley; believe me, it works.'

Kelley traced Zof's suggestion on the chart for
himself. The attractions of keeping hidden in the mass
of small islands were obvious. Not only would it be the
least expected area, but the choice of small sheltered
bays and inlets gave them hundreds of places to hole
up if they needed to. And coming into the Monte
Bellos from a direction that would surprise any
waiting forces, and at least a day later than anyone
would have expected, made sense.

He looked up. There was no doubt left in his eyes
now: no doubt, no room for disagreement. He had to
trust Zof completely. 'Go for it,' he said very quietly, so
that only Zof could hear. He turned away and left the
bridge.

Zof started the process of getting the big ship
moving. On orders from the bridge, the engine-room
crew turned the valves that released more oil into the

boilers, raising the pressure. Black smoke started to
pour from the stacks. As the pressure rose, other
valves were spun open to release the superheated
steam into the turbines, spinning them faster and
faster. The anchor was being noisily hauled up from
the muddy sea floor 300 feet below. The enormous
lump of iron and lead burst from the surface of the
sea like a rusty whale, shedding water and mud as it
was hauled up to its resting-place at the bow of the
ship. Once the anchor was clear, Zof ordered ahead all
engines, and the four propellers began to slowly turn
like marine windmills. The huge ship nosed forward
so slowly at first that the bow made hardly a ripple on
the surface. Zof ordered the *Stalin* on a heading of 180
degrees, due south, knowing he was being carefully
watched by the crew of the *Jackson* at least, and very
probably by at least one satellite. The ship gathered
speed southwards and, to the relief as well as the
anger of the whole crew of the *Jackson*, lumbered
towards the horizon trailing a thick haze of smoke
behind her until, half an hour later, only the smoke
trail was left, and that nothing more than a distant
smudge on the far horizon. *Stalin* had gone.

Zof felt as though he had just been caught stealing
apples when he was a small boy. The punishment
would be meted out later, and it would be a storm
when it came. That, at least, was a certainty. But for
now, before the final retribution thundered around
him, he could enjoy the fruits of victory; and to Zof,
simply winning was enough. He had brought the
Americans to heel, forced an abject surrender, and had
achieved his objectives. There was no more that you
could ask. The fact that the whirlwind was gathering
was, at least for now, a minor problem. So Zof told
himself. But he knew, deep down, that he could not
avoid the punishment. Did this, in a perverse way,

increase his pleasure in the crime? He gave no hint of what he was thinking. These were his deepest, private thoughts. Every now and then, the harshness of his childhood would come back to haunt him: the guilt, the unhappiness, the need to escape, the need to show his drunken father that he, Yakov Zof, was a greater man than any of them, He knew this was what drove him, but he was secretly ashamed of the power of his long-dead father to make him feel this way. Zof wanted to be in control of his own destiny; he hated his life being overtaken by the ghost of a drunken dock-worker. Pushing the thought deep back within himself, he quickly regained his composure as Captain, First Class, of the great *Stalin*. There was a job to be done.

*

The remnants of the encounter were gradually being mopped up. Crawford on the *Jackson* got his crew together, weighed anchor and set a course for the *Ocean Queen*. He spent some time on a secure radio link with Vieques and McEwan, also with Bell's staff at the Pentagon. He described the whole event and gave descriptions of Pine and Kelley that tallied with the others, though it didn't get anyone very far. They described the 'Kamikaze' attack and the subsequent shooting match to McEwan in some detail. He noted carefully the mistaken bridge position. Crawford ordered the nuclear magazine sealed shut, which for some reason made him feel better though Slatter thought the order was a joke.

Pawluk was cleaned up and hooked up to drips and tubes, though minus a leg and still out cold, but alive nevertheless, which would have maddened Pine had he known.

They caught up with the drifting *Ocean Queen*

after an hour. Crawford and Slatter were ferried over by the helicopter, which brought Weiner back to see what he could do for Pawluk. Crawford met Blake on his bridge. Apart from the damage to the propulsion system, the rest of the ship was working without problems. They were in no immediate danger. Crawford didn't like the idea of towing the huge ship – his biggest cables were not strong enough for the job. So they agreed to wait for a Dutch tug that had been called out by the British from Borneo. It would be another day and a half before it arrived, and Crawford offered to stay on station until it did.

Innocently, the *Komosuru* called up while they were discussing what to do. Blake formally acknowledged the offer of rescue but said that he was now well looked after, thank you, and the ship could proceed on its way. The Mexican Captain entered the conversation in his log and ordered the course changed back towards Tokyo. Once the ship settled to the new heading, he gave a quick glance at the radar, set an alarm ring at 24 miles, switched on the autopilot and went below to the mess where they were just starting a video of the South American football league games from two weeks ago. The bridge was left deserted and silent other than the occasional blip from the autopilot as it adjusted the ship's course. Only very much later would it be revealed that had the Captain not been so keen to watch the football and remained on the bridge, or at the very least left a competent officer on watch instead of allowing him to view the football at exactly the same time, he would have seen *Stalin* on radar, 26 miles distant, suddenly change its course from due south and turn through a right-angle to head off due east.

And a military satellite controller sitting at a small console in California would also, again somewhat later, be taken to task for finding the images of the *Ocean Queen* and the *Jackson* more interesting, and for ordering his camera to zoom in on the high-level view of the two ships as *Stalin*, the ship he had been asked to track, was clearly heading south. He assumed he could easily pick it back up again.

At a much later court-martial, the controller told them he was genuinely surprised when, half an hour later, he tracked his camera southwards and couldn't see a thing, even when he widened the angle of view of the camera. He then had to inform his supervisor that he'd lost the ship, which was duly relayed to Bell at the Pentagon who indulged in a stream of invective that was not recorded. The unfortunate man's replacement some hours later discovered a truth known to all mariners, though it was one that satellite operators found hard to believe – that the ocean is a very big place and even a big ship is very, very small. He failed, even after hours of scanning, to find the faintest trace of the huge Russian warship.

*

They were under way once more. With Zof's plan of escape now working, they all felt relaxed enough to go down to the mess where several of the crew had already opened a bottle. Even Kishkov was there. There was a sense of relief spreading around the ship: the worst of the job was now over. The new course that Zof had plotted would, he was sure, avoid any trouble for the next few days. He reckoned he had bought himself thirty-six hours at least, and maybe more. The final reckoning, he still knew deep inside himself, was on its way. But he'd delayed it sufficiently to be able to spend some time with his crew. They needed to see him relaxed, too. If Zof stayed tense, stalking the bridge, it simply kept the atmosphere at breaking point, and he knew the crew needed to have the break. They would have to work soon enough. For now, Yakov, take the lid off and let them see how calm you really are. Like all Russians, Yakov Zof was capable of hours of severe intensity, but it usually had to be followed by an evening of hard drinking where stories – and tears – would flow. Yakov wasn't a drinker: he'd seen his father succumb and swore he would never do the same. He'd take a small glass of the stuff just to show willing, but in truth he didn't like the taste and even that amount gave him a violent headache within an hour. Sometimes he wondered if his father's addiction to drink had in some perverse way left him with a physical reaction against the stuff.

The mess, like the rest of the ship, was a period piece from the Forties. The taste for Russian interior design at that time was towards the grandiose. The deckhead was high; a rigid chandelier hung from the centre. Fluted columns were moulded onto the bulkheads and the carpet remained in surprisingly good condition – it was a hand-woven example from Turkmenistan when that small and arid country was still part of Stalin's greater Soviet Union. The table was a vast black affair with a massive top and badly carved legs, presumably to give it an antique look. There were no windows, as the mess was inside the heavily armoured citadel, so the chandelier shed a musty yellow light in the room which gave the fittings an older appearance than they were entitled to.

On each bulkhead, flanked by the fluted columns, the brownish paintwork displayed large, pale rectangles where pictures had hung – flattering portraits of Stalin and important naval commanders of the day. One by one the portraits were removed as the leaders got shot, not by the enemy but by Stalin. One of the last to go was Stalin himself once his disgrace was announced by Krushchev; the pale patch at the end of the long room was the biggest of them all. When Zof first inspected the ship, a heavily retouched portrait of that fool Yeltsin was hanging there. He had personally removed it and flung it overboard.

The food was well up to Blokhin's standards. He worked miracles in the ancient galley; few of the men had eaten so well in years as on this voyage.

Icy pepper vodka was in good supply too. Zof had his small glass, and Kelley was already well into it; the rest of the crew were gathering in greater numbers and were starting to toast their exploits to each other.

'Miv I Druzhba ... Peace and friendship ... Here's to Captain Zof and his brave crew for winning the battle of the South China Sea,' toasted Kelley with his fifth glass, joining in the general swing of things. Zof politely nodded his appreciation, even though he had to interpret it for the others to appreciate the compliment. The glasses clinked and Zof slowly proposed a further toast in Russian to Kelley, who beamed happily at Zof, not understanding a word he was talking about.

'And here's to our good friends Kelley and poor Mr Pine, who we hope will make a speedy recovery, for their great good planning and for making us all very wealthy men. We toast you!' And the Russians jumped up, even Kishkov, and raised their glasses in the air. Zof's sarcasm was lost on Kelley. He was content to let them enjoy the moment. It might be their last chance to enjoy anything, but he kept his dark thoughts to himself.

Kelley applauded the toast in the Russian way, clapping himself along with the Russians, acknowledging the honour.

They sat down, and Kelley felt it was his turn again.

He refilled a glass, stood up and lifted his glass in the direction of Kishkov, who failed to understand a word that Kelley uttered but took it in good part anyway. Kelley fulsomely praised the genius of Kishkov, the brilliance of his original design, and the way the grand old ship had stood up to the recent pounding it had taken, and how this surely vindicated the excellence of the traditional Russian way of doing things. The old man nodded vigorously at whatever Kelley was saying and lifted his glass in return – far from the first of the day, suspected Zof, watching his pink waterlogged eyes. Zof translated Kelley's encomium. Kishkov nodded even more happily and, in the great Russian tradition, began to weep openly.

'Oh, Christ,' whispered Kelley to Zof. 'We're not going to have another of the old fool's turns, are we?'

'Don't worry,' Zof whispered back. 'It's our traditional Russian way of enjoying ourselves. The rest will start soon.'

They did. Once the tears started rolling down Kishkov's cheeks, Zof's engineering commander Zhadanov, with whom Kishkov had spent most of the voyage arguing, went and sat down next to him, wrapped his long arms round the tiny old man and started crying too, pausing only to lift his glass to drink. Zhadanov began a long oration about the miseries of Mother Russia now the communists had departed and that drunken fool Yeltsin had sold out to the West. Kishkov nodded in agreement. The rest of the Russians started to join in as a fresh bottle of pepper vodka was opened and passed around.

'I think it is best to leave them to it, Kelley. They could carry on like this all night. I'll make our excuses. We don't want to appear impolite, after all.' Zof stood up, complimented them all on their bravery, skilfulness and audacity, and explained that he and

Kelley were tired and had to retire. Kelley also rose, and the two of them moved towards the door.

Kishkov pulled himself to his feet, his cheeks glittering with tears spread across his wrinkled, sunburned leather face and snot smeared across the white scrub of his badly shaved upper lip. He raised his glass, his gnarled hand shaking so badly that slops of vodka flicked from the glass and spattered across the heavy table. The dim light of the chandelier accentuated the deeply etched lines stretched across his face, and he looked like an ancient Egyptian mummy brought to unsteady life.

'My very, very good friends,' he slurred in Russian, 'I would just like to say a few words to you before you retire. This has been a wonderful day for me. Under your leadership we have taken on the might of the American Navy and crushed and humiliated them before the eyes of the world.'

'What the hell's he on about?' Kelley demanded softly of Zof.

'He's being very nice. He's thanking us for beating the Americans.'

'Oh,' said Kelley dubiously, as Kishkov continued his speech.

'We have brought back the might of the old Soviet Navy. This is a truly great achievement. But, comrades, let us not forget that God is with us in this great enterprise. God alone protects us and makes all things possible. He has stretched out his mighty hand and crushed our enemies before our eyes.'

'Now what's he saying?'

'Apparently we need to thank God as well.'

'But sadly, my good friends and comrades,' continued Kishkov, 'God is unhappy with something that we have done. I too am unhappy. We must put this right.' He suddenly stopped and looked slowly around the room. His eyes had become sharper and brighter; he put both hands in his jacket pockets. 'The American has committed a great sin. This is a great sadness to me. I believed we were to relieve the Western decadents of gold and jewels they have only evil uses for. This is not so. The cargo taken from the filthy American ship was not gold or jewels. That cargo is an abomination in the sight of God!'

The whole room had gone quiet. Zof was staring straight ahead, wondering how long he should let the old man ramble on. Kelley, not following Kishkov at all, was trying not very successfully to suppress a smile. The old man presented a pathetic figure, swaying at the table, tears rolling down his cheeks, eyes raised to heaven and hands thrust into his jacket pockets as if trying to shield himself from something. He stopped talking and, with an even more mournful face, took his hands from his pockets, unbuttoned his cheap cloth jacket and carefully removed what looked like two candles wrapped in greaseproof paper neatly folded at each end, tied together, with a small metallic 'lipstick' stuck between them from which a length of wire led into Kishkov's coat.

His hands trembled with increasing violence as he placed the package on the table and he shook his head sadly and slowly while Kelley, across an instant of time that has no measure, changed from pity for the pathetic old man to heart-stopping terror at the sight of two sticks of Semtex explosive with the electronic detonator inserted between them, enough to thoroughly demolish the mess room and dispose of everyone inside it.

The rest of the room, half drunk as they were, took only a second or two longer to understand Kishkov's move and almost as one stood up and backed away, but with every eye rooted to Kishkov's hands, both of which were currently outside his jacket and, it was hoped, at that moment well away from the switch at the other end of the wire that disappeared inside it.

'Oh Christ,' muttered Kelley, who was backing away from the table under a dreadful compulsion to flee. He was stopped by the bulkhead.

Kishkov, having regarded the bomb with deep regret for a few seconds, continued his speech. 'God speaks to me at night and in the mornings as I pray to him. It is necessary to do this. We must take this evil cargo back to the Americans. It is required to do this now, please. You must understand, God has commanded me. It must be done.' Kishkov gazed at the crude bomb in front of him as if surprised to suddenly discover it. He looked squarely at Kelley and, even though his eyes were bloodshot and his gaze unsteady, it was quite clear that he was perfectly mad and perfectly serious.

Zof, astonished, moved back towards Kishkov. The old man flinched slightly and shook his head violently. Zof stopped, breathing heavily, and rapidly translated the old man's demand to Kelley, who was clearly terrified.

'Sure, sure! Tell him no problem. Tell him anything. Anything he wants. We agree, absolutely. Tell him, for fuck's sake,' said Kelley loudly, nodding his head violently and looking happily at Kishkov, hoping that smiling at him would make the old man relax. Zof translated somewhat more formally, trying to make it sound considered and sincere.

'Kelley respects your request, Comrade Chief Designer. He had no wish to offend you or God and would like to apologise very, very seriously. Of course we will immediately return the warheads. This is a terrible mistake and Kelley hopes we can remain friends.'

Kishkov nodded but remained standing, looking at his two stubby sticks of Semtex and showing not the slightest sign of moving until someone else did.

Zof broke the silence. He smiled at Kishkov and said something to him quickly, in Russian. The old man looked at Zof; then he began to visibly relax. A moment later the madness started to go out of his eyes; he nodded very slightly and then looked expectantly, first at Zof, then at Kelley.

'What the hell have you said?' whispered Kelley, still looking carefully at Kishkov.

'I told him we needed to go to the lower bridge, the battle bridge. I told him we're still cleaning up on the main bridge after the missile attack. We'll go there now and turn the ship round to find the *Jackson* again. I invited him to accompany us,' replied Zof quietly.

'Why?' demanded Kelley, not following Zof's plan.

'Remember the armour-plating on that bridge? It would stand up to anything. We get the old man going in, then we'll sort him out. Do you see?' replied Zof, still looking happily at Kishkov and talking from the side of his mouth.

Zof's idea suddenly dawned on Kelley. He nodded enthusiastically to Kishkov, as if to invite him to join them and some of his officers while they turned the ship around. Kishkov nodded, looking pleased, picked up his bomb, tucked it in his jacket pocket and kept his hand firmly over it. Following Zof, he led the way 'to the battle bridge, Comrade Chief Designer, as you know, because of the repair work'. Kishkov walked confidently but unsteadily from the room, to the very considerable relief of the remaining Russians.

It was a laughing, happy group that approached the battle bridge, Kelley trying desperately to keep up the atmosphere to distract Kishkov. Zof kept repeating the

abject apology and hoped Kishkov was feeling better.
The old man kept nodding. The group milled around
Kishkov, staying desperately cheerful, with Zof and
Kelley trying to distract him as much as possible. Then
before them was the dull grey steel outer door of the
battle bridge, a low squat room with the barest
minimum of controls and instruments to keep the
ship running, with two-foot-thick armour plate
surrounding the room and four armoured periscopes
facing each quarter to provide a blast-proof view
around the ship when the slit windows were
shuttered.

Zof unlatched the door and pulled it open, creaking
against the big steel hinges. Behind it lay another door,
which he also unlatched and pulled slowly open. This
was a foot thick with a line of steel bolts operated by
the handle, like a safe door. Designed as the last refuge
for the commanders of the ship when under heavy
fire, it was meant to keep the ship operational even if
the rest of the upperworks were shot away. Zof flicked
on the dim yellow lighting and stood by the door,
ushering Kishkov through. Kelley stopped, his heart
beating loudly, waiting for Kishkov to take the step. He
moved hesitantly, unwilling to pass the Captain and
now, even though swaying with the vodka and the
fear, suddenly aware that he was ahead and the others
behind him. He stopped again.

'Comrade Chief Designer, please enter the bridge.
Here we all are. After you, comrade. Let's get this mess
sorted out,' pleaded Zof.

Kishkov gave a blurred sort of smile to Zof and
carried on into the bridge. Kelley started breathing
again.

'Now, quick,' whispered Zof to Kelley, and with
Kishkov still wandering into the bridge both men
grabbed the thick steel door and heaved. Age, neglect

and the salt air of Vladivostok had told on the hinges. While the door moved, it groaned loudly and resisted any attempts to close it quickly. Kishkov turned at the sudden creak from the door, still smiling at Zof. He looked at Zof, he looked at the door. He looked again at Zof, who was still heaving against the slab of armour which moved with agonising slowness towards the frame.

Kishkov's face fell into a great sadness. He pulled the bomb from his pocket and started fiddling inside his jacket, presumably going after the switch or whatever it was that would detonate the thing. Zof yelled to Kelley, 'Shut it, shut it!' and dived into the disappearing gap after Kishkov before Kelley could stop him. The door had reached the point where the hinges were clear and, with Kelley pushing it snapped shut with Kishkov and Zof inside. Everyone waited for the blast.

Nothing came. The door remained shut and there wasn't a sound from inside.

Minutes passed, while Kelley wondered what on earth to do next. Then the door suddenly creaked again and was pushed open from the inside. They all shrank back. Zof came out, opened the door more widely and led out Kishkov, his arms around the old man's shoulders. A thin wire dangled loosely from his jacket. The old man was weeping once more, big tears that rolled silently down his withered cheeks. He held his arms out before him as though waiting for the communion bread, but at the end of his arms his hands flopped like rags, his fingers swelling and turning purple where Zof had apologetically taken each one of Kishkov's frail, withered hands in his own and tightened his powerful grip until the old man finally released his hold on the bomb.

21

The two American battleships worked their way steadily southwards, following McEwan's new course to bring them to the distant Australian coast to catch the *Stalin*, which they would reach in around eight days from leaving Pearl. They were leaving the palm-fringed Marshall Islands to the north, heading for the scatter of atolls that were the Solomons, and passing through the sprinkling of islands that littered this corner of the Pacific like sand spilt across a smooth blue table.

The weather, far out into the heart of the ocean, was serene and idyllic. McEwan had never seen sunsets like those he saw now. In a sky with faint smears of high cloud, the sun would quite suddenly dip down towards the polished blue sea, changing the sky from blue to orange to red to purple, and finally a star-scattered blackness, all in the space of five minutes. There was always an island on the horizon, more often a group, that provided a backdrop like a stage set for *South Pacific*, though they passed the islands too far away to enjoy the view with a silhouette of a palm tree or two.

The whereabouts of the *Stalin* still remained a mystery. The satellite trackers had completely lost sight of it. Cloud had closed down the visual search and the infra-red cameras, which should have located the huge ship boiling up hundreds of tons of water and spewing out hot smoke like a small volcano, couldn't spot the Russian vessel at all, looking as they were in entirely the wrong place. McEwan and the two Captains had given up with the intelligence people anyway. They trusted their own guesses far better. In the same position as Zof, none of them would have done anything other than take the straightest, fastest route out and, in their frequent conversations with Bell's staff back in the Pentagon, they backed their judgement too.

But now a new irritation had emerged. Legret, the captain of the *Madelaine*, had been tracked down by a press-man following a tip-off from a high official of the Hong Kong coastguard with whom he had an informal but useful financial arrangement. The press-man, an eager young Chinese, had got the story into the *South China Morning Post* as a world exclusive, complete with a picture of Legret and library photos of the *Ocean Queen*. The identity of the *Stalin* remained unrevealed, but the pirates were described as modern-day Long John Silvers.

The world's press, particularly the Australians, picked up the story within hours. Some chased down the young Chinese reporter and, following brief but heated negotiations, got his sources from him. It took hardly more than a day before the Pentagon was forced into making a statement that gave away little other than the barest facts.

The story was big enough to get the papers and the news stations chartering planes to fly over the region to see anything that could be seen. Eventually one spotted the drifting *Ocean Queen*. The story grew. A Reuters' stringer in Hawaii heard about the panic departure of the *Iowa* and *Missouri*. She contacted the Pentagon, who refused to say anything about it, which in her book was the nearest thing to a complete admission that they had sailed off to hunt down the pirates. She wrote and filed the story, and it was on the wires within the hour.

Thus, two days out of Pearl, a light aircraft set off the *Iowa*'s radar alarms: they were nowhere near any recognised routes for big or small aircraft. The plane, a twin-engined Piper, buzzed low over the ship, and the cameramen with the long lenses were clearly visible leaning out of the open door, oblivious of the fact that at least eight ship-to-air missiles had been activated and were carefully tracking them, a hair-trigger away from being fired.

There was a spirited exchange of language between the *Iowa*'s air defence officer and the Polynesian pilot of the plane who, in excellent French which fortunately the American didn't understand, informed him that he had as much right to be there as they did, while the American, in English that the pilot grasped, told him to fuck off anyway otherwise he'd blow him out of the air.

The Piper circled several times, then droned away to the south. An hour later another small aircraft arrived, took some pictures, then disappeared again. They were buzzed pretty constantly after that, with small planes popping up every few hours. Vieques ranted at the local air traffic control, who were in Tahiti, but they were not vastly concerned and told the Americans they could do nothing about it. The lazy French accent of the man he spoke to, who assured him he was in charge, suggested to Vieques that he wasn't going to get anywhere.

The two ships continued through the gentle seas of the South Sea Islands, racing through the emerald water, chasing an unknown quarry and watched by CNN crews who started to do real-time updates which were beamed around the world. But the *Jackson* and the story of its cargo remained secret; in a cool marble-lined room just outside Baghdad, a small group of uniformed men tuned into the CNN news via their private satellite link and began to grow anxious.

*

In the dark waters off Weigeo, north of the Moluccas, a low wooden boat with four brothers on board was quietly fishing with long lines, the baited hooks spread out behind them for a mile or more in the slow drift. Over the side of the boat a gas-powered lantern glared white in the dark night, attracting to the surface the squid which in turn brought the fat tunny-fish up from the depths where they would take the baits.

The fishing was slow that night. The lantern began to burn dim as the gas bottle started to run out. One of the brothers got up from the warm deck to change over the bottle, but another stopped him, asking why he wanted to waste good gas when it was perfectly obvious that there were no fish to be had tonight. He lay back again and left the lantern to grow dimmer and fade away into the darkness. They would drift a little longer and then, before dawn, start the long process of hauling the lines back in by hand, for they were poor and couldn't afford big power winches like the Japanese who raided their home waters with big ships and sucked the seas dry of fish.

The gas finally failed, and they were left gently rolling in the darkness. Only the oily phosphorescence of the sea gave any light.

Stalin came upon them suddenly. Zof was steaming without lights and navigating by radar, and had slowed to a modest but still fast 20 knots. He was now getting worried about his oil tanks giving him the range to the Monte Bello Islands; he'd decided to slow down to extend them as much as possible, but his margin was very tight. He would soon have to talk to Kelley about replenishing if his present rate of consumption continued. His mind was filled with thoughts about possible places to raid for refuelling when he noticed on his starboard side what looked like a long log in the water, rapidly falling astern and bobbing in the wake of the bow wave. The light was so dim he could barely make it out and, as he didn't actually hit it, he carried on worrying about the fuel situation.

The four brothers were only very briefly aware of the *Stalin* as it roared past 20 feet away from them. It rushed out of the darkness with a hissing sound as the crisp bow cleaved through the water, throwing it aside into a bow wave that hit their small boat like a tsunami. The approaching wave turned them nearly 90 degrees; they quickly righted as the sharp wave passed rapidly under them but, with the rolling motion already set up, as the small craft slipped again down the steep back of the wave, it passed the point of no return and rolled smoothly upside-down into the warm water. They were good swimmers; all four brothers climbed on to the upturned hull of their boat. The curses they shouted at the now receding *Stalin* were the most expressive their fishermen's minds could imagine, but all that happened was that the wash from the stern of the ship struck them and threw them off the hull again.

Stalin was now burrowing deep into the maze of islands gathered between Borneo and Celebes that made up Eastern Indonesia. Known in Dutch colonial days as the Moluccas, the ancient Spice Islands, their official name these days was Maluka; the islands of Buru, Ambon and Seram lay 100 miles to the south, and the ship was sticking close in to the New Guinea side. Zof planned to run down past Kofiau and Misool, leaving them to starboard so as to stay within reach of the hidden anchorages of the coast if he needed a bolt-hole. He watched his radar and his depth-sounder carefully. He still had over 500 feet of water under his keel, but it had started to come up in the last hour and the radar, though still blank of coastline features, was picking up the tops of distant mountains at the extreme limit of its range.

Dawn was approaching on the fourth day since they had relieved the *Jackson* of its cargo. Zof was approaching the island of Misool about 20 miles distant. He now had to figure out which way to pass through. From the chart the waters all looked hazardous, and he was far from confident that he wouldn't run into some small, unmarked lump of rock such as were scattered through these seas. He possessed an ancient copy of *Sailing Directions for the Pacific* issued by the Soviet Hydrographic Institute at St Petersburg, but they were notoriously unreliable outside Russian home waters.

His main problem remained the fuel. The decision to take the longer route had meant that his earlier calculation of the fuel load for the one-way trip was now well out of date. If he believed the fuel calculations, and also the calculation of the rate that the boilers were slurping fuel, then he had just about enough to make the Monte Bello Islands. But even dipping the tanks by hand left a margin of error, big enough to make him uncertain as the tanks emptied. And the boilers were certainly burning fuel at a faster rate than Kishkov had promised; judging by the black soot that now caked the top of the stack, they were burning the fuel much too richly.

Zof looked at the chart again, worrying about hazards in the water, and now he started looking at the various ports within the area where he could take on fuel. None of them was known to him, and the *Sailing Directions* were hardly helpful.

As the sky lightened, he saw the distant smudges of land on the horizons around him. He would have to slow down even more while they nosed through the narrow strait. The fuel situation preyed on his mind. Once the sun had risen, he picked up the internal phone and roused Kelley.

'What the hell is it, Zof? It's bloody five in the morning,' complained a sleepy and irritable Kelley.

'I'm sorry, my friend, but you must get up here on the bridge. The fuel is running low and we have only limited opportunities to take on some more. I have been up most of the night worrying about this. Kindly get yourself up here and help me out, please.' Polite as it was, it was not a request.

Kelley hauled himself out of bed and walked grumpily to the bridge in the early-morning light. He found Zof pouring over a chart.

'What's the problem?' he yawned.

Zof pointed out their current position and the planned course. For 600 miles they could stick close to the coast of New Guinea, which would provide plenty of cover and keep them near the few ports where they could get oil if they needed it. Zof liked the look of Manggawitu on the island of Adi; the water was deep, and being a small island would mean the authorities would be non-existent. The only drawback was that the waters were littered with islets and rocks that their chart didn't show; the Soviet pilot book only mentioned the bigger hazards to navigation.

The other option was to turn due south towards Kepulaun Gorong, where the water was deeper and safer, but this took them well out of range of any port that was small and discreet.

'Basically, Kelley, Manggawitu is our last chance for fuel if we need it. Once we go past, we have to make our current fuel load last another 1,800 miles. I do not know if we can make it. Only Kishkov could calculate it safely for us, and I think he is not exactly in any mood to do anything at all. So. You see, I think, my dilemma?'

Kelley saw the problem. 'How long to this port of yours?'

'We can make it by tonight.'

Kelley said he wanted to think about it and turned to go. It was too early to make decisions.

'No problem, Kelley. Take your time. You have exactly one minute.'

'For Christ's sake, Zof!' complained Kelley.

The Russian stubbed out his cigarette and lit another one. 'Sorry, Kelley. You have to decide now or else I'm stopping for fuel anyway.'

'Do we really need to stop? How much range have we got left?'

'Too close to call,' replied Zof. He could see the rising annoyance on Kelley's face and explained that the boilers were burning more than expected. If he believed the fuel calculations, they would arrive at the Monte Bello Islands with exactly eight tons of fuel oil left. It was simply too close a safety margin. Did they want to risk it?

Kelley began to calm down. What was eight tons the equivalent of? he asked. Zof told him the ship burned a ton of fuel every half-hour at top speed. Even at 20 knots it was a ton every forty-five minutes. Eight tons was no more than six hours' steaming, or about 130 miles. Over a total distance of nearly 1,800 miles, even Kelley admitted it was too close.

'What's this place like?' asked Kelley.

'I remember it from a training visit when the

Indonesians and the Russian were very great friends. It's a small port for the local coastal trade. I cannot tell if they carry much fuel oil, but I presume they must carry some. Even a few hundred tons will make the difference.'

'So we just sail in, tie up and ask for a load of fuel. What do we pay with? American Express?'

'Kelley, the ship's littered with gold bars. They'll send the local governor to give us a welcome party when we turn up.'

Kelley smiled and nodded. 'OK, Zof. What did you say the place is called?'

'Manggawitu. On Adi.'

'Manggawitu, here we come!'

*

The big ship moved slowly through the waters a mile off the port before finding a spot where Zof was happy dropping anchor. There was a huge splash as the anchor disappeared towards the sea-bed 60 feet below, as shallow as Zof dared go in. Once the ship had settled, they made ready the inflatable. Zof and two of the Russians were to go to the port to start negotiations, carrying two gold bars from the *Madelaine's* haul wrapped in sacking.

They returned an hour later with a small Indonesian dressed in a white but grubby uniform and a blue naval cap which didn't match. They led him up to the foredeck where Kelley was waiting.

'This is the harbourmaster, or says he is. He claims to have about four hundred tons of fuel oil, but will need a day to ferry it out here and another half a day to pump it in. He says he is happy to do this, but would like to see the rest of the gold,' explained Zof, as the Indonesian nodded cheerfully.

'The rest of the gold? How much does he want, for Christ's sake?'

'He says that to make sure our presence is not noticed will take a further ten bars. This will make him and the rest of his family rich for ever, and they will be eternally grateful.'

'Tell the sonofabitch he'll get another two bars, and he only gets that if the fuel is loaded within twenty-four hours. One bar more if he does it in less.'

'Tell him yourself, my friend. He speaks English.'

'OK? You understand? Two bars, plus the two you've seen. Loaded within the day, or forget it!' Kelley almost shouted.

The Indonesian shook his head sadly. 'Not enough. Very risky business. You don't look official, see what I mean? More gold or no fuel.' The man suddenly grinned, showing his few, very stained and crooked teeth.

'Go to hell! Three more bars, that's it. Otherwise no deal. There's plenty of other places we can go,' said Kelley, his voice getting louder.

The Indonesian figured that as the four, maybe five, gold bars were worth more than he and the rest of the town were likely to earn over their entire lives, this particular gift horse should not be looked in the mouth for too long. He didn't like the look of Kelley, anyway. Not like the fine naval officer who had spoken to him so nicely in the first place.

His grin quickly vanished. 'OK. three more bars. Get me back.'

The inflatable took him back across the small bay to the port. Two hours later a barge rounded the harbour wall, its blunt nose pushed into the air and its stern all but under water as it was driven steadily across the mile of water between the harbour and the anchorage. It slowly chugged up to the *Stalin*. The first of the fuel started to be transferred.

Four barge-loads had been pumped into *Stalin*'s

bunkers when a small aircraft flew overhead. It wasn't exactly common in those parts, but then it was hardly the most exciting event either. It droned out across the bay, passed by *Stalin* and then flew off. It made no suspicious noises and flew quite high. Neither Zof nor Kelley took any notice; it was just a local aircraft, after all.

*

'It's the Pentagon, sir, and they sound a little upset,' said a young Marine trying to rouse Vieques from a late-afternoon break in the *Iowa*'s air-conditioned Captain's suite.

What did they want? 'Put them on,' ordered Vieques, swinging his feet out from his bunk. The Pentagon staff normally sent orders by secure teleprinter. Direct voice links were considered bad security, even via scrambler, and were only used when something had gone badly wrong.

'Captain Vieques, we've found your Russian ship,' said the cold voice of one of Bell's senior staff officers. From the tone the man used, Vieques could tell all was far from well.

'*Stalin*? Where is it?' responded Vieques, swallowing hard and wondering how on earth they had found it.

'Holed up taking on fuel. Perhaps you'd like to know how we found this huge ship, the biggest battleship in the world, with all the technology available to us? And to you, Vieques, come to think of it?'

'I'm sure you're going to tell me.'

'CNN is how, Vieques. The CNO is sitting down to watch TV after dinner and, apart from some nice pictures of you and your men cruising the South Sea Islands, there's then a nice bit of film of the *Stalin* sitting quietly in a harbour taking on fuel. What do you think of that?'

'Very annoying. How did they find it and we didn't?'

'Sounds like pure luck. Just happened to be leaning out of the window and there she was. I've got hold of CNN and they've confirmed it. *Stalin*, two hours ago, was anchored off the island of Adi, 134 degrees east, 4 degrees south. Get there, Vieques! Get there now.'

Vieques hurried to the bridge and hauled out the chart. The island of Adi was tiny. The navigation officer quickly started working out a course while Vieques waited impatiently.

'Give or take an hour, we can make it by dawn, sir. But we'll have to maintain 28 knots.'

Vieques rubbed his hands. He quickly called Murray and got the officers together.

As the light began to fade and the shimmering orange sun dropped like a sinking globe towards the horizon, the *Iowa* and the *Missouri* slowly turned their elegant bows towards the north-west, the *Iowa* leading and the *Missouri* following in her wake, up towards New Guinea and the Equator where, if their luck held, they would come across *Stalin* like a sitting duck – which didn't seem to Vieques exactly the right expression to use, but he couldn't think of anything better.

*

They had been loading through the afternoon and into the night. By ten in the evening, long after the tropical sun had gone down, the Indonesian had delivered 600 tons of fuel oil. Kelley and the small official had a flaming row over the extra bar of gold, which Kelley wasn't going to hand over; Zof eventually persuaded him that the gold was hardly important and that they couldn't really afford to lose the goodwill of the locals. Kelley relaxed and finally handed over the last bar as the Indonesian stood in the inflatable, shouting curses in a language that no one seemed to know, until the gold appeared. With that, he vanished quickly into the night.

Kelley and Zof decided to wait at the anchorage until first light. Zof was not happy moving the big ship out into the maze of rocks and islands until he could see where he was. In any event, reasoned Kelley, the general idea was to take time to allow any pursuers to pass safely by. They turned in for the night, leaving a heavy guard outside to protect them from any thieves that might be tempted to come out under cover of darkness from the port; to Zof's great amusement, Kelley warned the guard that pirates had been known to operate in these parts.

Zof went back to his sparse cabin. Tomorrow would be the day, he decided: it was time to let the crew know what was really happening. They had started asking questions, and some of them wanted to know what the warheads were for. Some of them had asked about Harvey, and he had to tell them the story that Kelley had come up with.

His men would have to be trusted. Most wouldn't like it, of course, but he'd brought them this far and he couldn't see any reason why they wouldn't go along with it. He needed them sharp, anyway: they had the most dangerous part of the voyage still before them. They had got so far without trouble, but he knew it couldn't last.

Now he lay on his bunk going through what he would say. The glory of Russia. The power of the Navy. Their great victory over the Americans. The last run before they were home and rich. How they could be even richer. He'd tell them that a foreign power wanted the warheads. Some crazed Middle-Eastern dictator. They'd know who he meant. Most of them had a sneaking regard for Saddam anyway; he was an enemy of the Americans, after all, and therefore in their minds couldn't be all bad.

He would gather them on the foredeck. He could address them from the top of the forward turret. The three huge guns would be pointing out over them. It was the right setting, he thought: enough to impress them.

The night was close and the small cabin was still and sweaty. The porthole was wide open and the hot, damp air drifted slowly in and prickled the skin. It was like sitting in a steam bath. Zof knew he was going to find it difficult to sleep. His mind drifted away from the speech he would give first thing in the morning, and images of Polina and Yekaterina forced their way into his imagination. Polina was smiling at him but Yekaterina was screaming something, although no sound was coming from her mouth. Behind her was a huge ship flying the Red Banner, but then it suddenly changed to a Stars and Stripes. Yakov Zof turned over, and turned over again, drifting in and out of a fitful, restless sleep haunted by strange dreams.

*

By four in the morning, an hour before dawn, the radar operator on *Iowa* was certain that he could distinguish the echo of the *Stalin* from the background clutter. Vieques started to position his forces, bringing *Missouri* round in a wide circle to his port, while *Iowa* carried on straight at the island of Adi, holding *Stalin* in a pincer movement that, if they got the chance, would allow them to cascade shells on to her from both sides – forcing *Stalin* to fire at one or other of them, but only with great difficulty at both together. This was the basic technique worked out by Vieques and McEwan; they hadn't expected to have the process made easier by the Russian ship sitting asleep at anchor.

Missouri was slowly moving away from the *Iowa*, the distance between the two vessels widening gradually as Murray pulled his ship away. *Stalin* was just 30 miles distant, an hour's steaming. As they approached, the sun would be coming up almost behind them. The sky was clear and it would be a perfect sunrise. Once the sun was up, no one on the *Stalin* would be able to look into it and see the *Iowa*. And for the *Iowa*, with the sun behind them, it would light up the *Stalin* as if in a stage spotlight.

The *Iowa*'s radar officer kept a patient watch at his screen, waiting for any signs of movement which would suggest that *Stalin* had spotted them. But as far as he could tell from the steady image, there was no movement, no movement at all. The radar's computer was unable to detect any sign of life; both the bearing digits and speed digits displayed next to the blip remained unflickeringly at zero.

After another ten miles, Vieques ordered the ships to slow down to 10 knots. Now he wanted to creep gently up on his target, getting as near as he could to improve his guns' accuracy before opening fire.

If surprise was on his side he had, McEwan assured him, a substantial advantage. 'After the first shot wakes them up they'll be running round in a panic. It will take five minutes to get the gun crews into position, if not longer. Then, oh, say another five minutes to load and get their first shot off. That gives you at the very least ten solid minutes of shooting, in which time you can drop a pretty big heap of HE on the old ship. Then they've got to figure out which one to shoot at first. It's a bloody good chance, Captain.'

The gentle vibration of the ship under full power

diminished as its speed dropped away and it settled to the 10 knots ordered. The *Missouri* was now several miles distant to port of the *Iowa*.

Vieques ordered his crew to prepare for battle. Without rushing, the crew eased themselves into their allotted places and started getting the 16-inch guns ready. The operations centre, deep in the heart of the ship, started to glitter into life as computer screens flickered on and wall plots displayed the positions of the combatants. Young men and women, born long after the days when *Stalin*'s namesake was alive, now busied themselves with headsets and keyboards to plot the destruction of the second Man of Steel.

The target remained small on the distant horizon. The sun had started to lighten the sky behind them and in a few minutes would rise above the horizon to light up the old battleship. In the absence of any movement, Vieques had decided to wait until they were five miles off before opening fire. The ships slowly crept up on the slumbering giant in the water.

*

Zof had given up the unequal struggle by four that morning. Now he was wide awake, and his mind was churning over not only past events but the voyage ahead of him and the final handover. He would be a rich man; so would his crew. He planned to return to Russia as he couldn't think of anywhere he'd prefer to live. Could he find Yekaterina? How could he remain hidden? How could the crew remain hidden? There were a hundred other problems; the more he thought about it, the more problems he began to see. His mind raced on.

There was a knock on the cabin door. Zof rolled from his bunk to open it. In the early morning darkness a young seaman was standing there, carrying a tray with a large mug of strong, steaming coffee, brewed like fuel oil, the way Zof liked it.

'Comrade Blokhin thought you would like this, Captain,' said the young man.

How the hell did Blokhin know he would be up, worrying, he smiled to himself? The cook knew him too well. Zof nodded appreciatively and took the mug; it was a welcome relief. He recognised the youngster.

'Zavic, isn't it?'

'Yes, sir,' said the lad.

'Enjoying the trip?'

The seaman looked up at Zof. Enjoying it? his face seemed to say. What's enjoying it got to do with why I'm here? I was starving and the Navy threw me on the streets, then you came along and offered me half a chance. We could all be going to our death for all I know, Comrade Captain Zof, but what choice do I get?

'Oh, yes, sir,' he said doubtfully.

'Good. Thank Blokhin for the coffee. Tell him I'm looking forward to breakfast. On your way, now.'

'Yes, sir,' said the young seaman, and vanished.

Zof saw the look on the boy's face and read it like an open book. He hoped to whatever God there might be that the lad ended up with a great deal more than half a chance. He felt a sudden stab of guilt; where was he leading these people?

It was still hot; but now there was a hint of freshness off the sea that started to calm his racing brain and, although it was still inky black with just a few pale yellow lights on the quay, dawn would soon break. He would watch the sun come up. He walked slowly to the prow of the ship, lighting a cigarette. In the flame from the lighter, he could see the old teak planking was splitting in places. It creaked loosely under his feet. He would be sad to see the old ship go;

she would have to be scuttled, of course, once they reached the Monte Bello Islands. In spite of being worn around the edges, *Stalin* was a superb ship, the best he had ever sailed. Kishkov might be as mad as a hatter, he thought, but he must have been pretty impressive when he was fifty years younger.

At the prow, surrounded by the huge anchor chains and windlasses, he leaned comfortably on the guard-rail and stared out to sea. His eyes had grown used to the dark now, and the inkiness had relented to a deep, velvet grey in which the shadows of the ship were just visible. There were a million stars sprinkled across the sky but no moon. He looked towards the horizon. Dawn was due soon. Was it his eyes or was there a streak of dim distant light? He averted his eyes and then, after a few moments, looked back at the horizon. It was dim, but now there was a hazy veil of pale blackness spreading upwards across the sky. As he watched, the horizon emerged into view while the pale light grew stronger second by second.

Then he saw the *Iowa*.

It was dimly backlit, head on, and all he could make out was a vague shape that didn't appear to be moving. He thought it was a distant oil-rig at first. But his eye scanned along the horizon, where he then saw the *Missouri*. It had turned to encircle him, and presented a near-perfect side view. At first it looked just like an ordinary ship on the horizon, and he very nearly ignored it. But then the long, low shape of the *Missouri*, and its high central superstructure, stirred something in him. Old, dull lessons in warship recognition flickered into his memory. He walked quickly back along the splintering planks of the deck, ducked under the chains, and pulled himself up the several ladders that led to the bridge where he grabbed his old Nikon binoculars for a better view.

Seconds later, the ship was shaking with the alarm bells clanging over the loudspeakers as the passageways filled with panicking, half-dressed sailors who desperately struggled with each other to reach their battle stations.

22

Vieques was 18 miles distant when his radar officer suddenly broke the tense silence of the approach. 'Target moving, sir. Course 200 degrees, 2 or 3 knots.'

'Double-check that!'

'Aye, sir!' the radar officer yelled back. He punched the keyboard, asking the computer to verify the readout that suggested the *Stalin* had weighed anchor. Scanned once every second by the big antenna mounted high on the ship, the computer looked for the slightest changes in the target's position and was able to measure them far more accurately than the human eye.

'Target confirmed as moving, sir. Now 210 degrees and 5 to 6 knots,' yelled the radar officer as the screen flashed 'verified' at him.

'They must have seen us. Get *Missouri* and warn her. Have the guns loaded. We'll open fire when ready.'

Iowa, and then a few moments later *Missouri*, now also echoed to alarms, but this time from howling sirens as the gun-crews loaded their shells and the computers drove the turrets around and pointed the big guns to the required positions. Most of the activity inside the turrets was automatic.

The shrieking sirens were quiet now. There was a silent atmosphere of expectation on board the ship. 'All turrets ready, sir', called the fire-control officer, otherwise known as 'Guns'.

Vieques could feel the tension spreading out like ripples on a pond. The *Stalin* was slowly turning, slinking away like a thief in the night, hoping to be overlooked. But Vieques would deliver a massive blow at the ship. He paused for a second to savour the moment.

'Aye, Guns. Fire when ready,' Vieques finally ordered in a quiet voice.

There was a moment of silence. Then the first turret erupted with flame and smoke, each gun firing a microsecond after the other. Just as the immense noise hit them on the bridge, like the sound of two huge doors being slammed in quick succession, the second turret opened up. The horizon disappeared completely in the smoke, but the ship moved through it and left it hanging in the air behind them. Some miles away, Vieques counted six orange flashes as *Missouri* too opened up with all three turrets. Even as the ten shells were in the air the computers were watching them fall towards the target and feeding back adjustments to the gunners, who quickly reloaded.

*

Zof had got his ship moving, but it was painfully slow. After he'd sounded the alarm he urged the crew to their fighting stations over the PA system. Now there was no need for his much-rehearsed speech that had kept him awake most of the night. No need, and no time. The Americans were on them, he shouted. Now they had to fight, fight for the Navy, for Russia, and most of all for themselves.

The low steam pressure meant he wouldn't have top speed for another quarter-hour. But at least he had his gun-crews in their turrets, and they were working frantically to load the big shells and get a fix on the two ships. The optical system, looking into the now rising sun, was difficult to use.

Then Zof saw the orange flashes, first from the *Iowa*, then from the *Missouri*. Kelley, roused by the racket of the alarms and the sudden movement of the ship, had burst on to the bridge wearing just trousers and a vest, as Zof shouted a warning over the PA.

Everyone froze. They couldn't see the ten shells spinning towards them, but every man on the ship could feel their approach. The computers had judged their first attempt well. Shots one and two fell 50 yards behind the ship, thumping into the sea and bursting two pillars of white water hundreds of feet into the air. Shots three and four had been corrected by hundredths of a degree and plunged into the water 20 yards from the stern, having missed the ship by a matter of feet. *Stalin* shuddered from the two underwater detonations, but was unharmed.

The second salvo, from the *Missouri*, started badly: the first two shells landed nearly half a mile away. But then the computers seemed to get a better measure of the ship. Shots three and four landed a few hundred yards away, and five and six connected. There was a sudden, bone-shaking explosion at the bow of the *Stalin* as one shell pierced the thin armour of the fo'c'sle where a few minutes beforehand Zof had been watching the rising dawn. The shell ripped a hole in the deck but the explosion failed to do any real damage. With a level of cynicism that only a Soviet designer could dream of, the crew's quarters were at that point and it was not thought worth the bother of armouring them. They were empty now anyway.

The second hit connected further down the ship, where the heavily armoured deck took the blow. Kishkov's design paid off handsomely. The shell exploded with a crackling violence, but once the smoke had cleared, all it had done was rip apart the old teak decking. The grey armour plate underneath was stained black, but was unbreached.

All the shells had landed in quick succession, stuttering across *Stalin* within half a second of each other like a vast machine gun. Once a few seconds had passed after the last shell exploded, it was clear that the salvo was over. Kelley, on the bridge, was now crouching against the bulkhead, looking shaken. This was not in the plan.

'The salvo's over! You've got about thirty seconds before they reload and fire!' shouted Zof to Morin in the fire control room. Zof was quickly scanning the smoking area at the bow of the ship to see what damage had occurred. He shouted more orders, this time to the helmsman, and the big ship started turning to present a broadside to the distant American warships. The shuddering under their feet grew more pronounced as the engineers, panicked by the explosions from the shells, poured more fuel into the boilers to get the pressure up. As the *Stalin* swung, the three big turrets started to turn and the long barrels to elevate. The two forward turrets trained on the *Missouri*, which had got off six shots at them, and the after turret aimed at the *Iowa*.

'Sink the bastards,' muttered Zof under his breath as though he was talking directly to the gun-crews sweating inside the armoured turret.

There was a series of shuddering blasts as the nine huge guns spat their four-ton shells outwards towards the Americans. Kelley grinned at the sight, and on the bridge they peered eagerly through the acrid smoke, waiting for it to clear.

On the *Iowa*, the fire-control officer had just told Vieques he was ready for his next shot when the distant outline of the *Stalin*, lit up clearly by the rising

sun, sparkled with tiny white flashes. Like Zof a few
moments earlier, it was now Vieques' turn to warn his
ship. There was nothing he could do except wait for
the shells to fall.

Stalin's ancient optical system was no match for the
American's electronic aim; but the difference didn't
really matter. *Stalin*'s huge shells, each one carrying
nearly four tons of high explosive, had an effect over a
much wider area. The *Missouri* was first to feel their
awesome power. None of the *Stalin*'s shells actually hit
the ship, but all six landed close by and the shock
waves from the underwater blasts threw the whole
crew off their feet. Even a ship the size of *Missouri*
reacted to the detonations as though it was a piece of
rag in the jaws of a small dog, being shaken from side
to side.

The *Iowa* was less lucky. The first shell from *Stalin*'s
after turret missed and exploded just next to her; but
the second shell connected with a glancing blow along
the side of the ship. A direct impact would probably
have gone clean through; but as it was, the shell
ricocheted off before exploding. The impact was
enough to momentarily slow the *Iowa* right down.
Vieques started yelling at his damage-control people.
He was worried the blow had holed her. On the
Missouri, Murray was back on his feet and trying to
check that his crew was still functioning.

'Christ almighty, Lieutenant, that's one hell of a set
of guns they've got there,' said Vieques to the equally
shaken McEwan. 'I'm holding off until we re-think
this one. Full ahead all engines! Helm hard a-port and
come about. Tell *Missouri* to haul off and get out of
range,' he ordered.

He needn't have worried. Zof was equally shaken by
the attack and, at the same time as the Americans were
turning round, he ordered his ship to get away too. It

wasn't that he refused to do battle. He just preferred to do it in his own time, not when the Americans wanted. Rather than stay, he would prefer taking the occasional lucky hit in order to open some distance between them. He had no idea what these ships were, or what they were capable of, though they were clearly big, brutal and effective. But he knew that once he got up full speed he could outrun anything on the ocean. Big as they were, they'd have to catch him first.

The ship turned towards the north and, pouring thick smoke from its stack, slowly wound up the revolutions. With *Stalin* heading north and the two Americans turning away to the south, the gap between rapidly opened to 40 miles or more. No one was yet ready to join battle.

But at least the quarry had been spotted. As Vieques and Murray were re-grouping, they watched *Stalin* start to turn and creep away northwards. Vieques quickly re-thought his strategy and changed his course yet again. *Stalin* was on the run, and he wasn't going to let her out of his sight now. The distance between the Americans and the Russians soon stopped widening and, instead of fleeing themselves, *Iowa* and *Missouri* now started a deadly pursuit of the distant Russian, keeping a respectful distance between the ships.

*

'It's going to be a fight but we've nothing to worry about, Kelley. Please stop shouting at everyone. We knew it was only a matter of time before they found us,' Zof was saying. The American was visibly shaken and cursing everyone in sight.

'But how the hell did they find us, Zof? And how the hell did they get two big warships out here? They must have been following us.'

'Kelley, it really doesn't matter how they found us. They're here, and that's it. But they can't possibly stop us. All we need to do is draw them on to a spot where we can get some good shots at them, and you'll see them disappear after a couple of shells have hit them. Believe me, Kelley, no one in their right minds is going to take us on.'

Kelley looked unconvinced, but had to admit to himself that he had no alternative. Anyway, he told himself, they hadn't done so badly so far.

'OK, Zof. I guess we got no choice anyway. What's your grand plan?'

'Close them up. Sail through some narrows where the two of them are forced to follow each other if they want to follow us. That means only one can bring their guns to bear. Then we start shooting: first at one, then at the other. We can either sink them or they give up and leave us alone. Now we've got full speed, we should turn south to the Kai Islands. We can squeeze through plenty of gaps there, and they'll be forced to close up.'

'Why not just outrun the bastards? We're faster than them. Leave them behind. Why not?'

'Fuel is why. We only took on a few hundred tons. If we run at full speed we'll burn our way through it in no time, and we'll be left sitting in the middle of the sea with no engines, which is not a prospect I like very much, Kelley. We should take them on now. Bring them to battle. We'll pick them off one by one and then we can make good our escape. Trust me, my friend.'

'Jesus, Zof, you're enjoying this, aren't you?' said Kelley. The light in the Russian's eyes gave away his excitement.

Zof paused. 'Yes, I am. This is what I was trained for, what I was taught to believe in. This is what my life had been about. I suppose that sounds strange to someone like you, but believe me, Kelley, this is a battle I intend to fight and one I intend to win. If I can bring the Americans to face me fairly, I can crush them utterly. No more compromise. No more drunks playing at politics. No more dishonesty, no more taking orders from the White House. This is my time, Kelley. If you don't like it, just keep out of my way. We'll win. We'll get you to your Islands, warheads and all. Just let me fight the battle.'

Kelley didn't quite know what to say. Instead of threatening him, Zof sounded sad. But there was no mistaking the man's ruthless determination. Kelley hadn't seen much of that before in his life. He'd seen most things, but rarely had he come across someone like Zof. He found he admired it, even though he thought the Russian was going crazy.

'Sure, Zof. We fight. What the hell. Where do we go now?' asked Kelley. There was nothing he could do to change the Russian's mind anyway. Might as well go along with it. Maybe Zof was right. Maybe they would win.

Zof explained his new course. The Kai Islands were about 50 miles off, and they offered at least four good, narrow passages which it seemed they could get the big ship through, but which would force the Americans to close up together if they wanted to follow them. He gave the orders to change course and the *Stalin* started to come round on to the new heading, speeding up all the time to convince the Americans they were on the run.

And now Zof got back on the PA to address his crew once more. It wasn't the speech he had planned to give; he found the words came from his mouth as though someone else was saying them.

'Comrades, this is your Captain. I had hoped to speak to you all earlier about our plans, but as you have seen events have rather overtaken us. First of all, comrades, we are not running away. My plan is to close up the two American ships so that we can concentrate our fire on them. This will happen in a few hours' time. I want you all to be ready. We need to win this one, comrades. The Americans are on to us and will not let us rest. We need to bring them to battle and we need to win that battle. They have sent two old battleships after us. They are nothing compared with the mighty *Stalin*, even though there are two of them. They have chosen the strongest ships they have, and even then they are no match for us. We need to man our guns, keep up the speed, and fight like Russian sailors. Then we will sink them, and go on our way. Comrades, we are creating a legend. The last voyage of the *Stalin* will be its greatest. For us and for Russia. Think of all your friends left behind in the motherland who will hear of this battle. Think how many of them are starving. Think how many of them will greet you on your return and wish that they too could have seen this moment. Comrades, to battle! For the service, for Russia, for glory and for the *Stalin*!'

Kelley couldn't follow a word of Zof's speech as it echoed around the ship. But when Zof put down the microphone and turned away from him to stare out of the bridge windows at the prow of the ship now cleaving its way through the calm waters, he swore he could see the man's eyes were watering.

*

Vieques was standing in front of the radar as Zof gave his orders. 'McEwan, what do you make of this?' he asked once *Stalin* started to turn.

McEwan looked at the radar screen, watching the glowing blob that was the image of the *Stalin*. It was now clearly coming round, not directly towards them but on a course that was becoming more or less a right-angle away from them, towards the east.

'Can't say, Captain. Perhaps they want to bring us to battle?'

'I doubt it, Lieutenant, I doubt it. They're keeping up their speed, maybe even increasing it. I guess we'll just stick as near as we can and see what happens.' Vieques altered course to follow the Russian ship and asked for more power.

McEwan noted the bearing and looked at the detailed chart of the area. He drew a freehand line from *Stalin*'s current position and followed the new course, which ran straight into the Kai Islands. Now why on earth would they want to go there? He pulled down a new, very thick Indonesian pilot book and looked them up. There was nothing of interest in the islands. Just a few fishing communities, a couple of open-cast mines and a small population. Whatever their plans, they would be there in two hours or less. He snapped the pilot book shut and replaced it on the shelf. Still trying to figure out what they were up to, he went back to the bridge window and watched the distant battleship steaming steadily towards the still invisible islands.

'Damn!' he shouted twenty minutes later, suddenly turning away from the window. Everyone on the bridge jumped.

'Lieutenant, please don't do that. Everyone's nervous enough as it is,' reprimanded Vieques.

McEwan ignored him and called him over to the chart table. 'Vieques, look at this. This is *Stalin*. These are the Kai Islands. *Stalin* carries on so ... through this narrow strait. What happens?'

'What happens? We go in after him. What's wrong with that?'

'Here's what's wrong. Look. You and *Missouri*, you'll have to close up. You'll probably have to go in line. Once you're in line behind *Stalin*, *Missouri* can't fire. *Stalin* can concentrate the fire on you, pick you off, then work on the *Missouri*.'

'Oh, shit!' muttered Vieques to himself. Now he could see the neatness of Zof's plan. If he wanted to follow, the strait was so narrow that both ships would be forced to close up and follow each other. It was a trap that, faced with the awesome power of the *Stalin*'s huge 22-inch guns, he didn't want to get into. 'Maybe one of us goes round to catch *Stalin* on the other side?' he suggested.

'You don't have the speed, I'm afraid. Besides, you'll still be leaving one of your vessels open to the full force of the old ship. Sorry, Captain, we're going to have to stop *Stalin*, and quickly.'

'How?'

McEwan explained his plan. Vieques, after listening for a few minutes, nodded his agreement. He got back on the radio to the Pentagon.

*

The cloudless sky had become hazy in the oppressive heat. The *Stalin* was not pleasant in the tropics. There was no air-conditioning, and the forced ventilation simply pushed hot, wet air into the ship. The old boilers made a filthy black smoke that covered the after part of the vessel in a film of soot that clung like paint.

The Kai Islands were drawing closer. Zof had already chosen a half-mile-wide strait between two of the largest; the strait was not visible, but the islands were. They were now 15 miles away. Behind the ship, unseen from the bridge and half-obscured by the oily smoke that hung unmoved by any breeze over the

Stalin's wake, a dozen low-flying aircraft were speeding over the calm sea. It was only when they were several miles away that Zof noticed them on the radar. They had wave-hopped to stay radar-invisible, but now they were climbing and the radar caught them clearly and suddenly.

Zof yelled at Kelley. They ran to the end of the wings at the side of the bridge, looking towards the stern to see what the aircraft were. After the F-15 attack, neither man had imagined another air strike against them. The black shapes were distant but coming in fast, leaving light grey trails of smoke behind them, their engines now ramming them through the air at full power as they pushed to gain height.

As Zof and Kelley watched, the aircraft rapidly approached the ship, still climbing. Then they fanned out, splitting down the middle of the group, six passing on one side of the ship and six on the other. They drew closer. Suddenly, bombs were dropping from each aircraft, but the aircraft were still some distance from the ship. The bombs didn't look as though they had even been aimed at the ship, but were falling in a wide circle around it and ahead of it.

Zof shouted at his bridge officer to slow down as they waited for the explosions. But instead of the big blasts they were expecting, each bomb cruised down straight into the water and then burst into a thick black billowing smoke of napalm; the petrol jelly cascaded across the water, burning as it went. Once all the bombs had hit, a wide circle of fire and thick smoke surrounded *Stalin*. Within seconds, the thick murk climbed to several hundred feet, above the height of the optical fire directors located at the top of the mast.

Stalin was now blind.

*

Vieques was pleasantly surprised by the speed with which the bombers reached *Stalin*. Bell still had faith in air power and wanted his ships backed up by every trick in the book. Once Vieques had called him with McEwan's idea for putting the Russian's eyes out, Bell knew exactly who to yell at. The huge carrier *Independence* was 400 miles to the north and had loaded its planes with napalm and launched them screaming off the deck within twenty minutes of the order coming through from the Pentagon.

Carefully briefed by McEwan, the first bomb run was perfect, completely shrouding the ship in the billowing black smoke, obscuring *Stalin* from view but leaving the *Iowa* and *Missouri* with full radar vision which was all the computers needed.

With *Stalin* blinded and slowing, Vieques and Murray ordered their gunners to open fire. Though the range was close to maximum the first pair of salvoes were good, bracketing *Stalin* and, as far as anyone could tell, scoring several hits. Vieques ordered salvoes to keep pouring in while *Stalin* was still obscured by smoke and unable to fire back. They got four salvoes off until finally *Stalin* pushed out of the surrounding pall into clear air. Both the *Iowa* and *Missouri* had closed up a little; now each Captain inspected *Stalin* for signs of damage. Smoke poured from at least two points on her superstructure.

Within seconds of pulling out into the clear, *Stalin's* side sparkled with red and white flashes as she blasted out a full broadside while she could. Already the aircraft were coming back for another run of napalm to render her blind one more. The shots were poor. All nine shells fell a mile short of the *Missouri*, but even at that distance the explosions were awesome and reverberated through both ships.

The *Iowa* and *Missouri* continued to pump shells at

Stalin. Their turrets were aimed by computer and the process of lifting the heavy shells up from the magazines had, over the various modernisations, been highly automated. Every thirty seconds or so, the turrets spat their steel venom towards the ancient Russian, maintaining a merciless rate of fire. They paused briefly to allow the flight of bombers to sweep past both sides of the distant ship, releasing their napalm bomb loads. Once more *Stalin* vanished in the black billowing smoke, and as soon as the bombers were clear the cascade of steel resumed.

Vieques was sure that shells were hitting *Stalin;* what effect they were having was another question, but he continued to exhort his men to keep firing. The air around both ships stank of the sweet smell of cordite, and the gun-crews poured with sweat as they kept the turret machinery hauling the big shells and propellant bags. Both ships were firing so often that the noise turned into a constant roar in the battered ears of the crew, individual shots now melting one into the other. Everyone's hearing was affected; on the bridge, where the soundproofing was best, even Vieques was now routinely shouting at his officers to make himself heard.

The scent of bloody battle was now in the air. Vieques wanted to press home his advantage, and urged his ship and the *Missouri* further forward to narrow the gap. If he could close the distance by a few more miles, then he could bring his smaller guns to bear and add even more weight to the awesome tonnage of shells he was dropping on *Stalin.*

Again, *Stalin* burst from the enveloping murk. To Vieques' utter astonishment she was now heading directly at them, and across the bows of the ship appeared once more the evil glitter of the big guns firing.

*

Shrouded by the stinking black smoke, the shells were thudding and blasting into the *Stalin* from what felt like all directions. It was a black roaring hell. As each shell hit, the ship shook a little but even then the great vessel merely shuddered and carried steadily onwards. It was like mosquito bites on the hide of an elephant. Zof and Kelley crouched as each shell connected. Between salvoes, Zof managed to get damage reports from his crew scattered around the ship.

'No real damage yet, Kelley. Just a few fires which the crew are coping with. It feels worse than it is. Don't worry. We'll be fine,' shouted Zof across the din of another shell blasting its way over the after deck. It didn't seem to Kelley that anything could stand up to this rain of fire, yet Kishkov's thick steel carapace continued to absorb blow after blow without failing.

But Kishkov had never imagined an enemy being able to maintain such a rate of fire. The steel armour held, but the massive bolts which held the plates of armour to the frame were now beginning to work loose as the shells rammed home and wrenched each plate violently against its seating.

'Jesus, Zof, do we just sit here?' asked Kelley, who was braced in the corner of the bridge, visibly shaken by the onslaught.

'Hang on, Kelley. We're about to come out firing!' yelled Zof, who kept peering out through the slit windows. An acrid, stinging reek drifted in; something nasty was burning nearby.

After the second wave of napalm hit, Zof had decided to use the tactic to his own advantage and spin the ship quickly round to take them head on. He hoped the turn would be quick enough to fool the radar. *Stalin* plunged through the wall of smoke and flame and burst out into the clear air on the other side. Now they could see the *Iowa* and *Missouri* clearly, puffing little balls of smoke into the air each time the guns fired. Zof's sudden move had confused the radar system; the shots were starting to fall wide. In the clear air, the *Stalin's* optical aiming system could function again, and it took less than a minute to train the forward turrets on the Americans. Once the aim was confirmed, Zof ordered his gunners to open fire.

The big guns on the forward turret blazed again. Zof then ordered his ship into another tight turn; the second turret came to bear, and it too loosed its load of 12 tons of steel and high explosive. As the ship continued its turn, keeping the enemy radar confused by the constantly changing profile, the after turret finally was brought into action.

The time for aiming had been short, but Zof's shooting had improved. All the fire was concentrated on the *Missouri*. The first three shells fell beyond the target by 200 yards. The second group of three shells was closer. But of the final three, one clipped the mainmast and destroyed it, while the last two found their mark.

The first shell to hit struck the side of the *Missouri* with an awesome force. It felt as though the whole ship had been lifted up out of the water and shaken. The shell rammed itself into the side armour of the main hull and split it apart just forward of the main engine room. The following explosion tore the split wide open, but such was the strength of the armour that it still managed to absorb most of the blast. The second shell struck the bow square on and simply tore away the forward 20 feet of the ship in a blast of flame and flying splinters of steel.

The two hits were clearly visible from *Stalin*. The crew was cheering. Zof kept his ship running in a circle while the gunners reloaded for the next shot, even though the Americans' shells were still now and then striking the ship, though as Kishkov had always promised they were having little effect.

Back on *Iowa*, McEwan was under some pressure. Murray on the *Missouri* reported his damage but said he was still fully operational; his problem was that he doubted he could take another few shells like those. McEwan was damn sure he couldn't. Vieques had called in another napalm strike to blind *Stalin* again, but the aircraft had just used their last bombs and the next flight would be some time arriving.

Watching *Stalin* slowly turning, McEwan reminded Vieques about her weak spot. Was it worth trying? Following his study of the old plans of the ship from the Pentagon archives, McEwan had realised – as he had explained to Murray and Vieques earlier – that the armour plate on the ship stopped short of the stern but then re-started after a gap. This was to save weight and to offer protection to the vulnerable stern gear. But the problem was that it created a weak zone at the stern of the vessel, with heavy armour plate separated by lighter plating. If they could concentrate their fire on the weak spot, they might be able to inflict some substantial damage.

He spoke quickly to Vieques, who consulted his gunnery staff. Was the aim that precise? He pointed out the section of the ship that McEwan was interested in. Could they aim at the after part of the *Stalin* and actually hit it? The gunnery officer looked carefully at *Stalin* through powerful binoculars. The area they'd need to hit was small, but on average, he reckoned, with enough shells being directed at it, a sufficient number of them should connect. They'd try, he said, and ran back to the consoles to set up the computers to aim at McEwan's chosen spot.

The turning *Stalin* was moving into a position where it was presenting the perfect target for such an idea. Soon, the fire of both ships was concentrating on the after section of the big Russian.

*

Zof was willing his ship to turn round faster, but the huge vessel having reached full speed was more difficult to turn. Shells now started raining down again, this time dropping around the stern. In the mixture of smoke and spray it was impossible to see where they were falling, but the thuds he felt through his feet were a clear indication that some of them were connecting. The ship came round again to face the attackers, but once more, to Zof's fury, the aircraft roared in and dumped burning napalm around them, this time close in so that one bomb struck the top of the foremost turret, spreading dense black smoke right into the bridge itself. Still the shells kept pouring in, and the distant explosions of others hitting somewhere around the stern were easily felt, if not actually seen.

As each shell was fired, the computers on the American battleships followed the track and watched it fall, feeding back the trajectories of the hits so as to correct by tenths of a degree guns' aim for the next shot. The more shots hit, the more correction could be fed back to the processor that adjusted each gun's aim, and so the accuracy steadily and menacingly increased. The shells striking the weak area at the stern of the *Stalin* became more and more frequent. On the ship itself, it felt like a constant rain of hammer blows. The *Stalin* was now taking hits at the rate of one every minute.

This was worse than Zof had imagined. He was beginning to doubt the wisdom of sustaining this kind of punishment. He hadn't expected the napalm attack, and he was starting to realise the failings of the old ship. Brute force was one thing; but when you were blinded, you begged for a good radar-controlled gun. Grimly, he began to appreciate the enemy that was ranged against him. The only experience he'd had of Americans had convinced him that they were a loud, boasting people, with little real substance. Kelley just reinforced that view. He was realising his mistake. Equally grimly, Zof began to conclude that he should be planning to abandon ship.

For one moment he wondered if he should go down with the *Stalin*. Make sure the crew were off, then die the hero's death? It had an appeal. In any other circumstances, he wouldn't have hesitated. But the reality of the whole situation began to become clear. He knew he was no longer the heroic naval Captain fighting the last great battle and upholding the noble traditions of the service. Now, he was just a pirate. If he was caught, he'd probably be hanged or shot. And if the ship went down under him, it was not in some noble cause but simply for the destruction of a group of … well, he might as well admit it, now nothing more than a group of thugs and pirates.

He'd carry on fighting, of course. But when it came to the time, he knew what he would do.

For now, the *Stalin* was still running and the guns could still fire, but the steady pounding with tons of steel and high explosive was starting to inspire raw terror in the battered crew. Zof could see it on the faces of his bay-chay commanders and the crewmen who, black with smoke and sweat, would run shaking on to the bridge to report the damage. The ship itself was standing up well, according to the reports, but Zof was now hearing about the crewmen killed and mutilated by the flying shrapnel. He knew that he wouldn't be able to put his men through much more of this terror, even if the ship itself could take it, and even if the men wanted to keep on fighting. Already, twenty of them were dead and maybe thirty had been carried into the makeshift sick-bay deep in the bowels of the ship. Morin had already told Zof that he didn't think they had much left in them.

'Kelley, it's time to think about getting out of here. I don't think we can take a great deal more,' said Zof in the brief lull between shells.

'Christ, Zof! You wanted the fucking fight. You've got to keep going, get some shots in. You give up now, you and your crew have had it. These people mean business, Zof. You can't run and you can't just wave a white flag. They'll get you either way,' said Kelley, white with fear. As far as he was concerned, there was no chance of escape, least of all on a small boat on the open sea.

'Maybe. But these poor Russian bastards didn't come on this trip to be killed, Kelley. These are my men and my friends. Five more minutes and I order the ship abandoned,' yelled Zof above the din.

A series of three sudden thumps behind them in quick succession made them all flinch. This was followed by a long screeching sound, like somebody tearing steel plate.

'What the hell was that?' demanded Kelley.

Zof crouched down and looked outside on the wing bridge, ducking as another shell screamed overhead. The after part of the ship was covered in smoke which was only slowly drifting away. As the smoke cleared, what Zof saw made him swear loudly in Russian: the after hundred feet of his ship, more or less immediately behind his aft turret, was split across the deck from side to side, and was bending away at a slowly-increasing angle. With the drag of the water, his whole stern section was gradually breaking away. McEwan's plan was working.

Zof ducked back into the bridge to see what damage had been done to his power and steering systems. His speed seemed unaffected, but his helm was now dead: the wheel spun uselessly and the bow didn't move an inch. Whatever had happened had not affected his propellers but had rendered his rudder useless. He started yelling for damage reports. His fear now was that the stern breaking away would flood out the ship so that his engines would desert him. In the meantime, the drag of the breaking stern was starting to pull the ship round in the opposite direction.

Still the American shells came at them, and still they were concentrated on the damaged after part. Explosions jarred the ship again and again. Their only chance now was to get rid of the dragging stern. Zof ordered a crewman to go aft to see what they could do, if the Americans' shells didn't take it off first. He was burning with anger. While he knew the last moments were approaching, he now wanted to teach the Americans a final lesson. If he was going to be beaten, he wanted to leave behind more than a bloody nose.

He told Morin to order his artillery spotters to ensure the next shots connected, or else the whole crew had a problem. The man needed little encouragement; like the rest of them, he could see that unless they could deliver some real damage to the Americans they were all in mortal danger. He rested his eyes back against the rubber cups and with a steady hand carefully brought together the two images of the *Missouri* until they overlapped with total precision.

His task was made easier when suddenly the rain of shells stopped. From a hell of explosions and screaming metal, an eerie silence settled over the ship like a thick blanket. The *Stalin* carried on thundering through the sea, but in comparison it was as peaceful as a rowing boat on a pool. Now what?

Vieques had ordered the shelling stopped. His radar officer told him that *Stalin* had suddenly developed an erratic course. Had they damaged her? It was impossible to see through the smoke from their guns that surrounded the ship. He ordered the guns silenced to allow the smoke to clear for a moment, then inspected the after part of the *Stalin* through powerful binoculars. Smoke was billowing from four or five places on the ship, which continued to obscure the view, but the murk parted now and then and Vieques was sure he could see major damage at the stern. Certainly the stern appeared to be sitting at a slightly different angle from the rest of the ship, though according to the radar it was powering through the water unaffected.

'The weak point is behind the screws but ahead of the rudders. If we've taken it off, they'll lose their steering but not their power,' confirmed McEwan. 'Then the sea will start to flood out the ship. The bulkheads round there are pierced with all sorts of openings for controls and what-have-you. If you've damaged it badly, she could soon start losing power when the water reaches the engines.'

'Well, McEwan, whatever we've done, we certainly haven't affected the guns. Watch out!' called Vieques, who saw the forward turrets on the *Stalin* open up with six brilliant flashes. Seconds later there was a huge spout of water directly in front of the *Missouri*, followed by five huge explosions one after the other, marching right across the deck of their sister-ship. The force of each explosion was stunning even from that distance. All those on the bridge of the *Iowa* fell into an appalled silence. They looked on as the

Missouri was quickly enveloped in flame and smoke that climbed slowly into the air. Then the smoke started to drift away.

A moment of peace descended. Then, with the distance making it appear to be happening in slow motion, a boiling yellow spout of flame started to climb upwards from the centre of the *Missouri*, rapidly growing. For a couple of seconds there was no sound, but then a distant rumble rolled in and quickly turned into a roar. The great yellow flame erupted into a white brilliance almost the size of the ship itself, and then a boiling smoke spilled out of it, nearly hiding it from view. The roar became a massive, growling explosion.

Slowly the fireball turned red, then orange, then purple, and was finally overtaken by the growing cloud of smoke that continued to boil upwards into the sky. As Vieques and his officers watched in stunned silence, the smoke slowly drifted away. The *Missouri* was no more. The ship that over fifty years ago had sailed into Tokyo Bay to take the Japanese surrender, a ship that had become almost a national monument, was now a sinking wreck. Just the bow of the ship was visible above the water, and as they watched that too slipped silently beneath the sea.

23

Pine lay in a bunk deep in the heart of the ship. The improvised hospital was a dim, stinking room, crowded with frightened, sometimes screaming, crewmen who had been brought in with burns, mutilations, missing limbs, missing eyes ... all the flesh-tearing carnage of a battleship at war. They were brought in and dumped; the Russian doctor was working with a party of just four untrained orderlies, and the best they could do was mop up the blood and inject greater and greater doses of morphine.

The rain of shells was hard to hear this deep inside the ship, but the shaking and jarring was clearly felt. The bigger impacts were powerful enough to shift the old iron bedsteads, jumping them across the metal deck with a shriek drowned the screams of the wounded men. The constant thumping and crashing, together with the comings and goings of the injured, was slowly bringing Pine out of his drug-induced sleep.

His puffy face was swaddled in a loose blood-soaked bandage that covered almost his whole head except for his nose and eyes. He could see, blearily, from just one eye, the other having closed up long ago – folded into a blackened, puffy ball of stretched flesh. He blinked his good eye several times in the dim light, painfully pushed himself half up on his elbows and turned his head a little.

He was puzzled to see Kishkov in the bed next to him. He was sure he knew the man, sure he was somehow a problem, but he couldn't quite figure it out in the peaceful morphine haze that he wallowed in. Little was connecting in Pine's battered and addicted brain, but there was enough of his street-fighter's natural intelligence left to make him watch this strange, crooked old man.

Kishkov was sitting up and pulling with his teeth at the bandages that wrapped each of his hands like boxing gloves. Pine wondered what was going on. He couldn't grasp why, but he felt this wasn't what Kelley would have wanted. He watched Kishkov slowly unravel the bandage from one hand and then painfully go to work on the other. Once that was completed, he saw the old man look furtively around and then painfully get to his feet and start shuffling towards the door.

There was a sudden, violent shake and three dull thuds jarred the whole room. They were powerful enough to penetrate even Pine's dim consciousness. What was going on? In his disconnected mind, he suddenly felt he should be doing something but he just couldn't figure out what. He sat upright with difficulty, slowly swung his legs to the floor and then moved unsteadily to his feet, hanging on to the iron bed-frame. There was no pain; the massive shots of morphine had rendered his nervous system immune to almost all feeling.

Pine pushed his massive bulk from his bed and shuffled past the injured crewmen. They took no notice of him. There was another jolt above him and he put out his arm to steady himself, but instead grabbed a blinded sailor – his face a charred, crusting mask – and he screamed and cursed in Russian at Pine. He was oblivious to the injured man. All his

wrecked brain could cope with was following
Kishkov, who by now had almost disappeared from
the sick-bay The crashing and banging appeared to
have stopped now, and Pine lumbered after him as
quickly as he could manage.

On the bridge, there were whoops of delight as the
smoke cleared from around the spot where the
Missouri had been. One of their shots must have
penetrated the armour and detonated the entire
magazine to make such a huge explosion. Apart from
a slowly drifting cloud in the otherwise hazy blue sky
there was nothing to suggest that minutes before one
of the biggest battleships in the American Navy had
been pouring fire at them.

Kelley was clapping Zof on the back with
unrestrained joy. 'See? I told you we could do it,' he
exclaimed loudly. 'One hit and down she went. Now go
for the other bastard' he said, and then the internal
intercom rasped insistently. It was the engine room for
Zof. He listened and nodded and, as he did, any
pleasure he felt at his victory soon drained away.

'Bad news, my friend,' he said to Kelley, putting the
handset down. 'That was the engine room. We are
taking on water through the stern at quite a rate. In
fifteen minutes or so it will reach the turbines.'

Kelley didn't want to come to the conclusion that he
knew he must reach. 'Which means what, Zof?'he
asked, quietly.

'That's it, Kelley. If we have no turbines, we have no
power. No steerage. Dead in the water. It's over, Kelley.
I'm sorry.'

Kelley looked desperately at Zof. There was a long
silence. Zof refused to say anything to encourage the
American; he knew now that it was all finished, and it
was time to go. If he couldn't steer the ship and he
couldn't move it, it was only a matter of time before

they were blown to hell. He remembered the story of the *Bismarck*, cornered and powerless before the Royal Navy, which had to take hours of bloody punishment before it finally went to the bottom. It was an evil way to die. For him. For the crew. For the ship. He wanted no part of it.

'We can survive!' Kelley insisted, a note of pleading in his voice. He had no place to go. Even if he escaped, the Americans would be hunting him down from one side and the Iraqis from the other. He knew he was trapped.

'Kelley, please listen,' reasoned Zof. 'If we sit here we will just be pounded to hell until we go slowly to the bottom. I can think of better ways of dying. It's time to get out.'

'No way, Zof. No fucking way! If you think I'm gonna end up as meat in some US Navy sandwich, no chance. We fight, Zof, are you listening?'

'Kelley, you are crazy. Get out of here,' said Zof calmly.

'Order the guns to open fire. Now.' Kelley demanded.

Zof walked slowly to the handset and picked it up. He spoke quickly in Russian, then replaced it.

'We can do it, Zof, we can do it,' pleaded Kelley.

'Kelley, I've just given the orders to abandon ship. I've got my crew launching boats on the blind side of the ship, and they're bringing up the wounded. In less than half an hour we'll be on those boats and we'll get away. We'll fire a few more salvoes to keep them busy and cover our tracks. With all the smoke they won't see us go; we are too small to be seen on the radar. By the time they pluck up the courage to board the *Stalin*, we'll be long gone. Get ready, Kelley. We're going.'

Kelley stood rooted to the spot. He had no arguments left. 'What about the gold, for Christ's sake?' he asked.

'Forget the gold, Kelley. Get off while you can,' pleaded Zof. He didn't greatly like the man, but he didn't want to see him die like this.

Suddenly Kelley seemed calmer, as though he'd made a decision. 'Not a chance, Zof. I've come this far, at least I'll come out of it rich. You make your arrangements, I'll get the gold,' he said, and before Zof could say anything he disappeared off the bridge to see if he could force his way through the twisted, crushed decks and companionways to where the gold was waiting

Zof shook his head. He ordered the gun-crews to deliver covering fire while they loaded the boats, and then looked around the bridge for one last time. Ahead of him, through the splintered windows, all he could see was a pile of twisted, smoking wreckage that had once been the greatest battleship in the world. He lit a cigarette, swore, and turned and walked from the bridge for the last time.

*

And so the final battle between the two greatest warships the world had ever seen entered its last bitter and bloody phase. *Stalin*, her stern ripped away, battered by shells but still afloat and alive, now started to slow in the water as the sea steadily crept through the mangled stern towards the vital innards. The *Iowa*, stunned at the unbelievable fate of her sister-ship, was hardly touched and was overwhelmed with a desire to wreak awesome revenge on the grim killing machine lying menacingly on the horizon. If the ship had eyes, the light of battle now blazed fiercely in them.

Vieques was in no mood for anything other than total annihilation. Whatever the crippled *Stalin* could throw at him now, he would return a hundred- and a thousand-fold. His mood was dark and vengeful and he wanted to make the evil Russian suffer. He knew many of the men who minutes ago had been alive on the *Missouri*.

First, although McEwan sensibly told him it would make little impact, he asked the incoming flight of bombers, now just minutes away, to drop everything they had squarely on the *Stalin*. He would feel better for it, and he wasn't quite sure that McEwan was right. The pilots, now informed of the fate of the *Missouri*, performed better than any training manual demanded. Each aircraft swooped in fast and low, lower than they should have dared, taking time to aim carefully, each pilot now intent on inflicting the maximum damage with no thought as to any fire *Stalin* might throw up at them. Each bomber unloaded all the high-explosive ordnance it carried, then wheeled round for the follow-up strike with napalm directly on to the ship. Pilot after pilot swept in, and almost every bomb found a mark.

Within moments *Stalin* was ablaze from the fiercely burning petrol jelly but, with nothing for the flames to grip, soon subsided. McEwan was right in that the thick armour plate stood up to the bombing, but the battering it was now being subjected to continued to work loose the bolts that held the whole armoured structure together. Vieques was right to wreak this havoc too, not because it mortally damaged the ship but because the crew of the *Stalin* were now cowed into a silent, frozen inaction by the sudden violent onslaught. Even the gunners in the massive turrets crouched fearfully in dim corners. And, vitally, the mainmast that supported the optical director for the main guns was now blasted away and hung over the bridge like a collapsed pile of scaffolding. Other director positions were available, but were lower and smaller and therefore less accurate.

The aircraft flew on. The cowering gun-crews gathered enough courage to load another round and once more the nine big guns spat their shells at the *Iowa* . The aim was hopeless and all the shells missed, dumping noisily but harmlessly into the sea a mile beyond the target. Zof had wanted enough fire to keep the *Iowa* busy, but all he seemed to do was provoke a hornets' nest.

The *Iowa* returned the salvo with relish, and three of her shells connected with the side of the *Stalin*. The armour belt worked itself a little looser each time the shells blasted into it, though still it held against the shattering impacts. Now the *Iowa* turned from broadside on to bow on; she was getting her aim for a torpedo strike. Six fast torpedoes wormed out of the underwater tubes towards *Stalin,* and Zof was too busy launching the escape boats to stay on the bridge and give orders for evasive action.

Two passed harmlessly by, leaving the other four to connect, all of them towards the stern of the ship. Each explosion threw a fountain of oil-stained water hundreds of feet into the air, drenching the ship as it erupted. Again, Kishkov's genius for construction withstood the blasts, though the bottom of the ship was now grievously dented and whole sections torn away, even though the last of the triple layers remained unbreached. But the force of the blasts had loosed internal bulkheads; those which had held the sea back from the loosened stern section now began to open up, and the black water started to creep quickly forward.

The power system that ran the shell hoist for the after turret was soon underwater. The old insulation around the thick copper cable was no protection against the sea-water; it quickly shorted in a shower of unseen blue sparks, and the after turret was rendered useless with no shells to feed the gaping breeches of the 22-inch guns.

*

Deep in the tangled bowels of the ship, Kishkov stumbled along the poorly lit passageways. When a shell or torpedo struck and the whole ship heaved, he had to wrap his arms around the nearest stanchion. Lacking such a support, he was simply thrown to the deck. His purple hands were astonishingly painful and he found it nearly impossible to lift himself back up after each blast, but with a grim determination he managed to continue his slow journey.

He knew exactly where he was going, He had drawn the final plans for this very part of the ship with his own hands, nearly sixty years ago.

Pine moved more steadily than Kishkov. He was still trailing the old man, his drugged brain unable to work out exactly what he was doing, except that some deep instinct told him that Kishkov should be followed. It was what Kelley would have wanted.

The old man stumbled his way down several dim passageways and some flights of ladders, until at last he came to a grey steel door. He stopped in front of it and stared. To open it, he would have to grip a red wheel and spin it to release the latches. He rested his swollen hands on the wheel; slowly he tightened his bruised fingers around it. The pain made tracks of sweat course down his temples and his breath came in short bursts. Once he had gained enough grip, then he turned the wheel. It wasn't stiff, but to Kishkov the effort and the pain were almost beyond what he could bear. He turned it a quarter-turn and then rested, releasing his grip slightly. Waves of agony cascaded over him. Then another turn. Rest. Another turn. Rest. Slowly Kishkov unlatched the door and pushed it open.

Inside, stacked neatly in rows, were the twenty small nuclear warheads removed from the *Jackson*.

*

Now the *Stalin* began to feel the full force of the *Iowa's* anger. Sitting motionless in the water with only the forward two turrets operational and her main gunnery director wrecked, she could return fire only sporadically and with little effect. The *Iowa* redoubled her efforts, her computers now able to aim the big guns precisely, unaffected by any movement from the crippled target. *Iowa* let loose salvo after salvo which punched into *Stalin*, rocking the huge ship from side to side as shell after shell rammed home. It had become a turkey-shoot, and Vieques revelled in it. He was now close enough to bring his smaller 8-inch guns into play. He drove his gun-crews to fire faster and faster, and they willingly answered his orders with grim pleasure as they poured fire on to the shuddering, dying monster.

The upperworks were being crushed into a desolate wasteland of twisted, smoking steel. Most of the single massive funnel had been blasted away, leaving a stump like a broken tooth. Each time another shell powered into the armour belt, it loosened even more. A section of armour at the forward part of the ship finally gave way and under the impact of yet another shell simply disintegrated, sending splinters of hardened steel spinning hundreds of feet into the air.

The forward section of the hull had been breached, and now water begun to gush in through the growing number of holes. The stern of the ship had settled low in the water already; now the bow began to fill and inch by inch the waterline crept slowly upwards. But still *Stalin* stubbornly refused to breath her last.

Vieques was far from done. He ordered in another strike of high explosive from the circling aircraft. While he waited, he launched another half-dozen torpedoes for good measure. Still Kishkov's triple armour held; but the old ship would take little more. The boilers had now given up. The fuel lines split away and the vast steam pipes crumpled like straws, sending dense clouds of scalding steam into the engine room where the few remaining crew perished in agony. The creeping water had penetrated the generator hall too, and the four big diesels finally stuttered as the spinning alternators shorted out and stopped.

All that worked now was the stand-by system which automatically cut in to provide emergency power to critical parts of the ship. It was enough to keep most of the main circuits alive, or at least those sections of it which hadn't been shorted out by damage or water; but the turrets and the ammunition hoists used too much power and the stand-by system didn't supply them. The big guns couldn't get ammunition, and they couldn't aim either. The *Stalin* was now crippled, but even now she was not finally dead.

Zof, working on the blind side of the ship, furthest from the Americans, was managing to complete the launching of the boats. Helped by his bay-chay commanders, he'd already got one away, carrying the wounded together with sixty of his crew, mostly the younger ones, and it was standing off a few hundred yards waiting to be joined by the others. There were four boats in all, each one carrying around 100 men. He would go in the last one with the officers and with Kelley. In the meantime, he was hurrying the next batch of men down the ladder into the boat. He knew many of them by name; he gripped their arms or hands or just the scruffs of their necks as they jostled past him; he mumbled words of good luck as they passed. They looked at Zof, some gratefully, some in a state of shock, as he bade them farewell.

Just as he was ordering the second boat to cast off, the rain of shells suddenly ceased. In the silence, his ears rang, and he turned to see what his tormentors were about to do next.

The distant *Iowa* sat low on the placid sea about 7 or 8 miles off, and a small group of aircraft were wheeling round in the sky and turning once more for the *Stalin*. They were coming in low now, confident the battered ship could put up no resistance.

Zof ordered the second boat away and started to lower the third and then the fourth. Most of the crew had come up by now, but he noticed that neither Kishkov nor Pine were with the wounded. And where the hell was Kelley? An orderly told them that they couldn't be found. Damn them: they would drive him mad even at this last desperate moment. What in the name of hell were they all playing at? He was tempted to leave them; but however much he disliked the lot of them, it was a matter of pride to Zof to get everyone who could still walk off the ship.

'Morin!' he yelled to the artillery bay-chay commander who was counting off his gun-crews into the fourth boat. 'Go and find those damned Americans and our mad friend Kishkov. Get them up here and into the boats.'

Morin looked at Zof. Had his captain gone crazy too? After all this he wanted to rescue the very people who had got them into this shit? 'Those bastards? Captain, let them rot in hell. We need to get our men off. Don't worry about those criminals, for God's sake!'

He showed no signs of leaving his station near the loading lifeboat.

Zof swore. Morin was right, but still he couldn't just

leave them. He looked at the faces in the lifeboat; then he tore himself away and ran across the littered deck to the doorway leading down to the bowels of the ship. The door was half obstructed with a fallen section of mast. He struggled to heave it away; the mast suddenly moved – Zhadanov was behind him, helping.

'Get back to the boat, Yuri!' shouted Zof.

'Oh, shut up, Yakov! Leave this to me. I'll find the bastards. You're needed back at the boats,' grinned the engineer. Zof helped to shove the torn mast section aside and they pushed through. Inside only the dim emergency lighting glowed eerily. There was a flight of ladders leading down, but a pall of smoke drifted upwards and obscured the light; the smoke stung their nostrils and made Zof catch his breath.

'Kelley?' he yelled. 'Kishkov!' he yelled again. There was no reply.

'Yakov, for Christ's sake just leave this to me,' insisted Zhadanov, and he disappeared down the ladder into the smoke. Zof paused as he watched Zhadanov go. Yuri was right; he should get back to his crew and the escape. The planes were droning in; they had only minutes left. He stood for a moment. Suddenly he heard a voice outside, echoing through the doorway.

'Zof!' came the distant voice. It was Kelley. Zof turned and ran back to the door. The American was half-way down the deck, dragging a trolley loaded with boxes behind him. 'Zof! Get someone to help me!' he called.

'What in the name of hell are you doing?' Zof demanded.

'It's the fucking gold, you bastard! Give me a hand,' called Kelley, still struggling with the trolley. He'd managed to get it up two flights, carrying each box by hand, but the wreckage strewn across the deck blocked his progress. The ripped timbers stood up like jagged splinters, and snakes of black cable lay like a jungle across the deck.

The man was crazy. Damn him! His crew was far more important; if this madman wanted to struggle with the gold, he'd have to leave him to it. He was disgusted with all of them. Zof just shook his head, turned away and went back to the boats; one of them had a cable stuck in a rusty pulley and the boat was swinging dangerously in the air; while a young seaman beat the pulley with a spanner in an attempt to free it. Zof was about to jump up to the davit to lend a hand when he heard Kelley again. This time, closer. This time, right behind him.

'Zof, turn round.' There was rage in the American's voice.

Zof turned to see Kelley standing there, sweat pouring from his face, his shirt filthy and black. He was holding a gun which was pointed directly at Zof's face.

'Get someone to help me move this gold. Now!'

'Kelley, we're trying to get away. We don't want the gold. Put that gun away and get in the boat.'

'Don't fuck about with me, Zof,' shouted Kelley, a warning panic in his voice.

Zof didn't give a damn. His crew were waiting for him, drifting at the water's edge, 100 faces looking up at him expectantly; another 200 men further away. Everyone was waiting on Zof. His own chance of escape was hanging there, just about ready. Kelley was stopping him. He looked sadly at the American, then with an almost casual movement he seized his wrist, twisting it like a chicken's neck and forcing the gun away.

Kelley had threatened people with guns many times. Nobody had ever treated the threat so disdainfully. The big Russian's grip tightened on his wrist, painfully.

But Kelley was no snotty-nosed sailor kid; he tried to pull away, but Zof wouldn't release him. Kelley pulled the trigger and the gun went off with a crash, but the bullet went spinning harmlessly into the air. Zof was now angry.

'My friend, listen to me. This is your last chance. Get on the boat and get away. What the hell do you want? Gold or freedom? Get off, Kelley. We'll look after you, God knows why,' he said urgently.

'Fuck you, Zof,' hissed Kelley. 'I didn't come all this fucking way to end up with a bunch of deadbeat Russian sailors. Help me get the gold, Zof. Help me or I'll kill you.'

Zof shook his head. It was the American's life, his decision. After all they had been through, he had grown to almost like the short, stocky man who had so nearly made rich men of them all but who now threatened to kill them.

'I'm sorry for you, Kelley,' he said.

'Save it, Zof. I don't need it' Kelley spat.

'Good luck, my friend.'

'Damn you.' And Kelley turned and ran back towards the smoking ruins of the central superstructure, where he vanished through a doorway.

Zof watched him disappear, then started yelling at the crewman – who had stopped trying to free the pulley to watch the argument between the two men – to get on with his job. The young seaman gave the pulley one massive blow, and the cable started to run free again. The last boat now reached the water. Zof turned to look again at the *Iowa*. The planes were drawing closer, but still the American ship held its fire. Now Zof hurried the remaining crewmen down the ladder to the boat.

The planes continued their approach. There was

the dull thump of more napalm bombs bursting around the ship, but they stayed on the side nearest the *Iowa* , and Zof and his boats remained unharmed. In the smoke and haze of battle, they were invisible to the pilots. Where the hell was Zhadanov? None of his other men were left, except the bodies that would get a decent burial soon enough. The other three boats had already rowed a good distance off. Now he needed to find his engineer.

Zhadanov was standing there. He was looking sheepish.

'Yuri, did you find them?'

'Sorry, Yakov. No luck,' replied the younger man.

Zof was suspicious. 'Yuri, did you . . . ?' he started.

Zhadanov came up close. Although Zof was a good six inches taller, the engineer managed to stare him directly in the face. 'Listen, Yakov. I didn't look too hard, you know what I mean? There was no way I was going to let you, or me for that matter, waste time looking for those bastards. Yakov, I know what you're like. You'd never have gone if someone hadn't looked for them. Well, tough, Yakov. Now it's too late. Leave them. Bury them with the fucking ship. Yakov, it's time to go,' urged Zhadanov.

Zof stared back at him. Only Zhadanov could get away with something like that. But he had to admit that the engineer was right.

He looked around one last time. Yes, Yuri – finally, it was time to go. He glanced quickly up towards the mast, but there was no sign of the flag. It had been blown away hours ago, and the wreckage of the mast lay in a jumble, like collapsed scaffolding, over the jagged stump of the funnel. He whispered a silent farewell to the *Stalin* and to the dead seamen he was leaving behind, then hurried down the ladder, following Zhadanov. Half-way down, he thought he heard Kelley again. He turned and looked up; there he was, screaming something at him, leaning over the side of the ship high above Zof's head. But Zof couldn't hear what he was saying.

The aircraft had wheeled away, and the *Iowa* took up the battle once more. The whole side of the distant battleship sparkled with gunfire as every one of the big guns and then the smaller guns opened up, one after the other. The *Iowa* disappeared in the cloud of white smoke.

Distracted by the American and then by the sudden sound of the *Iowa* opening fire, Zof stayed where he was, huddling back against the protective side of the ship. There was another, desperate sound. He looked up again. Kelley had cupped his hands to his mouth and started screaming again, but his voice was drowned by the blast of shells that suddenly rained down around him.

As the echoes of the explosions died away, Zof resumed his hurried journey down the ladder. He reached the boat and tore the line from the cleat. The engine was useless, and he ordered the crew to row like demons to get away; they didn't need telling twice. Zof's was the last boat away – the other three were rowing just as furiously in a desperate attempt to escape. Now they had seen Zof join them, they put their very souls into it.

Another salvo of shells fell on the other side of the ship. Some fragments spun over their heads, but Zof and his boats were untouched. They managed to gain some distance, and then yet another salvo of shells landed, this time almost all of them on the *Stalin*. The sound of the explosions crashed across the sea and Zof could clearly hear metal being torn. She couldn't last much longer.

As the smoke cleared again, he yelled at the crew to

row faster. The next salvo would arrive in seconds. Zof glanced back.

Distant now, a small and desperate figure on the deck of the ruined ship was screaming soundlessly, waving a fist in the air. Zof shook his head sadly and murmured another silent farewell but this time to Kelley – then turned to urge the rowers onwards. As he did so, the aircraft swooped in once more from the other side of the ship, and the screaming figure disappeared in a huge explosion that started to detach the bow sections.

And still the *Stalin* refused to slip under the water...

On the *Iowa*, Vieques' anger rose and he poured more shots on to the old battleship. More armour fell away, more bulkheads were breached. He fired yet another round of torpedoes, and the ship shuddered and settled even lower in the water, but still Kishkov's work was steadily defying everything that Vieques could throw at it.

McEwan found it hard to believe that the wreck could still float. The whole of the upperworks had been smashed into twisted, burning wreckage. There were gaping holes punched in the side of the ship where smoke poured in rising columns to mix with the smoke from the shattered upperworks. The stern was missing and much of the bow section had come away. She lay low in the water, down by the stern, and was starting to list. The ship was black, scorched by fires and explosions.

Vieques ordered a pause in the firing. He wanted to finish the task but Bell, back in the Pentagon, told him to lay off. The old ship still had the warheads on board. And more than anything else, he wanted the American and the Russian arrested and paraded before the world. They would have their revenge, Bell assured Vieques, but not a private one. For their temerity in challenging the might of the American Navy, the ringleaders would be all but publicly executed. Bell was looking forward to it. He ordered Vieques to cease fire once the Russian ship fell silent, and to send across a boarding party, together with a Navy video crew, to arrest Zof and Kelley and bring them back in chains.

The *Stalin* had not returned fire for several minutes and, judging by the angle of the guns and the gradual settling of the ship into the water, was unlikely to do any more.

'I think she's finished, Captain. Nothing could stand a bombardment like that any longer,' said McEwan, looking at the old ship through his binoculars.

'I guess so, McEwan. Tell Kraft to get a boarding party ready and the video crew. We want those bastards taken off there. He knows what to do.'

McEwan relayed the message to Kraft, the *Iowa's* XO, and rejoined Vieques. They watched *Stalin* together. It was silent now and the smell of propellant had drifted away. The distant Russian ship was sending a pall into the air that was being lifted on a breeze which had sprung up with the heat of the sun. The pall billowed up into the sky like a storm cloud. The gun crews had come up onto the deck to watch the final moments. Wiping sweat from their heads with their T-shirts, they passed cold cans of Coke to each other. The tropical heat was cool compared to the ovens of the turrets.

After a few minutes, a small motor launch emerged from under the cover of the hull and slowly droned off towards the silent, smoking wreck in the distance.

*

Kishkov didn't notice the sudden silence. He was concentrating on the task before him, which was being made painfully difficult with his swollen fingers, but in his frame of mind it was not impossible. This was a task he *had* to complete.

Kishkov knew enough about nuclear warheads. After his release he had kept up his reading of the scientific and engineering journals for a few years. He knew what had to be done.

The old man looked carefully at the warheads in front of him and the job didn't seem to difficult, apart from these bloody stupid fingers. God will give me strength, he prayed, and set to work with a painful and deliberate slowness. The codes were what worried him: but he imagined they would come from the electronics within the delivery system. Once the electronics had done their job, they would simply trigger the pulse. One of the sockets had to carry it through to the warhead itself. Hot-wiring the obvious ones should do the job. There were bound to be cut-outs within the warhead; Kishkov simply banked on being able to override them by using plenty of power. It was crude, and the old man had no idea if it was going to work. But God was on his side.

Pine had followed him into the room and leaned, unseen, against a bulkhead. He couldn't make out what Kishkov was doing. His drugged, dull brain was attempting to make sense of the whole strange scene. But he still remembered dimly that Kishkov was somebody important: somebody who should be watched. Kelley would want him to do this, he felt. So Pine watched through his one useful eye as the old man twisted a pair of wires onto two small terminals on the side of one of the warheads. He heard him groaning with the pain, but it didn't register. He watched Kishkov as he slowly uncoiled the wire and opened up a junction box on the bulkhead carrying mains power at a considerable voltage. He watched as the Russian, with a struggle, pushed the lever downwards to the 'off' position, then slowly started work to connect the wires. This took some time and still Pine couldn't fathom what the old man was trying to do, but it caused him some concern.

Once Kishkov had connected the wires, he closed the junction box. Then he fell to his knees and started praying, crossing himself frequently. He remained like this for a full five minutes, and Pine began to get worried.

The old man struggled to his feet, crossed himself once more and reached up for the power switch. But it was now beyond his strength to push it upwards into the 'on' position. He cursed and tried again, but the lever was too stiff for his stiff and crushed fingers.

Through the drifting clouds inside his brain, Pine reached the conclusion that this was all wrong: the wires and the gleaming metal warhead, the old man praying. Something was going on, and he decided that Kelley would want him to put a stop to it. He walked unsteadily through the door towards Kishkov, who now spotted him for the first time. Kishkov spun round, staring wildly at the spectre of the bandaged Pine lurching towards him with hand outstretched.

'Stay away!' screamed Kishkov in Russian. 'This is my ship. Stay away!' He backed away from the advancing Pine.

Pine didn't understand a word the old man was yelling, but knew he had to stop whatever Kishkov was trying to do. He looked at the junction box and decided it should be turned off. He gripped the lever and pushed it upwards to what his fogged brain assumed was the 'off' position. The switch connected. He had done his job. Kelley would be pleased, and he smiled once more, but there was a sudden very bright white light and he wondered very briefly where Kishkov had gone . . .

Vieques and McEwan had watched the launch motor slowly away, and McEwan was talking to Vieques about the best way to finish off the listing wreck once they'd got the men off. They were looking at the old Russian plans of the ship as McEwan went through the weak points. Then there was an overwhelmingly brilliant white light that suddenly flashed through the bridge windows behind them. The light was burning. It lasted for less than a second and then just as suddenly died away.

Vieques and McEwan looked briefly at each other, then turned to the windows. Several of Vieques' officers had been looking through the windows and were holding their hands to their eyes with looks of surprise on their faces, blinded by the brilliant white flash. When Vieques and McEwan looked out on the scene, there was a vast boiling orange fireball where *Stalin* had been. It was climbing quickly up into the air, turning from orange to purple and green, shot through with white flashes; as the fireball rose, a thick cloud was being drawn up behind it. In the foreground, less than half a mile from the *Iowa*, the small motor launch had already veered off to port, the helmsman blinded by the light.

The fireball rose quickly to 1,000 feet and was turning black, and now starting to spread out at the top into a mushroom-shaped cloud. Then, rolling across the few miles of sea, the blast hit them. It was like being inside a huge drum struck with a massive hammer; the blow first, then echoes as it reverberated from side to side, booming and grumbling as it died away. The blast passed over them. Still the cloud spread, now rising thousands of feet into the upper air, the top glowing brightly in the sunshine, pulling away to one side as the wind high up in the atmosphere caught it and drifted it away.

There was nothing on the surface of the sea where the *Stalin* had been other than a soft grey ash that fell slowly from the rising cloud. *Stalin* had at last gone to her grave, at the hands of her maker, not her enemies. The last voyage was finally over.

McEwan stared at the spot where *Stalin* had been. There was a complete silence now on the ship and across the sea, from horizon to horizon. Thousands of tons of steel, built to withstand the most violent onslaught that the military machine of the day could devise, had vanished in the blink of an eye. McEwan couldn't but help feel sad, even though he'd spent the last weeks hunting down the ship and trying to destroy her. Somehow, he'd have preferred to sink her in a fairer fight. He respected her tenacity, the way she had hung on, the way she had absorbed blow after blow. It was heroic the way Zof had fought them all to the bitter end. At least, thought McEwan, he hadn't really lost at all. But here it was: the end of Zof, the end of the Soviet Navy, the end of the *Stalin*, and the last great battle that would ever be fought between these dinosaurs of the sea. McEwan knew he was witnessing a small footnote in history. In amongst the death and destruction, it was a brief moment of an older glory.

After some time, McEwan slowly and stiffly brought his arm up to a salute, which he held for several moments. Then Vieques, turning his back on the drifting cloud, ordered his ship to collect the launch and set a course for home.

*

Zof had urged his men to keep rowing. Some inner sense told him to get as far from the *Stalin* as possible, although he didn't know why. Already his four boats had covered five miles of the smoke-shrouded sea when Pine, in his final act of senselessness, helped Kishkov complete the detonation of the warhead. Zof's crew were heaving and sweating against the oars; they all had their heads down, and when the blinding flash burst where the *Stalin* had been, now little more than a crippled ghost in the smoke, they were stunned but otherwise unharmed. The quickly-rising mushroom cloud told everyone what had happened.

The blast wave hit them a second or two later. Had the warheads been any bigger, Zof's fleeing boats would have disappeared in the explosion. But Kishkov's bomb was a tactical warhead; and the old man's crude method of detonation meant that only some of the internal explosive used to compress the plutonium core had gone off, limiting the size of the nuclear blast to less than a quarter of what the designer had intended. Thus it was small enough to confine the damage to a modest – by nuclear standards – area. The boats were low on the water, too, and presented an insignificant cross-section, providing less target for the blast wave. There was a dull roar; a wave of hot air rippled over them in a boiling surge, and then spread out across the sea. As it passed it condensed the moisture in the air and left behind a pale white mist that drifted away with the wind. Nothing worse happened. The shock passed, and Zof knew his ship had finally gone.

The *Iowa* too had vanished from sight in the smoke and the haze. They couldn't see her slowly make her turn away. The sea around them was now silent and empty.

Zof had found Zhadanov when he finally scrambled into the last boat to get away. Now the two sat together, watching the mushroom cloud rising from where their great ship had been. They were huddled amongst their crewmen.

'Well, Yakov, some mess, eh?' said Zhadanov finally, resting on the thick oar. The crewmen rowing had stopped, too. Zof was suddenly aware of the silence that had fallen. The other boats nearby had also ceased moving and were bobbing gently on the water. They were waiting for him. Waiting for Zof.

Zof looked around at them all and just shrugged his shoulders. What more did they want from him?

'All this death. All this destruction All this work. What a bloody waste. Nothing to show for it, either,' continued the engineer gloomily. Zof could see, and feel, the eyes looking at him, waiting, wondering what was going on. What was he going to do now?

He got carefully to his feet. The Pacific swell rolled the boat gently and loaded as it was, the freeboard was down to a foot. Too much movement would have tipped them all into the sea.

Zof looked around. There were faces he recognised, others he didn't know. He rested an arm on Zhadanov's shoulder to steady himself. 'So. I give you no apologies, comrades' he started in a low voice that carried across the still sea. 'No regrets, either. We tried, and damn nearly beat them all. We took on the best of the American Navy and showed them what we could do. We didn't do so bad, comrades. We didn't do so bad at all. You can be proud of what you achieved. I salute you,' and he brought up his hand in a slow salute.

A voice came from the back of a boat. Zof couldn't see who was speaking.

'To hell with your salute, Captain! We fought a good battle and we lost a lot of good men, and for what? We come out of it with nothing, Comrade Captain, nothing at all.' There was a shocked silence from the rest of the crew. Heads turned to see who dared speak: you simply didn't talk that way to Zof.

Zof didn't mind. He didn't mind at all. To everyone's

surprise, he smiled. 'I wouldn't be so sure,' he said.

'I would, Captain. The gold went up with that mad American. We should have stopped to collect it.'

'The gold stayed on the ship. But this didn't,' said Zof. From beneath his feet he produced a battered leather briefcase and opened it. Inside were the diamonds that had been stolen from the *Ocean Queen*.

'Yakov, you bastard,' grinned Zhadanov. The anonymous crewman kept quiet. The rest of the men nodded to themselves, grinning now. Of course, they said. Of course. He planned it all along. This is Yakov Zof you're dealing with. The crew murmured back into action and started pulling on the oars once more, but there was less desperation now.

Zof sat down, staring out across the sea. 'Yuri, you know something? At long last the debt has been paid. Who would have believed it would be paid by Stalin himself?'

The haze drifted across the still waters of the Pacific and the four boats gently merged into the warm yellow light that now covered the ocean and the sky so that neither sea nor sky, nor ships, nor lifeboats, were any longer to be seen.